R. A. SALVATORE
NIGHT OF THE HUNTER

NIGHT OF THE HUNTER

©2014 Wizards of the Coast LLC.

Published by Wizards of the Coast LLC. Manufactured by: Hasbro SA, Rue Emile-Boéchat 31, 2800 Delémont, CH. Represented by Hasbro Europe, 2 Roundwood Ave, Stockley Park, Uxbridge, Middlesex, UB11 1AZ, UK.

Printed in the U.S.A.

Cartography by: Robert Lazzaretti
Cover art by: Tyler Jacobson
First Printing: March 2014

9 8 7 6 5 4 3 2 1

ISBN: 978-0-7869-6511-3
ISBN: 978-0-7869-6550-2 (ebook)
620A6535000001 EN

Cataloging-in-Publication data is on file with the Library of Congress

Contact Us at Wizards.com/CustomerService
Wizards of the Coast LLC, PO Box 707, Renton, WA 98057-0707, USA
USA & Canada: (800) 324-6496 or (425) 204-8069
Europe: +32(0) 70 233 277

Visit our web site at **www.dungeonsanddragons.com**

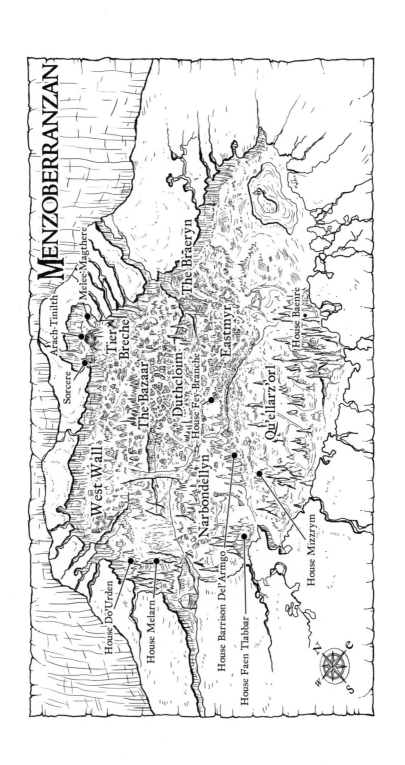

MENZOBERRANZAN

Arach-Tinilith
Melee-Magthere
Sorcere
Tier Breche
The Bazaar
Duthcloim
West Wall
House Fey-Branche
The Braeryn
Eastmyr
Narbondellyn
Qu'ellarz'orl
House Baenre
House Mizzrym
House Do'Urden
House Melarn
House Barrison Del'Armgo
House Faen Tlabbar

PROLOGUE

So much blood.

Everywhere, blood.

It followed Doum'wielle wherever she traveled. She saw it on her silvery skin, skin that spoke of her mixed elf and drow heritage. It followed her in her dreams, each night, every night. She saw it on the footprints she left in the snow. She saw it on her keen-edged sword—yes, on the sword most of all.

It was always there, reflected in the red edge of the sentient weapon, Khazid'hea.

A thousand times had she stabbed that blade through her brother's heart. His screams echoed between the beats of her every waking thought and filled her dreams, sweet music to the sensibilities of Khazid'hea.

Her brother Teirflin had tried to stab her with that very sword, with her sword, as she slept one day. But she had been quicker.

She had been better.

She had been more worthy.

She felt the blade entering his chest, easily shearing through skin and muscle and bone, reaching for his heart so that the delicious blood might flow freely.

She could never wash that blood from her hands, but at that time, in the thralls of the weapon, with the warm words of her father whispering into her ear, she didn't want to wash the blood from her hands.

Perhaps Teirflin's dying screams were music after all.

1

Two, the drow's fingers indicated, and the motion continued in the intricate silent hand-language of the cunning race, *Moving stealthily.*

Tsabrak Xorlarrin, noble wizard of Menzoberranzan's Third House, carefully considered his next move. He wasn't comfortable out here, so far from both Menzoberranzan and Q'Xorlarrin, the new drow city his family was creating in the mines of the ancient dwarven homeland of Gauntlgrym. He was fairly sure that he knew why Matron Zeerith had sent him, particularly him, on this distant reconnoiter: Zeerith wanted to keep him far from Ravel, her son, who was a bitter rival of Tsabrak.

And a bitter rival who had surely gained the upper hand, Tsabrak had to admit. With his successful infiltration of the ancient dwarven homeland, Ravel had become the shining faerie fire to accent the glory of House Xorlarrin—and he had done so in the company of a Baenre, no less, and with the blessing of that powerful clan. The city of Q'Xorlarrin was well on its way to becoming reality, and Ravel had played the paramount role in that development.

The wizard's fingers moved quickly, speaking to the point, demanding more information from the scouts. He sent them forth and headed back the other way, where his cousin Berellip, Ravel's older sister, waited. He spotted her among the entourage, still in a small natural chamber off to the side of the underground river that had been guiding them thus far. Berellip Xorlarrin was rarely hard to find, after all. Brash and loud, she kept the inferior commoner males far away, with only her two young female attendants allowed to even address her.

Tsabrak moved across the small room and waved those attendants away. "You have found them?"

Tsabrak nodded. "Two, at least. Moving along the lower tunnels."

"Orcs?"

The mage shrugged. "We do not yet know. Stealthier than orcs, it would seem. Clever goblins, perhaps."

"I can smell the orc stench all about us," Berellip said with obvious disgust.

Tsabrak, again, could only shrug. They had come here, to these tunnels underneath the northern reaches of the Silver Marches, with full expectation that they would encounter many orcs. After all, up above them was the land of King Obould, the Kingdom of Many-Arrows.

"I view your smirk as an invitation to play," Berellip warned, her hand moving near to the hilt of her snake-headed whip.

"My apologies, Priestess," Tsabrak said, and he bowed deferentially. This one did so love to put that whip to its painful work on the flesh of drow males. "I was merely wondering if a goblin tribe taken as prisoners would suffice upon our return to Q'Xorlarrin."

"You still believe that we were sent out here to secure slaves?"

"Partly," the wizard answered honestly. "I know of other reasons why I might be moved aside for the present. I am not certain, however, why you would be so removed in this time of great upheaval and glory for the House."

"Because Matron Zeerith determined it," the priestess answered through tight lips.

Tsabrak bowed again, confirming that such an answer was, of course, all that he needed or deserved. She closely guarded her thoughts, as was often her way, and Tsabrak could only accept it for what it was. He and Berellip had spoken many times of the purpose of their mission, in conversations where Berellip had been far more open, and even critical of Matron Zeerith. But such was the nature of Berellip Xorlarrin that she could simply, stubbornly, pretend that those previous discussions had never taken place.

"It was not only Matron Zeerith who determined our course and the composition of our troupe," he boldly remarked.

"You do not know this."

"I have known Archmage Gromph Baenre for two centuries. His hand is in this."

Berellip's face grew very tight, and she muttered, "Baenre's hand is in everything," a clear reference to Tiago Baenre, the First House's official escort to Ravel's mission that had conquered Gauntlgrym. Berellip had made no secret to Tsabrak of her distaste for the brash young noble warrior in the early days of their journey east.

Berellip's scorn for Tiago came as no surprise to Tsabrak. He knew Tiago fairly well, and the young warrior's propensity to forego the station afforded mere males and to throw the weight of House Baenre behind his imperial attitude was well-documented among the lesser Houses in Menzoberranzan. Besides, rumors whispered that Tiago would soon wed Saribel Xorlarrin, Berellip's younger, and by all accounts and all measures, inferior sister, having chosen her above Berellip. No doubt, Tsabrak realized, Berellip thought much the same of Saribel as she did of Ravel.

"What business would the archmage have with us out here?" Berellip asked, despite her smug superiority. "He would bid Matron Zeerith to send a high priestess and a master of Sorcere off on an errand to collect simple slaves?"

"There is more," Tsabrak said with confidence. He reminded her of a previous conversation by continuing, "The Spider Queen is pleased with our journey, so you have assured me."

He held his breath as he finished, expecting Berellip to lash out at him, but was pleasantly surprised when she simply nodded and said, "Something larger is afoot. We will know when Matron Zeerith determines that we should know."

"Or when Archmage Gromph determines it," Tsabrak dared to say, and Berellip's eyes flashed with anger.

He was quite relieved then, at that very moment, when his scouts returned, rushing into the side chamber.

"Not goblins," one reported, clearly excited.

"Drow," said the other.

"Drow?" Berellip asked. She and Tsabrak exchanged looks. There were no drow cities out here that either knew of.

Perhaps we will soon find our answers, Tsabrak's fingers silently flashed to his cousin, the mage taking care to keep the signal out of sight of the scouts and others in the room.

The two lithe figures sat on a ledge, halfway up an underground cliff face. Water poured from the tunnel opening above them, diving down to an underground lake below. Despite the narrow and seemingly precarious perch in the meager light of a few scattered lichens, neither shifted around nor clenched uncomfortably.

"Why must we ascend this cliff?" asked the woman, Doum'wielle, the younger of the elves. She hauled up the rope from below. She had to speak loudly to be heard over the sound of the falling, splashing water, which made the other, older figure, her father, wish that he had properly instructed her in the ways of drow sign language. "I thought

4

our plan was to *descend* through the Underdark," Doum'wielle added sarcastically.

The darker-skinned drow at her side took a bite of an Underdark mushroom, then looked at it distastefully. "This is the path I took when I left my home," he answered.

The young elf woman, half-drow, half-moon elf, leaned out a bit from the ledge and twirled the grapnel end of the rope, preparing to throw. She stopped mid-swing and stared at her companion incredulously.

"That was a hundred years ago," she reminded. "How can you remember the path you took?"

He tossed the rest of the mushroom from the ledge, gingerly stood, one leg showing garish wounds, and wiped his hands on his breeches. "I always knew I would return some day."

The woman spun the rope once more and let fly, the grapnel disappearing into the black hole of the tunnel entrance above.

"So I never let myself forget the way," he said as she tested the grip of the grapnel. "Although the waterfall wasn't here last time."

"Well, that's promising," she quipped and began to climb.

Her father watched her with pride. He noted the sword she carried sheathed on her hip, his sword, Khazid'hea, the Cutter, a sentient and powerful blade known for driving its weaker wielders into savage madness. His daughter was gaining control of the bloodthirsty weapon. No small feat, he knew from painful personal experience.

She wasn't halfway up to the tunnel when he jumped onto the fine, strong elven cord, his sinewy arms propelling him upward quickly behind her. He had nearly made the ledge as she rolled herself over it, turning to offer him a hand, which he took and scrambled over.

She said something to him, but he didn't hear her. Not then. Not when he was looking at a line of approaching enemies, arms extended, hand crossbows leveled his way.

Standing in the mouth of the tunnel opposite the waterfall, the same course his prey had taken, Tsabrak Xorlarrin watched the pair ascend the cliff face from across the underground lake. He had found them quite easily, and with his considerable magical abilities, had trailed them closely, and indeed with a wide smile (though it could not be viewed, since he was under the enchantment of invisibility), for he was fairly certain that he knew this wayward drow.

He wondered what Berellip Xorlarrin would do when she discovered this one's identity as a once-favored son of Menzoberranzan's Second House, the greatest rival family of House Xorlarrin.

"Tread cautiously, witch," he whispered, his words buried beneath the din of the waterfall. He could have used one of his spells to magically send a word of warning to Berellip's ambush group, and indeed, he almost began the spell.

But he changed his mind and smiled wider, and wider still when he heard the female cry out and saw a flash of lightning just within the tunnel entrance.

As a precaution, Tsabrak moved to the base of the cliff, noting two solid anchor points, stalagmites, as he began to cast a spell.

Pops and crackles sounded above the rush of water as Doum'wielle's lightning sheet intercepted the incoming hand crossbow bolts. Their momentum stolen, they fell harmlessly to the ground.

"To my side!" she cried to her father, but she needn't have bothered, for the veteran warrior was already moving to that very spot, sliding in beside her up against the tunnel wall. Like her, he clearly had no desire to battle the incoming warriors with his back to a cliff ledge.

He drew out his two swords, she her one.

She only held one blade, for Khazid'hea would not allow a sister weapon, would not share in the glory of the kill.

Three drow males swept in before the pair. They kept their backs to the rushing river, with practiced coordination, one sliding, one leaping, another running in to defend his comrades, and all three with two swords drawn. The sliding drow popped right to his feet in front of Doum'wielle's father with a double-up cross of his blades, driving his opponent's swords up high.

The leaping, somersaulting drow landed beside him, and before the drow had even touched down, he stabbed one blade out toward Doum'wielle and one out at her father. And with the third drow coming in hard at her and demanding a double parry, Doum'wielle only barely avoided being stabbed in the face.

"Do not kill!" her father cried, though whether he was speaking to her, or imploring their enemies, she could not tell. Nor would she have followed the command in any case, her sword thirsting for blood, demanding blood . . . any blood. She swept Khazid'hea across with a powerful backhand, taking her attacker's two swords aside. He rolled his trailing blade as she rolled Khazid'hea, both stabbing out.

Doum'wielle couldn't retreat with the wall against her back. But her strike drove her opponent back so that his sword, too, could not reach her. One against one, and with Khazid'hea in hand, she was certain she could defeat this formidable warrior.

But she wasn't one against one, and neither was her father. The drow centering the trio of enemies worked his blades independently, left and right, stabbing at both between the twirl of counters and parries.

No! Khazid'hea screamed in her thoughts as it sensed her intentions.

The demand of the sword carried little weight, though, for Doum'wielle's movements were driven by desperate need, not choice. The young half-drow battle-mage stabbed straight ahead, swept her blade out to deflect a strike from the centering enemy, then stabbed ahead again, driving her immediate opponent back.

She timed his retreat perfectly with the release of magic, a spell that sent him skidding into the river on the slippery stones. He thrashed and cried out, and was caught by the current and washed past his companions and out over the ledge.

"No!" her father cried at her, but for far different reasons than had the sword she held. Khazid'hea's cry was in denial of her use of magic, she understood, for the sword wanted all the glory and all the blood. Her father, however, apparently still thought that they could find the time to barter and diffuse the situation—a notion Doum'wielle thought all the more ridiculous because of the mocking response of Khazid'hea in her mind.

Noting that other enemies were near at hand and closing fast, Doum'wielle turned fast on the second drow in line, thinking to drive him into the enemy facing her father.

But this time, he proved the quicker, and as she advanced he leaped back and leaped high, one hand going to a brooch on his cloak tie, his House insignia. The magic of that jewelry brought forth a spell of levitation, and the drow floated out across the underground river.

7

Doum'wielle thought to pursue, but Khazid'hea drove her forward instead, sensing the vulnerability of the third in line, who was already entangled with her father. That enemy turned to meet her rush, and managed to partially deflect her leading strike.

Partially, but the devilish Khazid'hea got through, and so easily pierced his fine drow chain mail, and so beautifully slid into his skin. A look of delicious horror on his face, the drow threw himself backward, and flew from the ledge into the open air of the vast chamber beyond.

Doum'wielle turned with her father, side-by-side once more and facing into the tunnel, where four drow warriors, including the one who had levitated away across the river, stood in a line, lifting hand crossbows once more.

"And now we die," her father said with resignation.

"Enough!" came a loud cry, volume clearly magically enhanced, from behind the enemy line. It was a call that would surely carry the weight of command among any raised in Menzoberranzan, for it had sounded in a female voice.

The drow line parted and between the warriors passed a female, dressed in fine black robes adorned with spider-shaped charms and elaborate designs. Even Doum'wielle, who had no experience with drow culture other than the teachings of her father, could not miss the significance. This was a priestess of the goddess Lolth, and one of great power.

For she held the terrible weapon of her high station, a snake-headed whip, four living serpents weaving eagerly in the air at her side, ready to strike at her command.

"Who are you and why are you here?" Doum'wielle asked in the language of the drow, which her father had taught her.

"Ah, yes, introductions," her father said. "I would have offered them earlier, but your warriors were too busy trying to kill me."

The snakes of the female's whip hissed, reflecting her ire.

"You dare speak to a high priestess with such insolence?"

Doum'wielle was surprised to see her father fall back a step, clearly intimidated. He had underestimated her rank and did not seem overly confident now that it had been revealed.

"Forgive me," he said with a graceful bow. "I am . . ."

"Tos'un Armgo, of House Barrison Del'Armgo," Doum'wielle finished for him. "And I am Doum'wielle Armgo, of the same House." She stepped forward, Khazid'hea at the ready, its red edge shining angrily, hungrily.

"You will escort us to Menzoberranzan," she ordered, "where we will rejoin our House."

She couldn't tell if the stately priestess opposing her was impressed or amused.

"Children of House Barrison Del'Armgo, Menzoberranzan does not rule here," she said evenly.

She was amused, Doum'wielle realized, and that did not bode well.

"The city of Q'Xorlarrin, though, will greet you," the priestess said, and Tos'un sighed, and Doum'wielle thought it and hoped it to be an expression of great relief.

"Q'Xorlarrin?" he asked. "House Xorlarrin has built a city?" He half-turned to Doum'wielle and whispered, "My little Doe, our new life may yet prove more interesting than I had planned."

"Yes, House Xorlarrin," the priestess responded. "Once the Third House of Menzoberranzan, now greater. Greater than the Second House, it would seem."

The way she had spoken seemed to take the hope from her father's face, Doum'wielle noted.

"Tos'un Armgo," came a male voice from behind, and Doum'wielle and Tos'un turned in unison to see a drow floating in the air just beyond the ledge. Doum'wielle moved as if to lash out with magic, but her father grabbed her arm and held her still. When she looked at him, she understood that he thought them clearly overmatched.

"Tsabrak?" he asked.

The floating mage laughed and bowed, which seemed almost comical while hanging in mid-air.

"A friend?" Doum'wielle whispered hopefully.

"Drow don't have friends," Tos'un whispered back.

"Indeed," Tsabrak Xorlarrin agreed. "And yet, I have done you a great service, and likely saved you from summary execution." He pointed down below him, and Doum'wielle and Tos'un dared to inch closer and glance down over the ledge, to see the two drow warriors they had driven over caught helplessly, but safely, in a magical web strung near the bottom of the watery cavern.

"My cousin, the eldest daughter of Matron Zeerith, has only recently been granted, by the will of the goddess, a fourth snake for her implement of Lolth's mercy, and is eager to put the serpent to use, I would expect. Berellip is not known to show mercy on those who kill Xorlarrins."

9

"Perhaps, then, she should not send Xorlarrins to attack the children of House Barrison Del'Armgo!" Doum'wielle imperiously replied. Tos'un gasped and moved to stop her, and indeed, she did bite off the end of that retort.

But only because four living snakes, the heads of Berellip's mighty whip, bit her in the back for her impudence.

Khazid'hea screamed at her to retaliate, but the poison and the agony denied that, driving Doum'wielle to her knees.

And so her lesson had begun.

PART ONE

TOGETHER IN DARKNESS

Do people really change?

I've thought about this question so many times over the last decades—and how poignant it seemed to me when I happened once more upon Artemis Entreri, shockingly alive, given the passage of a century.

I came to travel with him, to trust him, even; does that mean that I came to believe that he had "changed"?

Not really. And now that we have once more parted ways, I don't believe there to be a fundamental difference in the man, compared to the Entreri I fought beside in the Undercity of Mithral Hall when it was still in the hands of the duergar, or the Entreri I pursued to Calimport when he abducted Regis. Fundamentally, he is the same man, as, fundamentally, I am the same drow.

A person may learn and grow, and thus react differently to a recurring situation—that is the hope I hold for all people, for myself, for societies, even. Is that not the whole point of gaining experience, to use it to make wiser choices, to temper destructive instincts, to find better resolutions? In that regard, I do believe Artemis Entreri to be a changed man, slower in turning to the dagger for resolution, though no less deadly when he needs it. But fundamentally, regarding what lies in the man's heart, he is the same.

I know that to be true of myself, although, in retrospect, I walked a very different path over the last few years than that I purposefully strode for the majority of my life. Darkness found my heart, I admit. With the loss of so many dear friends came the loss of hope itself and so I gave in to the easier path—although I had vowed almost every day that such a cynical journey would not be the road of Drizzt Do'Urden.

Fundamentally, though, I did not change, and so when faced with the reality of the darkened road, when it came time for me to admit the path to myself, I could not go on.

I cannot say that I miss Dahlia, Entreri, and the others. My heart does not call out for me to go and find them, surely—but I am not so certain that I could confidently claim such a casual attitude about my decision to part ways had it not been for the return of those friends I hold most dear! How can I regret parting with Dahlia when the fork in our road led me directly back into the arms of Catti-brie?

And thus, here I stand, together once more beside the Companions of the Hall, rejoined with the truest and dearest friends I have ever known, and could ever hope to know. Have they changed? Have their respective journeys through the realm of death itself brought to these four friends a new and guiding set of principles that will leave me sorely disappointed as I come to know them once more?

That is a fear I hold, but hold afar.

For people do not fundamentally change, so I believe. The warmth of Catti-brie's embrace is one inspiring confidence that I am right. The mischievous grin of Regis (even with the mustache and goatee) is one I have seen before. And Bruenor's call that night under the stars atop Kelvin's Cairn, and his reaction to Wulfgar . . . aye, that was Bruenor, true to the thick bone and thick head!

All that said, in these first days together, I have noted a change in Wulfgar's step, I admit. There is a lightness there I have not seen before, and—curiously, I say, given the description I have been told of his reluctance to leave Iruladoon for the mortal world once more—a smile that never seems to leave his face.

But he is Wulfgar, surely, the proud son of Beornegar. He has found some enlightenment, though in what way I cannot say. Enlightened and lightened. I see no burden there. I see amusement and joy, as if he views this all as a grand adventure on borrowed time, and I cannot deny the health of that perspective!

They are back. We are back. The Companions of the Hall. We are not as we once were, but our hearts remain true, our purpose joined, and our trust for each other undiminished and thus unbridled.

I am very glad of that!

And, in a curious way (and a surprising way to me), I hold no regrets for the last few years of my journey through a life confusing, frightening, and grand all at once. My time with Dahlia, and particularly with Entreri, was one of learning, I must believe. To see the world through a cynical perspective did not hurl me back to the days of my youth in Menzoberranzan, and thus encapsulate me in darkness, but rather, has offered to me a more complete understanding of the consequence of choice, for I broke free of the cynicism before knowing what fate awaited me atop Bruenor's Climb.

I am not so self-centered as to believe that the world around me is created for me! We all play such self-centered games at times, I suppose, but in this case, I will allow myself one moment of self-importance: to accept the reunion of the Companions of the Hall as a reward to me. Put whatever name you wish upon the gods and goddesses, or the fates, or the coincidences and twists that move the world along its path—it matters not. In this one instance, I choose to believe in a special kind of justice.

Indeed, it is a foolish and self-serving claim, I know.

But it feels good.

—Drizzt Do'Urden

CHAPTER 1

THE SEASONED MATRON BAENRE

IT SEEMED JUST ANOTHER DAY FOR MATRON MOTHER QUENTHEL BAENRE as she went to her evening prayers. Her magnificent black robes, laced like flowing spiderwebs, swirled around her as she regally moved along the center aisle, passing the inferior priestesses at the many side altars of the Baenre House Chapel. The slightest breeze could send the spidery ends of that robe drifting upward and outward, blurring the form of the matron mother, giving her the appearance of etherealness and otherworldliness.

Quenthel's sole surviving sister, Sos'Umptu, the first priestess of the House and keeper of the chapel, had preceded her to prayer this evening, and now prostrated herself, face down on the stone floor, legs tucked in a tight kneeling position. Quenthel considered that image as she neared, noting that Sos'Umptu had her forearms and hands flat on the floor above her head, up toward the altar, a position of complete supplication and apology, even, and not the typical form for daily prayers by the leading priestesses. A priestess of Sos'Umptu's station rarely assumed so humble an entreaty.

Quenthel walked up close enough to hear her sister's chanted prayer, and indeed, it was an apology, and a desperate one at that. The matron mother listened for a bit longer, hoping to catch some hint of why Sos'Umptu would be apologizing, but caught nothing specific.

"Dear sister," she said when Sos'Umptu finally broke from her fevered chant.

The first priestess raised her head and turned to glance back.

"Supplicate," Sos'Umptu whispered urgently. "At once!"

14

NIGHT OF THE HUNTER

Quenthel's first instinct was to lash out at Sos'Umptu for her disrespectful tone and for daring to order her to do anything. She even put a hand to her snake-headed whip, where the five writhing, sentient serpents continued their eternal dance. She was surprised as she grasped the weapon, though, for even K'Sothra, the most bloodthirsty of the serpents, warned her away from that course—and rare indeed was it for K'Sothra to ever counsel anything but the lash!

Hear her, purred Hsiv, the advisor serpent.

Sos'Umptu is devout, Yngoth agreed.

With the counsel of the serpents, the matron mother realized that only a matter of great importance would ever coax such irreverence from her sister. After all, Sos'Umptu was much like Triel, their deceased older sister, reserved and quietly calculating.

The matron mother straightened her robes out behind her and fell to her knees beside the first priestess, face down, arms extended in full surrender.

She heard the screaming—shrieking, actually—immediately, the discordant cacophony of demons, and of Lady Lolth herself, full of outrage and venom.

Something was very much amiss, clearly.

Quenthel tried to sort through the possibilities. Menzoberranzan remained on edge, as did most of Toril, as the world continued its realignment after the end of the Spellplague, some five years previous. But the drow city had fared well in that time, Quenthel believed. House Xorlarrin, Third House of Menzoberranzan, in league with House Baenre, had established a strong foothold in the dwarven complex formerly known as Gauntlgrym, and soon to be known as Q'Xorlarrin. The great and ancient Forge, powered by nothing less than a primordial of fire, had blazed to life, and weapons of fine edge and mighty enchantment had begun to flow back to Menzoberranzan. So secure did the new sister city seem that Matron Zeerith Xorlarrin herself had begun to make preparations for her departure, and had requested of Menzoberranzan's ruling council that it approve the name Q'Xorlarrin for the new settlement, and as the permanent abode for her powerful House.

Replacing that House on the Council of Eight could prove messy, of course, as was always the case when those Houses immediately below the top eight ranks saw a chance at ascendance, but Quenthel remained confident that she had those issues under control.

R.A. SALVATORE

Bregan D'aerthe, too, was thriving, with the resulting trade flowing in and out of Menzoberranzan. Under the leadership of Kimmuriel and Jarlaxle, the mercenaries had come to dominate the surface city of Luskan, and quietly, so as to not provoke the curiosity or ire of the lords of the surrounding kingdoms, particularly the powerful city of Waterdeep.

The matron mother subtly shook her head. Menzoberranzan was operating quite smoothly under her leadership. Perhaps these screams were prompted by something else. She tried to widen her focus beyond the reach of Menzoberranzan's tentacles.

But the sudden shriek in her head left no doubt that Lolth's anger this night was focused—and focused squarely on House Baenre, or at least, on Menzoberranzan. After a long while of accepting the telepathic berating, Quenthel lifted herself up to a kneeling position and motioned for Sos'Umptu to do likewise.

Her sister came up shaking her head, her expression as full of confusion as Quenthel's own.

The source of Queen Lolth's ire? Quenthel's fingers asked in the intricate drow sign language.

Sos'Umptu shook her head helplessly.

Matron Mother Quenthel looked at the grand altar, its standing backdrop a gigantic drider-like figure. Its eight spider legs were tucked in a squat, and it bore the head and torso of a female drow, the beautiful figure of Lady Lolth herself. Quenthel closed her eyes and listened once more, then fell to the floor in supplication yet again.

But the shrieks would not provide focus.

Quenthel gradually came back to a kneeling position no less confused or concerned. She crossed her arms over her chest and rocked slowly, seeking guidance. She put her hand on her sentient weapon, but the serpents remained silent, uncharacteristically so.

At length, she lifted her hands and signed to her sister, *Get you to Arach-Tinilith and retrieve Myrineyl!*

"Sister?" Sos'Umptu dared to openly question. Arach-Tinilith, the training academy for drow priestesses, served as the greatest of the drow academies, elevated on Tier Breche above the school of warriors, Melee-Magthere, and Sorcere, the school for promising young wizards.

Quenthel shot Sos'Umptu a threatening glare.

NIGHT OF THE HUNTER

I should retire to the Fane of Quarvelsharess, Sos'Umptu's fingers flashed, referring to the great public cathedral of Menzoberranzan, one Sos'Umptu had been instrumental in creating, and in which she served as high priestess. *I only visited Chapel Baenre so that I would not be tardy for evening prayers.*

Her argument revealed to the matron mother that Sos'Umptu thought the issue bigger than House Baenre, encompassing all of Menzoberranzan, and perhaps that was true, but Quenthel was not about to take the chance of allowing her House to become vulnerable in any way.

No! Quenthel's fingers flashed simply. She saw the disappointment on Sos'Umptu's face, and knew it was more a matter of the reason for the ordered diversion to Arach-Tinilith than the delay in her return to her precious Fane of Quarvelsharess. Sos'Umptu was no friend to Myrineyl, Quenthel's eldest daughter, after all! Soon to graduate from Arach-Tinilith, the whispers had already started concerning the expected struggle between Myrineyl and Sos'Umptu over the title of First Priestess of House Baenre, which was among the most coveted positions in the drow city.

You will work with Myrineyl, Quenthel's hand signs explained, and aloud she added, "Summon a yochlol, in this temple. We will hear the call of Lady Lolth and will answer to her needs."

Up and down the chapel, the matron mother's words were met by rising eyes, even rising priestesses, at the proclamation. Summoning a yochlol was no minor thing, after all, and most in attendance had never seen one of Lolth's Handmaidens.

The matron mother watched the expressions being exchanged among the lessers, wide-eyed, full of apprehension, full of excitement.

"Select half the priestesses of House Baenre to witness the summoning," the matron mother instructed as she rose. "Make them earn their place of witness." She threw the train of her spidery gown out behind her and imperiously strode away, appearing the rock of confidence and strength.

Inside, though, the matron mother's thoughts roiled, the shrieks of Lolth echoing in her mind. Somehow, someone had erred, and greatly so, and punishment from Lolth was never an easy sentence.

Perhaps she should take part in the summoning, she thought, before quickly dismissing the idea. She was the Matron Mother of House Baenre, after all, the unquestioned ruler of Lolth's city of Menzoberranzan. She would not request the audience of a yochlol, and would only accept the invitation of one, should it come to that. Besides, high priestesses were only supposed to call upon one of Lolth's handmaidens in a dire emergency, and Quenthel wasn't completely sure that's what this was. If not, and the summoning invoked the further displeasure of Lolth, better that she was not among those calling!

For now, she decided, she should visit with the one she believed to be her only other surviving sibling, the Archmage of Menzoberranzan, her brother Gromph, to learn what he might know.

The Elderboy of House Baenre, the first child of the great Yvonnel, Gromph Baenre now stood as the oldest living drow in Menzoberranzan, and had long before earned the distinction as the longest-serving archmage of the city. His tenure predated not only the Spellplague but the Time of Troubles, and by centuries! It was said that he got along by getting along, and by knowing his place, for though his station afforded him great latitude within Menzoberranzan, inarguably as the most powerful male drow in the city, he remained, after all, merely a male drow.

In theory, therefore, every matron mother and every high priestess outranked him. They were closer to Lolth, and the Spider Queen ruled all.

Many lesser priestesses had tested that theory against Gromph over the centuries.

They were all dead.

Even Quenthel, Matron Mother Quenthel herself, knocked lightly and politely on the door of the archmage's private chamber in House Baenre. She might have been more showy and forceful had Gromph been in his residence in the Academy of Sorcere, but here in House Baenre, the pretense couldn't stand. Quenthel and Gromph, siblings, understood each other, didn't much like each other, but surely needed each other.

The old wizard stood up quickly and offered a respectful bow when Quenthel pressed into the room.

"Unexpected," he said, for indeed, these two spent little time in each other's company, and usually only when Quenthel had summoned Gromph to her formal chair of station.

Quenthel closed the door and motioned for her brother to be seated. He noted her nervous movements and looked at her slyly. "There is news?"

Quenthel took the seat opposite the archmage, across the great desk, which was covered in parchment, both rolled and spread, with a hundred bottles of various inks set about them.

"Tell me of the Spellplague," Quenthel bade him.

"It is ended, mercifully," he replied with a shrug. "Magic is as magic was, the Weave reborn, and gloriously so."

Quenthel stared at him curiously. "Gloriously?" she asked, considering his strange choice of words, and one that surely seemed stranger still, given the typical demeanor of Gromph.

Gromph shrugged as if it did not matter, to deflect his nosy sister. For once, regarding the movements of Lady Lolth, this situation did not yet concern her. For once, the male wizards of Menzoberranzan had been entreated by the Spider Queen before and above the domineering disciples of Arach-Tinilith. Gromph knew that his time standing above Quenthel in Lolth's eyes would be brief, but he intended to hold fast to it for as long as possible.

Quenthel narrowed her eyes, and Gromph suppressed his smile, knowing that his apparent indifference to such godly games surely irked her.

"The Spider Queen is angry," Quenthel said.

"She is always angry," Gromph replied, "else she could hardly be considered a demon queen!"

"Your jests are noted, and will be relayed," Quenthel warned.

Gromph shrugged. He could hardly suppress his laughter. One of them would soon be exposing quite a bit of truth regarding the Spider Queen, he knew, but to Quenthel's surprise, it wouldn't be her.

"You think her current anger is regarding the Weave? The end of the Spellplague?" he asked, because he could not resist. He pictured the expression Quenthel would wear when the truth was revealed to her, and it took all that he could muster to not break out in open, mocking laughter. "Five years, it has been—not so long a time in the eyes of a goddess, true, but still . . ."

"Do not mock her," Quenthel warned.

"Of course not. I merely seek to discern—"

"She is angry," Quenthel interrupted. "It seemed unfocused, a discordant shriek, a scream of frustration."

"She lost," Gromph said matter-of-factly, and he laughed at Quenthel's threatening glare.

"It's not about that," the matron mother said with confidence.

"Dear sister . . ."

"Matron Mother," Quenthel sharply corrected.

"Do you fear that the Spider Queen is angry with you?" Gromph went on.

Quenthel rested back in her chair and stared off into nothingness, contemplating the question far longer than Gromph had anticipated—so long, in fact, that the archmage went back to his work, penning a new scroll.

"At us," Quenthel decided some time later, and Gromph looked up at her curiously.

"Us? House Baenre?"

"Menzoberranzan, perhaps." Quenthel waved her hand dismissively, obviously flustered. "I have set Sos'Umptu and my daughter to the task of summoning a handmaiden, that we might get more definitive answers."

"Then pray tell me, dear sister"—Gromph folded his hands on the desk before him, staring hard at Quenthel, pointedly referring to her in that less-than-formal manner—"why did you decide to disturb my work?"

"The Spellplague, the Weave," the matron mother flailed, again waving her hand.

"Nay, that is not the reason," said the old archmage. "Why, Quenthel, I believe that you are afraid."

"You dare to speak to me in that manner?"

"Why would I not, dear sister?"

Quenthel leaped from the chair, sending it skidding out behind her. Her eyes flashed with outrage as she corrected him once more, spitting every syllable, "Matron Mother."

"Yes," said Gromph. "Matron Mother of Menzoberranzan." He rose to face her directly, and matched her unblinking stare with his own. "Never forget that."

"You seem to be the one—"

Gromph rolled right over the thought. "And act the part of it," he said evenly.

Quenthel's eyes flashed again, her hands clenched and opened as if readying for a spell, but she quickly composed herself.

Gromph nodded and gave a little laugh. "If the Spider Queen is angry with you and you show any weakness, your doom will fall," he warned. "The World Above, and below, is in flux, Lady Lolth's own designs have only begun to spin, and she will brook no weakness now."

"Menzoberranzan thrives under my leadership!"

"Does it?"

"House Xorlarrin has settled Gauntlgrym. The ancient Forge is fired anew, and to the benefit of Menzoberranzan!"

"And House Barrison Del'Armgo?" Gromph asked slyly. "Do they view the move of Xorlarrin as one that strengthens the hand of Matron Mother Quenthel or as one that opens an opportunity for them here in the City of Spiders? You have removed a threat to them, have you not?"

"Their enemies the Xorlarrins are not far—Matron Zeerith is still within the city," Quenthel protested.

"But when she goes and the compound here is abandoned, as is soon to occur?"

"They will not be far."

"And if Matron Mez'Barris Armgo offers Zeerith a better deal than you have offered?"

Quenthel slid back into her chair, mulling over that dangerous notion. A long while passed before she looked up across the desk at Gromph, who stood towering above her now.

"Take heart, dear sister," Gromph said lightly. "We do not even know the source of Lady Lolth's . . . shriek. Perhaps it is naught but a residual scream of frustration over some event in the realm of the gods that has no bearing upon us whatsoever. Perhaps it was not, is not, directed at you or at House Baenre or at Menzoberranzan at all. Who can tell with these gods?"

Quenthel nodded hopefully at that.

"They will likely have engaged the yochlol by now," she explained, rising once more and turning for the door. "Let us go and get our answers."

"You go," Gromph bade her. He already had his answers, after all. "I have my work here—I will remain in House Baenre this day and throughout tomorrow in case I am needed."

That seemed to satisfy the matron mother and she took her leave, and Gromph remained standing until she had closed the door behind her. Then he sat, with a profound sigh.

He did not need a handmaiden to enlighten him. Another source, more ancient than he, had already told him of the stirrings of the Spider Queen and Lolth's mounting frustration with Menzoberranzan.

Quenthel would return to him shortly, he knew, and she would not much enjoy the journey he had planned for her.

21

The handmaiden's muddy voice, bubbly and scratchy all at once, fit its physical appearance, that of a half-melted blob of dirty wax, and with several tentacles waving around just to complete the nightmare.

"You extend, but you are not strong," the yochlol said, clearly irritated.

Sos'Umptu and Myrineyl exchanged nervous glances.

"We seek only to please the Spider Queen," Sos'Umptu replied, her voice thick with proper deference and supplication.

"She is pleased by strength," said the yochlol.

It was a surprising answer to both the priestesses, in that it did not include any variation or synonym to the word "chaos," which was the very edict and domain of Lady Lolth.

The gooey mass shifted then, turning slowly and thinning as it went. The tentacles shrank and became arms, drow arms, and drow legs, as the creature transformed into the guise of a female drow, naked and glorious. With a wry grin, the handmaiden walked over to Myrineyl and gently lifted her hand to stroke the drow's cheek and chin.

"Are you afraid, daughter of Matron Mother Quenthel?" the yochlol-turned-drow asked.

Myrineyl, now visibly trembling, swallowed hard.

"We sense that the goddess is in pain, or in distress," Sos'Umptu interjected, but the yochlol held up a hand to silence the older drow, and never turned her penetrating gaze from Myrineyl. The handmaiden's hand drifted lower, around Myrineyl's delicate jaw and gently, lightly, down her neck.

The young Baenre seemed to Sos'Umptu on the verge of panic. Despite her misgivings regarding Myrineyl, Sos'Umptu lifted her hand into Myrineyl's view and her fingers flashed the word *Strength!*

Myrineyl firmed up immediately and shook her head. "We are House Baenre," she said solidly. "If Lady Lolth is in need, we are here to serve. That is all."

"But you tremble at the touch of a handmaiden," the yochlol replied. "Are you afraid? Or do I so disgust you?"

Sos'Umptu held her breath, knowing that if Myrineyl answered incorrectly, the yochlol would likely drag her back to the Demonweb Pits for an eternity of torment.

But Myrineyl smiled, then suddenly embraced the handmaiden in a passionate kiss.

Sos'Umptu nodded in admiration, silently congratulating the play of the young priestess.

A long while later, Sos'Umptu and Myrineyl walked side-by-side through the halls of the Baenre main house, on their way to report to the matron mother. They had learned little from the handmaiden directly, which was typical of such encounters.

"Why?" Myrineyl asked quietly.

She didn't have to elaborate. Sos'Umptu could have allowed her to fail the handmaiden's test and been rid of her once and for all—and every drow in Menzoberranzan knew that Sos'Umptu Baenre would like nothing more than to be rid of Quenthel's troublesome and ambitious daughter.

"You thought it a test?" Sos'Umptu replied.

Myrineyl stopped walking and considered the older priestess.

"You think the handmaiden's call for strength is aimed at you?" Sos'Umptu asked, and scoffed. "Is it inexperience, then, or stupidity that propels you? Or arrogance, perhaps. Yes, that would be a proper failing for a child of Quenthel."

For many heartbeats, Myrineyl didn't respond, didn't even blink, and Sos'Umptu could see her rolling the insult over and over in her thoughts, looking for an angle of counterattack.

"You dare speak of the matron mother with such disrespect?" came the predictable retort.

"The test was for me," Sos'Umptu declared, and she started walking again, briskly, forcing Myrineyl to move swiftly to catch up. "And as such, for House Baenre wholly."

Myrineyl, who had, after all, just made love to a half-melted lump of dirty wax, wore a most delicious and perplexed expression.

"When a handmaiden takes the illusion of a drow, does she see through the eyes of the drow?" Sos'Umptu asked.

"What do you mean?"

"The yochlol physically watched me while she faced you, young fool," Sos'Umptu explained. "She saw my sign to you to show strength as clearly as you did, and that was the whole point of the exercise. Something is wrong. The Spider Queen is greatly upset, and demands strength."

"Unity," Myrineyl quietly breathed.

"Unity among the two nobles of House Baenre least likely to provide it." Myrineyl's eyes went wide.

"Do you think that the rivalry between the high priestess of House Baenre and the daughter of Matron Mother Quenthel would go unnoticed?" Sos'Umptu replied.

"I remain at Arach-Tinilith, serving Mistress Minolin Fey," Myrineyl said innocently.

"But you will never replace Minolin," Sos'Umptu said slyly, "or Ardulrae of House Melarn as Matron of Scriptures. With those appointments, the matron mother, your mother, satisfies two rival Houses, potential enemies House Baenre prefers not to deal with in this dangerous time of House Xorlarrin's departure. But then, you know this."

The innocent look was gone from Myrineyl's face now, Sos'Umptu noted, the young priestess assumed a rather brash posture.

"Unity now," Sos'Umptu said against that threatening pose. "The Spider Queen demands it." The words sounded quite curious to her as she spoke them, and to Myrineyl, as well, she realized when the younger priestess responded simply, "Why?"

Sos'Umptu could only sigh and shrug against that all-important question. The handmaiden had revealed little, her largest hint being an obscure reference that "The Eternal would understand."

They had arrived at Quenthel's door by then. Myrineyl lifted her hand to knock, but a look from Sos'Umptu warned her away. "Unity requires adherence to station, young one," Sos'Umptu explained, and it was she who knocked, she who answered the matron mother's call, and she who entered Quenthel's private chambers first.

Gromph smiled as his door swung open and, predictably, Matron Mother Quenthel swept into the room.

"She taunts me!" Quenthel whined. She moved up to the chair she had previously used and started to sit down, but instead just kicked it aside. "The Eternal would know, the handmaiden whispered to Sos'Umptu and Myrineyl. The Eternal! Our mother would know, but alas, mere Quenthel cannot!"

Gromph realized that his chuckle might not be appreciated at that moment, but he couldn't hold it back. The reference, the Eternal, was clear enough, speaking of their mother, Yvonnel, who was known as Yvonnel the Eternal, the greatest matron mother Menzoberranzan had ever known, and one who had ruled the city for millennia.

"And now you dare taunt me?" Quenthel fumed. "Would you ever have so responded to Yvonnel?"

"Of course not," the old archmage replied. "Yvonnel would have killed me."

"But mere Quenthel cannot, so you suppose?" The matron mother's features tightened into a dangerous scowl.

Gromph casually rose. "You won't," he replied, "whether you can or not."

"Are you so sure of that?"

"Only because I know my sister to be wise," he replied, moving to the left-hand wall of the chamber. There, he opened a large cabinet, revealing several shelves covered with various items: scrolls—so many scrolls!—coffers, sacks, and one large iron box. With a wave of his hand and a quick chant, Gromph cast a minor spell. A glistening, floating disc appeared beside him. He scooped out the iron box and placed it atop his enchantment.

"Of course I only dare to tease you because I have the answer to your riddle," he explained, turning back to Quenthel.

"In there?" she asked, indicating the box.

Gromph smiled all the wider.

"I have been waiting for this day for a long time, dear sister," the archmage explained.

"Matron Mother," she corrected.

"Exactly. It is past time that you are no longer referred to in any other manner."

Quenthel rocked back a step, then sat in the chair, staring at the archmage. "What do you know? Why is the Spider Queen angry?"

"That, I do not know," he replied. "Not exactly. But the handmaiden's reference to our dear dead mother tells me that I—that *we* can likely find out."

He gave another little laugh. "Or at least, I know how you can find out. Indeed, I know how you might learn many things. Good fortune lurks in the corridors of the Underdark just outside of Menzoberranzan. Good fortune and an intellect older than Yvonnel."

Quenthel stared at him hard for a long while. "Do you intend to forevermore speak in riddles?"

Gromph crossed the room behind her, to another cabinet near a display case. He opened the door to reveal a large, floor-to-ceiling mirror. The archmage closed his eyes and cast another spell, this one much longer to complete and much more intricate. The image of Gromph and the room in the mirror darkened, then disappeared altogether.

"Come," Gromph instructed, looking over his shoulder and reaching out for his sister's hand. The disc with the iron box atop it floated up beside Gromph.

"In there?"

"Of course."

"Where?" Quenthel demanded, but she reached out and took Gromph's hand.

"I just told you," he explained, stepping through and pulling Quenthel behind him. The floating disc came in as well, and with a word from Gromph, the magical construct began to glow, illuminating the area and revealing an Underdark tunnel.

"We are outside the city?" Quenthel asked, her voice a bit unstable. As the primary voice of Lady Lolth in Menzoberranzan, Matron Mother Quenthel was not allowed such journeys without a large entourage of soldiers and guards.

"You are quite safe, Matron Mother," Gromph replied, and his use of the proper title had the desired effect, drawing a nod from Quenthel.

"I discovered an old friend out here—or shall we call him an acquaintance?—quite by accident, you see," Gromph explained. "Although now I must presume that it was no accident, but a godly inspired discovery."

"More riddles?"

"It is all riddles—to me as well," he lied, for he knew well that Lolth had led him to these revelations and with definite purpose. "But you see, I am not the matron mother, and so our acquaintance will only reveal so much to me."

Quenthel started to reply, but stopped when Gromph pointed a wand out into the darkness of a side corridor and called upon its powers to create a small light in the distance, revealing a cave entrance blocked by lines of beads.

The archmage started for it, the matron mother and the floating disc right beside him.

Quenthel fell back when those beads parted at the end of a three-fingered hand, and an ugly biped stepped forth, the tentacles of its bulbous head waving excitedly.

"Illithid!" Quenthel gasped.

"An old friend," Gromph explained.

Quenthel steeled herself and stared hard at the approaching creature. Gromph took delight in her obvious disgust. Mind flayers were horrid creatures, of course, but this one was uglier still, having suffered grievous wounds, including one that left part of its brain-like, bulbous head hanging in a flap above its left shoulder.

"Methil," Quenthel whispered, and then called more loudly, "Methil El-Viddenvelp!"

"You remember!" Gromph congratulated.

Of course she remembered—how could anyone who had been serving in House Baenre in the last decades of Matron Mother Yvonnel's rule possibly forget this creature? Methil had served beside Matron Mother Yvonnel as her secret advisor, her *duvall*, as the drow called the position. With his mind-reading abilities, so foreign to all but psionicist drow, which were very few in number since Matron Mother Yvonnel had obliterated House Oblodra by dropping the whole of the place into the Clawrift during the Time of Troubles, Methil El-Viddenvelp had provided Matron Mother Yvonnel with great insight into the desires, the deceit, and the desperation of friends and enemies alike.

"But he died in the attack on Mithral Hall," Quenthel whispered.

"So did you," Gromph reminded. "And you are wrong in any case. Our friend here did not die, thanks to our bro—thanks to the efforts of Bregan D'aerthe."

"Kimmuriel," Quenthel reasoned, nodding, and Gromph was glad that he had corrected himself quickly enough, and that Kimmuriel Oblodra, one of the few surviving members of the fallen House, an accomplished psionicist, known associate of illithids, and, coincidentally, currently one of the co-leaders of the mercenary band, had reasonably come into her mind.

Kimmuriel had not even been involved in the efforts their brother Jarlaxle had expended in saving the grievously wounded illithid. But Quenthel didn't need to know that—or to know that Jarlaxle was even related to them!

"How long have you known about the mind flayer?" Quenthel asked suspiciously.

Gromph looked at her as though he didn't understand. "As long as you . . ." he started to reply.

"How long have you known him to be out here?" the matron mother clarified.

"Many months," Gromph replied, though as he considered the question, he realized it had probably been many years.

"And you did not think to inform me?"

Gromph again stared at her as if he didn't understand. "You think to use Methil as Yvonnel once utilized him?" Before Quenthel could reply, he added, "You cannot! The creature is quite damaged, I assure you, and would cause you considerable grief and nothing more in that role."

Quenthel's hand flashed up, palm outward, at the illithid, who had moved too close for comfort. She uttered a spell of command. "Halt!"

Normally such a spell would never have proven effective on a creature of such intellect, but when Matron Mother Quenthel uttered a command, it carried much greater weight indeed. That, perhaps combined with Methil El-Viddenvelp's clearly diminished mental capacity, had the illithid skidding to an abrupt and complete stop.

"Then why are we here?" Quenthel asked her brother pointedly.

"Because Yvonnel would know," he replied, and he turned to the iron box set upon the floating disc. He waved his hand over it, the cover magically lifting, and said, "Behold."

Quenthel gasped again as she peered into the box to see a withered head, split down the middle and somewhat stitched back together, a head she surely recognized, the split head of her long-dead mother!

"What is that?" she asked, falling back in horror. "You dare to blaspheme—"

"To preserve," Gromph corrected.

"How did you get that . . . her? Who?"

"Bregan D'aerthe, of course. The same ones who saved Methil, here."

"This is unconscionable!"

"You mean to resurrect Yvonnel?" The tremor was clear in her voice, Gromph noted, and rightly so—such an act would steal profoundly from the current matron mother, after all.

Gromph shook his head. "Our dear dead mother is far beyond that. The magic that had kept her alive for too many centuries is long dissipated. To bring her back now, well, she would just wither and shrivel and be dead once more."

"Then why do you have that?" Quenthel asked, pointing to the box, and she even dared to edge closer and glance in once more at the horrid thing.

"A curiosity at first," said Gromph. "Have you not complained to me many times about my collections?"

"This is beyond even your morbid sensibilities," Quenthel said dryly.

The archmage shrugged and smiled. "Indeed, you may be right, but . . ." He paused and nodded his chin past his sister. Quenthel turned and found the illithid in a highly agitated state, shivering and hopping about, with disgusting drool spilling down over the front of its white robe.

Quenthel turned an angry glare back at her brother. "Explain!" she demanded. "What desecration—"

"It would seem that I have preserved more than the physical head of our dead mother," Gromph replied casually. "For, as I have learned from Kimmuriel Oblodra of Bregan D'aerthe, and he from the illithids, the physical mind is full of patterns, tiny connections that preserve memories." As he spoke, he waved his hand, and the disc floated past Quenthel toward Methil, whose tentacles waggled insatiably.

"You would not dare!" the matron mother said, to both of them.

"I already have, many times," Gromph replied. "To your benefit, I expect."

Quenthel shot him an angry glare.

"The Spider Queen knows of it," the archmage explained. "So said the Mistress of Arach-Tinilith, with whom I spoke."

Quenthel's eyes flared with anger and her hand fell to her dreaded whip, but all five of the snakes screamed in her thoughts to hold back. Trembling with rage, for she knew well her conniving brother's confidante, the matron mother composed herself as much as possible and whispered through gritted teeth, "You confided in Minolin Fey, above me?"

"On Lolth's command," came the damning reply, so easily and confidently spoken.

Quenthel cried out, and she winced then and swung around, then fell back a step when she saw Methil leaning over the opened iron box, the creature's tentacles waggling within it, waggling within the skull of Matron Mother Yvonnel Baenre, no doubt!

"I revealed nothing to dear Minolin in specific detail, of course," Gromph casually continued. "Only in cryptic generalities."

"You would choose House Fey-Branche over House Baenre?"

"I would choose a powerful Mistress of Arach-Tinilith as a confidante in a matter most urgent to the Spider Queen. Minolin Fey understands that any betrayal on her part will be a move against Lolth and not one against House Baenre. Understand, Matron Mother, that the Spider Queen is not angry with me. Indeed, given the handmaiden's response to Sos'Umptu and Myrineyl this day, I hold confidence that Lady Lolth expected this all along, and certainly she sanctions it, and likely she orchestrated it. And it is, in the end, your own fault, dear sister."

Anger flashed in Quenthel's eyes. "Minolin Fey is a weakling," she said. "A fool of the highest order, and too stupid to even understand her own ignorance."

"Yes, accept the truth of my insult," Gromph came right back without fear. "How do you judge your tenure as the Matron Mother of Menzoberranzan?"

"Who are you to ask such a question of me?"

"I am the archmage. I am your brother. I am your ally."

"The city thrives!" Quenthel argued. "We expand to Gauntlgrym on my doing!"

"Are you trying to convince me, or yourself?" Gromph asked slyly, for they both knew the truth. Titanic events were going on all around them with the end of the Spellplague, and Lady Lolth herself was at play in the realm of arcane magic, Gromph knew, and yet, through it all, the denizens of Menzoberranzan had been mere spectators, after all.

And while House Baenre's hold on the city seemed as solid as ever at a cursory glance, the Baenre nobles knew the truth. The departure of House Xorlarrin, the Third House of the city and the one of greatest arcane power, was a tremendous risk that could bring great tumult to Menzoberranzan. Perhaps it would be seen as an opportunity for ascension to the ultimate rank by Matron Mez'Barris Armgo of House Barrison Del'Armgo, Baenre's rival, who had long coveted the title held by Yvonnel and now by Quenthel.

Appearances aside, Gromph knew it and Quenthel knew it: Menzoberranzan teetered on the edge of civil war.

"Our friend is ready for you," Gromph said.

Quenthel looked at him curiously for a moment, then, catching the reference, her eyes went wide as she spun around to face the illithid, who was standing right behind her. Quenthel took a fast step away, or tried to, but Gromph was quicker, casting a spell of holding upon her—a dweomer that never should have taken hold on the Matron Mother of Menzoberranzan.

NIGHT OF THE HUNTER

Unless Lady Lolth allowed it, Quenthel realized to her horror as she froze in place.

Still, she fought against the magic with all her strength, thoroughly repulsed, as Methil El-Viddenvelp's waggling tentacles reached for her tender skin, touched her neck and face, slithered up her nostrils.

Her expression became a mask of indignation, of outrage, and the purest anger Gromph had ever seen. He knew that if she found the power to break away at that moment, she would launch herself at him, physically and magically, to punish and bite and tear. She'd put her five-headed snake whip to work in short order, letting them strike at him, filling him with their agonizing venom, letting them chew into his belly and feast on his entrails.

Oh, if only she could break free!

But she could not, for Lady Lolth had sanctioned this most painful and profound lesson, and Gromph stood confident that by the time Quenthel was released, she'd more likely thank him than punish him.

For now, though, there was violation at a most intimate level, an outrage at the most primal depth, and pain of the most excruciating sort.

How she screamed! In terror and in the purest and most exquisite pain as the illithid did its work. Quenthel's agonized wails echoed through the corridors of the Underdark.

CHAPTER 2

OF MEN AND MONSTERS

"THEIR DECISION DOESN'T INTEREST YOU?" WULFGAR ASKED REGIS. THE two sat on the porch of Regis's small house late in the afternoon the day after their return from Kelvin's Cairn, and indeed it proved to be a wonderful spring day. They stared out across the waters of the great lake known as Maer Dualdon, the glistening line of the lowering sun cutting the waters. They each had a pipe full of fine leaf Regis had procured on his last ride through the Boareskyr Bridge.

Regis shrugged and blew a smoke ring, then watched as it drifted lazily into the air on the southern breeze. Any course Drizzt, Bruenor, and Catti-brie decided upon would be acceptable to him, for he was hardly considering the road ahead. His thoughts remained on the road behind, to his days with the Grinning Ponies and, more so, his remarkable days with Donnola and the others of Morada Topolino.

"Why did you change your mind?" he asked, cutting short Wulfgar's next remark even as the huge barbarian started to speak. He looked up at his big friend, and realized that he had broached a delicate subject, so he didn't press the point.

"You really enjoy this?" Wulfgar asked, holding up the pipe and staring at its smoking bowl incredulously.

The halfling laughed, took a draw and blew another ring, then puffed a second, smaller one right through the first. "It is a way to pass the time in thought. It helps me to find a place of peace of mind, where I can remember all that has come before, or remember nothing at all as I so choose, and just enjoy the moment." He pointed out across the lake, where a thin line of clouds lying low in the western sky wore a kilt of brilliant orange above the rays of the setting sun.

"Just here," Regis explained. "Just now."

Wulfgar nodded and again looked distastefully at the pipe, though he tried once more, slipping the end between his lips and hesitantly inhaling, just a bit.

"You could use that fine silver horn you carry to hold the leaf," the halfling said. "I could fashion you a stopper and a cover for the openings."

Wulfgar offered a wry grin in response and lifted the item. "No," he said solemnly. This one I will use as it is."

"You like to be loud," Regis remarked.

"It is more than a horn."

"Do tell."

"Three years ago, I traveled back to the lair of Icingdeath," Wulfgar replied, and Regis sucked in his breath hard and nearly choked on the smoke.

"There remain many treasures to be found in the place," Wulfgar added, "and many enemies to battle, so I discovered."

"The dragon?" Regis coughed. "You went back to the dragon's lair?"

"The long-dead dragon, but yes."

"And you found that?" the halfling asked, pointing to the horn.

Wulfgar held it up and turned it a bit, and only then did Regis note its true beauty. It was a simple horn, similar in shape to one that could be procured from a common bull, but was made of silver, shining in the morning light, and with a thin gray-brown band encircling it halfway along its length. That band, actual horn, Regis thought, sparkled in the light even more intensely than the shining silver, for it was set with several white diamonds. Clearly this instrument had not been crafted by a workman's hands alone, and certainly it was no work of the tundra barbarians. Elves, perhaps, or dwarves, or both, Regis thought.

"It found me," Wulfgar corrected. "And in a time of great need, with ice trolls pressing in all about."

"You called to your allies with it?"

"I blew the horn in hopes of giving my enemies pause, or simply because it was louder than a scream of frustration, for truly, I thought my quest at its end, and that I would not live to see my friends atop Kelvin's Cairn. But yes, allies did come, from Warrior's Rest."

Regis stared at him incredulously. He had never heard of such a thing. "Ghosts?"

"Warriors," Wulfgar said. "Fearless and wild. They appeared from a mist and went back to nothingness when they were struck down. All but one, who survived the fight. He would not speak to me, not a word did any of them utter, and then he, too, disappeared."

"Have you blown it since?" Regis asked breathlessly.

"The magic is limited. It is a horn, nothing more, save once every seven days, it seems."

"And then it brings in your allies?"

Wulfgar nodded and tried another draw on the pipe.

"How many?"

The barbarian shrugged. "Sometimes just a few; once there were ten. Perhaps one day I will summon an army, but then I will have but an hour to put it into action!"

Regis dropped his hand to his own dagger, with its living serpents, and understood.

"So why did you change your mind?" he decided to ask once more, changing the subject back. "You were determined to enter the pond in Iruladoon when last I saw you, rejecting the idea of living as a mortal man once more."

"Do you recall the time I first happened upon Bruenor?" Wulfgar asked, pausing every word or two to cough out some smoke.

Regis nodded—how could he forget the Battle of Kelvin's Cairn, after all?

"I was barely a man, little more than a boy, really," Wulfgar explained. "My people had come to wage war on the towns and on the dwarves. It was not a fight Bruenor and his people had asked for, yet one they had to endure. So when I, proud and fierce, and carrying the battle standard of my tribe, saw before me this red-bearded dwarf, I did as any Elk warrior might do, as is required of any true disciple of Tempus."

"You attacked him," Regis said, then laughed and added in his best dwarf imitation, "Aye, ye hit 'im in the noggin, silly boy! Ain't no one ever told ye not to hit a dwarf on the head?"

"A difficult lesson," Wulfgar admitted. "Had I been swinging a wet blanket, my strike would have had no lesser effect against the thick skull of Bruenor Battlehammer. How easily did he lay me low. He swept my feet out from under me. That should have been the end of Wulfgar."

"Bruenor didn't kill you, of course. That is why you chose to leave the forest edge instead of the pond?" Regis knew that he didn't sound convincing, because in truth, he wasn't convinced.

"Bruenor didn't kill me," Wulfgar echoed. "But more than that, Bruenor didn't let any of the other dwarves kill me! They were within their rights to do so—I had brought my fate upon myself. Not a magistrate of any town in all Faerûn would have found fault with Bruenor or his kin had my life been forfeited on that field. Nor was there any gain to them in keeping me alive."

Regis held his pipe in his hand, then, making no move to return it to his lips as he stared up at his huge friend. The tone of Wulfgar's voice, one of reverence—but more than that, one of warmth and profound joy— had caught him by surprise here, he realized. As did the serene look on Wulfgar's face. The big man was staring out over the lake now, as calmly as Regis had just been, and the pipe was in his mouth, and was settled there quite nicely, Regis thought.

"He didn't kill me," Wulfgar went on, and he seemed to be speaking more to himself than to Regis—and likely giving voice to the internal conversation that had found him in the waters of the pond in Iruladoon. "He took me in. He gave me life and gave me home, and gave me, with all of you and with the dwarves of Clan Battlehammer, family. All that I became after that battle, I owe to Bruenor. My return to my people and the woman I came to love and the children I came to know . . ." He paused and flashed Regis an ear-to-ear smile, his white teeth shining within the frame of his yellow beard. "And the grandchildren!" he said with great enthusiasm.

"They are all gone now?" Regis asked somberly.

Wulfgar nodded and looked back out at the lake, but his expression was not one of loss or sadness, or even resignation. "To Warrior's Rest, so I must believe. And if that promise holds truth, then there they will be when I am no more again, when the road of my grave is straight to the halls. What are a few decades of delay against the hopes of the eternity of godly reward?"

"If?" Regis said, picking up on that curious reference. They had all been dead, of course, and through the power of a goddess had returned to life. Could there be any doubt for any of them now regarding an afterlife?

He studied Wulfgar carefully as the big man shrugged and answered, "I do not know what lies on the other side of the cave beneath the waters of the pond, any more than I knew the reality of life after death before my journey to that strange forest."

"Yet you died and went there, by the power of a goddess."

"Perhaps."

Regis stared at him incredulously.

"Who can know the truth of it?" Wulfgar asked. "Perhaps it is all a wizard's trick, yes? A magical weave of deception to twist us and turn us to his desires."

"You cannot believe that!"

Wulfgar laughed, took a deep draw, and almost managed a smoke ring—and one accompanied by only a minor fit of coughing.

"It does not matter," Wulfgar said absently. "And only when I came to appreciate that truth, that I could not know the end of the road through the cave at the bottom of Iruladoon's pond . . ." He paused again and seemed to be fighting for the right words. It seemed to Regis that his friend had found an epiphany beyond his ability to explain it.

"Whatever the gods have planned for me after I am truly and fully dead is theirs to determine," Wulfgar went on. "Only when I came to truly appreciate that was I able to stop asking myself what Tempus wanted from me."

"And ask instead what course was best for you," Regis finished for him.

Wulfgar looked down at him and smiled once more. "What an ungrateful son I would be, what a foul friend indeed, had I gone through the other way and dived into that pond."

"None of us would have judged you."

Wulfgar's expression reflected sincerity as he nodded his agreement. "Yet more confirmation that I was right to return," he said, and his next smoke ring actually looked like a ring.

Regis wasted no time in sending a smaller ring right through it.

"I wasn't coming," Bruenor admitted to Catti-brie and Drizzt. Catti-brie sat by the drow's bed as Drizzt leaned back, half-sitting, half-lying, still weak from his wounds. The dwarf shook his hairy head—his beard was growing in thick once more—and paced around the small room as if it were a cage.

The admission didn't really shake Drizzt, but he noted the surprise on Catti-brie's face.

"Reginald Roundshield, Guard Captain o' King Emerus himself, at yer service!" Bruenor said with an almost-graceful bow.

"It's an incredible tale," Drizzt replied, shaking his head and considering the adventures his four friends had shared with him in the last couple of days. Regis had taken center stage in those bardic games, and if only a portion of what the halfling had claimed was true, then he had lived a thrilling second life indeed. "You, all of you, lived as children of others, and with full recollection of your life before. I can hardly believe it, though I do not doubt you."

"Knocked me brains about near to batty. Aye, took me to the drink, it did!" Bruenor said with an exaggerated wink.

"King Emerus," Drizzt mused. "Citadel Felbarr?"

"Aye, the same."

"And how fares the good king?"

Bruenor shrugged. "All the land's on edge. And all the land's smellin' with the stench o' orcs."

"That is why you almost turned aside from your course here and your pledge to Mielikki," Catti-brie reasoned, and once more, Drizzt noted a bit of surprise, and even a bit of annoyance, in her reaction to Bruenor's claim.

Bruenor started to answer, but held back and seemed to Drizzt to be weighing his words very carefully. Uncharacteristically so.

"You just said—" Catti-brie prompted.

Bruenor waved a hand to silence her. "I came to fight for me friend, so let's find the fight and be done with it." He looked to Catti-brie as he finished, as if expecting her to lead them right out on the hunt.

"What fight?" Drizzt asked.

"Who can know?" Catti-brie answered, speaking to Bruenor, not Drizzt. "We have done as the goddess bade us. And had we not—"

"I would have died up there on Kelvin's Cairn that night," Drizzt interrupted. He took Catti-brie's hand and she looked into his eyes and nodded. His wounds would have proven mortal, she had already told him, as she had explained that Mielikki had guided her and the others to that particular spot on that particular night.

"Then we're done here, and I've a road to be walking!" Bruenor declared.

"You intend to leave us?" Drizzt asked.

"Oh, yerself's coming with me, don't ye doubt," the dwarf replied. "Got something I need to fix—something yerself needs to fix with me."

"Many-Arrows?"

"The same."

Drizzt shook his head helplessly. "There is no war," he said quietly. "Surely that is a good thing."

"There'll be war," Bruenor argued. "Soon enough if it ain't started already, don't ye doubt! In me days with Felbarr, then with Mithral Hall—"

"You returned to Mithral Hall?" the other two asked in unison.

Bruenor stopped his pacing, finally, and took a deep and steadying breath. "Aye, but they're not for knowin' me as anything but Reginald Roundshield—Little Arr Arr, as Emerus's boys called me. Spent the better part of '79 there, and I'm tellin' ye true. War's coming to the Silver Marches, and coming soon if it ain't already on."

"You cannot know that," Drizzt insisted. "It was averted before, and so it might be again."

"No!" Bruenor shouted, and stamped his boot. "No more! Wrong I was in signing that damned treaty! Did nothin' more than hold it off."

"We had little choice."

"We had every choice!" Bruenor came back, again loudly as he clearly grew more and more agitated. "I should've put me axe right through the skull o' that stinkin' Obould and been done with it! And Mithral Hall . . . aye, but we should've stood strong."

"The other kingdoms refused to help!" Drizzt reminded.

"Stood strong!" Bruenor shouted, and stamped his boot again. "And they'd've come in, don't ye doubt! And we'd've been done with Obould and his ugly orcs then and there."

"With thousands killed on both sides."

"No shame in dyin' when ye're killin' orcs!"

The door pushed open and Regis and Wulfgar rushed in, looking around as if expecting to find a fight in progress.

"You took a chance," Drizzt said, and he tried to calm his voice, though mostly unsuccessfully. "One that might reshape the relationship of the races to the orcs throughout the Realms, if the peace holds."

"Maybe I ain't wanting that."

"You would prefer war?" Drizzt asked. He looked to Catti-brie for support, and was surprised by her stern expression—directed at him, not

Bruenor. "King Obould offered us a different way," Drizzt pushed on anyway. "We could not defeat him, not alone, perhaps not even if all the kingdoms of the Silver Marches had joined in with our cause, which they would not. The peace has held there, by all accounts."

"I been there," Bruenor muttered. "Not so peaceful."

"But not war, either," said Drizzt. "How many have been born, or have lived out their lives peacefully, who otherwise would have known only misery and death under the trample of armies?"

"And how many now will know the stamp o' them boots because we didn't put Obould back in his hole a hunnerd years ago?" Bruenor shot right back.

"It was never going to be an easy road to a lasting peace," said Drizzt. "But it was worth the chance."

"No!" Catti-brie cried. Both the drow and the dwarf stared incredulously at the usually gentle woman. "No," Catti-brie said again, quieter now, but no less insistently. She shook her head to accentuate the point and declared, "It was no more than a fool's game, a false hope against harsh reality."

"You were there," Drizzt reminded. "On the podium in Garumn's Gorge beside the rest of us as Bruenor signed."

"I wished to go out and hunt Obould with you and Bruenor and Regis," Catti-brie replied, "to kill him and not to break bread."

"But in the end, you came to agree with the intent and terms of the treaty."

"And I was wrong," came her simple admission. "You, my love, were wrong, most of all."

The room held silent for a long while after that, the others mulling over the surprising reversal and accusation from the woman. Drizzt stared at her hard, as if she had just shot an arrow through his heart and soul, but she didn't back down an inch.

"It seems that I missed eventful times," said Wulfgar, who had left his friends and Mithral Hall before the advent of the Treaty of Garumn's Gorge, never to return. He gave a little laugh, trying to break the tension clearly, and just as clearly, he failed.

"I advised Bruenor as I thought best," Drizzt said quietly.

"It was a good plan," said Regis, but no one seemed to notice.

"Ye could'no've bringed me to sign the durned paper if me heart didn't agree with ye," Bruenor said.

"Bad advice is often given from a place of good intent," Catti-brie remarked.

"Did you drag us back to the world of the living so that you could play out some unexpected anger over a decision made a century ago?" Regis demanded, and this time, he commanded center stage, stepping out in front of Bruenor to boldly confront the woman.

Catti-brie looked at him, her expression showing surprise for just a moment before a smile widened on her pretty face.

"It was a mistake, and a grand one," she said. "We all need to know that now, I believe, for the choices we will find before us will likely prove no less momentous than those we made before."

"Those we made wrongly, ye mean," said a clearly agitated Bruenor.

"Aye," Catti-brie agreed without the slightest hesitation—and again, without the slightest caveat against her assertion to be found in her tone, her expression, or her posture.

"Ye seem awful sure o' yerself, girl," Bruenor warned.

"They are orcs," she replied, her tone deathly even and unforgiving. "We should have killed them, every one."

"Their women, too, then?" Drizzt asked.

"Where's the babies' room?" Catti-brie replied in her best dwarf voice as she echoed the merciless battle cry usually reserved by the bearded folk for when they broke through the defenses of a fortress of goblinkin or evil giantkind. It was an old joke among the dwarves more than anything else, a reason to smash their mugs together in bawdy toast. But when Catti-brie spoke it then, it seemed to the other four as if she was as serious as death itself.

Drizzt visibly winced at the proclamation. "And you would take the blade . . . ?" he started to ask.

"Yes," she said, and the other four shuddered a bit as the cold wind of sheer indifference blew through them.

Drizzt couldn't tear his incredulous stare from the woman standing before him, suddenly so tall and beautiful and terrible all at once in her white gown and black shawl. He felt Regis staring up at him from the side, but couldn't manage to glance back at the halfling, and knew that he had nothing to offer that likely plaintive expression anyway. For none in that room were more confused at that moment than Drizzt himself!

"What is this about?" Regis quietly asked him.

"The burden you carry blurs your judgment," Catti-brie said to Drizzt. "As you see yourself, you hope to find in others—in orcs and goblins, even." She shook her head. "But that cannot be, with only very rare exception."

"Ye've become very sure o' yerself, girl," Bruenor warned.

Behind him, Wulfgar laughed, and that surprising interjection turned them all around to consider him.

"Mielikki told her this," he explained, and he nodded to Catti-brie, turning them all back to face the woman.

Who still did not blink, and indeed, even nodded her agreement to confirm Wulfgar's assessment.

"The goblinkin are not as the other races of the world," Catti-brie explained. "They are not as the humans, the halflings, the elves, the dwarves, the gnomes . . . even the drow. That is your mistake, my love. That was the mistake all of us made that long-ago day when we agreed to the Treaty of Garumn's Gorge. We hoped to see the world through our own perspectives, and projected that common sense to the hearts of the orcs. Perhaps because we wanted so badly to believe it, perhaps because we were given little choice, but in any case, we were wrong. Mielikki has shown me this."

Drizzt shook his head, though more in confusion than disagreement.

"They are evil," Catti-brie stated simply.

"Have you met my kin?" Drizzt sarcastically replied.

"The difference is not subtle," she immediately replied, as if expecting that very line of questioning. "Your people—most of your people—are nurtured in the webs of a demon goddess, who has built within your culture a structure of control that oft leads to acts of evil. The ways of the drow, often evil I agree, remain a matter of choice, of free will, though the institutions of the drow distort that choice in the direction the Spider Queen's demands. This is not the case with goblinkin or most giantkind."

"Ye think a ranger might know this," Bruenor said off-handedly, and when everyone turned to him, the dwarf shrugged and laughed. "Well, ain't that the whole point o' yer training, elf?" he asked of Drizzt.

Drizzt turned back to Catti-brie. "I met a goblin once who would argue against your point."

"Nojheim, I know," she replied. "I remember your tale."

"Was I wrong about him?"

Catti-brie shrugged. "Perhaps there are exceptions, but if so, they are greatly deviant from their race. Or perhaps he was not full with goblin blood—surely there are examples of goodly half-orcs, even full communities of half-orcs who coexist in peace."

"But not full-blooded goblinkin?" Drizzt asked.

"No."

"We should assume then that they—all of them—all orcs, all goblins, gnolls, and kobolds are simply that? Simply evil?" Drizzt asked, letting his skepticism and dismay shine through his tone. "We should treat them without mercy, and strike without parlay?"

"Yes," she said.

"You sound very much like the matron mothers of Menzoberranzan when they speak of other races," he scolded.

But again, Catti-brie didn't blink and didn't back away a step. "Were Bruenor to claim such against . . . say, Nesmé, then his claims would be compatible to those of your matron mothers," she explained. "Not my claims. Not regarding goblinkin. They are created to destroy, nothing more. Their godly design is as a blight upon the land, a scourge and challenge to those who would serve goodly purpose. It is not a king they serve, or even a goddess, as with the drow. Nor are these the words designed by kings who would conquer, or races seeking supremacy. This is the simple truth of it, I tell you as Mielikki has told to me. The goblinkin are not nurtured to evil. Evil is their nature. That distinction is not subtle, but profound, and woe to any who blurs that line."

"King Obould saw a different way," Drizzt reasoned. "A better way for his people, and by his strength . . ." He stopped in the face of Catti-brie's scowl.

"That was the deception, to us and to Obould," Catti-brie said. "He was granted great gifts by the magic of the shamans of Gruumsh One-eye, and indeed, by Gruumsh himself. Physical gifts, like his great strength—greater than any orc should know. But also, he was given wisdom and a vision of a better way for the orcs, and he believed it, and through his strength, so they have pursued that course."

"Then your point does not hold!" Drizzt argued.

"Unless it was all a ruse," Catti-brie continued, undaunted. "Through Obould, Gruumsh led the orcs into society, a sister-state to the kingdoms of the Silver Marches, but only because he believed they could better destroy that society from within. Even with the army he had constructed, Obould could not have conquered the Silver Marches. Tens of thousands of goodly folk would have died in that war, but the kingdoms of the Silver Marches would not have fallen. This time, it would seem that Gruumsh demanded more of his fodder minions."

"And we gave it to him," Bruenor said with great lament.

Drizzt looked at him in alarm, and then turned back to Catti-brie, whose eyes finally showed a bit more regret—some sympathy, perhaps, but not disagreement with the grim assessment.

"They are not people," she said softly. "They are monsters. This is not true of the other races, not even of the tieflings, who claim demonic ancestry, for they, unlike goblinkin, have free will and reason in matters of conscience. Indeed, they *have* a conscience! True and full goblinkin do not, I say; Mielikki says. Were you to find a lion cub and raise it in your home, you would be safer than if you found and raised a goblin child, for the goblin child would surely murder you when it suited him, for gain, or even for the simple pleasure of the act."

Drizzt felt as if the floor was shifting beneath his feet. He didn't doubt Catti-brie's words, and didn't doubt her claim that they had been inspired by the song of Mielikki. Ever had this been an issue of great tribulation for the drow—the rogue drow who had found the heart to walk away from the wicked ways of the city of his kin. Was she correct in her assessment? In her assessment of him most of all?

Her words rang loudly in Drizzt's thoughts. *The burden you carry blurs your judgment.* He didn't want to believe it, wanted to find some logical counter to her reasoning. He thought of Montolio, his first mentor when he came to the surface, but a quick recollection of those days affirmed Catti-brie's words, not his own heart in this, for Montolio had never offered him any advice about judging the content of the character of a goblin or orc. Drizzt considered Montolio Debrouchee to be as good a man as he had ever known—would Montolio have signed the Treaty of Garumn's Gorge?

Had Montolio ever suffered goblinkin to live?

Drizzt could not imagine that he had.

He looked plaintively at Catti-brie, but the woman loved him too much to offer him an easy out. He had to face the accusation she had just uttered—words that had come from the insights of Mielikki, from a common place in the hearts of Drizzt and Catti-brie.

He wanted to believe that Obould's actions were wrought of noble intent. He wanted to believe that an orc, or a goblin like Nojheim, could rise above the reputation of their respective races, because if they could, then so could he, and so, conversely, if he could, then so could, or so should, they.

"The goblinkin are not people," Catti-brie said. "Not human, not drow, nor any other race. You cannot judge them and cannot treat them by or from those perspectives."

"Ye durned right," Bruenor put in. "Dwarfs've knowed it for centuries!"

"Yet you signed the treaty," Regis said, and all eyes flashed at the halfling, Bruenor's scowl most prominent of all.

But that glare was met by a wide, teasing, and ultimately infectious smile.

"Bought yerself a bit more o' the intestinal fortitude this time around, did ye?" Bruenor asked.

Regis winked and grinned. "Let's go kill some orcs."

Any anger Bruenor might have had about the comment washed away instantly at that invitation. "Bwahaha!" he roared and clapped Regis on the back.

"The trails will soon open, and we can navigate them in any case," Catti-brie said. "To Mithral Hall, then?

"Aye," said Bruenor, but as he spoke, he looked at Wulfgar. The barbarian had left the Companions of the Hall in the days of Obould, after all, returning to his first home and people on the tundra of Icewind Dale.

"Aye," Wulfgar heartily replied.

"Ye got no mind to stay with yer folks, then?" Bruenor asked bluntly.

"I returned to fight beside Drizzt and the rest of you," Wulfgar said, completely at ease. "For adventure. For battle. Let us play."

Drizzt noted Catti-brie's stare coming his way. He shared her surprise, and a pleasant surprise it was, for both of them.

"Mithral Hall," Drizzt agreed.

"Not straight away," Bruenor declared. "We got other business, then," he explained, nodding with every word. "We got a friend in trouble, elf, one ye saw and left to die."

Drizzt looked at him curiously.

Bruenor went to the side of the room, bent and reached under his cot and brought forth a familiar helmet, shield, and axe. The others were not surprised, but Drizzt, who had been too groggy and dazed that night on Kelvin's Cairn to fully register Bruenor's garb, surely was. For in light of the tales he had heard of his companions' rebirth, he understood what they meant: Bruenor had visited his own grave!

"Except our old friend was already dead," Bruenor explained, "and not as strong as he thinked himself."

"Pwent," Drizzt breathed, only then remembering the poor fellow. He had found Pwent outside of Neverwinter, outside of Gauntlgrym, inflicted with vampirism, and had left the dwarf in a cave, awaiting the sunrise to end his curse.

"What of him?" Catti-brie asked.

"He's in Gauntlgrym, killing drow," said Bruenor.

"That would make him happy," Regis remarked, and then with surprise, breathlessly added, "Gauntlgrym?"

"Cursed as a vampire," Drizzt explained.

"Aye, and I ain't for leavin' him," said Bruenor.

"You mean to kill him?" Wulfgar asked.

Bruenor shrugged, but Drizzt turned to Catti-brie. "Is there another way?"

The woman matched Bruenor's shrug with a helpless one of her own. She was a priestess, but surely no expert in the issues regarding undeath, a realm foreign to, and indeed contrary to, the tenets of Mielikki.

"Gauntlgrym?" Regis asked again.

"Aye, we found it," said Bruenor. "In the Crags north o' Neverwinter. Pwent's there, lost and dead, and so're some drow, and I ain't much likin' that thought o' them folk with the Forge o' me ancestors!"

"We'll find our answers along the road, then," said Catti-brie.

"Jarlaxle's in Luskan," Regis remarked, and the others perked up at that name.

But Catti-brie was thinking along other lines, Drizzt realized, for now she was shaking her head. She mouthed "Longsaddle."

Drizzt couldn't hide his astonishment, for the home of the Harpells was not a place that typically inspired confidence!

45

CHAPTER 3

THE FESTIVAL OF THE FOUNDING

AND NOW YOU UNDERSTAND WHY I HAVE NEVER BOTHERED TO HUNT Drizzt Do'Urden down and kill him," Gromph said to Quenthel when they were back at the Baenre compound and the matron mother had recovered from the illithid's attack.

"The goddess uses him." Quenthel nodded.

She was not smiling, though, Gromph noted, and given the memories, the core of Yvonnel, which Methil had imparted to his sister, the archmage doubted that he would ever see her smile again, unless it was from the pleasure of exacting pain upon another.

He noted his sister's pensive pose, so similar to the one his mother often used to wear, and one he had never before seen from the inferior Quenthel.

"Why tempt him?" she asked. "With so many other greater needs arising all about us, why now?"

A good question, the archmage thought, and one he had discussed at length with Minolin Fey just the previous tenday. The Spider Queen was expanding her power now—in the realm of the gods, not among mere mortals—so why would she bother with a rogue drow of such little real importance or consequence?

"That is a matter for priestesses, not wizards," he replied.

Quenthel narrowed her eyes for she understood now, of course, the direction of Lolth's designs, a course that surely elevated Gromph and his wizardly ilk. "And you have spoken to priestesses . . . one in particular," she reminded him. "And about this very topic."

Gromph sat up straighter behind his desk, matching his sister's intense stare with careful scrutiny of his own. "My dear sister—" he started.

"Never call me that again," she interrupted, her voice even and confident and clearly threatening.

"Matron Mother Quenthel," he corrected.

Gromph brought his hands up to tap-tap his fingers before his pursed lips, his typical posture when digesting some rather startling possibilities. He knew that he was looking at a being much greater than the one he had led out of Menzoberranzan only a short while before. Methil El-Viddenvelp had infused Quenthel with so many of the memories of Matron Mother Yvonnel Baenre, with their dead mother's understanding of Lolth, and, it would seem, with more than a little of their dead mother's personality as well. He had known this would be a possibility—bringing Quenthel out to receive the collected insights of an illithid had been an exercise to fortify her in this time of Lady Lolth's need. She was the Matron Mother of Menzoberranzan, and so ruled supreme in the city, but in truth, all who knew the inner workings of House Baenre understood that Gromph, the eldest, the most veteran, the most wizened, had been working his will behind the scenes.

It had always been a risk that taking Quenthel to Methil would empower her enough to change that dynamic.

"The gods are in turmoil, so said Mistress Minolin Fey," he answered, lowering his hands, though surely not lowering his gaze. "The realignment is well under way, in many different corners."

"The Spider Queen has bigger concerns."

"Why are you asking me, and not her? You are the Matron Mother of Menzoberranzan . . ."

"Do not deign to tell me who I am or how I am to act," Matron Mother Quenthel replied. "I would not bother Lolth for answers that others can provide, nor trouble her handmaidens in unweaving the web that I might learn what others in my city already know."

"Do you think personal pettiness is above the gods?" Gromph asked bluntly.

Then came a smile, surprising him. A wry and knowing grin, an evil one that the Elderboy of House Baenre knew well, though he had not seen it in well over a century.

"Then the insolent rogue remains inconsequential," Matron Mother Quenthel reasoned. "A thorn to be used against a rival goddess, turned

47

to the glorious darkness for no practical reason than to pain the witch Mielikki."

"Or turned into failure yet again for the Spider Queen, and thus the scream of pain you heard that began your most recent journey."

"In heart and soul, the rogue Do'Urden betrayed Lady Lolth yet again."

As when the rogue Do'Urden killed you, Gromph thought, but did not say, though he might as well have said it, he realized, for his grin had surely betrayed the notion.

"Mielikki won that minor battle for the heart of Drizzt Do'Urden." Gromph nodded as he spoke, looking away from his sister. Indeed, he was looking into the past, trying to figure out how his mother might have handled such news. How might Quenthel ultimately weigh against that standard, he wondered?

"Shall I go and exterminate the rogue Do'Urden?" the archmage asked.

Matron Mother Quenthel fixed him with an incredulous, almost pitying stare, and Gromph had his answer. The mind flayer had given her so much! For of course, that was the correct answer, the answer Gromph would have given, the answer Yvonnel would have given, the answer Lolth needed from Matron Mother Quenthel of the City of Spiders.

Possessed of this information regarding the source of Lady Lolth's scream before her encounter with the illithid, petty Quenthel would have already sent Gromph and a dozen other assassins on their way to exterminate the puny rogue of House Do'Urden, a useless endeavor that would reap nothing but a momentary flash of vengeful joy, soon to be lost in the knowledge that the rogue was then with his goddess, and that goddess was not Lolth, and that Lolth was not sated . . . and then, with such a simple matter of the finality of death, the goddess could never be.

"To take with the sword is easy," Matron Mother Quenthel stated. "To take with the heart is desirable."

"And yet the goddess could not take his heart."

Quenthel smiled again—no, Gromph couldn't think of her as Quenthel any longer, he realized. Matron Mother Quenthel smiled again, an awful, wicked, delicious, inspiring smile.

"What we cannot take, we break," Matron Mother Quenthel quietly observed.

Yes, Gromph knew, he had relegated himself to subservient status once more, in more than official rank. All of the years he had nurtured Minolin

Fey, his student in the ways of intrigue, his puppet in his plans of dominion over his pathetic sister, his lover—all of that would likely unwind now that Quenthel had looked so intimately into the mind of Yvonnel.

Yvonnel the Eternal, he thought, remembering the moniker he had often heard attached to his powerful mother, one that had seemed a cruel joke when the axe of the dwarf king had so sundered Yvonnel's withered old skull. But perhaps that moniker had been more than a passing reference after all. Perhaps, through Methil's waggling tentacles, "eternal" remained a fitting description.

And Gromph had just given that "eternal" insight to his sister.

As Lady Lolth had demanded of him.

So be it.

"Tomorrow is the Festival of the Founding," Matron Mother Quenthel said.

Gromph stared at her incredulously, but only at first, only until he reminded himself that this was not merely Quenthel seated across from him. Then his look turned to suspicion. After all, when had House Baenre observed the festival in any but the most cursory, and even cynical, way? The twentieth of Ches, the third month, was heralded as the anniversary of Menzoberranzan's founding, and on that day, the collective defensive crouch of the city relaxed into a profound communal sigh. House gates were less guarded, indeed even opened, for passersby, for Lolth was known, occasionally, to appear in some avatar form in the city, and a blessing it was upon the whole of the city in that case.

To House Baenre, so much closer to the goddess, and with so much more to lose by letting down its guard, the Festival of the Founding had, in the days of Yvonnel (the Sable Years, they were called in Menzoberranzan), been a mere formality, rarely mentioned, lightly observed, and used by the House—through Bregan D'aerthe spies, typically—to gain information on the defenses and weaknesses of those other noble Houses.

"Matron Byrtyn Fey has extended . . ." Matron Mother Quenthel paused and gave a wicked little laugh, then corrected, "Matron Byrtyn will extend a most gracious invitation for us to dine in her worthy home, and we will accept, of course, as the Founding requires of us."

"We will go to Narbondellyn?" Gromph asked with open and determined skepticism, referring to the neighborhood of manor houses, theaters, and arenas, and the compounds of two of Menzoberranzan's eight ruling

Houses. While Narbondellyn was a fashionable enough address in the City of Spiders, and indeed Gromph often visited the area, rarely before had all the nobles of House Baenre left Qu'ellarz'orl, the grandest district of the city, wherein resided the greatest of the noble Houses—except to go to war. The tradition of the Festival of the Founding called upon unallied Houses to dine together in a rare show of unity, but House Baenre usually used that tradition to host Matron Mez'Barris and her Second House, Barrison Del'Armgo, or vice versa.

"I await Matron Byrtyn's invitation," Matron Mother Quenthel said slyly, her grin now firmly aimed at Gromph. With that, she rose and departed, leaving the old mage quite flummoxed.

House Fey-Branche, the Sixth House of Menzoberranzan, the House of Minolin.

Why had Quenthel—Matron Mother Baenre—arranged this, Gromph wondered, and indeed, how?

She was among the oldest drow in Menzoberranzan and the longest-serving matron mother, even though her House, Barrison Del'Armgo was the second youngest of all the great Houses in the city, having formed a mere eight centuries earlier. Under her guidance, House Barrison Del'Armgo had climbed the ranks swiftly to the penultimate rank in the city. Barely a quarter-millennium before, the little known House had been considered no higher than the forty-seventh House of the city, barely known and with little consideration of any of the true powers of Menzoberranzan. The leap in ranking, all the way to sixteenth, had caught their attention, though, and when the matrons of the Ruling Council had at last bothered to look more closely at the Armgo ways and powers, it had become quite obvious that Mez'Barris would not be watching the Ruling Council from afar for long.

Mez'Barris had found her niche of power. Other Houses competed for the favor of Lolth by building chapels and training priestesses, but Matron Mez'Barris had veered her family down an opposite path. Barrison Del'Armgo was known for its House wizards, as were their arch-rivals, the Xorlarrins, but more than that, this House was the home of many of Menzoberranzan's greatest warriors. Every year, the ranks of

NIGHT OF THE HUNTER

Melee-Magthere, the drow academy of warriors, included a full complement of budding Armgo warriors.

The thousand soldiers of Barrison Del'Armgo formed the backbone of the city's martial garrison and granted Mez'Barris the firmest foundation for her House army, one not subject to the whims of a fickle deity or the ebbs and flows of magic.

And now things had become more interesting. Matron Mez'Barris was well aware of the growing instability within the one House, House Baenre, that kept her from the pinnacle of Menzoberranzan's power.

"They march as if the entire city should stand and gape in awe," High Priestess Taayrul said to her mother as they stood together on one of the more obscure balconies in the sprawling compound. Only recently had Barrison Del'Armgo relocated to Qu'ellarz'orl from their previous location in Narbondellyn, and so their compound was not nearly as magnificent or magic-highlighted yet as the great Baenre compound.

"They are Baenre," said Malagdorl, Elderboy and Weapons Master of Barrison Del'Armgo. "Let Menzoberranzan embrace them with awe, for those are the admiring looks we will know soon enough."

"Do not speak of such things openly, my impetuous child," Mez'Barris scolded, but her tone showed more pride than anger. She could well imagine the parade below her being the march of her own House someday soon.

But she couldn't deny the pageantry and beauty of the procession of House Baenre, soldiers marching crisply, in disciplined precision, in their battle armor, so finely cut and fitted. The glint of hundreds of weapons shone and sparkled in the accented magical lighting, all done to exacting precision, with spells set and aimed perfectly to catch the gleaming metal of sword or battle-axe or javelin tip. Faerie fire of purple, blue, and orange highlighted the group commanders and their great subterranean lizards. Light spells seemed to emanate from within the accompanying magical jade spiders, pony-sized versions of the great monstrosities that guarded the Baenre compound and several other Houses on Qu'ellarz'orl. Those spiders flanked the most important contingent, the noble priestesses, and it didn't take Mez'Barris long to spot Matron Mother Quenthel as she glided out of the Baenre gates, floating on a translucent disc of purple and blue energies, her eldest daughter and Sos'Umptu close behind and flanking, left and right, on discs of their own. A magical red flame burned in the center of their triangle, backlighting Quenthel perfectly so that she seemed seated in a halo of red light. That hue caught the matching color of her eyes so keenly that Mez'Barris could see her eyes even from this distance. For just a moment it seemed that Quenthel was staring right back at her.

Undeniably, the Baenres knew how to march, and all the city would tremble at their passing. It took breathless Mez'Barris many heartbeats to realize that this procession was not normal, even for the Festival of the Founding. Not any more, at least. She had not seen such a thing from the vaunted Baenres in decades, a century and more, even, not since . . .

"Yvonnel," she whispered, and it was clear to her that Matron Mother Quenthel was making an important statement, to the entire city, and likely, given the departure of Matron Zeerith and the Xorlarrins, most keenly of all, she was sending a warning to Matron Mez'Barris.

Malagdorl gave a little growl as the lead of the procession moved past House Barrison Del'Armgo, barely fifty feet from the balcony where the Armgo nobles had gathered. Weapons Master Andzrel Baenre led the procession, riding a lizard with a barding of jewels and bells, sitting tall and proud.

"Indeed," Mez'Barris said, noting the source of his ire, and so full of her own spittle. "Tell me again why you have not found the opportunity to kill that one?"

Malagdorl lowered his eyes. The great rivalries between the weapons masters of the first two Houses went back many decades, to the legendary fights between Uthegental Armgo and Dantrag Baenre. So it had seemed would be the case with their successors, and Malagdorl wanted nothing more. But Andzrel had shied from any conflicts of late.

Mez'Barris knew why. She knew of Tiago, growing strong and building a great name for himself, and she knew of Elderboy Aumon, Quenthel's oldest son, who had just completed his first year at the Academy. Andzrel was playing cautiously, because any mistake he might make would see him supplanted as weapons master by one of the two eager upstarts.

On and on, the procession went. Finally Mez'Barris noted Gromph, surprisingly far back in the long line, riding a spectral mount of shifting hues and amorphous magic. It seemed a hellhorse, then a rothé-like creature, then something in between, then something entirely different.

A smile creased Mez'Barris's tight lips. Gromph hated Quenthel as much as she did, she knew—or thought she knew—and with the rise of the stature of wizards among Lolth's flock, he would be the downfall of Mez'Barris's rival.

NIGHT OF THE HUNTER

"They will not dine with the Xorlarrins?" Priestess Taayrul asked when it was clear that the Baenre army was moving past the wizard spire of the Third House and out of Qu'ellarz'orl altogether. By that point, the Baenre line stretched all the way from the Baenre gate to the giant mushrooms that separated Qu'ellarz'orl from the rest of the city.

"It is the Founding," Malagdorl reminded her with confidence. "They are to dine with a House that is not allied . . ." His voice faded with his confidence as the two priestesses stared at him with clear amusement that he would be so concerned with such a quaint tradition.

"Matron Mother Quenthel seeks to make new inroads, no doubt," said Mez'Barris. "With the impending departure of the Xorlarrins, she has perhaps finally realized her open flank." She nodded as she spoke, confident of her assertions. House Xorlarrin and House Baenre, First and Third, surrounded Barrison Del'Armgo, but while both of the next Houses in line, Faen Tlabbar and Mizzrym, were allied with Baenre, the two remained bitter rivals, a competition that would only intensify with House Faen Tlabbar's greatest ally, House Xorlarrin, removed from Menzoberranzan. Indeed, the coveted rank of Third House would be opened, likely for one of these to fill the void. In terms of the relationship between Houses Baenre and Armgo, then, this could not be seen as good news for Matron Mother Quenthel. While Faen Tlabbar and Mizzrym together might be more powerful than Xorlarrin alone, the Matron Mother of House Baenre could never count on them, together or separately, to hold back the ambitions of House Barrison Del'Armgo as she had counted on Matron Zeerith Xorlarrin.

"And so the meticulous detail in the grand parade of Baenre," Mez'Barris remarked quietly, and nodded knowingly. Her daughter and the weapons master stared at her. "They try to project strength and order to quell the chaos that will surely reach Quenthel's front door."

Taayrul's eyes popped open wide at that remark, and even dull Malagdorl caught on to the reference of Quenthel without the appropriate title offered in deference.

Houses in Menzoberranzan had gone to war for less.

The march of House Baenre wove through every neighborhood in Menzoberranzan, even up to the raised area of Tier Breche, where stood the three houses of the drow academy, and then across the West Wall, across the whole of the city, before winding back to the neighborhood known as Narbondellyn, which was immediately across the mushroom forest from Qu'ellarz'orl. From every balcony and every window, drow looked on, and as was so typical of Menzoberranzan, half did so with trepidation, the other half with appreciative nods at the constancy Baenre represented.

The procession split as it neared Narbondellyn, select guard groups taking position outside of House Fey-Branche's opened gates. Only the royal group passed through, including the siblings, Quenthel, Sos'Umptu, and Gromph; Quenthel's daughter Myrineyl; Weapons Master Andzrel Baenre; and Patron Velkryst, Quenthel's current chosen mate and once a Xorlarrin House wizard.

Even if this had not been the Festival of the Founding, this particular group of six would not have walked with fear, though surely almost every drow who saw them coming would cower.

Matron Byrtyn Fey met them at the door, flanked by Minolin and Patron Calagher. Byrtyn seemed a bit surprised by the small number in attendance, and both Gromph and Quenthel caught a flash of something else—annoyance?—as Brytyn looked past them and noted the army the Baenres had set in place outside her compound.

Matron Byrtyn's stride revealed nervousness as she led the way to the dining hall, where a feast had been set out on a table flanked by nearly two score chairs. Half were filled by Fey-Branche nobles, the other half clearly intended for the Baenres. Byrtyn waved her hand, a signal, obviously, to dismiss all but her closest family members.

"Do let them all stay," Matron Mother Quenthel whispered to her. "You may fill the rest of the chairs if you so please." She looked at Minolin. "Your brother is not about? It would please me to see him again."

The uncharacteristic gesture rocked Minolin, clearly, and she and her mother exchanged nervous glances, as if to silently question whether the Baenres were gathering them all together for a slaughter.

"We are the eldest two Houses in the City of Spiders," Matron Mother Quenthel remarked. "Time has frayed our bonds, it would seem, but in this new era of the goddess's resurgence, we do well to rewind those ties."

A flash of surprise and a flash of hope crossed Byrtyn's face, subtly, but Gromph certainly caught every bit of it. It was common knowledge that Zeerith Xorlarrin was already moving many of her resources to Gauntlgrym, and whispers hinted that the pressure was on for Zeerith to surrender her House rank and her place on the Ruling Council. Fey-Branche was the Sixth House of Menzoberranzan, so surely in the line of ascension; was Matron Mother Quenthel offering her support for the third rank?

Gromph noted the gaze of Minolin Fey, which he returned with a tiny shrug, his indifference eliciting a bit of a snarl from the priestess. She was on edge, the archmage realized, and he silently congratulated his sister, if he could still think of Matron Mother Quenthel as such, for her blunt and devious twist of the mood.

Matron Byrtyn filled the chairs with the worthiest members of her House, the six Baenres sorted themselves out among the group, mingling appropriately and not all in one area. Andzrel and G'eldrin Fey, old friends from the Academy, both heralded weapons masters, gathered at the far end with other warriors to discuss the recent events at Melee-Magthere, while Patron Velkryst and Fey-Branche House wizard Zeknar led the discussion about the return of the Weave. Gromph, though, did not join his wizard fellows, and instead kept himself near to Matron Mother Quenthel, who sat at the head of the table, of course, with Matron Byrtyn to her right and Minolin Fey to her left.

The food was scrumptious, the music magnificent and not overbearing, and the celebration handled with all the meticulous detail that one would expect of a noble House second only to House Baenre in longevity and tradition among the ranks of Menzoberranzan. As was customary, the conversation remained light, with few words of scorn for Houses that were not in attendance, and with each of the Matrons taking turns in directing the others to voice opinions about one or another promising situation. In the City of Spiders, after all, this was the day, typically the only day, of communal hope and renewal, the one day reserved for the premise that the whole of Menzoberranzan was greater than the familial parts.

"I was so thrilled to receive your invitation," Matron Mother Quenthel said to Byrtyn at one point.

Gromph watched Minolin stiffen, for the invitation had been solicited in no uncertain terms, of course. "We are the elders, the cornerstones of Menzoberranzan, the constancy within the swirl of continually shifting power and allegiance." Baenre gave a little, almost embarrassed, laugh and added, "Although some things, like the pinnacle of Menzoberranzan's power, are indeed eternal."

An amazing show of hubris by that self-proclaimed pinnacle, Gromph thought. He wasn't surprised as, obviously, were both Byrtyn and Minolin, or taken aback, but rather, more intrigued. Had his sister made this remark only a day earlier, Gromph would have thought it a clumsy blunder, but now, after her intimate melding with the experiences of Yvonnel, he knew it to be a cunning twist.

Matron Mother Yvonnel the Eternal did not make mistakes, and so Gromph now expected—to his own surprise—the same competence from Quenthel.

"Where has the trust and friendship between Baenre and Fey-Branche gone?" she asked with an exaggerated sigh.

"Thinned by death, no doubt," Matron Byrtyn replied, a subtle hint of annoyance creeping into her voice.

Gromph coughed to cover his chuckle. "Thinned by death" was a perfect description, the old archmage thought, for House Fey-Branche had lost so many nobles over the last few decades to untimely death. Byrtyn and her House had retreated, defensively crouched, with more than a little suspicion that House Baenre had played a role in many of those untimely deaths—with good reason.

"Yes," Quenthel agreed, playing along. "Too much thinned."

Minolin Fey shifted in her seat, clearly uncomfortable, on the verge of blurting out the obvious and totally inappropriate question as to why Matron Mother Quenthel had demanded this shared dinner.

"I am told that Matron Zeerith will soon depart," Matron Byrtyn said. "What will become of the Xorlarrin tower on Qu'ellarz'orl, I wonder?"

"It will not be open to the new Third House," Matron Mother Quenthel replied.

"Whomever that will be," said Matron Byrtyn, somewhat slyly.

"It will not be Fey-Branche, if that is your thought," Matron Mother Quenthel replied, and now even Gromph could not suppress his incredulity. Minolin shifted again—and seemed on the verge of lashing out. Matron Byrtyn rocked back away from Quenthel, her mouth hanging open. Around them, everyone at the table quieted suddenly, and Gromph began considering the words to a spell that would efficiently evacuate him from this potentially lethal bar fight.

"You are no ambitious child, Byrtyn," Matron Mother Quenthel went on, undeterred, and indeed even upping the stakes here by leaving off the female's title. "It is no secret in the city that Fey-Branche is considered without allies and that Matron Zhindia of the fanatical Melarni has set her eyes on ascending the ladder. Were you to reach for Matron Zeerith's seat at the Ruling Council, you would have three superior Houses coveting your downfall."

"Such banter is not appropriate on the Festival of the Founding," Minolin Fey interrupted.

"Nor is it an excuse for a priestess to forget her place," Matron Byrtyn scolded.

"Your exchange will cost both our Houses the favor of Lolth," Minolin pleaded with Matron Mother Quenthel.

"Dear child," Matron Mother Quenthel, who was no older than Minolin, replied, her voice dripping with condescending sweetness, "do not ever again make the error of explaining to me the desires of Lolth."

There was an old saying among the drow that the ears of a Matron Mother were so keen they could catch the rustle of a strand of hair falling to the floor. In that moment, the room became so suddenly quiet that Gromph believed the proverb was not an exaggeration.

Matron Mother Quenthel looked to Matron Byrtyn, as if inviting her to speak, but the other woman did not oblige, and instead went back to her meal, as did everyone else. Not another word was spoken for a long, long while.

House servants cleared the plates quickly when the meal was ended, and Matron Brytyn led the group to an adjacent, even larger room where the attendees milled around in smaller groups. Gromph made his way to Velkryst and the other wizards, but kept his attention quietly attuned to the focus of the evening, the matron mothers and their respective high priestesses. He watched as Sos'Umptu rushed over to speak with Matron Byrtyn, pointing off to the south, to another set of rooms. A moment later Brytyn, Sos'Umptu, and Myrineyl moved off that way, leaving Matron Mother Quenthel—so conveniently!—alone with Minolin Fey.

That pair headed off as well, but to the west.

Gromph rubbed his thumb against a ring on his index finger, secretly sending an invisible projection in their wake, his senses following the duo as they crossed out of the room, down a small corridor, and through a set of double doors onto a balcony looking out to the pillar of Narbondel, and beyond it to the western reaches of Menzoberranzan.

Matron Mother Quenthel looked back, her expression curious. A wave of her hand shut the door—and did more than that, Gromph realized, for his spell was no more, the connection broken. Beside him, Velkryst chattered on about something to do with the Xorlarrin expedition to Gauntlgrym, the Fey-Branche mages hanging on his every word. The success of the Xolarrins, the one drow House that elevated arcane magic to the level of the divine, held great implications for them as wizards and as male drow. Gromph pretended to listen. Of course he knew far more about the goings-on in Gauntlgrym than Velkryst ever would, since he had arranged the expedition in the first place. But he kept his gaze to the west, to the doors through which Matron Mother Quenthel and Minolin Fey had exited, almost expecting an explosion of some kind to tear the western wing off the compound of Fey-Branche.

He couldn't predict the movements of Quenthel any longer, he realized then, and he could not control them or even influence them to any great extent.

The implications of his gift to his sister weighed heavily upon his old shoulders.

"I owe you a great apology," Baenre said to Minolin when they were alone. The heat glow of Narbondel had begun to diminish by then, the day growing late.

The priestess stared at Baenre, suspicion dominating her expression.

"For years now, I have been abusing you, thinking you worthy of my disdain, thinking you a sniveling child and nothing more," the Matron Mother of Menzoberranzan went on. "I only allowed you to remain in a position of power at Arach-Tinilith because doing so spoke to the city of the glories of old. House Fey-Branche should be powerfully represented in the Academy of Lolth, of course, but then, since it was pathetic you, how powerful would the position truly prove?"

Minolin stiffened at the insult, her eyes narrowing, one fist clenching at her side. She wanted to lash out, but Baenre knew Minolin would not summon the courage to do so. This one was not a fighter but a plotter, working with subterfuge and caution within the shadows.

"Little did I understand the adamantine of your bones," Baenre went on, "or the cleverness lurking behind your dull eyes."

Those eyes flared at that remark! Minolin was obviously off-balance, insulted and angry, indeed, but also cornered by an enemy she knew she could not hope to defeat.

"You thought you had Gromph in your web," Baenre openly taunted. "You truly believed that you could turn his distrust and disapproval of mere Quenthel against the Eternal Baenre?"

The blunt remark had Minolin falling back a step. Her game was over, clearly. For years she had quietly worked on Gromph, using every wile, whispering undermining words against Quenthel—the witch Quenthel!—whom Gromph had hated through the decades.

Matron Mother Quenthel watched all of those thoughts play out on the trapped priestess's face, circling through anger and fear, the willingness to throw herself into the fray against the hope that somehow, some way, she could mitigate this personal disaster. And that circle was a spiral, Baenre knew, and one driving Minolin ever downward into despair. Yes, she would play through the logic here—she was no fool, but a calculating and devious witch, a true devotee to Lady Lolth!

And so Minolin knew, without doubt, that the sudden insight of her arch-enemy, this Matron Mother standing before her, had to have come from Lady Lolth herself.

And so she knew that she was surely doomed.

Minolin lifted a hand—even a mouse would fight in such a corner—but of course Matron Mother Quenthel was the quicker. The Scourge of Quenthel appeared in her hand, the five writhing snake heads hungrily striking at poor Minolin, taunting her telepathically as they invaded her tender flesh. The priestess's eyes widened with horror as she felt the pleasure of K'Sothra, who would taste blood to be content. Minolin gasped and fell away as Zinda's fangs reached for her face, for it was fear that Zinda most desired from her enemies.

Do not resist, the third serpent, Hsiv, advised, a soothing melody whispering through Minolin's thoughts, and one so discordant with the excruciating pain of serpent Qorra's fiery poison.

The fifth snake, Yngoth, did not strike, but swayed tantalizingly before Minolin's eyes as the priestess slumped back against the wall. In those black eyes, Minolin would see hope, Matron Mother Quenthel knew, for the living serpents of her scourge imparted to her their methods, of course, and asked her permission to continue.

Minolin Fey was overwhelmed. Only the wall held her up as the snakes retreated.

Then it was the iron grasp of Matron Mother Quenthel, taking her by the arm and dragging her away through another door from the balcony and into a small sitting room. Baenre shoved Minolin forward. The priestess crashed through some chairs and barely held her balance.

She struggled for a few moments, seeming on the verge of collapse, but then stood straight and spun around to face her adversary.

"You dare strike me in my own house? And on this day of festival?" she started to growl, but the words caught in her throat as Baenre lifted a clawed hand and reached out with her magic.

"Yield," she said simply.

Minolin wanted to spit, of course, but instead, she fell to her knees, driven there by the power of the spell, held there by the will of Quenthel Baenre.

"I will never underestimate you again, clever assassin," Matron Mother Quenthel said. "Indeed, my scorn for you is removed, replaced by—"

Gromph Baenre burst into the room.

" —admiration," Matron Mother Quenthel finished, smiling wickedly and looking at the archmage as if to ask him what had taken him so long.

"On—on this day?" Gromph stammered with obvious shock. "In this time?"

Matron Mother Quenthel lowered her scourge, the snakes going to their writhing dance and sleep as the weapon fell to the end of its wyvern hide loop at her hip. She held her hands up innocently, as if in surrender.

"Decide where your loyalties lie," she said to Gromph. "The Spider Queen will not have her archmage divided in his loyalties, not in this majestic time. You would secretly lead House Baenre, so you hoped, and a tenday ago, your choice would have been an easy one."

"Dear sister," Gromph said, and in that instant, the face of the Matron Mother of Menzoberranzan darkened with rage and twisted with the weight of centuries, and for just a flash of time, glared at him with an awful power bared.

"Matron Mother," he quietly corrected, lowering his gaze.

"No!" cried Minolin Fey, her eyes wide, her expression shocked to see mighty Gromph so cowed.

"You will never lead Baenre," the matron mother calmly remarked.

"Strike at her!" Minolin cried. "It is just Quenthel!"

NIGHT OF THE HUNTER

Gromph's gaze snapped up, full of anger, but it fell over Minolin and not his sister. The priestess of Fey-Branche fell back, her arms coming up defensively as if she expected Gromph to destroy her utterly, then and there. "I am with child!" she shrieked as she fell away to prostrate herself on the floor. "Your child!" she begged pathetically.

Matron Mother Quenthel smiled knowingly as Gromph turned his astonished expression her way. With a nod to Minolin, the matron mother began to cast a spell, and the wizard followed suit. A pair of spectral drow hands, one male, one female, appeared above the prostrated priestess, and together they reached down and grabbed her around the folds of her robes and jerked her back to her feet so abruptly that it took her a moment to even realize that she was standing.

She started to speak once more, both Gromph and Matron Mother Quenthel moving to silence her, but then all three fell silent as there erupted a great tumult from inside the Fey-Branche house, shrieks and screams and the clatter of dropped glasses and tumbling furniture.

"House Baenre wars upon us!" Minolin Fey said with a gasp.

"Matron Mother?" Gromph asked, turning Quenthel's way.

But the Matron Mother of Menzoberranzan wore a look of serenity, her expression telling the other two that this was no attack.

The interior door of the sitting room swung open and in strode a drow female of extraordinary beauty and presence.

"Yor'thae," Matron Mother Quenthel greeted, using the term reserved for the greatest Chosen being of Lady Lolth, a particular priestess who had become the vessel of Lolth in the War of the Spider Queen. Matron Mother Quenthel, the leader of Menzoberranzan, the supreme drow of the City of Spiders, ended her greeting with a deep and respectful bow.

Minolin swallowed hard before the specter, the avatar of the Spider Queen herself. Beyond the female, in the other room, the minions of House Fey-Branche and the four remaining Baenres followed the glorious creature, and all of them were on their knees, crawling, and with their eyes respectfully aimed at the floor.

Minolin shuffled uncomfortably, almost imperceptibly, but Matron Mother Quenthel caught it, and understood. Minolin knew that she should be kneeling, of course, particularly when Gromph fell to his knees beside her. She wanted to drop, but she could not, Baenre knew, because the avatar before them, a priestess who had once been known as Danifae Yauntyrr, would not let her fall.

Matron Mother Quenthel fixed Minolin with a knowing glance and a taunting grin. Any thoughts Minolin Fey had entertained of revenge against Matron Mother Quenthel had just been washed away, they both knew.

The incarnation of Lady Lolth glided across the room, passing before Minolin, and pausing there only to put her hand on the trembling priestess's belly, not yet swollen with child. She moved to stand before the matron mother, and nodded and smiled, then fixed Quenthel Baenre with the most passionate kiss.

"My Eternal Servant," the avatar said, gently stroking the matron mother's tender cheek.

Then she walked past Baenre, out onto the balcony, and floated off into nothingness.

"Lolth appeared!" cried one of the priestesses in the room beyond, several daring to climb to their feet once more.

"The festival is a success!" another yelled, for indeed, the Festival of the Founding was a day when all the drow of Menzoberranzan hoped that Lady Lolth would make an appearance among them, a sign that they remained in her good graces.

Cheers and chatter echoed around the compound, spreading out to the streets beyond. All the city would soon know of Lolth's appearance, Matron Mother Quenthel understood. Matron Mez'Barris Armgo would soon know.

Matron Byrtyn moved up beside her, and Baenre was glad to see the look of reverence splayed upon the old matron's face.

"It is a sign to us," Baenre quietly explained. "House Fey-Branche is vulnerable no more. You are no longer without an ally."

Matron Byrtyn bowed before the supreme Matron Mother of Menzoberranzan.

"You will marry," Matron Mother Quenthel instructed Gromph and Minolin.

"Marry?" Gromph chortled, for indeed, Minolin was hardly the first priestess to bear one of his children, and, if he had his way, she would hardly be the last.

Matron Mother Quenthel turned and waved Sos'Umptu and Myrineyl back, then waved the door closed in their faces, leaving only Byrtyn, Gromph, and Minolin in the room with her.

"You are with child, and that child is a girl," she explained to Minolin. "She will be raised in House Baenre, where you will forever more reside, at my side."

"Minolin is the High Priestess of Fey-Branche!" Matron Byrtyn protested, but Baenre silenced her with a look.

"And your child will be groomed as my successor," Baenre said. Byrtyn gasped. "And you will name her . . ." She fixed Gromph with a sly look.

"Yvonnel," he finished for her quietly, catching on.

The matron mother sidled up to Minolin, who trembled visibly. Baenre reached up to stroke her smooth cheek and the priestess tried unsuccessfully to shy from the touch. "If you fail in this, you will suffer eternity at the feet of the Spider Queen, her poison burning in your blood with an agony that will never relent," she warned.

"I will serve," Minolin said, her voice thin and shaky. "When the child is born, I will properly train—"

"You are an egg and nothing more," Matron Mother Quenthel sharply interrupted. "Do not think yourself worthy to train Yvonnel Baenre."

Minolin didn't dare respond.

"Yvonnel the Eternal," Matron Mother Quenthel said, turning back to Gromph. "The babe's instruction will begin at once."

It took Gromph a moment to figure out what she meant, but when he did, his eyes widened and he gasped audibly, in disbelief, "No."

Baenre's smug smile mocked him. Both she and Gromph imagined the tentacles of Methil crawling over the naked flesh of Minolin Fey-Branche, finding their way to the growing consciousness of the life inside her, imparting the memories and the sensibilities that Gromph had saved within the split skull of his dead mother.

CHAPTER 4

UNFORGIVEN

A MUDDY GANG OF FIVE CROSSED INTO THE NORTHERN END OF THE PASS that led south through the Spine of the World. Their trip from Ten-Towns across the tundra had been uneventful, but hardly easy in the days of the early spring melt, where bottomless bogs hid cleverly among the patches of ice and sludge, where sinkholes opened suddenly to swallow a rider and his mount whole, where mud bubbles of trapped gasses grew like boils as the ice of winter relinquished its hold. Such bulbous sludge mounds appeared all about the trail, sometimes blocking it, and were known to explode, sending forth a shower of cold mud.

This group had found more than their share of those natural mud bombs, particularly the three walking beside the tall mount that carried the man and the woman. They appeared almost monochrome, head-to-toe layered in brown, where even their smiles, on the rare occasions they managed one, showed flecks of mud. Heavy boots pulled from the grabbing ground, sucking sounds accompanying each step.

"Sure but I'm not to miss this foul land," said the dwarf, and she lifted her boot and turned her leg, scraping at the mud pack. Her effort cost her balance, though, and she stumbled to the side, crashing against the large steed, which snorted in protest and stamped its fiery hoof hard, splattering mud and sending the dwarf and her two cohorts ducking.

"Ah, but control yer smelly nightmare!" the dwarf bellowed.

"I am," Artemis Entreri casually replied from his high perch. "It did not stomp you into the ground, did it? And believe me when I tell you that the hell horse would like nothing more."

"Bah!" Amber the dwarf snorted in reply, and she wiped a patch of mud from her shoulder, then snapped her hand out at Entreri, throwing the mud his way.

"It is not the best season to be crossing the tundra, I expect," said Brother Afafrenfere. The monk had trained in the Bloodstone Lands, in the mountains of Damara, right beside the frozen wastes of Vaasa, so he was the most experienced of the troupe in the manner of terrain found in Icewind Dale. "Another tenday in one of the towns would have served us well."

Afafrenfere never looked up as he spoke, just kept his head low under the cowl of his woolen hood, and so he did not see the scowl from the woman riding on the nightmare behind Entreri.

"Another tenday deeper into the spring would have meant more monsters awake from their winter nap, and prowling around, hungry," Entreri said, and the others all recognized that he made the remark merely to calm Dahlia, who had been in a foul mood since they left Drizzt Do'Urden on the slopes of Kelvin's Cairn a dozen days before. None of the five hardy adventurers were afraid of such monsters, of course, and indeed, they were all itching for a fight.

They had awakened from a sleep in an enchanted forest, a slumber that had seen the passage of eighteen years, though had seemed no more than a night's sleep to the band. After their numb shock at the revelation, they had tried to look on the bright side of their magically created dilemma, for, as Amber had pointed out, they had gone to sleep as fugitives, with many powerful enemies searching for them, yet had awakened in freedom, in anonymity even, if that was their choice, likely more so than any of them had known in decades.

But since that night on Kelvin's Cairn, the mood had turned sour, particularly with Dahlia, and none had found much relief from the dismal pall while tramping through the endless mud of Icewind Dale.

"We're not yet in civilized lands," warned Effron, the fifth of the group, a small and skinny tiefling warlock with a broken and twisted body, his collar and shoulders mangled so that his right arm swung uselessly behind him.

All eyes turned his way. These were among the first words he had spoken since their departure from the mountain.

"You have seen them, then?" Entreri asked.

"Of course, shadowing us, and it frightens me that I travel with companions who have not noted the clear signs."

"Ye think ye might be talkin' less in riddles for the rest of us?" Amber asked.

"We are being followed," Afafrenfere answered. "For more than a day now. Large forms, bigger than goblins, than hobgoblins, even."

"Giants?" the dwarf asked with a glint in her eye.

"Yetis," Afafrenfere replied.

"Do tell." Entreri crossed his arms on the neck of his conjured nightmare steed and leaned forward, seeming amused.

"Vaasa is known for such beasts," the monk explained. "They are quite ferocious, and a mere scratch of their claws is known to cause disease and a lingering death—that is, if you are fortunate enough to avoid being eaten alive by them."

"Never heared o' them," said the dwarf.

"Nor I," Dahlia added.

"Then let's hope they remain no more than the warning of a tired monk on a muddy trail," Afafrenfere said, and started away.

"Well, since you two are up high and not crawling in the mud like the rest of us, perhaps you should keep your eyes to the horizon," Effron said. There was a clear undertone of disdain in his voice, underlying the general discontent that had followed the quintet out of Ten-Towns, an argument that had become particularly virulent between the twisted tiefling warlock and his mother, Dahlia.

Dahlia returned his words with a sharp glare, but Entreri continued to lean, and to wear his amused grin.

They climbed a narrower trail through a maze of tumbled boulders, which had them all on edge since the huge stones provided fine cover to any would-be ambushers. The path soon leveled off, then began a descent into the gorge cutting through the towering mountains. Any who ever crossed this way could not help but imagine enemies far above, raining death upon them in the form of arrows or stones.

Entreri and Dahlia led the way on the nightmare, and it was a fortunate choice. Barely had the group returned to level ground, walking amid a boulder-strewn, wider section of the trail, when the ground before them exploded. A large and thick, hairy creature leaped up from the concealment of a puddle of mud.

Seeming like a cross between a tall man and a burly bear, the hulking creature lifted up to its full height in the blink of an eye, heavy arms raised high above its head, dirty claws ready to swipe down.

NIGHT OF THE HUNTER

The nightmare reared and snorted puffs of black smoke from its wide nostrils, but it was not afraid as a normal horse surely would have been. Hellsteeds did not know fear—only anger.

Dahlia went with the movement, gracefully rolling off the back of the mount as its forelegs rose up into the air. She landed on her feet, though the mud nearly took them out from under her, and skidded aside quickly, scrambling away from the dangerous rear legs of the battling nightmare. She started as if to charge around the horse and Entreri, her magical quarterstaff at the ready, but no sooner had she landed than Amber called out from behind. Reflexively glancing that way, Dahlia saw that this tundra yeti had not come after them alone.

As surprised as he was, for the tundra yeti had blended perfectly into the muddy tail ahead, Entreri managed to hold his saddle, although only barely, tightly gripping the reins against his chest with all his strength.

The nightmare lashed out with its forelegs as the yeti brought its claws sweeping down, both monsters striking hard, both crying out in response—the yeti with a heavy grunt as the blow from the hoofs sent it skidding backward, the nightmare with an otherworldly shriek that sounded of pain, perhaps, but more so of anger.

The steed fell to all fours and tugged back against Entreri with such power that it almost flipped him forward over its head, and indeed, he smashed his face into the nightmare's neck. He felt the warmth of blood trickling from his nose, and a wave of pain that again had him holding on desperately as his mount leaped forward to engage.

Entreri shook the dizziness away and, wanting no part of this monstrous tangle, threw himself off the side of the nightmare right before the powerful combatants collided. He hit the ground in a roll, sloshing through puddles and mud, and came around to one knee just as the area behind him uplifted in a spray of mud and stones, a second yeti lifting up from concealment, towering over the kneeling, seemingly helpless man.

At the back of the line, Effron spun around to see a yeti leap up from behind a boulder to stand high atop the rock. It beat its powerful chest and issued a great roar.

"Yell louder," Effron quietly implored it as he lowered his bone staff and lashed out with a bolt of dark magic that shot from the eyes of the small skull that topped the powerfully enchanted weapon.

The ray hit the yeti in the belly, sizzling its brown coat, and indeed it roared all the louder, nearly falling off the back of the rock from the impact.

Effron, hardly about to wait around for the creature to regroup, cast a second spell, one he always kept ready, and his body flattened, becoming two-dimensional, more like a shadow than a living being; and the yeti roared all the louder, in protest then, when the twisted warlock slipped down into the ground.

"Where ye goin'? Amber cried out as he disappeared. Just before her, Afafrenfere joined Dahlia, the two sprinting off across the trail from the yeti Effron had hit, at yet another beast that had appeared between a pair of flat-topped rocks, each about waist-high to the monk.

"Wait, what?" the dwarf called, hopping all around, looking for Effron, who was gone, then turning to the yeti the twisted warlock had stung, which was clearly outraged, then turning to the pair running off the other way.

She chased Dahlia and Afafrenfere. Three against one, she thought, and liked the odds.

But then two more yetis appeared, one rising up behind each of the rocks flanking the trio's intended target.

"Oh, by the gods," the dwarf muttered, and she skidded up against a nearby boulder and cast a spell that made her sink right into it, melding with the stone.

"Find a strike behind my move!" Afafrenfere instructed, and he sprinted in front of Dahlia, fearlessly bearing down on the three hairy behemoths. He leaped atop the stone to the left, right before one startled yeti, and right beside the initial target.

The yeti behind the stone roared and swung hard, but Afafrenfere moved ahead of the blow, leaping above it into a back flip that also brought him above the reach of the yeti in the middle. That centering beast watched him rise, and so it didn't take note of the heavy follow-through of its companion, and caught the swipe of the first yeti right in the face.

The monk landed lightly on the other stone, launching immediately into a circle-kick that smacked the third yeti right in the face. But even with that tremendous force behind it, the kick did little to drive the monster back, and it responded with a slash of its claws that had the monk diving back for the center of the trail.

The yeti half-leaped, half-rolled over the boulder, in close pursuit. So focused was it on the human that had kicked it in the face that it hardly noticed Dahlia rushing past it the other way.

She thought that a good thing.

In she charged at the tangled other two, leading the way with a straight-forward stab of her powerful staff, Kozah's Needle, driving its tip right into the torn flesh of the yeti standing between the stones. That strike alone would have brought forth a howl of agony, but Dahlia made it all the more devastating, releasing a blast of lightning through the staff.

With a crackle of energy and a puff of gray smoke, the yeti fell away.

"Hold them!" Afafrenfere cried from far behind her.

"Of course," she replied dryly, as if in agreement that holding back two giant-sized hulking monsters would obviously be no problem at all!

The yeti, of course, thought it had the man helpless. Any onlooker would have believed the same.

Unless that onlooker understood the skill of the monster's intended victim.

From his half-kneeling position, Entreri threw himself over wildly, spinning out to the side ahead of the descending yeti claw. The beast tried to keep up, stomping its foot in an attempt to pin him down or crush him.

But Entreri stayed ahead, and his sidelong spin turned into a forward roll that brought him back up to his feet. He broke aside immediately, dodging the lunging yeti, and whirled around, his momentum strengthening the stab of his sword, the blade tearing through flesh to nick off the thick rib of the beast.

With a frightening howl, the yeti spun around to face him.

But Entreri was already gone, out the other way, and he struck again with his sword, but did not plunge it in deeply this time. He stayed ahead of the turning beast, sticking it again, goading it around and around. And as soon as he seemed to become predictable, Entreri stopped abruptly and ducked low, the turning yeti sweeping its grasping arms up over him as he cut back the other way.

From the other side, he leaped up and drove his dagger hard into the yeti's right armpit, the vampiric weapon slicing through tendon and muscle with ease. And Entreri let his magical dagger drink deeply, stealing the very life force of the huge creature.

How it howled!

It swung back violently, swinging arm clipping Entreri, who was already diving out and away, and the force of the blow helped him along as he put several strides between himself and his beastly enemy. He rolled back up in perfect balance and turned around, facing the beast.

In came the yeti in a running charge, but with one arm now hanging dead at its side. Entreri charged as well, and at the last second, the beast lunging wildly, he dived aside, managing a slash as the monster tumbled past. A quick turn had him in pursuit, behind the yeti, and he struck with sword and dagger now, chasing it and sticking it repeatedly, never giving it the chance to stop and turn back. His sword bashed against the beast's remaining good arm, but Entreri stabbed with the dagger, poking little holes, inconsequential wounds except that with each bite, the vampiric dagger fed.

But then the yeti turned the tables back. It was gone so quickly it took Entreri a long heartbeat to even realize it had leaped straight up into the air. He ran past and the beast landed heavily behind him, and pursued him.

Entreri angled for the wall, knowing he could not stay ahead of this foe for long and in no position to try a blind and desperate dive to either side.

He could hear the breaths of the monster so close behind. In front of him, the mountain wall climbed high, barely five strides away.

But he didn't slow.

Instead he leaped, throwing his shoulders back, running up the stone, one step, two steps, then leaping higher and inverting, back-flipping high in to the air. He threw his sword as he did, as high as he could, and he came over above the yeti, which had bent low to grab at him at the last moment. He crashed down atop the yeti's back, legs straddling, both hands grasping his dagger hilt and all of his momentum driving that vicious blade straight down atop the yeti's head. A boulder split asunder by a stroke of lightning would have sounded no louder than the crack of that skull, and the yeti's legs simply gave out under it.

NIGHT OF THE HUNTER

Entreri caught his descending sword and rolled aside, far from the tumble as the beast thrashed crazily in its death throes, the jeweled dagger's hilt still sticking like a unicorn's horn from the top of its head.

Entreri took a deep breath and tried to reorient himself, turning back to view the battle. A quick glance to the side showed him his nightmare and the other yeti locked in a death grip, smoke and blood and torn hair all around them. The nightmare had been pulled down to its front knees, but bit hard at the yeti's arm as the beast clamped around the steed's head, trying to twist its neck apart. Entreri rushed to retrieve his dagger from the now-dead beast, thinking to go to the nightmare while the yeti was so vulnerable, but a horrid cry sounded from behind, demanding his attention.

He whirled around to see another of the yetis, the one on the same side of the trail as he, frantically thrashing around, tearing its own skin with its claws as spiders climbed out of a gaping wound in its belly. Entreri had witnessed Effron's handiwork before, and he held faith that this yeti, too, was out of the fight for the time being.

He scanned out toward the center of the trail to see Afafrenfere in full retreat, a yeti in close pursuit.

Entreri yanked his dagger free and started out to help his companion, but before Entreri had gone two steps, the monk cut before one large boulder and as the yeti crossed it in pursuit, a form materialized from out of the rock.

Ambergris, her melding spell ended, came out swinging. She had both hands on Skullcrusher, her huge mace, and it was obvious that she had seen the yeti coming from within her meld with the rock, for the level and angle of her sidelong swipe was perfect, sweeping across to crunch the yeti's knee and sending it sprawling to the ground.

Clearly anticipating the move, Afafrenfere was already turning, and was fast back to the spot, leaping with a double knee drop onto the back of the prostrate yeti's head. The monk sprang up and stomped again, then leaped out before the yeti as it started to rise, demanding its attention.

And so the beast never saw Amber coming as the dwarf landed on its back and executed a tremendous overhead chop with Skullcrusher, the weapon once more living up to its name.

One on one, Dahlia figured she might have a chance against a tundra yeti, even though her weapon was not particularly effective against their tough hides and thick bones. When the second beast climbed back to its feet and came forward, though, the elf woman knew that she was in trouble.

She banged her staff against the stone before her nearest opponent several times in rapid succession, building a charge, then thrust it out against the returning yeti and released the energy, driving the monster back a couple of steps.

Dahlia thought to turn and flee. Indeed, she started to do just that, but then another form materialized before her—and behind the yetis—as her half-tiefling son slipped out of a crack in the mountain wall and became again three-dimensional. He was already into spellcasting as he reformed, Dahlia noted, so she redoubled her efforts at holding the yetis in place with a series of jabs and sweeps of Kozah's Needle.

A cloud appeared, sickly green and steaming with putrid aromas, its stench forcing Dahlia back, though it was not aimed at her. It sat in place up above and in front of her, engulfing the heads of the tall beasts. Their arms flailed more at the gases than forward at Dahlia. She heard them choking, half a roar and half a cough, though she could no longer see much of their heads within the steamy, opaque veil of the spell.

Dahlia fell back another step, broke her staff into a tri-staff and sent it into a spin. Clutching the middle pole, she launched into a twirling dance, exaggerating her movements to enhance the spinning flow of the outer poles. Her hands lifted and thrust alternately on the center pole, angling the spinning side bars to crack against the stones and occasionally against each other, throwing sparks that were immediately gobbled up by the enchantment of Kozah's Needle.

Within the stinking cloud, the yetis flailed. One finally found the good sense to duck low out of the gases, but when it came clear, it began to jolt and roar and twist all around—behind it, the warlock sent forth black bolts of stinging magic. The whole of the beast burst into flame then, magical darkfire eating at its flesh and hair.

Down that yeti went, streams of smoke rising. The second came forth, though, from the cloud, tumbling over the rock, its chin and chest covered in vomit, but with claws stubbornly raking at Dahlia.

She got in a hard blow, and let forth her lightning burst to doubly sting the beast. She dropped her hands to the outermost pole and twirled the other two around, whip-like, gathering momentum and speed, then snapping it like a biting snake, again and again as the beast stubbornly rose up on its hind legs once more.

She felt as if she were beating the dust from a hanging tapestry, and so doing no real damage to the tapestry itself!

Dahlia cursed and wished for a broadsword.

She cursed some more when the second yeti stood once again, still burning and smoking, but no longer bothered, it seemed, by the roiling putrid cloud. When it, too, came forward, moving between the rocks, the elf woman began her retreat, her nearest opponent pacing her, the second closing in.

But not closing in on her, she only realized when that trailing yeti scraped a clawed paw across the back of her opponent's head, and when the leading beast spun around to react, the second leaped upon it, bearing it to the ground.

Dahlia fell back, unable to decipher the riddle—until she spotted Effron once more, moving around the putrid cloud and the stones, his bone staff extended, the eyes of the staff's skull glowing red with inner fire. She figured out then that this second yeti was quite dead, and in death, it served Effron!

Her son had done this.

She watched, mesmerized, overwhelmed, half-proud but more than half-horrified.

The otherworldly shriek of Entreri's nightmare broke that trance and had Dahlia spinning around to see Amber and Afafrenfere standing around another dead yeti. Another beast, still alive, retreated back to the north and tore at its stomach as it went, a trail of spiders crawling behind it in pursuit. And finally, to see Entreri bashing in the skull of the yeti in the middle of the trail, the first of the beasts to appear, as it continued to twist and tear at the throat of the nightmare. The hellsteed now lay on its side, beginning to dissipate into black nothingness.

Amber and Afafrenfere rushed up to join Dahlia, and all three turned to regard the nearby struggle. Effron's zombie seemed no match for the living yeti, but it served to keep the beast engaged as Effron once more began to throw his blackfire magic. The living yeti finally managed to extract itself, the zombie falling still, quite destroyed, but the wounded beast had no more heart for the fight, obviously, and it ran off to the north, one last bolt of energy reaching forth from the warlock's bone staff to bite at it as it fled.

"Formidable," Afafrenfere remarked as Entreri finished off the last of the enemies.

"Thank you," replied the warlock.

"All of us, I mean," said the monk. "A capable band of five."

Effron just chuckled as he walked past the trio.

"Let us not tarry," Entreri called out to them. "Let us be far from this place before those two return, and likely with more friends." He ended by leaping to the side, in seeming alarm, and his motion and gaze had Dahlia, the monk, and the dwarf beside her turning fast.

The yeti Amber had killed stood up once more, brains dripping from the back of its exploded skull. It lumbered after Effron as he went on his way to the far side of the trail. A moment later, the eyes of the tiefling's bone staff flared yet again and the yeti Entreri had killed by the wall shifted and stiffly rose to its feet.

"I'm not much liking this," Amber remarked, and the dwarf priestess lifted her holy symbol.

"Get used to it," Effron replied without humor, and indeed, with a clear warning in his tone that he would not much appreciate any attempts the dwarf might make to drive his new pets away. The twisted warlock looked to Entreri and bade him, "Lead on."

Entreri's eyes never left the warlock, or his two new pets. The assassin moved in front of his latest kill and retrieved the obsidian nightmare statuette. He could not summon his mount again, so soon after the fight, so he tucked the figurine away into his pouch and waited for Dahlia and the others to catch up.

"Ye keep yer beasties far back," Amber ordered Effron as she and Afafrenfere fell into line behind Dahlia and Entreri. "I'm only tellin' ye once."

Effron only gave a cynical little laugh.

Despite the protests of the dwarf, and the clear uneasiness of the others, when they made camp that night, the zombie yetis stood guard. Indeed, Effron kept the beasts beside them all the way through the mountain pass and onto the rolling hills south of the Spine of the World, only releasing them back into death when the towers of Luskan came into sight, for even in that scurvy town, such monstrous undead guards would not likely find a warm welcome.

They made their way to the city outskirts north of the River Mirar, where a group of the city garrison stood guard at the north gate.

"What business have you in the City of Sails?" asked one. He looked at Dahlia as he spoke, but with apparent lust, not recognition. She had been a fugitive in Luskan, of course, and quite high in profile, having murdered one of the high captains and taken his enchanted cloak, which she now wore openly.

But none of the group seemed to recognize her, or any of them, reminding them of the benefit of their multi-year sleep. They had gone to Icewind Dale as fugitives, with many powerful enemies in pursuit, but now nearly two decades had passed.

"Passing through," Amber replied, and she moved in close and offered a handshake, cleverly slipping a gold coin into the guard's hand as he accepted her grip. "Or might be stayin', or might be signing on with a ship. Who's to say?"

The guard nodded and glanced back over his shoulder, pointing to a structure not far down the road. "One-Eyed Jax," he said. "That'd be the place for you."

"One-Eyed Jax?" Entreri echoed suspiciously, holding out his arm to bar any others from walking past him.

"Aye, a fine inn and a common room for postings, ship or caravan," the guard replied.

"Jax?" the assassin pressed.

"That's what he said," Amber interjected, but Entreri ignored her.

"The proprietor?"

"Aye, that'd be a shortened version of his name," the guard replied hesitantly.

"Jarlaxle!" Ambergris blurted, catching on.

The guard and his companions all blanched and looked around nervously, for such was clearly not a name to be spoken openly and loudly in Luskan!

Entreri moved back, signaling his group around him. "We go around the city," he told them quietly.

"Been wantin' a warm bed," Amber argued.

"No."

"Bah, but I'll meet ye on th'other side after one good night!" the dwarf bargained.

"No," Entreri flatly answered and he pointedly turned away from the guard and mouthed silently to his companions, "Would you so quickly tell all the world that we have returned to the land of the living?"

That gave Amber, and the others, pause. Entreri moved them away, motioning for the guard to remain behind.

"You don't believe we can trust Jarlaxle?" Dahlia asked quietly when they were off to the side.

Entreri snorted as if the question itself was perfectly ridiculous.

"He saved us," Dahlia reminded him.

Entreri snorted again. "Yet another reason for me to hate him."

"We were statues, we three," Afafrenfere put in, indicating himself, Entreri, and Dahlia, all three who had been turned to stone by a medusa in the dark environs of the Shadowfell, in the House of Lord Draygo Quick. "Trapped forever in nothingness, unable to even go on to our afterlife."

"Sounds like heaven," Entreri said dryly. "We go around the city, all of us, and not another word."

"Are you deigning to speak for the whole group now?" Dahlia asked.

"As you did in going to battle against Drizzt, you mean?" Entreri quickly retorted, and the woman backed off.

The dwarf, the monk, and Effron exchanged glances.

"Well, lead on then, ye dolt," Amber said. "Next city in line—Port Llast if she's still standing. I'm in need of a beer and a bed, don't ye doubt!"

"And a bath," Afafrenfere added.

"Don't ye get all stupid," grumbled the dwarf, and with a farewell nod to the confused Luskan guard, the band turned east, around the city, and moved off down the road.

CHAPTER 5

HUZZAHS AND HEIGH-HOS!

A RAY OF MORNING SUNLIGHT PEEKED IN THROUGH THE WINDOW AND tickled Catti-brie's senses. She slowly came out of her wonderful night's sleep. She was naked, but huddled under piles of blankets and delightfully warm—and warmer still as memories of the previous night flooded through her.

She reached back behind her at that warm thought, feeling for her companion, but he was not there. Surprised, Catti-brie moved up to her elbows and peeked out from under the edge of the blankets.

Drizzt was across the room, near the hearth, the flames shining off his ebon skin, orange highlighted reflections showing in his long white hair. He, too, was quite naked, and Catti-brie took the moment to admire his form, the grace of his movements as he tossed another log onto the fire. It bounced around the half-consumed faggots within and settled too near to the front, and she heard Drizzt's sigh as he considered it. She thought he would reach for the poker, but he did not. Indeed, he moved the small iron screen farther off to the side and reached in with his bare hand to retrieve the log, which had not caught yet, though tiny sparks could already be seen within the folds of the bark.

Drizzt laid that log aside and turned back to the low-burning fire, bending low, then instinctively jumping back as one burning log popped, sending a spray of sparks up the chimney.

Catti-brie muffled her laugh with the blankets, not wanting Drizzt to know that she was spying on him. She pulled the blankets down from in front of her face, though, her mouth hanging wide open, when Drizzt reached into the fire to rearrange the smoldering logs within. He grabbed one glowing log, flames erupting all around his forearm, with hardly a wince, and reset it upon the others.

Apparently satisfied with his handiwork, he retrieved the new log he had set aside and carefully placed it on the others. He stood, brushed his hands together, and replaced the screen.

"How?" Catti-brie asked from the bed and Drizzt turned to regard her. The woman's gaze moved across the small room, to the far wall where Drizzt had hung his sword belt. She noted the gem-encrusted, black cat-shaped pommel of the scimitar Icingdeath, which she knew could offer Drizzt such protection from the bite of fire. Had he grown so attuned to the blade that it could lend him such even when he was not carrying it?

"Good morning!" he greeted. "And oh, it is a fine one, though the stubborn wind of winter's end bites hard this day. The others are off to gather mounts and supplies."

"How did you do that?"

"Do what?"

"You reached into the fire. It should have curled the flesh from your finger bones!"

Drizzt came over to the bed and sat beside her, lifting his left hand to reveal a ring, made wholly of ruby, a sparkling red band around his finger.

"I took it from a mage, a drow noble," he explained as he slid it off and held it up for Catti-brie. "In the bowels of Gauntlgrym—it is a long tale, and a good one for the road." He reached his hand out, offering the ring to the woman for a closer look.

"It protects you from the flames?"

"As surely as my scimitar," Drizzt replied. "Indeed, when first I put it on, I felt a sense of affinity between the two, scimitar and ring. It was almost as if their magic had . . . nodded respectfully to each other."

Catti-brie looked at him curiously, and skeptically, for she had never heard of such a thing. Drizzt's weapon, powerful though it was, was not sentient in any way that she knew, and rings such as this ruby band were not uncommon, not overly powerful, and not known to possess any type of empathy or telepathy.

She handed it back, but Drizzt caught her hand before she could retract it.

"In many cultures, the ring is the sign of fidelity and undying love," he explained as he slipped it onto her finger. "Take this in that spirit, and with the added benefit of the protection it offers. With my scimitar in hand, we two can walk across hot coals!"

Catti-brie looked curiously at the jewel. For just a fleeting second when it had gone onto her hand, she had felt something . . . something like a call from afar, or as if the ring was feeling her as surely as she was feeling it. The sensation was gone in a moment, and then it seemed just a ruby band once more, but one that had shrunken already to perfectly fit her, as magical rings were wont to do.

She held her hand up to better view it with the ring on, and looked through her fingers to the violet eyes of the drow she so loved.

"The others are gone?" she asked.

"They left with the dawn," Drizzt replied.

Catti-brie lifted the edge of the blanket, and Drizzt didn't need to be invited into the bed twice.

"I thought we had returned for Drizzt," Regis said to Catti-brie, the two at the back of the line of five as they made their way into the rocky dells around Kelvin's Cairn, the long and winding approach to the dwarven complex. He didn't even try to hide the regret from his voice, and Catti-brie caught it, he knew, when she turned to regard him with obvious concern.

"Were you hoping for a fight?"

"I was hoping that I would be of use," Regis replied. "I left much behind me to get to Icewind Dale."

"He would have died without us," the woman replied.

"Without you, not me. You arrived armed with healing spells. My potions were not needed—indeed, I was not needed. Had I remained in the south, the outcome here would have been the same."

"You cannot know that," said Wulfgar. He slowed to let the other two catch up to him. Drizzt and Bruenor were far in the distance, already around the next bend. "Something you might have done, someone you might have met and influenced, perhaps played a part before we ever came upon him atop the mountain."

"Or perhaps those assassins we fought on the bank of the lake would have come for me instead, and, alone, I would have been slain," Catti-brie added.

But Regis shook his head, having none of it. His thoughts were to the south, with the Grinning Ponies. His memories drifted across the Sea of Fallen Stars, to sweet Donnola Topolino and a mercantile empire he could claim beside her. It was wonderful to be among the Companions of the Hall again, of course, but there remained the question of why. Duty had brought him here, running. But what duty might that be?

To fight a war for Bruenor and Mithral Hall? To go and do battle with a vampire? Laudable missions, both, he reasoned, but neither seemed above the work he was doing with the Grinning Ponies.

Catti-brie stopped her walk and grabbed him by the shoulder to halt him, too, then called Wulfgar close to join them. "Drizzt won his fight on the night we rejoined him," she explained. "Even if we had not been there and he had succumbed to his wounds, that night, victory was his."

Regis looked to Wulfgar for some clarification of the surprising remark, but the barbarian could only shrug, obviously as much at a loss as he.

"The battle was for his soul, not his body," Catti-brie explained. "For the very identity of Drizzt Do'Urden, and such a fight must be won or lost alone. And yet, Mielikki bade us to return, and facilitated it—and that is no small thing, even for a god!"

"Because she knew he would win," Wulfgar put in, and Regis stared at him, trying to catch up to the reasoning.

"And because he won against the desires of a vengeful goddess, one Drizzt has cheated since his earliest days," Catti-brie added. "This is not ended, I expect. Lolth cannot get his soul, but she will exact retribution, do not doubt."

"She will try," Regis corrected, his voice steeled, his shoulders squared. He was glad that he had kept most of his doubts private, for how trivial they suddenly seemed to him. Yes, he would like to ride beside Doregardo and the Grinning Ponies once more—those were fine years of camaraderie and adventure. And yes, of course, he desperately wanted to find Donnola again—he had been away from her for years, yet his love for her had not diminished. Indeed, it seemed to him that he loved her more now than he had when she had forced him to flee the ghost of Ebonsoul.

But even that love had to wait, he resolutely reminded himself. He was only alive again because of this, because of Mielikki.

A sharp whistle up ahead turned the trio to see Drizzt back at the bend, waving for them to hurry along.

Soon after, the five had crossed into the dwarf complex. Only Drizzt had revealed his true identity, and unlike the snarling folk of Bryn Shander, Stokely Silverstream's dwarves were more than willing to hear the drow's side of the Balor story. The guards escorted the group straight to Stokely, who was taking his breakfast in proper dwarf fashion, with a heaping plate of eggs and breads, and a flagon of beer to wash it down.

"Well now," the dwarf leader greeted, rising and offering his hand to Drizzt. "Heared ye might be about. Some friends o' yers came looking for ye. A monk fellow, the pretty Amber Gristle O'Maul . . ."

"Of the Adbar O'Mauls," Drizzt said before Stokely could, and the dwarf chuckled and went on.

"They came looking for ye, and surprised we were! Where ye been, elf? Near to twenty years gone by . . ."

"It is a long tale, my friend, and one I am anxious to tell," Drizzt replied. "But trust me when I say that it will be the least interesting of the tales you hear this day."

Drizzt nodded from Stokely to the other dwarves in the room, his look begging for some privacy.

"Bah, but ye ain't to be trusted, Drizzt," said another of the dwarves in the room, a mining boss named Junky. "That's what them o' the towns're sayin'!"

"Then them in the towns're stupid," Bruenor retorted.

"We need to speak with you," Drizzt said quietly to Stokely. "On my word, and on the graves of Bruen—" He paused and flashed a little grin. "On the graves of Bonnego Battle-axe and Thibbledorf Pwent," he corrected.

Stokely nodded, considered the words for a moment, then waved the other dwarves out of the room.

As soon as they were gone, Drizzt stepped back and swept his arm out toward the other four, standing at his side. "You know my friends not, and yet you do," Drizzt said.

"Eh?" Stokely looked them over, shaking his head, then focusing mostly on Bruenor, as would be expected. Soon his inspection became more than a simple perusal, though, for there seemed a spark in the clan leader's eye, as if he should know this young dwarf standing before him, but couldn't quite place him. He silently echoed the name Drizzt had just spoken.

"Might that I should be introducin' meself as Bonnego Battle-axe," Bruenor said, and Stokely scrunched his face up with confusion and fell back a step.

And his face unwound as the blood drained from it, as his jaw began to inevitably drop open.

"I give to you, King Bruenor of Clan Battlehammer," Drizzt said.

"It can no' be," Stokely breathed.

"Ain't ye seen enough craziness in yer life to believe a bit more craziness?" Bruenor asked with a great "harrumph" and a derisive snort.

Stokely moved up to stand before him, studying him closely. Stokely had never known King Bruenor at the age of this dwarf before him, of course, for Bruenor was much older than he, but poor flummoxed Stokely wasn't wearing an expression of denial on his face.

"I seen ye die in Gauntlgrym," Stokely said. "Put a stone on yer cairn meself."

"And ye was in Mithral Hall when Gandalug come back after a thousand years of deadness."

Stokely tried to respond, but flapped his lips indecipherably for several heartbeats. "But I seen ye die," he tried to explain. "More personal this time."

"Aye ye did, and now I'm back. Been back to Gauntlgrym, too, and goin' that way again, don't ye doubt. Any o' yer boys been there since the fightin'?"

Stokely continued to stare at him and didn't seem to register the question for many heartbeats. Then he cleared his throat nervously and shook his head. "No. Them halls be a long walk through the Underdark, and the way's full o' damned drow . . ." He paused and looked at Drizzt. "Word's that them drow've taken over the lower tunnels."

"Aye, they have," said Bruenor.

"Ye meanin' to do something about that?"

Bruenor nodded, but looked to Drizzt, who was shaking his head emphatically. "Might, in time," Bruenor explained to Stokely.

"King Bruenor will rouse Clan Battlehammer, then?"

"Much to do. Much to do," said Bruenor. "And I'm askin' ye now not to be spreading word of me return."

"If ye be who ye say ye be, more an order than an ask," Stokely remarked.

"If I be who I say I be, and I do, then I'm askin' as a friend and not tellin' ye as yer king."

The two exchanged a long look then, both slowly nodding. Then Bruenor stepped back to introduce the others, but before he even started, Stokely rattled off their names. Any dwarf of Clan Battlehammer needed no introductions to the Companions of the Hall.

"What a glorious day it be!" Stokely said soon after, as the shock began to wear off. "Ah, but why, I'm wantin' to ask, but it's not to matter! Only that it be, that King Bruenor's back from Moradin's Hall in Dwarfhome. A good day for Clan Battlehammer!"

Bruenor did well to hide his wince at the reference to Dwarfhome, enough so that Stokely didn't catch it. Drizzt did, though he wasn't sure what it meant. He looked to Catti-brie, who had similarly noted it, and she returned his inquisitive expression with a subtle shake of her head, telling him that this was neither the time nor the place for that particular discussion.

"Here's to a hunnerd years o' good days for Clan Battlehammer, then!" Bruenor said, managing a fair amount of bluster.

"So where's yer road? Ye meaning to spend the summer with us here in the Dale, are ye?"

"Nah, got to be going," Bruenor replied. "I just came here to gather me friends, and now we've a long road to walk."

"Mithral Hall?"

"Soon."

Stokely paused and pondered things for a moment. "And I can't be tellin' no one?"

"Not a one," said Bruenor. "I'm asking ye."

"Then why'd ye come here?" Stokely asked. "Why not just ride out to the south? Are ye needin' something from me, then?"

"Not a thing."

"Then why'd ye come here?"

Bruenor put his hands on his hips and pasted on a most solemn expression. "Because I owed it to ye," he said in all seriousness. "If I'm livin' another thousand years, if I'm back after that for another thousand more, I'll not be forgettin' the charge o' Stokely and his boys in Gauntlgrym. Ah, but we were lost, all of us and all our hopes, and there ye were, Pwent beside ye. No king could ask for a better clan and no friend for better friends, I tell ye. And so I'm owin' ye."

"Then ye're owing us all, living here under the mountain, for I didn't go there alone," said Stokely.

Bruenor looked at him curiously.

"Ye tell 'em who ye be," Stokely said. "I'll give ye a send-off—oh, and she'll be one to fit the miracle that bringed ye back to us, don't ye doubt. And ye'll get up on the durned table and tell yer tale, to meself and to all me boys."

"Telling the world presents . . . complications," Drizzt interrupted.

"And ye tell all me boys what ye told me, about keepin' our mouths shut," said Stokely.

"It would be better—" Drizzt started to say, but Bruenor, whose eyes remained locked with Stokely's, cut him short.

"Ye bring many the keg," Bruenor agreed, "for I've a long tale, and one beggin' a huzzah and heigh-ho at every turn."

He clapped Stokely on the shoulder, and the other dwarf smiled from ear-to-hairy-ear, and shouted out for the dwarves who waited on the other side of the door.

"Call all the boys in from the mines," Stokely ordered. "And ye tell Fat Gorin to cook us a feast fit for a king!"

"Huzzah!" the dwarves cried, as dwarves always yelled when an excuse was offered for libations.

***

No dwarf in attendance that night of the celebration of the return of King Bruenor would ever forget it.

Dwarves prided themselves on their storytelling, of course, epic adventures laced with solemn songs of long-lost lands and hills of gold, heroic feats tinged ever with sadness and ever gleaming with the hopes that the next round—aye the next—would bring them to a better place.

So many were the songs of old, so many the tales of places lost, places waiting to be found again, that the celebration of King Bruenor that night in the smoky halls under the mountain in Icewind Dale started out as a typical celebration, with few understanding that this would fast become a special occasion.

Not to the height it became, at least.

For when he rose upon the table, the introductions of his friends still ringing in the air with the echoes of huzzah, King Bruenor took Stokely's boys to a place they'd never been. His song was not of lament, not of kingdoms lost. Nay, not that night. That night, King Bruenor spoke of friendship eternal, of fidelity and fealty, of purpose greater than that of any one dwarf.

He spoke of Iruladoon and the curse that he meant to make a blessing. He openly admitted to his boys his mistake in not going on to Dwarfhome, and begged forgiveness, which came from every corner. He spoke of Mithral Hall and of Adbar and of Felbarr, of King Connerad and Emerus Warcrown, and Harbromme's twins, who ruled in Adbar. He spoke of the Silver Marches and of an orc kingdom that should not be.

And he wound it all back to Gauntlgrym, to Delzoun, the heritage, to all that had been, and to all that must be again.

Not all that could be, but all that must be.

And he was King Bruenor, the living legend, and so when he said it, the dwarves of Clan Battlehammer believed it, and when he said it would be so, so they determined they would make it so.

And the flagons raised and the cheers echoed, and the flagons raised again.

"Ah, but the dwarves, always up for a toast," Regis remarked, sitting in the corner at the back of the hall beside Wulfgar.

Wulfgar gave him a wry smile, and said with sly irony, "You only live once."

"Twice," Catti-brie corrected, and she slid into the chair between the two.

"Aye," Wulfgar agreed. "And for some, it seems, it takes the second turn around to understand the joy of it."

Both Regis and Catti-brie looked at him curiously, and looked at each other, each offering a shrug.

"I loved you, you know," Wulfgar said, and Catti-brie's expression turned to one of sympathy and sadness.

"Oh no," Regis whispered under his breath.

"Honestly, and with all my heart," said Wulfgar.

"Wulfgar . . ." she started to reply, her eyes scanning as if searching for some way to stop this course.

But Wulfgar pressed on. "I just wanted you to know that."

"I do—I did," she assured him, and she took his hand and stared into his eyes, and he into hers, and a great grin spread over his face.

"My heart does not ache," he said.

Catti-brie looked at Regis again, neither having an answer.

Wulfgar burst out laughing.

"Am I missing a finer tale than the one Bruenor is telling again?" Drizzt asked, moving up to the table.

"No," Catti-brie said.

"You are missing an apology, my friend," Wulfgar said.

Drizzt moved to the chair opposite Catti-brie. "An apology?"

"I was simply telling your wife that my love for her was honest and true," Wulfgar said matter-of-factly.

"And it still is, then?" asked Drizzt.

Wulfgar laughed again, heartily, without the slightest hint of sarcasm or regret to be found.

"Aye," he said. "Aye! How could it not be?"

Drizzt didn't blink.

"Look at her!" Wulfgar cried. "As beautiful as the sunrise, as warm as the sunset, with the promise of peace close behind. Would you have me lie to you and tell you that I have no love for fair Catti-brie? Would that make it easier for you to travel the road beside me?"

"Yes," Catti-brie said, at the same instant that Drizzt emphatically answered, "No!"

Drizzt and Catti-brie turned to each other, both appearing as if they had been slapped with a cold, wet towel.

"I'll tell no lies to make our journey more comfortable," Wulfgar said. "Of course I love her. I always have and I always will."

"Wulfgar . . ." Catti-brie started to reply, but he spoke right past her.

"And I'll always love him, fool dwarf, who gave me a life with mercy he ever denies he possesses. And you," he added, looking to Regis. "Once I traveled to the end of Faerûn to find you, and I would do so again, with a song on my lips, and should I die trying, then know I died well!"

He turned to Drizzt and held up his huge hand, and Drizzt took it.

"And you, my brother, my friend," Wulfgar said. "Do you fear my love for your wife?"

Drizzt stared into Wulfgar's eyes for a long time, and gradually his lips curled into a confident smile. "No."

"I would never betray you," Wulfgar said.

Drizzt nodded.

"Never," Wulfgar said again. He glanced over at Catti-brie. "Nor would she, of course, but then, you know that."

Drizzt nodded.

"You spoke of a second time around," Catti-brie said, drawing their attention. "What have you learned?"

Wulfgar grabbed her hand and brought it to his lips for a gentle kiss. "My friend," he said, "I have learned to smile."

Catti-brie looked to Drizzt, and to Regis, the three passing around a grin none could quite decipher.

"And now if you will grant me your pardon," Wulfgar said, hoisting himself to his feet with great effort, and clearly, he had offered more than a few huzzahs and heigh-hos of his own through Bruenor's continuing tale. He nodded his chin to the far corner of the room, and following that motion, the friends noted a dwarf lass staring back at him.

"A pretty thing and I've always wondered," Wulfgar said with a laugh.

"Truly?" Regis said.

Wulfgar straightened his shirt and pants, turned back to the halfling, and winked. "You only live once, eh?"

He sauntered away.

Regis gave a little snort, shaking his head.

"Go and watch over him," Catti-brie bade the halfling, but as Regis started to stand, Drizzt put a hand out to stop him.

"What do you know?" Catti-brie asked him.

Drizzt was still staring at the departing barbarian. "I know that he is content. His heart is full."

Catti-brie started to argue, but stopped before a single word had come forth. She looked back at Wulfgar, noting the unmistakable lightness of his step.

"He completed his journey the first time," Catti-brie remarked, as much to herself as to the others, thinking those words would solve any riddle here. But when she turned back, she found the other two both staring at her to elaborate.

"He was married, with children," she explained.

"Grandchildren," Regis added. "All gone now."

"So he lived by the rules and traditions," said Catti-brie. "He did his duty to his people and to his god."

"And now?" Drizzt asked.

Catti-brie looked back at Wulfgar, who was dancing with the young dwarf lass by then. "Now, he will play," she said.

"It's all a game to him," Regis said, nodding as he reasoned it out. "Time borrowed from the calendar of the gods for pleasure and adventure, beyond what any man could ask or expect or hope to know."

"He is free," Catti-brie said as if only then understanding it.

Drizzt looked at the big man, and found, to his surprise, that he envied Wulfgar at that moment. But that moment passed, and instead the drow determined that he would learn from his large friend.

For in looking at Wulfgar, Drizzt couldn't deny the light, the joy, which surrounded the man like a halo sent from the gods. With a burst of heartfelt laughter, Drizzt lifted his hand and snapped his fingers, gaining the attention of a dwarf handing out flagons.

Why not, indeed?

CHAPTER 6

D'AERMON N'A'SHEZBAERNON

RIDERS," THE SOLDIER REPORTED. "A TRIO AT LEAST, HOLED UP IN THE rear chamber of the former chapel."

Matron Mother Quenthel looked to Gromph.

"Melarni," he confirmed.

Quenthel Baenre looked to Vadalma Tlabbar, one of the other three matron mothers who had accompanied her this day. Vadalma had ruled her fanatically devout House, Faen Tlabbar, for less than a century, but in that time had earned herself an amazing reputation for sadism and promiscuity. She would copulate with anything or kill anything, so it was said, and sometimes at the same time.

And Vadalma was always plotting, Matron Mother Quenthel knew, much like Vadalma's dead mother, Ghenni'tiroth. Yes, like her. The memories of Yvonnel, given to Quenthel by the illithid, explicitly warned of the fanatical Tlabbars.

"Should I have them killed then?" Matron Mother Quenthel asked her three escorts.

"Yes," Matron Miz'ri Mizzrym of the Fifth House answered immediately, drawing a laugh from Zeerith Xorlarrin. Miz'ri pointedly looked to Vadalma as she answered.

Miz'ri had heard the rumors, too, the others understood, for by all whispered accounts, a quiet alliance was being forged. House Faen Tlabbar and House Melarn, considered the two most fanatical in their devotion to the Spider Queen but each taking their rituals and practices in different directions, were hardly friendly with each other. Their priestesses at Arach-Tinilith argued constantly, sometimes violently, over the proper ways to show their love of Lady Lolth. Still, despite the disputes, the quiet whispers about Menzoberranzan now hinted that Matron Vadalma had recently been approached by agents for House Melarn, offering a truce of sorts.

It made sense, as these four matrons understood all too well. With House Xorlarrin leaving, there would be a major opening on the Ruling Council, and every House below Xorlarrin would vie for that coveted position. Perhaps House Melarn would go to war with House Mizzrym, the Fifth House, then ascend to the fourth rank as House Faen Tlabbar, House Melarn's secret ally in their endeavors against Miz'ri's family, climbed into the vacant third spot.

"Matron Vadalma?" Matron Mother Quenthel asked innocently.

"I do not think it wise to destroy driders of any House, or of no House at all," the Tlabbar leader answered. "They suffer by living. That is why they are driders."

Matron Mother Quenthel turned her smirk to Gromph.

"She has a point," the archmage agreed.

"Flush them out and capture them," Baenre ordered. "Take them in webs to House Baenre for . . . retraining."

"Matron Zhindia of House Melarn will protest," Zeerith Q'Xorlarrin warned. "But then, she is always protesting, is she not?"

"How many have we defeated already who are quietly associated with her House?" Matron Mother Quenthel asked, and she moved to the balcony of the loft and looked down over the wide audience chamber below, where the defeated resistance, some alive and shackled, others dead and piled, had been brought. "By what right does Matron Melarn utilize this place?" She spun on the others fiercely. "By what right do any enter here, in this most cursed of locations?"

"Until now?" Matron Zeerith asked, right on cue. She and Matron Mother Quenthel had practiced this very exchange, after all.

"Until now," Matron Mother Quenthel replied. "Now we are sanctioned by the goddess. So says First Priestess Sos'Umptu Baenre, who is First Priestess of the Fane of the Goddess, which is near to this place."

"And so says First Priestess Kiriy of Xorlarrin," said Zeerith.

"And Sabbal, First Priestess of Mizzrym," Miz'ri was proud to add, turning to Matron Tlabbar with a smug expression as she spoke. And why shouldn't she appear so? Matron Mez'Barris Armgo hadn't been invited along—indeed, it was likely that some of the wayward dark elves the Baenre forces had chased out of this compound had belonged to House Barrison Del'Armgo, while others had been merely Houseless rogues, and most others had been of House Melarn. If the rumors of House Melarn trying to ally with House Faen Tlabbar were true—and it seemed from Vadalma's sour expression that such was indeed the case—and that House Faen Tlabbar was entertaining the possibility, this expedition had likely put a screeching end to that unified march.

"And First Priestess Luafae of Faen Tlabbar," said Vadalma, clearly trying to bring some determination and exuberance to her tone.

Matron Mother Quenthel almost laughed at her.

Almost.

Just close enough so as to let the others, Vadalma included, know that she wanted to laugh at her, but, out of deference to Vadalma's station, the temperate Matron Mother Quenthel had restrained herself.

Matron Mez'Barris Armgo paced around her chapel, huffing and snorting and shaking her head. "What are you about, Quenthel?" she whispered to herself.

House Baenre had sent a sizable force to West Wall, to the old Do'Urden compound, scouring the place, and beside Quenthel had gone the matrons of the three Houses ranked immediately below Baenre and Barrison Del'Armgo. It seemed an almost unprecedented power play, so startling from the weakling Quenthel, a warning to any Houses thinking to climb into the top hierarchy that any such attacks would be met by a unified alliance of overwhelming power.

And perhaps it was, as well, a threat to House Barrison Del'Armgo. Matron Mez'Barris did not fear any of the other Houses individually; even House Baenre would never openly attack her. The cost would prove far too high.

But all four of these together? Might this be the start of a great realignment? The creation of a grander tie between Menzoberranzan and the fledgling city of Q'Xorlarrin before Matron Zeerith and the rest of her family departed for their new home?

Weapons Master Malagdorl entered the chapel then, his stride fast and anxious.

He nodded back at Matron Mez'Barris's inquiring look.

"Witch," Mez'Barris said under her breath. Malagdorl had been sent to Melee-Magthere to speak with spies House Barrison Del'Armgo had placed about Aumon Baenre, Quenthel's son. It was an open secret in Menzoberranzan that House Baenre had sanctioned House Xorlarrin's journey to the complex known as Gauntlgrym, but in light of these new developments, Mez'Barris suspected more than a simple sanction. Malagdorl's nod spoke volumes: Quenthel had arranged that expedition, Mez'Barris knew now, for as she had suspected, the brash upstart warrior, Tiago Baenre, had traveled with the Xorlarrins.

Tiago was the grandson of Weapons Master Dantrag, whom Mez'Barris hated. Dantrag had been the greatest enemy and rival of Uthegental, her beloved warrior son, the greatest weapons master Menzoberranzan had ever known, so Mez'Barris believed and preached.

"Gol'fanin, too," Malagdorl said, and Mez'Barris nodded, her lips disappearing in a profound scowl. Gol'fanin, the greatest blacksmith in the city, had traveled with Tiago Baenre to the legendary Forge of the Delzoun dwarves. Mez'Barris could well imagine what that might portend.

She looked at Malagdorl pitifully, and dismissed him with a wave. Did he understand, she wondered? Did her rather dimwitted grandson realize that Tiago would come back armed to kill . . . him?

No sooner had Malagdorl departed than First Priestess Taayrul poked her head in through the ornate door. "Minolin Fey has arrived, Matron," she said quietly.

"Take her to my private chambers at once," Mez'Barris answered. "Quietly. And let no word go forth that she is here. House Melarn will likely come calling soon enough. Matron Zhindia is surely outraged by the brash move of Quenthel Baenre, and no doubt House Melarn has lost many foot soldiers this day."

"Driders and captured drow foot soldiers were just carted from West Wall to Qu'ellarz'orl," Taayrul solemnly replied. "To House Baenre, it is presumed."

Matron Mez'Barris snorted and shook her head. Quenthel had truly surprised her with the boldness of this move. She had never thought the sniveling Baenre whelp was possessed of such courage.

To openly abduct Melarni driders?

"Put the garrison on war footing," Matron Mez'Barris said suddenly. Taayrul's red eyes widened. "Matron?"

It had been an impulsive command, and one of great consequence, but as she considered the events transpiring, Mez'Barris found herself agreeing with that impulse even more. "Recall all of Barrison Del'Armgo, noble and commoner. Close the gates and prepare every defense."

"Matron," Taayrul said with a respectful bow, and she scurried away. Leaving Mez'Barris alone with her worries.

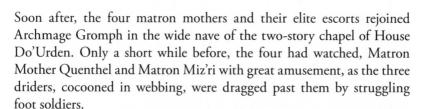

Soon after, the four matron mothers and their elite escorts rejoined Archmage Gromph in the wide nave of the two-story chapel of House Do'Urden. Only a short while before, the four had watched, Matron Mother Quenthel and Matron Miz'ri with great amusement, as the three driders, cocooned in webbing, were dragged past them by struggling foot soldiers.

"It has been so long since I looked upon this place," Matron Mother Quenthel said. "I had forgotten how much it resembles the Baenre Chapel, although far less magnificent, of course."

"Indeed, it is amazing that a House with a chapel of such design could have fallen so far from the Spider Queen's favor," Matron Vadalma put in, the sweetness of her tone doing little to cover the cattiness of her remark.

But Matron Mother Quenthel merely smiled at her. It didn't matter, Baenre knew, because the plan was in full execution and the other three had bought in wholly. When first they had entered this abandoned compound in Menzoberranzan's West Wall district, following an army of Baenre foot soldiers and wizards and beside the archmage himself, Vadalma Tlabbar and Miz'ri Mizzrym had both worn sour expressions. They had learned soon after the secret invitation the gist of this little adventure, no doubt, particularly since those invitations had come from Matron Zeerith and not from House Baenre, but had been sent in deference to the demands of House Baenre.

Through the maze of the complex's entry caverns, the four matrons had been greeted over and over by Baenre warriors, dragging out the many rogues who had come into this place unbidden and without permission.

None were supposed to be in here, by order of the Ruling Council, but it was an ill-kept secret in the city that Houses Melarn and Barrison Del'Armgo used this place as training quarters.

In a powerful stroke, then, Matron Mother Quenthel had struck a blow against both of those Houses, the uneasy Second House and the ambitious Seventh. If Baenre's choice of dining with House Fey-Branche during the Festival of the Founding hadn't warned House Melarn to temper those ambitions—indeed, if the appearance of Lolth's Avatar at the dinner, if the rumors were to be believed, hadn't done so—then surely this bold strike would make the demand crystal clear to Matron Zhindia Melarn.

And Zhindia could not even raise her grievance at the next iteration of the Ruling Council, because this place, once the home of Malice Do'Urden, the birthplace of the infamous Drizzt Do'Urden, could not be inhabited or visited, by direct and unambiguous edict of the Ruling Council.

Until now, when the First Priestesses of the four Houses in attendance had independently confirmed to their matrons that this mission was Lolth's will.

And so by Lolth's will and by Baenre's power, House Do'Urden was cleared that day of vagabonds and secret militia.

And so by Lolth's will, in accordance with Lolth's demand, House Do'Urden was ready to be reconstituted.

Minolin Fey noted the agitation in Mez'Barris's movements as the Matron swept into the room.

"You have seen the events of this day?" she asked, moving right to the point.

Minolin Fey nodded. "They have not been secret about it."

"Four Houses, striking together."

Minolin Fey shrugged as if it should not matter. "The Do'Urden compound is forbidden ground," she said quietly and calmly.

"I note that Fey-Branche was not invited to Matron Mother Quenthel's little excursion," Mez'Barris said slyly. "House Baenre pulls her allies in close in this time of upheaval, and yet, there you are, alone and with a hungry and ambitious House Melarn watching."

Minolin Fey forced herself not to wince. House Baenre had guaranteed its alliance to House Fey-Branche at the Festival of the Founding, but indeed, the events of this day had not reassured Minolin's family.

"Matron Mother Quenthel makes more of a statement by those she did not invite, it would seem," said Mez'Barris, twisting the knife a bit.

"As with your own?"

Matron Mez'Barris laughed easily and took a seat on a chair of over-stuffed pillows just across from Minolin Fey. "We refused her invitation," Mez'Barris said. "They have more than enough force to expel a few Houseless rogues, and I have better things to do than follow Matron Mother Quenthel on her ridiculous excursions."

A few Houseless rogues, Minolin Fey thought, and didn't hide her knowing smile. Not so Houseless, most, she knew well, and not a few of them were tied right back here, to House Barrison Del'Armgo. Which was why, of course, there was no possibility that Matron Mother Quenthel had invited Mez'Barris along on the assault, despite the matron's claims to the contrary.

Mez'Barris's lie revealed her fears, and thus, her weakness, Minolin Fey silently reassured herself.

"Do you think Matron Zhindia Melarn will attack House Fey-Branche while the Baenre soldiers are still in the field?" Matron Mez'Barris asked. "Or will she wait until Quen—Matron Mother Quenthel's little play is ended?"

Minolin Fey merely smiled—not because she was confident that Mez'Barris was wrong, but because even if House Fey-Branche was wholly razed, she knew herself to be above the fray. Indeed, by Matron Mother Quenthel's private decree, one sanctified by the Avatar of Lolth herself, Minolin was of House Baenre now, the secret wife of Gromph, the expectant mother of the future Matron Mother of Menzoberranzan. But of course, Mez'Barris Armgo didn't need to know any of that.

"What are we to do about this?" Mez'Barris asked, rather sharply, shocking Minolin Fey from her contemplation.

"Do?"

"Be not coy," said Mez'Barris. "Matron Mother Quenthel has struck out against House Melarn this day . . ."

"And against your own House," Minolin Fey interjected.

Matron Mez'Barris looked at her as if she wanted to lash out.

"If we are being . . . not coy," Minolin Fey said.

The matron paused for a long while, staring at Minolin Fey hard. "Matron Mother Quenthel has gathered her power together, and is daring House Melarn to retaliate, but to the side. Indeed, she seems to be goading House Melarn to strike at House Fey-Branche, and were that to pass, and were I to support Matron Zhindia of House Melarn, Matron Mother Quenthel and her lackeys would not intervene."

"You have already said as much, in fewer words," Minolin Fey dared to reply.

"What are we to do about it?" Matron Mez'Barris asked slyly, leadingly. Minolin Fey looked at her blankly.

"What are *you* going to do about it?" Mez'Barris clarified, and after a few more heartbeats of uncomfortable silence, she added, "We are allies, yes? Long have we planned for this inevitable day. Perhaps it is time now for us to seal that alliance, Barrison Del'Armgo with Fey-Branche. I can hold Matron Zhindia at bay—House Melarn would not attack Fey-Branche without my blessing. Not now. Not when Matron Mother Quenthel has gathered her allies so tightly about her."

"What am I to offer the balor?" Minolin Fey asked.

"Errtu was banished by a son of House Baenre. Defeated on a cold field in the World Above. Surely he is not enamored of Tiago's family. You offer him the chance to repay Matron Mother Quenthel."

"Errtu is patient. Perhaps he would prefer to exact his revenge on his own, in time."

"You have spoken with the balor?" Matron Mez'Barris asked bluntly.

"Not recently, and not directly. I cannot summon him, of course, since he is banished from our plane of existence, and I do not often travel to the Abyss, particularly not to parlay with one as unpredictable and dangerous as Errtu. I do not wish to find myself as a cell mate to Matron K'yorl."

"We have discussed this," an agitated Mez'Barris said.

"The sword of Tiago Baenre has altered our . . . possibilities."

"We will go to Errtu together," Mez'Barris offered. "We will bring the archmage as well. Yes, it is time for him to assert control."

"Gromph will not go against Matron Mother Quenthel. Not now."

"He knows of our plan—indeed, it was his plan to begin with!" Mez'Barris argued.

NIGHT OF THE HUNTER

It was true enough, Minolin Fey had to admit. The three of them, none favoring Matron Mother Quenthel, had indeed plotted Quenthel's downfall. With Lady Lolth venturing into the realm of the arcane, the drow wizards, even though overwhelmingly male, sought to gain newer and higher stature, and of course, none stood to gain more than Gromph Baenre, the great Archmage of Menzoberranzan, the oldest and, by many estimations, the most powerful drow in the city. Perhaps Gromph would even be officially recognized as the Patron Father of House Baenre. Such things were unprecedented, but then, so were these curious and chaotic times.

Mez'Barris Armgo certainly would support the ascent of Gromph, mostly because her House would, in that circumstance, almost surely be elevated above House Baenre, at long and deserving last. But also because she and Gromph had developed a mutual understanding over the past few decades.

At least, that had been the case, Minolin Fey thought but did not say. Unbeknownst to Mez'Barris, much had changed in the Festival of the Founding.

"Errtu will give us Matron K'yorl," Mez'Barris insisted, referring to the Matron of House Oblodra, a drow family skilled in the strange magic of psionics. In the Time of Troubles, when normal magic had gone awry, K'yorl had tried to take advantage of her House's sudden imbalance of power, but alas, Matron Mother Yvonnel Baenre had channeled the power of Lolth and dropped House Oblodra into the chasm known as the Clawrift. For her insolence, K'yorl Odran, Matron K'yorl, had been gifted to the demon Errtu, where she remained, tormented, to this day. "Her hatred of House Baenre is beyond sanity, and her powers . . . yes, with House Oblodra a distant memory, Matron Mother Quenthel will not be prepared to deal with the bared powers of K'yorl. She will destroy Quenthel, and we will be rid of the witch!"

"Bregan D'aerthe's Kimmuriel is said to be of House Oblodra, and quite skilled—"

"He will never get to Quenthel's side in time!" Matron Mez'Barris insisted, so agitated now that she had dropped the use of the proper title for her rival.

Minolin Fey merely smiled. She had gone that morning for her first . . . encounter, with Methil El-Viddenvelp, who was now, it seemed, firmly in the court of Matron Mother Quenthel. Even if freed and their plan enacted, K'yorl would not be nearly as effective as Matron Mez'Barris hoped, Minolin Fey suspected.

"Gromph will not go against Matron Mother Quenthel," Minolin Fey said again. "Not now, perhaps never. And so our plan is moot."

"We do not need him!"

"*You* do not need him," Minolin Fey said. "If you wish to go to the Abyss to deal with Errtu, then may Lady Lolth go with you, because you will need her."

"Your House stands alone," Matron Mez'Barris reminded her. "I am your one hedge against the wrath of House Melarn!"

"My House? My House does not fear Matron Zhindia."

"Fey-Branche is no match for—"

"Fey-Branche is not my House," Minolin Fey said, tired of the discussion, and confident that she had learned all that she might this day.

Matron Mez'Barris stared at her curiously.

"I am Minolin Fey-Baenre," she announced boldly, standing, "wife of Gromph, servant of Matron Mother Quenthel Baenre."

"You dare?" an outraged Mez'Barris cried.

"The Avatar of Lolth appeared at House Fey-Branche in the Festival of the Founding," Minolin Fey explained. "It is not merely a rumor, Matron. It is the truth. And that truth has sealed a bond between House Baenre and House Fey-Branche. You might wish to relay that truth to Matron Zhindia Melarn before she does something rather stupid."

Minolin waved her hand and cast a quick spell of recall, and said, "I go . . . home."

The corporeal form of Minolin Fey seemed to fall apart then, bursting into a multitude of fast-dissipating black balls of insubstantial smoke, leaving Mez'Barris Armgo staring dumbfounded at this most curious, and surely most dangerous, turn of events.

CHAPTER 7

SUFFERANCE OF BAENRE

"E NTRERI," BENIAGO TOLD JARLAXLE IN THE DROW'S PRIVATE ROOM IN the bowels of Illusk, a room magically warded from any unwanted intrusions. "Not Drizzt, but Entreri and the others of that band."

Jarlaxle shifted his eyepatch from his left eye to his right, humming all the while as he considered the startling report. Entreri and his band, sans Drizzt apparently, had passed Luskan, heading south. After nearly two decades of complete absence, the group had returned.

And this so close on the heels of the report from Braelin Janquay, a most reliable scout, that a woman, powerful with magic, and the curious halfling who had come through Luskan the previous autumn were apparently going by names quite familiar to Jarlaxle.

"Catti-brie and Regis," he said, shaking his head in disbelief. He remembered when the two had passed on, when Drizzt and King Bruenor had begged him to find them. Well now, perhaps, he had, but with no sign of Drizzt anywhere and with Bruenor lying dead under the rocks in distant Gauntlgrym, or so he believed.

"They've been dead a hundred years," Beniago replied, though Jarlaxle had been speaking to himself and was startled by the response.

"You think it impossible?"

"Implausible," Beniago said. "But then, I find myself astonished that Entreri and his band of five have returned. Perhaps I have grown so cynical that nothing can truly surprise me anymore, eh?"

"Cynical?" Jarlaxle replied with a chuckle. "My dear Beniago, I would argue just the opposite. Believe in miracles, or in anything else that makes your day a better journey!"

"And be ready for anything," Beniago finished with a wry grin, one that Jarlaxle matched with a smile and a nod of his own.

"He would not come to Luskan," Jarlaxle said. "Likely he believes that I might still be here."

"Entreri? One would think him grateful. I can think of few fates worse than suffering eternity as a block of stone."

Jarlaxle's thoughts drifted back across the years, to the assault he had led on the castle of Lord Draygo Quick in the Shadowfell. He couldn't help but laugh as he replayed that most enjoyable adventure. He and his minions had thoroughly thrashed the castle guard, as indeed Jarlaxle had thrashed the castle itself, enacting an instant fortress of adamantine right within Draygo Quick's foyer! He could still see the expressions of the House guard.

After the rout, Jarlaxle had gone to the substructure of the castle, and there had found and rescued Artemis Entreri, Dahlia, and the monk Afafrenfere, all three turned to stone by Lord Draygo's pet medusa.

"Perhaps the nothingness of stone was preferable to Entreri than the torment he feels in his heart and mind," Jarlaxle heard himself saying, but absently, for his thoughts were already moving to the present, to the revelation that Entreri was up and about once more.

Jarlaxle didn't know why he cared so much. But he did.

"Where has he gone?" the mercenary leader asked.

"Port Llast, they said, and the five are probably halfway to the place already," Beniago answered. "Dangerous road these days, though, so we cannot—"

Jarlaxle's laughter cut him short. "I assure you that it will take more than a band of highwaymen to stop or even delay the likes of that group," he said, and he was already planning his own trip to Port Llast.

"Any further word from Braelin?"

Beniago shook his head. "Drizzt, do you think?"

Jarlaxle nodded, and muttered under his breath, "Let's hope." He looked up at Beniago, and noted the high captain's surprise at that statement, and indeed, Jarlaxle realized that such a sentiment must seem curious indeed to those who did not understand his own long history with the Do'Urden rogue, or worse, who did not understand what Drizzt Do'Urden had secretly come to symbolize for many of Menzoberranzan's drow, particularly drow males. Perhaps Beniago hadn't lived in Menzoberranzan long enough to properly appreciate that point.

Interesting times seemed to be upon them, and Jarlaxle was glad that Kimmuriel was not in Luskan, or even this part of the world, at that time. Jarlaxle's co-captain was off playing with his illithid friends at some horrid hive-mind, which offered Jarlaxle great latitude in directing Bregan D'aerthe, and in his own choice of roads.

He thought back to his raid on the castle of Lord Draygo, and could hardly believe that the attack had been his last real adventure. He looked down at his great desk, covered in parchment, in this, his private room in the Bregan D'aerthe enclave, carved out of a subterranean ruin crawling with ghosts and ghouls.

"I have become a clerk," he said absently.

Beniago's laugh reminded him that he was not alone.

"You take heart in my misery?" Jarlaxle asked, feigning upset.

"I laugh at the notion that mighty Jarlaxle would ever think such of himself," replied High Captain Kurth, who was really a drow of the same House as Jarlaxle—though Beniago didn't know that little detail about Jarlaxle's true identity. "A clerk!"

Jarlaxle waved his hand above the piles of inventories, payroll records, and purchase requisitions.

"So give the records to Serena or one of your other consorts or associates and go out and kill something!" Beniago replied heartily.

"I hope I haven't forgotten how to fight."

Beniago laughed all the harder and stood to leave. "If you decide to find out, please do so with someone other than me, eh?" he said.

"Why so?" Jarlaxle replied. "Perhaps you will defeat me and take over Bregan D'aerthe in Kimmuriel's absence."

"I would hardly want that," Beniago said sincerely. "And want even less to go to my grave at the end of Jarlaxle's sword, or dagger, or wand, or other wand, or giant bird, or enchanted boot, or belt whip, or . . . have I missed one?"

"Many more than one," Jarlaxle assured him.

"Go to Port Llast," Beniago said as he moved to the door at the side of the room. This led to a small alcove and a circular stairway that began a winding path that would get take him under the harbor and back up to Closeguard Isle and the Ship Kurth compound. "You know that you must. The trade with the Xorlarrins proceeds easily, the city is under our thumb fully, and I will be here when you return, with a smile, a pot of gold, and a bevy of lovely ladies to suit your tastes!" He tipped his cap and left the room.

Jarlaxle found that he believed every word. Indeed, never had Bregan D'aerthe run so smoothly. The trade brought enormous profits, the City of Sails was fully, if discreetly, cowed, tamed, and spiderwebbed with an intricate set of new tunnels, and not a hint of trouble darkened any horizon Jarlaxle could see.

"No wonder I am bored," he said, a lament he regretted as soon as he heard it.

"Are you indeed?" came the response from the corner behind him, spoken in the language of Menzoberranzan, and spoken in a voice he knew well, to his great dismay.

On Closeguard Isle in Luskan Harbor stood as secure a fortress as any in the city, the squat keep and tower that housed Ship Kurth. Beniago Baenre, who was known as High Captain Kurth, was the most powerful of the five high captains that ruled the city, as he would have been even if he didn't secretly have the forces of Bregan D'aerthe supporting him, as was his predecessor even before Bregan D'aerthe had thrown in with the Ship.

Ship Kurth claimed the largest fleet in Luskan, more than twice the number of foot soldiers as the next Ship in line, and an array of allied magic-users who split their time between Closeguard Isle and the haunted remains of the Hosttower of the Arcane, on nearby Cutlass Island. The only land route to Cutlass Island, other than the secret tunnels Bregan D'aerthe had constructed beneath the water, was a bridge between Closeguard and Cutlass, and so when the wizards had come to the city seeking to reclaim the lost glories of the Arcane Brotherhood, or at least trying to recover some of the secrets and artifacts from the ruins of the Hosttower, Beniago naturally invited them into an alliance with his Ship.

With all of that might arrayed around him, and Bregan D'aerthe's deadly mercenaries in easy reach, Beniago walked easily when he entered his thick-walled keep, and took no note that there seemed to be few others about this day, which he simply attributed to the fact that spring had at last come, and the ships and caravans were being prepared once more for their travels. The drow paused in front of a large mirror outside the door of his private chambers on the squat tower's second floor, noticing his human disguise. "Not human," he reminded himself aloud, for he had taken to telling people that he was actually half-elven. He had been in Luskan for decades, and had barely aged, after all, as more than a few had noticed. To keep his human guise properly aging was too much trouble, the Bregan D'aerthe wizards had told him, so he was Beniago the half-elf.

"Good enough for them," he muttered, shaking his head. After all these years, the drow still hadn't gotten used to his body—his gangly legs and "stretched" form, his pasty skin that turned red at the first hints of a sunbeam, and particularly his carrot-colored mop of hair.

Three keys disarmed the multitude of traps and unlocked his bed-chamber door, and the high captain pushed into the room. He would have much work before him, he knew. Jarlaxle was surely going to chase Artemis Entreri to Port Llast, and Kimmuriel was not due back until late in the year, at least. With that in mind, Beniago started for his large desk, covered in parchment more so than even Jarlaxle's had been, and with that in sight, he changed his mind and veered for the small hutch beside it, where he kept his fine and potent beverages.

It wasn't until he started reaching for his finest bourbon that Beniago at last realized that something was amiss. He paused, his hand outstretched for the bottle, his other hand discreetly seeking the fine dagger he kept in his belt sash.

He caught the slightest of sounds behind him: a light step, a soft breath.

He drew and spun around with practiced ease and the agility of a noble drow warrior.

And his eyes widened and he stopped his thrust mid-strike, trying to cover up instead against the coordinated strikes of a swarm of snakes.

Beniago lurched and fell back, crashing against the hutch, bottles falling and shattering all around him. He tried to re-orient himself, to sort out the confusing explosions of movement. He felt the burn of poison.

He heard the crack of the whip.

He saw that these were not snakes at all, but the serpents of Lolth's instrument.

"You dare raise a weapon against me?" the wielder of that awful instru-ment scolded in the language of Menzoberranzan, and the writhing swarm struck once more, the lightning speed of the vipers overwhelming poor

Beniago. He felt curving fangs tearing at his cheek, and a second snake biting around his belly.

"Or has your human disguise overcome your mind at last?" the wielder yelled as Beniago desperately threw himself to the floor, thinking to scramble under his desk for some cover. "Have you forgotten your place, son of House Baenre?"

The words froze him in place

House Baenre?

"Matron Mother," he breathed, and all thoughts of fleeing flew from him and he prostrated himself before the priestess . . . and tried not to squirm as the five snakes of Matron Mother Quenthel Baenre's scourge bit at him some more.

"If you cry out, I will kill you," she promised.

Beniago felt as if he had been thrust back in time, to his youth in Menzoberranzan, where he had known such beatings as a matter of course.

It went on until the pain and venom drove him to unconsciousness, but barely had he escaped that torment when the warm waves of healing magic washed through him, leaving him awake once more.

Just as it had been when he was a young boy: beaten to unconsciousness, healed back to the waking world, and beaten some more. He opened his eyes to find that he was sitting up in a chair, slumped but unhurt, and facing Matron Mother Quenthel, his great aunt.

"Please me," she told him bluntly, nodding. "Yes, even though you are *iblith* and ugly."

Beniago knew better than to look up at her, and staring at her feet, he saw her robes drop to the floor. "May I speak?"

"Be quick!"

"I have not worn my true form in many tendays . . . p-perhaps a . . . a year . . ." Beniago stammered. "I can revert . . ."

"No," she commanded. "I am curious." She walked up to him, cupped his chin with her hand, and lifted his face up so he could look into her eyes. "I have great promises for you. Do not disappoint me," she said.

Despite the torment, despite his very well-grounded terror, Beniago knew that he would not. Eagerly, he stood up before Quenthel.

Eagerly, despite the beating she had put upon him.

Hungrily, because this was how he had been trained, with punishment as prelude to seduction, with supplication as beggary for pleasure.

"And then you will tell me," Quenthel said, pulling him close and biting his lip.

"Tell you?"

"Everything," she said and she shoved him down atop his desk.

Jarlaxle figured that in all of Faerûn there were probably only a score of magic-users or priestesses powerful enough to get through the multitude of magical wards he had spent years enacting around his private quarters, and maybe half that number who could do so without him being aware of the intrusion.

Unfortunately for him, one of that select group was his brother, Gromph Baenre.

"Well met," he greeted, sliding his chair around to regard the archmage. "To what do I owe this most unexpected pleasure?"

"My generous personality."

Jarlaxle nodded.

"How fares Luskan?"

Jarlaxle shrugged. "It is a wretched place of wretched people, so not well, I presume. But I fare well here, profitably so."

"Fortunately so, I would say."

"The gems and baubles flow back to Xorlarrin, as agreed, and to the coffers of House Baenre, I would expect."

"Fortunately so . . . for you."

"Is there an issue? Do tell?"

"I am sure there is. I did not come here to see you, but merely as a guide for another who is about within the city."

"Yet here you are . . . fortunately, no doubt, for me."

"For another, who is at Ship Kurth," Gromph added, and Jarlaxle had to work hard to keep the concern from his face.

"Come to study the Hosttower's tendrils, then? To discern the important ties to the city now called Xorlarrin?"

"No, come to speak with Beniago Baenre."

Jarlaxle sat back and tried very hard to look unimpressed. "It is not a name he has used—"

"In a century or more," Gromph agreed. "But, alas, Baenre is a surname he cannot escape."

"Do you plan to speak openly, or continue in riddles?" Jarlaxle asked, starting to rise.

"Sit down," Gromph instructed, stopping him in mid-stand.

Jarlaxle stared at the old mage for a long while, measuring the possibilities. Had it come, at last, to a battle between them, he wondered?

There were many ways in which Jarlaxle could strike at Gromph in this room, traps he could strategically spring, including no small number of disenchantments that might strip much of his brother's magical armor away.

But no, Jarlaxle realized, his best action would be a swift retreat, and that, too, could be done with a mere tug on his earring.

"The barmaid at the inn across the river is one of your lovelies?" Gromph asked, and seemed quite pleased with himself for having discerned that information, or even that there was an inn across the river with which Jarlaxle was associated.

"A plaything," Jarlaxle replied nonchalantly.

"Pretty, for a human. Perhaps you will bring her along."

"Are we going somewhere?"

"Oh yes, I expect we are."

"More riddles?"

"It is not my place to tell you."

Jarlaxle started to respond, but bit it back, seeing the seriousness in Gromph's expression. That last claim hadn't been some off-handed remark; the mage had chosen his words purposely and carefully.

But who could claim a place above Gromph?

"When might I expect more guests, then?" Jarlaxle asked. "Should I prepare for a visit? Some food brought down for a proper feast of greeting, perhaps?"

"Just sit, and for once, dear brother, do shut up," the archmage replied.

There were times, as when he had first arrived here this day with Beniago, when Jarlaxle was glad that Kimmuriel was not around Luskan. And there were times when Jarlaxle truly missed Kimmuriel Oblodra and the drow's psionic powers, telepathically relaying information to Jarlaxle from a different perspective and a deeper understanding, or with Kimmuriel preparing to discombobulate an aggressive wizard with a blast of mind-scrambling energy, or with Kimmuriel ready and prepared to instantly send a telepathic call to all of Bregan D'aerthe's allies.

This was one of those times.

An exhausted and battered Beniago Baenre sat in his room, contemplating the dramatic changes. Luskan was his now, and he had just become directly responsible to House Baenre for any failures!

He wondered how Jarlaxle had survived all these years with such vile witches as the matrons flitting around the edges of his domain. Jarlaxle was a master of deception, perhaps the best Beniago had ever known at that intricate craft, but how to fool a matron, let alone the matron mother, given their abilities to magically detect lies?

"I need an eyepatch," the high captain quietly lamented.

He tried to sort out Matron Mother Quenthel's sudden interest in Luskan, in Bregan D'aerthe, even in Entreri's band, and by extension, in Drizzt. Likely it had to do with Tiago, since Tiago had made no secret of his desire to hunt down the rogue and claim his head as a trophy.

"Yes," Beniago mused. Jarlaxle had gone to great lengths to keep Drizzt hidden away from Tiago—but hadn't that come on advice from Gromph? Beniago shook his head. It all made little sense to him, except that it was clear now that a power shift had occurred in Menzoberranzan, one that had put his aunt Quenthel in absolute control. Gromph would likely not be happy.

He gave a resigned sigh, for what choice did he have in the matter? He was responsible now, and in charge.

The caveat to that level of power struck him, though, in his contemplations of his cousin Tiago. Matron Mother Quenthel had made it quite clear that when and if Tiago ventured to Luskan, Beniago was to serve him without question.

He wasn't overly fond of his cousin. Indeed, Beniago hated Tiago, and he knew the feeling to be mutual.

It was not a good day.

"Matron Mother," Jarlaxle said reverently, leaping out of his chair and bowing low when Quenthel Baenre unexpectedly joined Gromph in Jarlaxle's private quarters in underground Illusk.

"Such the diplomat," Quenthel replied sarcastically.

"The surprised diplomat," Jarlaxle said, daring to stand straight once more. "Rarely does a Matron Mother of Menzoberranzan venture from the city. Indeed, I am shocked that you are here, and more so that you have not brought an army with you." He paused and looked at her curiously. "You have not, have you?"

Despite her grim aspect, Quenthel laughed.

"We leave at once," she said.

"A pity!" Jarlaxle cried. "Do promise to return."

"We," Quenthel said again, and she accentuated the next word as she continued, "*three* leave at once."

Jarlaxle's eyes widened; he even lifted his eyepatch to let Matron Mother Quenthel see his shocked expression more clearly. "It is a complicated place, Luskan. I have many duties to attend to and preparations—"

"Dear brother, shut up," Matron Mother Quenthel ordered. "This pathetic city is no longer your concern. You are being recalled to Menzoberranzan."

Jarlaxle started to respond, but for one of the few times in his life, found himself choking on the words. "Menzoberranzan?" the mercenary leader asked.

"I need soldiers. Bregan D'aerthe will suffice."

"For?"

Matron Mother Quenthel's hand went to her scourge, and the five snakes came to life instantly, writhing around and focusing their flicking tongues on Jarlaxle. Something was very wrong, and on a large scale, Jarlaxle knew, and particularly unsettling was the behavior of his sister.

His stupid, weakling sister.

He looked to Gromph again and the archmage returned his inquisitive expression with the slightest, but most definite of nods. Quenthel would actually whip him, he realized to his ultimate shock.

"Take us home, Archmage," Matron Mother Quenthel ordered.

Later that same day, Jarlaxle wandered the corridors of House Do'Urden in the West Wall neighborhood of Menzoberranzan, coordinating a hundred Bregan D'aerthe foot soldiers as they scoured the place of any remaining vagabonds and secured each of the entrances.

He was glad that he had capable lieutenants around him, setting up the defenses of the House, exploring secret passages, and generally readying the place for proper inhabitation once more. Jarlaxle's thoughts were anywhere but House Do'Urden.

He was glad when Gromph finally found him, in a quiet anteroom to the Do'Urden House chapel.

"How? Who?" he asked bluntly, both questions obviously referring to the strange and powerful creature that seemed to be inhabiting Quenthel's body.

Gromph snorted. "It's a long story. She handled you fairly, and with wisdom."

"And I find that the most unsettling thing of all!" Jarlaxle replied. By Quenthel's order, to all looking in on this, it would seem as if Bregan D'aerthe had formally been hired by House Baenre to prepare House Do'Urden; indeed, House Baenre was even paying Jarlaxle for the service.

"All will be as it has been," Quenthel had assured him. "To all of Menzoberranzan, you are merely Jarlaxle, and your organization remains independent, and indeed that is the truth, as long as you serve me well."

If Jarlaxle didn't play this well, he realized, Bregan D'aerthe would be absorbed into the Baenre garrison, and everything he had spent his life building would come crumbling down around him.

"You knew it had to happen sooner or later," Gromph said to him, as if reading his mind, which truly, at that time, would prove no difficult task. The eyepatch might prevent such magical intrusions, but it could not hide the obvious.

And Gromph was right, Jarlaxle had to admit. His life and his organization was in many ways a charade. Indeed, it survived because of that very fact, forever on the edge of disaster, forever just at the edge of the sufferance of the Matron Mother of Menzoberranzan, forever just a power play away from wrecking that sufferance.

Unless Jarlaxle wanted open war.

In the halls of a place once known as House Do'Urden, the thought crossed his mind.

CHAPTER 8

SPINNING DARK ALLEYS

THE DROW CREPT UP TO THE LEDGE, FLAT ON HIS BELLY ON THE COLD stone, and peered down at the road below, shaking his head in disbelief. This side of the small hillock was a straight drop, perhaps thirty feet or more, affording him a splendid view of the troupe moving past him on the road below.

Braelin Janquay had heard of Drizzt Do'Urden, of course, but seeing him now, riding a shining white unicorn with a horn of gold and a coat of elaborate barding covered in bells—bells that were silent now, and obviously magically connected to the will of the rider—took the young scout's breath away. The rogue rode easily, very comfortable in the small saddle and using the unicorn's long white mane as his reins. His scimitars bounced along at his hips, the diamond edge of Icingdeath catching the morning light and reflecting it brilliantly, and the ease with which he carried a bow across his shoulders spoke of great skill with that weapon, as well.

And indeed, Jarlaxle had told Braelin of the bow called Heartseeker, and had claimed that Drizzt could take down a line of orcs with a single shot, or split stone, even, with the lightning arrows.

That last recollection had Braelin edging back from the stony ledge just a bit.

A huge black panther loped along beside the unicorn and seemed on edge, constantly turning at this sound or that.

The scout thought of Tiago Baenre. It was no secret among Bregan D'aerthe that the young warrior had been seeking Drizzt for two decades now, determined to claim the rogue's head as a trophy. The whispers said that Jarlaxle and Beniago had gone to great lengths to keep Tiago away from Drizzt, and now Braelin understood the wisdom of that choice.

He couldn't imagine Tiago surviving an encounter with this one.

To say nothing of Drizzt's companions, even, for beside him rode the human woman named Catti-brie, astride a spectral mount, another unicorn and one she had summoned with a magical spell, a steed nearly as impressive as the drow's own. Behind them came a wagon, pulled by mules and driven by a young and ferocious red-bearded dwarf wearing a one-horned helm and carrying an axe that had seen many battles—too many, if this one's age was to be believed. Beside him sat another human, one whose parents must have included an ogre, Braelin thought, given his great size and obvious strength. On the road beside that formidable pair rode the halfling, Regis, on a fat pinto pony.

The troupe bounced down the muddy road to the southwest, seeming a carefree bunch, though they were leaving the safety of Ten-Towns behind. Other caravans were forming in the towns, particularly the closest one, Bremen, on the southern bank of Maer Dualdon, but those caravans would not leave without a full escort of at least twenty guards, Braelin had learned. Not at this time of the year, when the roads were full of yetis and goblinkin and all sorts of beasts ready to begin fattening up now that winter was at last letting go.

Yet here they were, a group of only five, depending on a slow-moving wagon, riding into the wilds, seemingly without a care in the world.

Watching them, Braelin Janquay hadn't a doubt in the world that they would get through the Spine of the World safely.

And Jarlaxle and Beniago would be waiting for them. He slid back from the ledge. Perhaps he could at last leave this forsaken place and deliver this last report in person. He'd shadow the group to their first camp, then go past them in the dark of night—and perhaps even get in close to the camp to see if he might find a bauble or two of his own . . .

With a wicked smile on his face, the young Bregan D'aerthe scout crept back to the ledge and looked back to the companions, who had moved off. Something struck Braelin as different about the troupe then, but he dismissed it as unimportant—until he realized that the black panther was no longer beside them.

Sent home to the Astral Plane? he wondered. He had been well-schooled in the ways of Drizzt Do'Urden before being sent in pursuit of the strange halfling.

He nodded, thinking that must be it, hoping that must be it.

Then he realized that Drizzt Do'Urden, riding calmly and easily still, no longer had his bow slung over his shoulder . . .

"Likely a jackalope or wayward caribou," Catti-brie whispered to Drizzt as they plodded along. Something had attracted Guenhwyvar's attention, and Drizzt had let the panther run off.

"Guen will let us know," Drizzt assured her. He turned back to the other three. "If her warning call sounds, guard the wagon at all costs. We don't want to lose our supplies to a hungry yeti."

"Not a yeti," Wulfgar replied. "A yeti would have had to be closer, or even Guenhwyvar would not have noted it."

"You underestimate Guen."

"You have forgotten tundra yetis, then?" Wulfgar asked.

"Aye, elf, ye ain't remembering how many times I pulled ye out from under one o' them beasties when you runned right into them?" Bruenor added.

"Once," Drizzt admitted, to the laughter of his friends. "Only once."

"I'm thinkin' an elf's only good eatin' once, eh?" asked Bruenor.

"Stay with the wagon," Drizzt replied.

Wulfgar and Bruenor laughed, and Drizzt turned to Regis for support, to find the halfling apparently distracted and not paying attention.

"Regis?"

The halfling looked at him directly, seeming startled.

"Stay with the wagon?" Drizzt remarked again.

"Back among that swollen pile of boulders, I think," Regis answered, but didn't glance back, not wanting to tip his hand.

Drizzt wasn't quite what to make of the statement, but before he could inquire further, a low growl echoed across the muddy plain of the melting tundra, and indeed, it seemed to come from the very spot Regis had indicated.

Drizzt spun around and tugged Andahar hard to the left, the unicorn leaping off the trail and splashing off in full gallop. Catti-brie on her spectral mount paced him stride for stride, the two galloping hard and angling for the back side of the small mound of swollen mud and boulders.

"Drive them our way!" Bruenor called. "Bah, but I'm wantin' a good fight, I am!"

"I had thought you in a fine mood," Regis argued.

"Am!" Bruenor agreed. "What's yer point?"

But Regis wasn't listening any longer He noted the angle of Drizzt and Catti-brie's approach, and saw a potential problem. He, too, whirled his mount, and drove his heels into Rumble's flank, the pony leaping away.

" 'Ere, where ye going, Rumblebelly?" Bruenor shouted.

"That's my pony's name!" Regis called back, never slowing.

Bruenor tried to turn the wagon, but Wulfgar grabbed him by the arm, holding him steady and shaking his head.

"Aye, we'll be runnin' with muddy feet," the dwarf agreed. "Like old times."

Braelin Janquay didn't notice the mounts breaking from the group. His attention was held by the black form he'd noticed behind him, the panther stalking up the back side of the hillock around the scattered boulders. The drow scout thought to sprint for the trail, but realized the cat would surely cut him off.

He lifted his hand crossbow and started to draw his sword. Just then, Guenhwyvar came more clearly into view, cutting behind a small tumble halfway up the back side of the hill. Braelin wasn't thirty feet above her anymore, looking down at her. He had underestimated the size of the beast. Braelin shook his head, wanting no part of that fight.

Then he noted movement out on the plain, back and to the right—the two steeds charging along.

The drow turned and jumped from the cliff. He heard a shout from up the road but ignored it and concentrated on the situation at hand. He tapped his Bregan D'aerthe insignia, activating the levitation magic of the brooch, and his drop became a float, caught on the breeze and drifting out over the road.

He landed to find a new enemy close at hand: the halfling on his pony.

"Perfect," he said, thinking to shoot this one from the saddle and commandeer the mount, and up came the hand crossbow.

But the clever halfling fell over to the side of his mount, stealing the shot. Braelin growled and held steady, and glanced back up to the cliff, expecting a giant panther to leap down upon him.

He should have focused on the road ahead. The well-trained pony kept coming and even veered in a bit, and Braelin had to fall back a step to avoid being run down. He turned with the pony as it thundered by, aiming a shot at its low rider.

But the halfling wasn't there.

Braelin whirled, to face a hand crossbow much like his own. The halfling had the drop on him and fired true. The dart hit him in the chest and he staggered back under the weight of the blow, and felt the burn of poison.

But he was drow, and well-trained, and Braelin brought his own hand crossbow to bear quickly.

Except the halfling wasn't there.

Braelin felt the tip of a rapier prodding at his back.

"Yield or die!" came the command.

Drizzt studied the hillock as they came around the back side, picking a path to ride up. He kept circumventing the mound, though, and was startled indeed when Regis's pony appeared on the road to the north, riderless and galloping.

"Quick!" he called to Catti-brie, and put his head down and spurred Andahar on. He caught sight of Guenhwyvar then.

"To him, Guen!" he cried, and the panther roared and leaped back the other way.

Andahar cut around the north side of the mound, and Drizzt caught sight of Regis, behind a drow—a drow!—and holding his slender blade to the dark elf's back!

Hurry, Regis thought, considering his friends. Despite his initial success, he wasn't thrilled at the prospect, or his odds, of holding a drow at bay. He holstered his hand crossbow and reached for his dirk.

Sure enough, neither was the drow, who spun around faster than Regis could strike, a sword leading to drive the rapier blade aside.

Regis was already moving with the turn, crying out and falling back. His rapier went flying from his grasp and he tried to draw the three-bladed dirk, though what good that might do against a dark elf waving two fine swords, he did not know.

The drow came forward a step and Regis fell away, but the fellow turned to the left, to the north.

Regis, purely on reflex and purely in terror, drew not his dirk but a living snake, and threw it out before him even as he fell to the ground.

The drow didn't seem to know what to make of the quick serpent, which rushed up and around his throat like a living garrote. He turned back to Regis, even took a step the halfling's way, but then the specter appeared, the evil soul of the dirk. It tugged the snake garrote with wicked strength, so powerfully that the drow was thrown back and to the ground, his swords flying, his boots coming right off the ground.

At that same moment, something dark and ominous crashed down beside Regis, who yelped again and tried to scramble away—until he noted Guenhwyvar, leaping over to straddle his fallen enemy.

"Hurry!" Regis cried. "Please, oh please!"

He noted Drizzt and Catti-brie, riding hard from the north. He saw Wulfgar and Bruenor running up from the south, but he knew in his heart that his plea was not to any of them, but to himself. He wasn't going to let the ghost choke the life out of this one, not when Guenhwyvar had the drow under control.

He rushed to retrieve his rapier and scrambled to the fallen drow, who was struggling to pry at the snake with one hand, his other arm thrown over his eyes in a desperate attempt to stop the great panther from raking his face off.

Regis rushed up beside the fallen drow and stabbed down with his rapier.

"Rumblebelly!" Bruenor yelled in shock.

"Regis, no!" Drizzt cried.

But Regis wasn't aiming for the drow, instead prodding the leering face of the specter. This was the weakness of the garrote ability, he knew: a single strike at the undead monster and it would disappear in a puff of gray smoke—as it did now. The snake released its choking hold around the drow's throat and died instantly.

So half the drow's problems were solved, but there remained the little problem of six hundred pounds of feline muscle standing atop him.

"Wh-what?" Drizzt stammered, dropping down from Andahar and rushing to his halfling friend. "What was that?"

"A rather pleasant weapon, don't you think?" replied Catti-Brie, who had seen this particular dirk in play before, on the banks of Maer Dualdon.

Drizzt moved over to look down at the pinned drow, the captive's eyes wide with terror. Guenhwyvar kept her face near his own, and opened her mouth wide to let him see her deadly incisors.

"Who are you?" Drizzt asked.

"Don't kill me, Drizzt Do'Urden," he replied. "I meant you no harm."

"Baenre?" Drizzt asked.

"Bregan D'aerthe," the drow answered.

Drizzt looked at him curiously. He had heard this ploy before—indeed, he, Entreri, and Dahlia had used it before, claiming to be a member of Jarlaxle's band when confronted by the Xorlarrins and a noble son of House Baenre in Gauntlgrym.

"Jarlaxle sent me here, following the halfling from Luskan."

The others looked at Regis.

"I saw our old friend in Luskan," Regis confirmed. "At an inn called One-Eyed Jax—his tavern, from what I could gather. I didn't think he recognized me. It's been a hundred years, after all and—"

"Enough," Drizzt cut him short. Regis swallowed hard, likely realizing that he had probably just revealed far too much.

"I helped him, and the girl," the drow pleaded. "On the beach."

Again, all eyes turned to Regis, and to Catti-brie as well. The woman, looking confused, merely said, "I've never seen him before."

But Regis was already nodding. "The dart," he said, looking to Catti-brie. "The archer who was shot down into the sand. That wasn't my dart that put him to slumber."

They looked down at the drow. "My dart," he said.

"Why?" Drizzt asked.

"Jarlaxle wouldn't want him dead, I figured."

"Good choice. Let him up, Guen."

When the panther sprang away, Regis moved to offer his hand, but with agility only a dark elf could match, the drow leaped to his feet.

"Your name?" Drizzt demanded.

The drow hesitated, and Drizzt sighed.

"Braelin Janquay," he answered.

"Of Bregan D'aerthe?"

Braelin nodded.

"What will you tell Jarlaxle, then?"

"What would you have me tell him?"

Regis whistled sharply, startling them all. When they reflexively turned to the halfling, he motioned rather sheepishly down the road to his pony, which he had just called back. The little round-bellied pinto cantered along, tossing his head as if in complaint—which of course seemed fitting to the others for Regis's mount.

"Tell him that I pray he is well," Drizzt answered and laughed.

"Where have you been, Drizzt Do'Urden?" Braelin asked. "Jarlaxle has been looking for you for many years."

Drizzt considered it for a moment, then sighed. "I needed some rest, apparently."

"Eighteen years?" Braelin said skeptically.

"It has been a long road," Drizzt replied with feigned exasperation.

"Goin' to get longer, I'm thinking," said Bruenor.

"Where is Jarlaxle?" Drizzt asked. He turned to Catti-brie and said quietly, "We could use his talents, I expect," and the woman was already nodding, clearly thinking along the same lines. Jarlaxle knew the underground way from Luskan to Gauntlgrym, and if anyone knew how to deal with a vampire, it would be the mercenary leader.

"Luskan, and there I am bound," Braelin answered.

"Travel with us, then," Regis blurted. Many surprised looks came his way. Regis had just invited a drow, one they did not know, into their camp. Rarely would such a gesture prove to be a good idea.

Drizzt looked over the newcomer carefully, then turned to Catti-brie, who merely shrugged. "Do," he said to Braelin. "The road is dangerous this time of year. We could use another sword." He looked to the left, to one fallen blade, then to the other, across to the right. "Or two."

They set off soon after, Braelin taking point far out in front, on Drizzt's order.

"Rumblebelly beat himself a drow elf!" Bruenor said when at last Braelin was out of earshot.

"That's my pony's name," Regis replied, evenly and in all seriousness.

"Aye, and what's yer own name, then?" asked the laughing dwarf.

Regis straightened his shoulders. "Spider," he said. "Aye, Spider Parrafin of Morada Topolino."

"Aye, well there's a mouthful."

"And what of yourself?" the halfling asked.

"Was known as Reginald Roundshield, o' the Adbar Roundshields," Bruenor answered. "Little Arr Arr, some called me, but don't think o' doing that yerself, or know that I'll put me fist in yer eye!" He stomped his heavy boot on the footboard of the wagon and declared, "Bruenor's me name and none other. Bruenor Battlehammer o' Mithral Hall!"

"And you are Ruqiah," Regis said to Catti-brie, who walked her mount casually across the wagon from him and his pony. "Daughter of Niraj and Kavita of Desai, raised on the plains of Netheril." She had told him the tales, of course, over the long days of the previous winter.

"I was," she corrected. "And now I am who I have always been."

"What o' yerself, boy?" Bruenor asked of Wulfgar. "Ye ain't telled us. Who ye been?"

"Hrolf, son of Alfarin, of the tribe of the Elk," Wulfgar answered.

"Born o' yer own people, then," said Bruenor. "Ah, but ye found a bit o' good luck in that!"

Regis nodded, but as he considered the grand road that had brought him back to his friends, as he thought of beautiful Donnola Topolino and the Grandfather, and of Doregardo and the Grinning Ponies, he found that he could not agree with Bruenor's assessment.

"High Captain Kurth," Regis informed his four companions when they noted the red-haired man approaching their camp just outside of Luskan's northern reaches. With Braelin Janquay along, they had made an uneventful journey out of Icewind Dale and through the Spine of the World. The five companions had camped outside the city, sending Braelin in on his word that he would find and retrieve Jarlaxle.

"High captain? Then he ain't likely alone," said Bruenor. "Ye think the drow rat double-crossed us, elf?"

Drizzt was shaking his head, the others noted, but the look on his face was perplexed indeed. He knew this man from twenty years previous, but it seemed as if the red-headed fellow hadn't aged a day.

"Well met, and welcome back, Master Parrafin," High Captain Kurth greeted, offering a nod to Regis. "Or do you prefer Spider?"

Regis tipped his beret.

"Serena sends her regards."

"And mine to her, then," Regis replied.

"Beniago?" Drizzt asked, for of course he remembered the name. It had been nearly two decades, but to Drizzt, who had slept a magical night in Iruladoon where eighteen years had passed on Faerûn, it had only been a few tendays.

"Well met again, Master Do'Urden," Beniago replied, but in a whisper, and he glanced around and patted the air with his hand, signaling them to be quiet.

"High Captain now?"

The man shrugged. "Outlive your superiors and the world is yours, yes?"

"Especially for those who are friends of Jarlaxle, I would imagine."

Beniago grinned and shrugged. "Your other friends passed by here a tenday or so ago," he said.

"Other friends?" Catti-brie asked.

"Entreri and them strange ones," said Bruenor, who had seen an unusual trio indeed—a weirdly twisted tiefling, a boisterous female dwarf, and a gray-skinned human in monk's robes—on the side of Kelvin's Cairn on the night he and the others had rejoined Drizzt.

"Bound for . . . ?" Drizzt asked, nodding to Regis to confirm Bruenor's guess.

The man shifted uncomfortably, something both Drizzt and Catti-brie surely caught. "Who can say? I have come to tell you . . ." He paused and looked around.

"Where are our manners?" Drizzt asked. "A meal and a drink for our guest."

"I already have one set," Wulfgar said from behind them and they turned to see him rearranging the large stones they were using as seats to allow for one more. The ease with which Wulfgar hoisted those rocks threw Drizzt back in time, for the man had apparently lost nothing of his uncanny strength in this second incarnation.

They gathered around their campfire and Drizzt called in Guenhwyvar and set her off to make sure they were alone.

"Should I warn her of your associates?" Drizzt asked.

"I came out alone and dare not remain long," Beniago replied. He looked around into the darkness, again seeming nervous. "I only came here because of your . . . mutual friendship with one of my associates."

"Jarl—?" Drizzt started to ask, but Beniago held up his hand, as if he didn't want the name spoken aloud. Only then did Drizzt begin to fathom the gravity of the meeting.

"The one you seek is not in Luskan," Beniago explained, his voice going even quieter. "I doubt he will ever return. Nor should you go in there. Nor should you ever mention, to anyone, that you have traveled with Braelin. For his sake, I beg of you."

The surprising request, and the even more surprising humility from one who was High Captain of Ship Kurth, and thus, the nearest thing Luskan had to a ruler, set Drizzt back in his seat.

"Eat," Wulfgar offered, holding forth a bowl of stew, but Beniago shook his head and rose up.

"Fare well, wherever you travel."

"We're headin' for—" Bruenor started to say, but Beniago cut him short with an emphatic wave. The red-haired man bowed then, and disappeared into the night.

"Well, that was interesting," said Bruenor when he was gone.

Regis looked at Drizzt.

"Tiago Baenre," Drizzt remarked, his voice still a whisper, and the halfling nodded, and Catti-brie said, "Oh," and also nodded, apparently catching on.

"What're ye huffing about?" Bruenor demanded.

"I would guess more trouble has followed in Drizzt's wake than the demon fight at Bryn Shander's gate," said Regis.

"Demon fight?" Bruenor asked.

Wulfgar gave a laugh. "Such a simple life I left behind," he lamented.

"So Entreri's been by here and Jarlaxle is gone and won't return," said Catti-brie. "You said he had a secret way into Gauntlgrym, but that is lost to us, I would expect."

"I got me a map," Bruenor said. "We'll get there."

"But not straightaway," Drizzt said, looking at the woman who had once been his wife.

"Longsaddle," Catti-brie agreed.

"Perhaps we should use our new names," Regis suggested. "And find an alias for Drizzt."

"No!" Bruenor insisted and stamped his boot. "Carried that name too long already."

"Someone's hunting—"

"Then let 'em come," said the dwarf, and he was no longer whispering. "Me name's King Bruenor to any who're askin', and King Bruenor to any who ain't."

"How much can we trust this Beniago?" Wulfgar asked, and when Drizzt gave him a noncommittal look, the giant barbarian stood up, began re-rolling his bedroll, and packing up the wagon.

They set off soon after, heading east across the fields. Barely into the journey, Bruenor began to sing, a mournful song of loss and a grandeur and era that could not be again, the Delzoun song of Gauntlgrym.

There was no moon this night, and no clouds, and a million stars twinkled in the clear skies above, and the gray swirl of a distant galaxy—clouds in one of the overlapping celestial spheres, Regis named them—striped the sky directly above. It was one of those nights when the heavens seemed to reach down to the earth itself, lifting up the soul and the imagination, much as Drizzt had known in the quiet dark atop Bruenor's Climb on Kelvin's Cairn.

It was a night where the rogue drow felt tiny, and yet grand, a part of something ancient, eternal, and as vast as his imagination and as warm as the love among these five friends surrounding him in the wagon, even Guenhwyvar, for he could not bring himself to dismiss her back to her Astral home.

Indeed, on a night such as this, *in* a night such as this, it seemed to Drizzt as if Guenhwyvar's home had come to them.

Yes, it was good to be home, Drizzt decided.

And this, a rolling wagon bouncing across the farmlands east of Luskan, was home, because home wasn't a place, oh no, but a bond, and one that had never seemed stronger.

PART TWO

_ाੰ੨ਾੀੂੰਾ ∙᠊᠊⌒∙᠊᠊ ਾੰਾੂਾਾੀੀੰ_

CROSSING PATHS AND CROSSING SWORDS

I am haunted by the expression on Bruenor's face, and by the words of Catti-brie. "The burden you carry blurs your judgment," she told me without reservation. "As you see yourself, you hope to find in others—in orcs and goblins, even."

She alone said this, but Bruenor's expression and wholehearted nod certainly agreed with Catti-brie's assessment. I wanted to argue, but found I could not. I wanted to scream against them both, to tell them that fate is not predetermined by nature, that a reasoning being could escape the determination of heredity, that intellect could overwhelm instinct.

I wanted to tell them that I had escaped.

And so, in that roundabout reasoning-turned-admission, Catti-brie's description of my burden ultimately rang true to me, and so, were I not bound by my own experiences, and the uncertainty that has followed me every step out of Menzoberranzan, even these many decades later, my expression would likely have matched Bruenor's own.

Was the Treaty of Garumn's Gorge a mistake? To this day, I still do not know, but I find now, in light of this discussion, that my ambiguous stance relies more on the averted suffering to the dwarves and elves and humans of the Silver Marches, and less on the benefit to the orcs. For in my heart, I suspect that Bruenor is right, and that Catti-brie's newfound understanding of orc nature is confirmed by the goings-on in the Silver Marches. The Kingdom of Many-Arrows holds as an entity, so Bruenor claims, but the peace it promotes is a sham. And perhaps, I must admit, that peace only facilitates the orc raiders and allows them more freedom than they would find if Many-Arrows did not exist.

Still, with all the revelations and epiphanies, it hurts, all of this, and the apparent solution seems a chasm too far for me to jump. Bruenor is ready to march to Mithral Hall, rouse the dwarves, and raise an army, and with that force, wage open war on the Kingdom of Many-Arrows.

Bruenor is determined to begin a war. So determined is he that he will put aside the suffering, the death, the disease, the utter misery that such a conflict will wreak on the land, so that, as he puts it, he might right the wrong he caused that century ago.

I cannot start a war. Even if I embraced what Catti-brie has claimed, even if I believed that her every word came from the mouth of Mielikki herself, I cannot start a war!

I will not, I say—and I fear—nor will I allow Bruenor to do so. Even if his words about the nature of orcs are true—and likely they are—then the current situation still, in my view, remains better than the open conflict he so desires. Perhaps I am bound to caution because of my burden of personal experience, but Bruenor is bound by guilt to try to correct what he sees as his chance at redemption.

Is that any less a burden?

Likely it is more so.

He will run headlong into misery, for himself, his legacy, and for all the goodly folk of the Silver Marches. That is my fear, and as such, as a friend, I must stop him if I can.

I can only wince at the possibilities illuminated by this course, for I have never seen Bruenor more determined, more sure of his steps. So much so, that should I try to dissuade him, I fear we might come to blows!

As indeed, I fear my road back to Mithral Hall. My last visit was not pleasant, and not one I often consider, for it pains me to realize that I, a ranger, have worked openly against dwarves and elves for the sake of orcs. For the sake of the "peace," I tell myself, but in the end, that dodge can only hold true if Catti-brie's admonition, if Mielikki's claim, is not true. If orcs are not to be counted among the reasoning beings born of a choice in their road, then . . .

I will follow Bruenor to Mithral Hall. If the orc raiders are as prevalent as Bruenor insists, then I am sure I will find good use for my blades, and likely at Bruenor's side, vigilant hunters striking without hesitation or guilt.

But I will not start a war.

That chasm is too wide.

Am I wrong, then, in hoping that the decision is taken from us before we ever arrive? In hoping that the Kingdom of Many-Arrows proves Catti-brie's point in no uncertain terms?

"Where's the babies' room!" I hear her again, often in my thoughts, in that Dwarvish brogue of old, and with the ferocity befitting a daughter of King Bruenor Battlehammer. And though Catti-brie carried this accent for many years, and can fight as well as any, this time her cheer rang discordantly, painfully, in my ears.

What of Nojheim, then, the goblin I once knew who seemed a decent sort undeserving of his harsh fate?

Or am I really saying, what, then, of Drizzt?

I want to deny the message of Mielikki; once I claimed the goddess as that which was in my heart, a name for what I knew to be true and right. And now I want to deny it, desperately so, and yet I cannot. Perhaps it is the harsh truth of Faerûn that goblinkin and evil giant-kind are just evil, by nature and not nurture.

And likely, my perception of this truth has been distorted by my own determined escape from the seemingly inevitable path I was born to follow, and perhaps distorted in dangerous ways.

On a very basic level, this message wounds me, and that wound is the burden. Is there, in this instance, no place for optimism and an insistence that there is good to be found? Does that outlook, the guiding philosophy of my existence, simply have no place in the darkness of an orc's heart?

Can I start a war?

I walk this road tentatively, but also eagerly, for I am filled with conflict. I wish to know, I must know!

I am afraid to know.

Alas, so much has changed, but so much remains the same. The Spellplague is gone, yet trouble seems ever to be brewing in our wake. Yet we walk a road into deeper darkness, into Gauntlgrym for the sake of a lost friend, and then, if we survive, into the midst of a greater storm.

For all of that, have I ever been happier?

—Drizzt Do'Urden

CHAPTER 9

WHEN THE SUN WENT DOWN

"YOU SHOULDN'T HAVE STOPPED ME," DAHLIA SAID WITH AN ACCOMPA-nying hiss when Entreri walked back into the room they shared in Port Llast, a high room in the inn called Stonecutter's Solace tucked up against the eastern cliffs of the sheltered city. Dahlia sat at the room's lone window, looking west, to the docks and the ocean of the reclaimed city—reclaimed in no small part because of the actions of this very group of adventurers. The sun sat low on the horizon before her, ready to surrender to the twilight.

"That again?" Entreri asked with a snort. He was returning from a late supper with the other three of their party, a meal in which the pouting Dahlia had refused to partake.

Dahlia swiveled around in her seat to regard him, her face scrunching with that unrelenting anger. She wore her hair in the top-braid again, something she had not done in some time, and her magical blue facial woad seemed particularly angry to Entreri this evening, somewhat resembling a hunting cat, and she turned and tilted her head obstinately. At least, that was the impression it gave to him.

"Do you think he is following us?" she asked.

"No." In truth, the assassin had no idea whether Drizzt had decided to follow them out of Icewind Dale, nor was he overly concerned, in any case. At least, not for the reason Dahlia was clearly concerned. Likely Drizzt had remained in Icewind Dale, as he had indicated he would. He was probably licking his wounds and looking for some way to redeem his reputation among the folk of Ten-Towns, Entreri figured, for the assassin had seen the pain on Drizzt's face when they had been denied entry to Bryn Shander.

Drizzt should have come with them, Entreri believed, although Dahlia had made that road far more difficult.

Or perhaps Entreri was simply considering his own preferences, to have the capable and steady drow warrior at his side. That realization surprised him more than a little.

"He will seek revenge," Dahlia insisted. "You should not have stopped me!"

Entreri laughed at her.

"He deserved to die!" Dahlia spat, and she leaped out of her seat and stormed across the room to stand before the man.

"We were the ones who betrayed him, remember?" Entreri came back with a snicker. "And Drizzt forgave you, and never once confronted me—"

"He dismissed me," Dahlia interrupted, as if that explained everything regarding her outright attack on the drow. She poked her finger into Entreri's chest as she spoke, which brought another amused smile from the man.

So Dahlia slapped him across the face.

But he intercepted, catching her by the wrist and turning her arm down and around with a painful jerk.

"I am not Drizzt Do'Urden," he assured her evenly. "If you attack me, I will fight back."

"We have battled before," Dahlia reminded him.

"Yes, but then I didn't understand your strange weapon," the assassin replied, using that voice that had chilled the blood of so many victims over the decades, usually right before his blades had drained that same blood. "I know your style and tricks now. If you attack me, have no doubt, I will kill you."

He let go of her wrist, shoving the arm aside, and Dahlia fell back a step, staring at him with an expression caught somewhere between outrage and intrigue. Behind her, through the window, the sun disappeared, the long shadows giving way to dusk.

"Is that what you want?" Entreri reasoned. "Isn't that what you've always wanted?"

Dahlia straightened and squared her shoulders but couldn't seem to find a response.

"Because you are a coward?" Entreri asked.

The woman's hands reflexively moved toward her flail, the pair set in a belt loop on her left hip.

Artemis Entreri smiled again, and Dahlia stopped short of grabbing them.

"To what end, Dahlia?" he asked quietly. "You have your son back, and he forgives you, even if you cannot find the strength to forgive yourself. How long will you continue hating what you see in the mirror?"

"You know nothing of it."

"I know that you went after Drizzt because he rejected you," Entreri answered. "I also know your game."

She tilted her head in curiosity, prompting him to elaborate.

"To find a lover who will confirm what you hate about yourself," Entreri obliged. "And to find one who will, when you confront him, be strong enough to finally grant you peace. Well take heart, elf, for here I stand."

Dahlia fell back a step, staring at Entreri and seemingly at a loss.

"We are done, here and now," Entreri announced. "I will sail from this place without you."

Dahlia's expression went blank, and she mouthed "no," though she couldn't seem to find the breath to actually speak the word, as she shook her head slowly in denial.

"So draw your weapons as you will," Entreri said, and he made sure he did so rather flippantly. "I long ago lost count of those I've killed. One more shan't matter."

Dahlia continued to shake her head, and it seemed to Entreri that she might simply melt then and there before him. Tears gathered in her eyes, one rolling down her cheek. Her lips moved as if she were trying to find something to say to him, some denial.

What he didn't see, to his great satisfaction, was anger.

"Please," she finally managed to say.

Entreri laughed callously and turned for the door. He did so while moving his hands close to his weapons, fully expecting an attack.

And indeed, Dahlia came after him, but not with her weapon, throwing herself at him plaintively, crying out for him not to leave. He turned and caught her charge, and twisted around as they moved for the door so that he pushed her up against it, and not the other way around.

"Please," she said, trembling, and Entreri realized that he was the only thing holding her up.

"I grow tired of hearing of Drizzt," he said to her, and she was nodding with every word. "If you truly believe that I did you no favor in ending your fight on the mountain, then tell me now."

It took Dahlia a moment, and then she lowered her eyes and slowly shook her head.

Entreri pushed up against her, pinning her tightly to the closed door, his face a finger's breadth from hers. "Do you want me to lead you back to him, that together we can finish what you started?" he asked. "Would it please you to kill Drizzt Do'Urden?"

Dahlia's expression showed her shock at the blunt question.

"Say the word," he teased.

"No," she said, but calmly. She shook her head again, but with conviction now as she straightened against the door. "No."

Entreri smiled once more, and when she pressed in closer to kiss him, he did not resist.

Artemis Entreri understood the power and significance of Dahlia's epiphany, even though it was something that Dahlia did not yet fully comprehend.

"It took me many years to be able to look into a mirror honestly," he said quietly, pulling back from her just a bit. "And even still, shadows lurk—"

His sentence was cut short by a sudden explosion that shook Stonecutter's Solace to its foundation, threw Entreri up against Dahlia, and jolted both of them hard into the door.

Entreri jumped back and pulled Dahlia around behind him. He threw the door open and charged into the hall, cutting left for the stairway, drawing his weapons as he went. The corridor ran twenty feet before turning back to the right around the corner, at the top of the stairs.

The building rocked again, shaking under a tremendous blast, and a burst of flames exploded up from the stairs and into Entreri's corridor, rolling and dissipating, licking the walls to blackness. Beneath that gout came Afafrenfere, rolling low along the floor, tucked fully under his heavy robes. He came up as the flames disappeared, and glanced to Entreri.

"Drow!" he cried. "Many! Run!"

Darkness engulfed him, blacking out the end of the corridor.

Entreri took a step the monk's way, before falling back in surprise at a thunderous retort from the end of the hall—a lightning bolt, he knew, burned into the magical darkness.

The assassin skidded and turned around, crashing into Dahlia as she exited the room and shoving her back in before him. He swung the door closed and kept running, across the room to the small window.

"Drow!" he yelled back at Dahlia, who was repeatedly screaming, "What? What?"

"We've got to get out of here."

"Effron!" she cried.

Entreri kicked the window out. "He left for a walk with the dwarf when I returned to you," he said. "Be quick!" And out he went, catching hold on the top border of the glass, then standing atop the pane. Stonecutter's Solace was set up against the eastern cliff wall of the valley city of Port Llast, up high on a foundation of stone. The buildings before it were also below it, and when Entreri looked out this window, he could see over the rooftops of the lesser structures to the west.

Even in the dim light of dusk, Entreri saw that the fighting wasn't confined to Stonecutter's Solace. Down the street, a man staggered out of a building and fell face down in the road. On the porch below, patrons of the inn scrambled and ran—or tried to, for Afafrenfere's call had indeed been accurate, and murderous dark elves caught them and cut them down.

A bit farther along, Entreri noted another enemy, a bigger enemy, half-drow, half-spider. He had spent years in Menzoberranzan; he knew the power and sheer evil of the abomination known as a drider.

He shook his head and finger-crawled away along the side of the building, some ten feet from the window. He turned back to call to Dahlia, and motioned for her to follow, then continued on a bit more and pushed himself out from the wall in a great leap, landing lightly atop the roof of the building just below Stonecutter's Solace.

He turned back for Dahlia, thinking to catch her if her leap brought her in short, and he just shook his head when he realized that the dangerous elf woman wasn't following him at all. She came flying out of the window, literally, her magical cloak transforming her into a giant raven. She swept out of the window and circled tightly, climbing fast to land on the inn's roof.

Entreri glanced down. The building was burning and the sounds from the common room on the first floor told him that the fight was on in full.

NIGHT OF THE HUNTER

Bright blinding light filled all the windows in a sudden and thunderous flash, and splinters of wood went flying off the far side of the building, blown apart by a powerful stroke of some lightning-like magic. And out came a pair of men, staggering, jerking wildly, hair flying crazily.

A drow leaped out behind them, his shield and sword seeming like the essence of the stars themselves, translucent but spotted with bits of stones that sparkled like diamond lights in a night sky. The drow struck once, twice, and both men tumbled down, writhing and dying.

It occurred to Artemis Entreri that he had seen this drow before, though not outfitted so marvelously, surely. Still, watching the movements, watching the deference played toward this one by the other dark elves spilling out behind him, brought a name to Entreri's lips, one from a dark place in a dark time.

"Tiago Baenre." He shook his head. "Lovely."

"Whoa now!" Ambergris said, staggering and trying to hold her balance as the whole street reverberated with the shock of rolling thunder. She grabbed onto Effron for support, and caught his dead arm, which was swaying wildly behind his back.

"Dwarf!" he managed to call out before tumbling over backward.

"Eh, no," Ambergris answered, standing over him, one hand reaching down to help him up. "No dwarf."

A shaken and unsettled Effron reached up for the dwarf's offered hand, but he paused, noting Amber's face. He followed her gaze across the lane, to the front of a building, and more important, to the gigantic arachnoid creature standing in front of the building.

Its drow face smiling, the beast lifted a huge spear and let fly. The throw came in high, above Amber's head, but that was the design, for the spear trailed a net, a net that opened behind it.

"Bah!" Ambergris cried, grabbing her mace off her back and sweeping it across, right to left as she dived out to the right. Skullcrusher's bulbous head hit the side of the net and drove it across and the dwarf rolled free. She called out for Effron, though, certain that her companion was under the net, and when she scrambled around, she managed a glance that way, to confirm that yes, indeed, the twisted young tiefling crouched in the road, covered by the heavy cords of the drider net.

"Bah, ye dog!" the dwarf roared and started forward as the drider lifted another spear and charged off the porch. But another form came first, rushing around the skittering spider legs, out of the spider's twilight shadow, and Ambergris howled and batted her mace back and forth desperately, in full retreat as she parried the sudden strikes of drow swords.

"Get out, boy! Oh run!" she managed to cry out, staggering backward, trying to find some measure of a defensive posture against the overwhelming assault by the drow warrior.

A task made much easier a heartbeat later when a line of black fire swept between Ambergris and the drow, and to the dwarf's great relief, the hot side of the darkfire licked cruelly at her opponent. She saw the drow sprinting away, slapping at flames, and turned to thank, and hopefully support, Effron, but stopped before she had taken a step that way.

Where the warlock had been was now a roiling cloud of gooey black smoke, rolling over and popping like bubbling mud. And spreading, it seemed, like a hungry black ooze.

Not knowing what to make of it, Ambergris retreated across the street, running for the shelter of the house behind.

She reached the door and almost got through, when a second drider suddenly appeared meeting her in the doorway with a swing of a heavy cudgel that rattled off the side of Amber's head, sending her staggering backward yet again to smash through a hitching rail and stagger hard into a stack of water barrels, sending them and the stunned dwarf tumbling.

Pressed flat against the wooden floor in the magical darkness, his robes tight around him, Afafrenfere felt the burning and shocking power of the lightning bolt. He heard the wall splintering above him, and had to hope that it was broken apart enough for him to push through.

But he couldn't check it, he knew instinctively, and he wasn't surprised when he found that he was not alone in the darkness. These were dark elves, after all, who relished the blackness.

The monk came up fast, and on instinct even leaped as he rose, and he felt the cut of a sword beneath him, as expected, the drow figuring to finish what the fireball and lightning bolt had started. Afafrenfere landed lightly and struck out with his hands, left and right, and fell into a rhythm, feeling the movements around him, anticipating the attacks.

An out-turned downward slap moved a cutting sword aside, an uplifted leg, bent at the knee, starting in close and sweeping out wide, took a second sword with it, and as he moved that leg, Afafrenfere planted his foot firmly and bulled ahead.

His heavy right punch connected squarely, and he felt the lighter drow flying away and heard the dark elf tumbling down the stairs.

But the replacement was there almost instantly, and the fact that this newcomer had so easily avoided the flying swordsman told the monk that the area of darkness was very limited, likely just a stride or so.

Afafrenfere rushed to the right along the corridor. Hope rekindled when he came out of the darkness, as he had suspected, only two quick strides to the side.

And that hope fell away when he realized that he was alone, that Entreri and Dahlia were gone, and hope plummeted from a high cliff face when a shining sword chased him out of the darkness and caught up to him, under his late block, to stab him deeply in the side.

He lurched and stumbled toward the door of Entreri's room.

Then he stopped and spun around, his left arm leading and rising, lifting the pursuing drow's sword. Afafrenfere kicked his foot up straight between himself and the dark elf, as if he meant to stomp it down straight ahead— and indeed, the drow's second blade angled in to defeat just such an attack.

But Afafrenfere's leg swept out to the side and down instead, away from the blade, and the monk stepped in behind the feigned kick and leaned forward over his feet to drive his open hand into the drow's chin, staggering the swordsman back into the darkness. Afafrenfere kept going forward with a jump and somersault, and as he came over, he double-kicked straight ahead, into the darkness and into the drow. The monk felt the bite of a sword on one leg, but it was not a substantial hit, and certainly nothing to compare with the weight of his own blows.

He landed hard, but came up immediately and started for the door. He winced with every stride, not for his leg but for the first wound in his side, one much worse than he had initially realized, it seemed.

By the time he pushed through the door he was wheezing and fighting for breath, with one hand against his torn side, trying to quell the bleeding,

Afafrenfere stumbled to the broken window where Entreri and Dahlia had made their escape. He looked out at the street, now with fighting visible in many locations.

Stonecutter's Solace shook again with a tremendous explosion, one that put the monk down to the floor. He knew the drow were coming—he certainly hadn't killed either of his last two foes. Now fighting for every clawing inch, Afafrenfere pulled himself back up, and squeezed out of the window. He had to climb for the roof, he knew, his fingers settling on the top board of the frame. With great effort, the bleeding monk pulled himself to his feet on the sill. He picked his next handhold, then grimaced as he got slugged in the gut.

No, not punched, he realized, looking down to see the hand crossbow bolt sticking in his midsection.

Another joined it.

Afafrenfere knew about drow poison, of course, but that didn't trouble him nearly as much as knowing that there were a pair of dark elves, at least, coming into the room!

He let go of the top board and stepped off the sill.

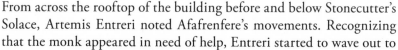

From across the rooftop of the building before and below Stonecutter's Solace, Artemis Entreri noted Afafrenfere's movements. Recognizing that the monk appeared in need of help, Entreri started to wave out to Dahlia, who stood atop the inn's roof as an elf woman once more. She looked down over the street. He tried to get her attention, but Dahlia seemed not to notice, her gaze set farther along to the west, down the road and the hill from the inn. Entreri brought his fingers to his lips, thinking to blow a sharp whistle to gain her attention, but before he could, Afafrenfere simply stepped away and dropped from the ledge. The shocked Entreri understood a moment later when a dark elf appeared at the window.

Down plummeted the monk, but his hands and feet worked furiously along the side of the building, catching holds and slowing his fall somewhat. But Afafrenfere was surely in a weakened state, Entreri could see, and he hit the ground hard, his legs buckling under him as he rolled away from the burning building.

And not far from him stood the drow with the sword and shield, the one Entreri thought he recognized as Tiago Baenre.

A drow noble.

Once more, Entreri turned to the rooftop, to call to Dahlia, and he was relieved to see her become a giant raven again, moving to the edge and springing off into the darkening night. He thought she must be going to Afafrenfere's rescue, but could only shake his head as Dahlia swooped out and away from the building, flying right past Entreri's perch and farther on down the street.

Hardly thinking of the movement, realizing only that he was the monk's only chance at survival, Artemis Entreri sprinted across the roof.

Tiago Baenre had noticed the fallen monk, who was then struggling to stand back up, shaky on his legs and lurching to the side, his hand tight there, obviously against a wound.

Tiago would have him dead before he ever readied a defense.

Weapons in hand, Entreri had leaped down to the ground and sprinted to Afafrenfere before he could even consider the seemingly suicidal move. He went by the monk and met the charge of Tiago, his sword blocked by that translucent, star-filled shield, his jeweled dagger ably taking the drow's strange sword aside.

In his head, the assassin spat curses at Drizzt Do'Urden.

Drizzt had done this to him, he knew. All those acts and talks of nobility and community and friendship . . . all of that, indeed, had put Artemis Entreri into battle with a drow noble, superbly armed and with many allies all around.

And all for the sake of a wounded friend.

"How has it come to this?" the assassin asked with a helpless laugh.

A golden translucent shield appeared at the front of the bubbling ooze of Effron's magical smoke, and not a heartbeat too soon, for the huge drider let fly another spear, this one aimed lower, to pierce the heart of the cloud and the heart of the warlock who had created the cloud.

The spear hit the shield and deflected wide, spinning and shaking, but still deadly, as one unfortunate citizen, fleeing the battle up the road at the inn, found out. The huge missile caught him in the side, lifted him from the ground, and threw him back across the street, not far from where Ambergris shakily tried to rise. The man groaned and rolled, grabbing at the spear as if hoping to tug its barbed head free.

He was dead before he closed his hands.

The bubbling ooze around Effron melted away, and melted with it was the heavy net, the thick coils, those that remained at all, reduced to twisted and charred lines of unconnected twine.

The young warlock stood up, leaned his bone staff against his shoulder, and dusted himself off, his expression aptly reflecting that he was more piqued than scared as he matched stares with the huge drider—and though Effron may have seemed a tiny thing indeed standing before a creature as large and imposing as this particular drider, who now produced a trident that was longer than Effron was tall, the twisted warlock was not the least bit intimidated by the half-spider, half-drow abomination.

No, he was just angry.

He swept his bone staff in front of him, releasing a wave of bolts of black energy, weaving around as they flew across the way to turn unerringly, burning into the drider. As the creature recoiled, stung but hardly defeated, Effron glanced back for Ambergris. He saw her, but she wasn't about to be much use to him, obviously. She had risen by then, and had her large mace in hand, but faced an enemy akin to his own, although a smaller abomination than this one, and, like the dwarf, female.

Effron noted another possibility, though, and he held forth his staff, the eyes on its small skull head flaring with the power of the negative plane. A line of red energy reached out from the weapon for the man lying dead at the end of the drider's spear.

Effron spun back and stamped his staff on the ground, and the area between him and the closing male drider began to bubble and boil, and octopus-like tentacles erupted from the morass, writhing and reaching for the arachnoid creature.

Just a few moments later, the newly created zombie shuffled by Effron, the long spear dragging at its side, and bore down on the drider, walking right through the black tentacles where the drider did not dare.

"Tricks will not save you!" the drider cried, ending with a grunt as Effron hit it with stinging black fire.

The zombie wandered through, lifting its arms to rake at the drider.

The drider impaled it with a single thrust of his huge trident, and easily lifted the undead thing high into the air, tossing it far over his shoulder in a movement that reminded Effron of a farmer throwing hay.

He nodded his admiration to the beast, then moved fast to his right as the drider skittered right, determined to keep the writhing tentacles between them.

Distance favored him, Effron knew, and he threw another wave of black energy missiles, weaving through the tentacles and stinging the mighty drider yet again.

"How many have you got, trickster?" the beast howled.

"Forevermore," Effron answered, and simply to prove his point, he sent forth another wave.

But the creature smiled through its grimaces, its expression so confident as to be more than a little unnerving. Effron glanced to the left to see Ambergris apparently holding her own on the porch of the building. As he continued moving to his right, the twisted warlock glanced over his shoulder.

A large black bird glided down toward him—his mother, he knew—but whatever comfort he might take in that powerful reinforcement was quickly lost. For the drider had allies as well, a group of dark elves standing in concentric circles, centered by one who served as the hub of a peculiar spider's web of blue-sparking electrical energy.

"Fly away!" the young warlock yelled to his mother, just as she came down beside him, and just as the drow flung the lightning web, spinning, turning, and sparkling.

Dahlia came back to her elf form.

The lightning net fell over the mother and son.

Effron melted away.

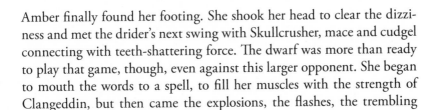

Amber finally found her footing. She shook her head to clear the dizziness and met the drider's next swing with Skullcrusher, mace and cudgel connecting with teeth-shattering force. The dwarf was more than ready to play that game, though, even against this larger opponent. She began to mouth the words to a spell, to fill her muscles with the strength of Clangeddin, but then came the explosions, the flashes, the trembling ground, violently shaking as the lightning net landed over Dahlia, who stood just a few strides from Ambergris.

The dwarf staggered, but the drider, so balanced on eight spidery legs, did not.

Cudgel and mace met again with crushing force. The shock wave of magical thunder continued. The ground rolled.

Ambergris was on her back then, her spell driven from her lips, her mace flown from her hand, the drider standing over her.

The drider's heavy cudgel descended.

The first exchanges seemed more a dance than a battle, with Entreri and Tiago circling, each offering weak thrusts that were easily blocked or parried.

"Where is he?" Tiago asked, and he turned back to his right, putting the now-burning Stonecutter's Solace behind him.

Entreri moved fast to intercept, seeing that the drow was creating an open line for the fallen monk.

"Any time you wish to join in would be welcomed," Entreri said to his companion.

Afafrenfere groaned and managed to stand, but barely, for one leg would not hold his weight and the side of his robe was soaked in blood. A quick glance at the man had Entreri realizing that he had been foolish indeed to leap down from the rooftop to come to Afafrenfere's aid. This one, he believed, wasn't about to survive the wounds he already bore!

The assassin went at Tiago in his frustration, sword leading, in and up, and he spun behind it in a sudden reverse to send his dagger thrusting forward.

But Tiago not only met the sword with his own wondrous blade, and got his shield in line with the dagger, he did so while resetting his feet. Before Entreri had even completed the maneuver, Tiago came forward in a rush, his shield sweeping out before him, but turned then so that its edge could cut across to take Entreri out at the legs.

Entreri barely retreated in time, and Tiago continued forward, sword chopping, shield cutting back the other way, then back again, with the sword quickly following in a dizzying display.

The assassin had nearly been caught off his guard with the sheer ferocity, balance, and coordination of the attack.

This was a Baenre noble, he reminded himself, and he knew well what that likely meant.

Entreri would be at his best here, or he would surely be dead!

He matched Tiago's assault with a fast riposte, then drove forward with three sudden thrusts, each forcing the drow farther from Afafrenfere and more to the middle of the lane.

"Monk!" Entreri called, and he winced as dark elves began to arrive, coming from the windows and door, and floating down from the higher windows of the burning building. "Run!"

In response, Afafrenfere took a step, nearly tumbling as his weight came upon his broken leg. He grimaced and fought through it, though, stumbling along for another few steps.

A globe of darkness engulfed him.

A hail of javelins swarmed into the globe. There came a grunt and the thud of the man falling to the ground, and Entreri noted his hand protruding from the edge of the darkness, fingers trembling and moving, as if they were trying to grasp at life itself.

Then stillness.

So it was over, Entreri realized, his gallant idiocy sure to leave them both dead on the street. He managed a glance behind him, down the lane toward the lower city, and caught sight of Dahlia in crow form touching down beside Effron, and Amber battling a horrid drider off to the side, and a spinning web of lightning descending right behind Dahlia.

The flashes and reverberations of that lightning net shook the ground all around this section of Port Llast; people were running, scrambling, tumbling as the ground moved under their feet.

Entreri held his balance, and even used the tremor to go at Tiago once more, hoping to at least take this miserable drow noble down before the other dark elves overwhelmed him.

But Tiago, with equal balance, was ready for the charge, and Entreri's slashing sword met a spiraling, widening shield—a magical shield expanding right before Entreri's eyes! Tiago dared to roll around, even putting his back to Entreri for a brief instant.

His back! Entreri saw the opening. His opponent had underestimated him.

He went for the target, or tried to, but found to his horror that his sword was stuck fast to Tiago's shield, as surely as if he had slashed it into the side of a thick spiderweb.

Tiago came around turning that shield, tugging hard and nearly taking the sword from Entreri's hand. Only the assassin's great speed and balance allowed him to twist and turn enough to hold on desperately as the drow's sword stabbed for him. Only a last-instant parry by his jeweled dagger turned that blade from his face, and only enough so that blade still nicked his ear as it passed.

Entreri felt the sting of that hit, and the added sting of drow poison.

And then the ground rolled under him suddenly, like an ocean wave, and he and Tiago were lifted into the air, deafened by a thunder stroke, and blinded by a flash so brilliant that it stole the night.

CHAPTER 10

EVERY DAY, EVERY EXPERIENCE, EVERY THRILL

"CA-RU-DELLY!" PENELOPE HARPELL SAID WITH GREAT ENTHUSIASM AND a loud clap of her hands when the five companions, led by Catti-brie, were escorted into her audience chamber.

"Eh?" Bruenor asked.

But Catti-brie was simply smiling in response at the affectionate nickname—one Catti-brie had earned in her initial meeting with Penelope a couple of years earlier. When asked her name in that first meeting, Catti-brie had nearly blurted the truth, then tried to change it with the name she had been given by her Bedine parents, and finally had settled on her alias, that of poor Delly Curtie. She moved swiftly across the room, catching Penelope, her mentor, in a great hug.

"I told you I would return," she said.

"To tell me the truth of your tale, so you promised," Penelope replied as they broke the embrace. The older woman looked past Catti-brie to her companions, and her expression turned to one of curiosity when her gaze settled on the dark elf.

"Drizzt Do'Urden?" she asked. "Truly?"

The drow bowed. "Well met, Lady Penelope," he said.

"Truly, indeed," said an old man as he came in the door. He walked around Drizzt, nodded and smiled to Catti-brie, then clapped the drow on the shoulder.

"Kipper Harpell," Drizzt said, nodding. He didn't really remember the man all that well, but the name was fresh in his thoughts, given Catti-brie's tutelage of the current state of the Ivy Mansion as the group had neared the place.

"I was a young man when last you came through Longsaddle," Kipper said.

"Aye, was half a century ago when last we seen ye," answered Bruenor, moving up beside Drizzt and offering his hand to Kipper.

The old man looked at him curiously.

"Half a century?" he asked, staring doubtfully at the young dwarf, who could not be half that age.

"I was older then," Bruenor said with a laugh.

"I was older still," Wulfgar said. "In human years."

Regis snorted and waved his hand dismissively at the other two. "I was dead!" he exclaimed.

Kipper turned to Penelope, but she wore a perplexed expression to match that of the old mage.

"I told you I had a tale to tell," Catti-brie said to her.

The older woman considered her former student, then turned to regard Drizzt and the others, her gaze settling on Bruenor. "Older then, but wearing the same crown?" she asked, and when the dwarf smiled, she added, "The one-horned helm of King Bruenor Battlehammer of Mithral Hall?"

"Aye, she's gettin' it!" said the dwarf.

Penelope turned to the beautiful young woman with auburn hair standing beside her and said, "Catti-brie."

Catti-brie nodded.

"Was she your mother, then?" Kipper asked Catti-brie. "Or your great-great-great grandmother at the least."

Penelope grabbed Catti-brie's arm and lifted it, pulling back the sleeve of her white gown to reveal the spellscar. She looked at Kipper and shook her head. "Catti-brie," she reiterated.

"The Companions of the Hall," Drizzt put in. "All of us. Once great friends to the Harpells of Longsaddle, who came to our aid in Mithral Hall in the Time of Troubles, when the drow returned."

"I am too old for riddles," Kipper complained.

"But are you too old for a fine tale?" Catti-brie asked.

Penelope's husband Dowell entered the room then, his smile going wide when he noted the return of the woman called Delly Curtie. He looked around, happily at first, but his smile vanished when he regarded old Kipper, who stood with his arms crossed, a frown on his face, and tapping one shoe impatiently against the wooden floor.

"It seems that I have missed something," Dowell said.

The door closed and all turned to see the foppish halfling leaning up against it. With a wide grin, Regis led the looks to the side of the room, where Wulfgar was already setting out an array of glasses, and inspecting the bottles of Penelope and Dowell's private stock as he went.

Apparently noticing the dumbfounded stares upon him, Wulfgar turned and met them with a beaming smile. "What is a fine tale without an appropriate toasting beverage?" he asked, looking at Regis as he did.

"Ye're gonna get me boy in trouble," Bruenor whispered to the halfling.

"Count on it," the halfling replied.

With a laugh, Penelope agreed, and she moved fast to clear enough of her desk for the large barbarian to bring over sufficient glasses and bottles. She settled back into her chair, Dowell and Kipper taking seats to flank her, and bade Catti-brie to spin her tale.

Even as the woman moved before the desk to begin, though, Penelope held up her hand to stop her. The Harpell leader then closed her eyes and whispered a spell—indeed, a spell referred to as the magical whisper. Soon after, there came a knock on the door. On Penelope's signal, Regis opened it, and in came a line of younger Harpells, all bearing comfortable chairs for the guests.

"Do begin," Penelope bade Catti-brie when the students were gone and the door closed once more.

A long while later, Penelope magically whispered once more, and soon after that, a grand dinner was brought in.

Through the meal, Catti-brie and the others continued their tale.

Long into the night, Drizzt finished. "And so we are here, with a dark road before us, and needing the friendship of the great Harpells of Longsaddle once more.

"For the sake o' me Pwent," Bruenor added.

Penelope looked to Dowell, and both deferred to Kipper.

"Already working on it," replied the old mage, who had appeared asleep until the weight of the gazes had stirred him.

"He will have to be resurrected," Kipper told Catti-brie around midmorning of the next day. "I see no other way."

The woman frowned and looked to the third person in the room, Penelope Harpell.

"There is no cure for vampirism," Penelope said with a shrug. "None that I know of, at least."

"Such a spell as resurrection is far beyond my abilities," Catti-brie said.

"Far beyond all but a few—and it won't come cheaply!" Kipper stated. "And I doubt your friend will survive it—you understand that, of course?"

Catti-brie nodded.

"Thibbledorf Pwent was old and in failing health at the time of his infection," Kipper went on. "So you have told me. And many decades have passed since then. You will likely raise him from undeath only to deliver him to true death."

"Better that," Catti-brie said, and the others nodded.

"Likely, yes," said Penelope, and she dropped a hand gently on Catti-brie's forearm to comfort her.

"But what is the point?" Catti-brie asked. "If Pwent is doomed in any case, we can simply destroy him as is—"

"You would not wish to offer him the peace of alleviating his curse before he ventures to the netherworld?" Kipper asked.

There came a knock at the door and Penelope went to answer it.

"I see no choice," Catti-brie answered. "How am I to procure the services of a properly skilled high priest? And one who will venture to Gauntlgrym?"

"Bring the vampire to the priest, when you find one," Kipper said, and as he spoke, Wulfgar entered the room. "Ah, good," Kipper said. "Do join us."

Wulfgar took the seat beside Catti-brie. She looked at him curiously, but he could only shrug in response, clearly as perplexed as she as to why he had been summoned to this meeting.

"You have brought it?" Kipper asked.

Wulfgar seemed confused for a just a moment as Kipper reached his hand out, but then moved quickly to remove his silver horn and hand it over to the old mage.

"A brilliant item!" Kipper said, rolling it over in his hands, then casting a spell to examine it more closely. He focused on the line of small but exquisite gemstones set in the silver.

"From a dragon's lair, you say," Penelope prompted, taking the conversation while Kipper continued his examination.

"Icingdeath."

"The dragon you and Drizzt killed many years ago."

"A lifetime ago," Wulfgar said with a grin.

"Have you used it?" Kipper asked.

"Yes—almost immediately after I found it," Wulfgar answered, "in the dragon's lair, on a hoard of treasure. Ice trolls had dogged me all the way to the treasure hoard and by then had surrounded me. I thought my new life near its end and blew the horn out of defiance and nothing more—well, perhaps I hoped its notes would bring the ice ceiling crashing down, affording me some chance against the odds, at least."

"And the trumpet brought in allies," Kipper said with a laugh. "Oh, how grand!"

"And have you used it since?" Penelope asked.

"Only once, to confirm . . ." Wulfgar answered sheepishly.

"It troubles you?" Penelope asked.

"He thinks he is disturbing the sleep of the dead, and his culture frowns upon that," Kipper answered before Wulfgar could. "Is that correct, son?"

Wulfgar started to answer, but chuckled instead. "When I died, I was decades older than you are now, mage," he said. "But yes, it is not my place to disturb the sleep of the dead."

"Well, rest assured, friend, that you are doing no such thing," Kipper said, and he blew the horn, a wheezing and broken note, but enough to enact the magic. Within a few heartbeats, the gems on the side of the silver horn sparkled and a trio of warriors appeared, each armed with either a pair of hand axes or an axe and sword. They danced around the room for a bit, unsure of what was required of them, it seemed, until Kipper cast another spell and dismissed them back to nothingness.

"It is a magic item, a tool," the old mage assured Wulfgar as he handed back the horn.

"Like Guenhwyvar," Wulfgar replied.

"Nay, the panther is much more than that," Penelope said. "This is more akin to the whistle that summons Drizzt's unicorn."

"These are not the souls of the dead warriors," Kipper assured him. "These are the magical manifestations of what the berserkers had been, physically, but rest easy that the souls who inhabited those bodies have long gone to Warrior's Rest." He looked at Penelope and nodded, "As I expected."

"What am I missing here?" Catti-brie asked. "How is the horn relevant?"

"The magic of the horn is—or was—a spell meant to trap the soul," Kipper answered. "Part of it, at least. There is much more imbued there that I do not understand, for it is a very ancient item, one long, long pre-dating the Spellplague or even the Time of Troubles, likely. But the victims of that magic, the warriors who have since passed on, were caught there through the spell I mentioned, and such a spell might well aid you in catching your vampire friend."

"Trap his soul in a gemstone and bring the stone to a powerful high priest to finish the grim task," Penelope offered.

"I do not know this spell," said Catti-brie.

"No, and it is a powerful one," Kipper said. "Perhaps beyond you, but I do not think so—with the help of a scroll, at least, and a gemstone worthy of containing such a treasure as a soul."

"And you have such items," Wulfgar assumed.

"We prepared many things for the Bidderdoos, just in case," Penelope answered.

"Werewolves," Catti-brie explained to her large friend.

"I remember him," Wulfgar agreed with a nod.

"He left a legacy. In the forest."

Penelope Harpell rose and offered Wulfgar her hand. "Come," she bade him. "Let us leave Catti-brie and Kipper to their work. She has much to learn."

When they had left the room, Catti-brie turned to the old mage with a smile. "I knew you would help."

"The world is a dark place," Kipper replied. "But when friends join hands, it lightens."

Catti-brie nodded as she considered the generosity, and she wondered how much more the Harpells might offer when the Companions of the Hall finished their business in Gauntlgrym and turned their warrior eyes once more to the Silver Marches.

"Do you feel better about your . . . toy?" Penelope asked as she led Wulfgar away. He walked with her down many halls and through a few rooms, and finally, out into the grand garden in back of the Ivy Mansion.

"I do," Wulfgar admitted. "I feared disturbing the sleep of the dead. It is not my place—"

"But you didn't destroy the horn," Penelope noted. "Or put it away."

Wulfgar smiled at her, conceding the point. "It saved my life once," he admitted.

"Yes, in a dragon's lair, so you and your halfling friend before that, have told me," said Penelope. "I would love to hear more about the fight."

Wulfgar paused and looked down at her. "Were you once an adventurer? Have you known the thrill of battle?"

"Or of theft?" Penelope asked, and reached up to tug the silver horn.

"Proper pillaging!" Wulfgar corrected with a laugh.

"When I was younger, I found adventure," the woman admitted. "In fact, it was on the wild road, in a steading full of hill giants, where I met Dowell and fell in love. In the midst of battle, no less."

"He saved you?" Wulfgar asked slyly.

"Quite the opposite," the woman replied, and she walked on down the garden path, moving between tall rows of high flowers and coming out into the full sunshine on the far end. "Dowell is quite skilled at his craft, but he was never much of an evoker, and giants are not the most receptive creatures to charm spells."

"Ah, but Penelope was, apparently."

The woman laughed. "He didn't need them against my resolve!"

"His powers of persuasion must be great indeed to convince you to join this family," Wulfgar remarked, and Penelope looked at him with a puzzled expression, as if she did not understand.

"I convinced him," she corrected when she had sorted it out. "I am Penelope Harpell by birth, not marriage."

It was Wulfgar's turn to wear the puzzled expression.

"Dowell joined my clan and took my name," she explained. "It was the least he could do after I pulled him from the grasp of the hill giant king—a hungry hill giant king, no less!"

Wulfgar laughed.

"I find your return to Toril the most curious tale among those of your group," Penelope went on. "Catti-brie was bound by her goddess, Bruenor by his sense of friendship, the halfling by a need to prove his worth—be wary for him, for I suspect that his demands of his own courage will land him in dire straits in short order. But what of Wulfgar? You admitted that you did not immediately choose this path, yet here you are."

"Bound by friendship, as with Bruenor, and including my friendship and debt to Bruenor as much as to Drizzt," Wulfgar answered.

"You owed nothing, and that friendship was long past, by your own admission." She stopped and looked up at Wulfgar intently, forcing him to look her in the eye.

After a long pause, he admitted, "Perhaps I fear death, after all."

"A strange admission from one who has existed on the other side of life."

"What is to be found in Warrior's Rest?" he asked.

"Family, friends, comfort? Is that not what you expect?"

"Eternally."

The way he said it tipped her off. "Eternal boredom, you mean."

"I cannot say, but it matters not. If it is eternal, then it will wait, yes? And now I was presented with a grand adventure, another life of memories to make and a worthy band of friends to make them beside. Why would I not return?"

"You seem quite the opposite of Drizzt," Penelope replied. "He could not let go of Catti-brie and his former life, and you seem eager to do so."

Wulfgar pondered her words for a few moments, then slowly began shaking his head. "Nay, not that, but merely to expand that experience," he explained. "More battles to fight, more women to love, more food to eat, and more spirits to drink."

"So it is a grand game to you, then? Is there nothing more?"

"I know not," Wulfgar admitted.

"So the aim of living is pleasure?"

"A fine goal!" Wulfgar said lightheartedly, but Penelope would not let it go so easily.

"There is a religion to support your theory," she said, and Wulfgar's expression immediately soured. "More a philosophy," she quickly corrected. "But it presupposes the absence of just reward. It calls the gods false, relegating them to superior mortal beings posing as deities for the sake of their own enjoyment, and at the expense of the lesser rational beings who inhabit the world, and also, that they might control us."

"You seem to know a lot about it."

It was Penelope's turn to laugh, "I have been called unconventional. I think it a badge of honor."

Wulfgar stared at her intently. "You miss the open road and the thrill of adventure," he stated.

"I am too old . . ." she started to reply, but his laughter cut her short.

"I have lived a century and a quarter!"

"You have the body of a young man."

"I have the lust of a young man, but only because I have lived through the dullness of being an old man," Wulfgar corrected. "I have passed through pain and grief—"

"And love?"

He didn't deny it. He lifted Aegis-fang from over his shoulder and swung it easily at the end of one huge arm. "Every day, every experience," he said with a nod. "Every thrill."

"Like talking to an old lady in a sunlit garden?"

Wulfgar's smile was wide and genuine, and his crystal blue eyes sparkled. "Not so old," he said mischievously. "Perhaps one day, you and I will go kill some giants."

Now Penelope was smiling, too, and that was her answer, and it was a sincere hope that such an event might come to pass.

"Truly, you remind me of a caged animal," Regis said to Bruenor on the front deck of the Ivy Mansion one bright morning a few days later. Spring was in full bloom, the air light, the wind warm, and the road beckoned—and beckoned none more than the grumbling dwarf.

He paced back and forth, back and forth, thumping his heavy boots against the wooden porch. He paused for just a moment, to snort at the halfling, then went along again.

Just down the path from the pair stood Drizzt and Wulfgar, working their weapons slowly and methodically in mock battle, with Wulfgar asking questions of his old mentor every few twists. Regis thought he should go down there and further his own training—who better for him to learn from than Drizzt, after all?

"Long road ahead," Bruenor remarked, passing the halfling by on one of his pacing lanes.

Regis nodded.

"Gauntlgrym—ah, wait till ye see it," Bruenor went on. "We'll catch us a Pwent and be on our way. Silverymoon, I say! Aye, we'll find us a priest there to do the deed, and then we'll set to chasing Obould and his dogs back into their holes!"

He continued on, muttering to himself as much as anything, for the notion of a "long road ahead" had sent Regis into some of his own ruminating. Yes, he'd travel to Gauntlgrym, but might that be the end of the journey for him? Should he choose to go south from there instead of east to the Silver Marches, he was fairly confident that he could find Doregardo and the Grinning Ponies early in the summer—with enough time to go back to Delthuntle and the waiting arms of his lovely Donnola.

The door to the mansion opened then, and Catti-brie came out, Penelope and Kipper beside her.

"If he fights off the first try, you might consider just killing him then and there," Kipper was saying.

Drizzt and Wulfgar moved back to join them.

" 'Ere now, what's that?" Bruenor asked.

Catti-brie showed him a ring on her hand, golden and set with a black gemstone. "Stored within this ring is the spell we need to trap Pwent's soul." She rolled her hand, revealing a huge gemstone, red as blood.

"Ruby?" Drizzt asked.

"Sapphire," Regis corrected, staring at the gem and licking his lips.

"Phylactery," Catti-brie corrected, and she tucked it away.

"Ye said if it don't work," Bruenor said to Kipper. "Ye thinkin' it might not, then?"

Old Kipper sucked in his breath. "It is a difficult spell—"

"Me girl can cast it!"

"Oh, indeed," said Penelope. "The ring Kipper has loaned her holds the spell intact. But still, it is a difficult conjuration, and one an unwilling target can fight, sometimes successfully."

"An unwilling dwarf," Kipper added, "is never an easy target of any magical spell!"

"Nor an easy friend," Regis quipped, drawing a glare from Bruenor.

"Kipper has shown me the spell—I have practiced," Catti-brie said. "If the ring fails, I have this." She reached under the fold of her white gown and produced a silver scroll tube.

But Kipper couldn't help but shake his head. "Better to just destroy the vampire if he resists the magic," he said. "Trap the Soul is difficult to enact—only a mage of great experience can do so without the scroll, and even with it . . . I fear that you are not ready."

"Do not underestimate her," Penelope put in, and put her hand on Catti-brie's shoulder. "She has the favor of a goddess shining upon her, and is wiser in the ways of the world than her youthful appearance suggests."

"Yes, yes, I know, I know," Kipper said. "Well, to you all, then, a farewell and a fair road. I hope you find your lost friend."

He bowed and went back inside, and the companions took turns bidding Penelope farewell, then started off down the hill for the gate to the Ivy Mansion, the road beyond and the trails beyond that.

"There are rumors of giants roaming the foothills of the Spine of the World," Penelope called after them. Wulfgar grinned.

"Aye," Wulfgar answered her. "We might have to see to that!"

"What was that about?" Catti-brie asked when they were on their way again.

"Adventure," Wulfgar replied. "The same thing it is always about."

CHAPTER 11

PAWN TO QUEEN FOUR

SPEAK NOT A WORD UNLESS YOU ARE DIRECTLY COMMANDED TO DO SO! Tos'un Armgo's fingers flashed to his daughter Doum'wielle, the two standing side-by-side, as ordered, on marks Berellip Xorlarrin had scratched on the ground.

"Do not move," she had warned them, the gravity in her voice impossible to miss. Something was going on here, Tos'un understood, and it terrified him. Never had the Xorlarrins been friendly to the House of Armgo, of course, but this was even beyond that measure of animosity.

Berellip, a noble daughter and a high priestess, had been scared when she had ordered them to their spots.

"What do you think . . . ?" Doum'wielle started to ask, but her whisper became a shriek as the heads of four venomous snakes bit into her back one after another. The girl swooned under the burn of poison and the shock that Berellip was still so close nearby. Her legs wobbled beneath her as she slumped to the floor, and she went to one knee. She would have slumped lower, except that a strong hand grabbed her under her upper arm and yanked her back upright.

"Weakling," Berellip whispered in her ear. "*Iblith!* Perhaps I should drag you away and feed you to my driders so that the matron mother will not have to suffer the disgust in looking upon such an abomination as you!"

"She is a noble daughter of House Barrison Del'Armgo," Tos'un said.

Berellip laughed and roughly shoved Doum'wielle before walking around to stand before the pair once more. "That says so much about the fraudulent Second House of Menzoberranzan, does it not? That they seek the beds of *iblith* to expand their ignoble family?"

Tos'un's eyes flashed and Doum'wielle expected him to return a verbal barrage at that, but surprisingly, he stood perfectly quiet and perfectly still, except that his jaw quivered just a bit. Doum'wielle thought that curious and out of character, but then she realized that her father was not looking at Berellip any longer but was staring *past* her. The younger Armgo sucked in her breath, and despite the continuing burn of the snake bites, forced herself to stand taller.

Behind High Priestess Berellip Xorlarrin came a procession of drow such as she had never seen before, such as she had never imagined before. Male warriors flanked the central figures left and right, marching with precision, in perfect step, arms and armor sparkling with magical power.

Between those ranks, on a floating translucent disk that shined purple and blue, sat a woman bedecked in grand robes, laced and bejeweled with intricate designs of spiders and webs. A five-snake scourge rested across her lap, the serpent heads alive and writhing and clearly aware of the scene before them.

Berellip spun around and fell to her knees, eyes lowered to the floor.

Should she do the same, Doum'wielle wondered? She glanced at her father, who stood perfectly still, his eyes lowered. Her gaze dipped to the floor and she swallowed hard. The sight of her father, so clearly terrified, sweat upon his brow, had further unnerved her.

"Matron Mother Quenthel," Berellip greeted, but did not look up.

"This is the son of House Barrison Del'Armgo?" Matron Mother Quenthel Baenre asked, stepping off her disc and moving up beside Berellip, waving for the high priestess to stand up as she did.

"Yes, Tsabrak caught him in the tunnels to the east."

The matron mother turned a curious eye over Doum'wielle, first with intrigue but with her face quickly scrunching up with open disgust. "What is this?"

"My daughter, Matron Mother," Tos'un dared interject, and Berellip slapped him across the face.

Quenthel pushed Berellip back, though, and bade Tos'un to look up at her. "Your daughter?" she asked, using the common tongue of the surface.

"Yes."

"A noble of House Barrison Del'Armgo?"

Tos'un swallowed hard, something Doum'wielle surely did not miss.

"How lovely," Matron Mother Quenthel said. "Such a thoughtful present you have delivered to me."

All three—Doum'wielle, Tos'un, and Berellip—looked at the matron mother with puzzlement.

"I wonder how proud your mother will be to know that her line is no longer pure," Quenthel remarked, her voice like the purr of a contented cat. "Or will it be a secret she will want kept, do you suppose?"

Tos'un swallowed hard and cast a plaintive glance at Doum'wielle, and the young half-drow saw the sudden regret in his eyes. He had erred in bringing her here. They should never have left the Silver Marches.

"Andzrel!" Matron Mother Quenthel called, looking back to her line. A tall warrior rushed forward. "Take her and teach her what it is to be *iblith* in Menzoberranzan."

"As I please?" he asked.

"Just keep her alive," Quenthel instructed. "How much alive, I do not care."

"No!" Doum'wielle cried, grabbing for her sword, but Quenthel lifted her hand and uttered a single word and the poor girl was sent flying backward.

Khazid'hea, the sentient blade, screamed in her head, telling her to stand down, but the headstrong girl picked herself up from the floor and stubbornly drew out the sword.

"Little Doe, no!" Tos'un cried.

Matron Mother Quenthel laughed wickedly. At her side, Andzrel drew out his two swords and calmly walked toward the poor girl.

"Back, I warn!" Doum'wielle said.

The Weapons Master of House Baenre came at her then in a blur of movement, spinning and dodging, his blades flashing brightly as they cut in circles and stabs. Doum'wielle thought herself a fine swordswoman, but never had she seen anything of this tempo and skill. And worse, Khazid'hea would not cooperate, filling her head with doubt and calls for surrender.

Andzrel's blade slapped hard against her sword, and Khazid'hea sent a charge of discord into her head, dizzying her.

Doum'wielle didn't know what to make of any of it. She saw her cherished blade go flying out to the side, clanging down on the stone floor. She saw Andzrel stepping in closer, saw the pommel of his weapon rushing to smash her in the face.

Then she saw black spots flitting around her swirling vision. She felt the strong hands of the drow upon her, dragging her back. He was behind her, holding her upright . . .

Five snake heads danced before her eyes.

Berellip's whip had hurt her, so she had believed, but compared to the scourge of Matron Mother Quenthel, that strike had been nothing at all.

In moments, Doum'wielle was on the floor, screaming and writhing in agony. Blow after blow descended upon her, viper fangs tearing at her flesh, burning poison streaming into her veins.

"Matron Mother, I beg of you!" Tos'un cried.

The matron mother turned an angry glare upon him. "You have lived on the surface," she said. "How long?"

Tos'un hesitated, and Doum'wielle paid for his slip with another beating.

"Since the attack on Mithral Hall!" the son of House Barrison Del'Armgo blurted.

Quenthel stared at him incredulously. "I did not return to Menzoberranzan," he explained. "I was lost and wandering . . ."

"And you went to live with elves?"

"Yes . . . no! I found others, drow of Ched Nasad, of House Suun Wett and Khareese . . ."

"Where are they?"

"Dead. Long dead."

"And you stayed?"

"I had nowhere to turn, nowhere to go," Tos'un explained.

"Until now."

"It was time to find my way home, with Doum'wielle, my daughter, who is drow in heart and soul. She killed her brother, who was not akin to our weal, who could not follow the Spider Queen, and I, too, struck down her mother."

"Dead?"

"Dead," he said. "I have left the surface behind and only wish to return home."

The matron mother mulled it over for a few moments, then looked down at the battered girl. "Perhaps . . ." she said, but then shook her head. "Take her away," she instructed Andzrel.

"And teach her?" he asked with a smile.

"Gently," Quenthel Baenre said.

Andzrel motioned for another of the Baenre soldiers to retrieve the fallen sword. Noting the commoner drow's movement, Tos'un cried out again, "Take care! The blade is sentient, malicious and powerful!"

That drew curious looks from both Baenre nobles. The matron mother nodded to the weapons master and he went over and personally retrieved the sword, gingerly picking it up. His eyes widened with shock immediately and he held the blade aloft, clearly involved in a mental struggle for dominance with it.

And then Andzrel threw Khazid'hea to the ground once more and stared at his matron mother with a look of shock.

"The *iblith* child wielded it!" Matron Mother Quenthel scolded.

"With much preparation," Tos'un explained.

"Dantrag!" Andzrel cried, and he rushed back and scooped up the sword once more, now wearing a determined expression and squeezing the blood from his knuckles as he gripped the hilt.

"Dantrag?" Quenthel Baenre echoed, for Dantrag, her brother, was long dead, a century or more. Andzrel had known him, but what . . . ?

Quenthel's eyes went wide with the shock of recognition as she stared at the sword Andzrel held.

"Khazid'hea," she whispered. She snapped her angry glare over Tos'un.

"My sword?" he asked innocently.

"The sword of Dantrag Baenre!" the matron mother corrected, and it was Tos'un's turn to gasp in surprise.

"It cannot be," he mouthed.

"How did you get this?" Matron Mother Quenthel asked sharply, her threat clear in her tone.

"It . . . it found me," Tos'un stammered, and he sounded very much like he knew he was about to die horribly. "In a rocky canyon, in the World Above."

"A sword of such power?" Quenthel snapped back incredulously.

"It had abandoned its wielder, I expected, or the wielder was slain. I do not know!"

"Liar!"

"The sword agrees!" Andzrel said through chattering teeth, and when the matron mother and Tos'un turned to him, the weapons master threw the sword down once again. He stood there gawking and gasping for his breath. "It is a blade of considerable power!"

"Dantrag mastered it," Quenthel reminded him spitefully. She turned back on Tos'un angrily. "Where did you get it?"

"As I told you, Matron Mother," he said desperately. "I believe that one of the companions of Drizzt Do'Urden carried it, or perhaps the rogue himself." He dared look up as he spoke that cursed name, and was relieved to see that it had the desired effect, for the matron mother visibly backed down, considering his words. She was weighing the region, no doubt, the Silver Marches, where Drizzt was known to roam, where Drizzt's friend had once been the dwarven King of Mithral Hall.

Matron Mother Quenthel walked over and casually picked up Khazid'hea. "A Baenre blade," she said quietly, as if talking to herself, or perhaps to the sword. "Ah, my brother, a pity you were lost to us."

Quenthel's eyes widened suddenly in shock. " 'Deceived by Drizzt,' it said to me."

"It has told me the same, Matron Mother," Tos'un dared reply.

" 'Traitorous rogue,' it calls him," Quenthel said softly, and she focused on the blade again and seemed to be holding a telepathic conversation with it. A short while later, she walked back over, sword in hand. She moved to Andzrel, then with a mocking grin moved right past him to stand before Tos'un.

"Your blade," she said.

"It was," Tos'un said, keeping his eyes low, and to his shock, and indeed, to Andzrel Baenre's gasp, Matron Mother Quenthel handed the blade back to the son of House Barrison Del'Armgo.

"Sheathe it and keep it there," the matron mother ordered, and Tos'un accepted the blade with trembling hands and quickly put it away.

The matron mother offered a look of disgust to Andzrel and motioned for him to gather up Doum'wielle and be gone. She then instructed Tos'un to walk immediately behind her as the procession left the chamber.

"Deceived by Drizzt Do'Urden," she said, turning back to him, and Tos'un noted that she spat every word with utter contempt. What Tos'un did not know was that this Matron Mother, Quenthel Baenre had great personal history with the rogue named Drizzt, and indeed, she had been slain by his blades in the very battle that had left Tos'un alone in the tunnels and mountains around the place called Mithral Hall.

———————〜◁ ◁〜———————

"It is fortunate that you arrived when you did, Matron Mother," Tsabrak Xorlarrin said. The matron mother had cornered him in his private chamber in the Xorlarrin Gauntlgrym complex, a situation that had made him clearly uncomfortable.

"Do tell," Matron Mother Quenthel replied, coolly, and without any hint that the wizard should relax. She liked having her subjects balanced on a precarious edge.

"The son of House Barrison Del'Armgo," Tsabrak replied, as if that should have been obvious.

"I did not come for him," Matron Mother Quenthel said, and then, slyly, she added, "I came for you."

The Xorlarrin wizard swallowed hard. "Matron Mother?" he asked.

"You were dispatched to the east to find the tunnels that would lead you to the land known as the Silver Marches," Matron Mother Quenthel explained.

"Yes, Matron Mother, and I have!" Tsabrak quickly answered, and it was clear that he was fighting hard to keep his voice steady. "The Armgo pair are but an added benefit."

"We will see," Matron Mother Quenthel replied. "But they are not nearly as important. Do you know why you were sent on your journey?"

"No." The hesitance in Tsabrak's voice was palpable.

"I do," Matron Mother Quenthel assured him. She offered a smile, but it was not a comforting one. "And know that you will be returning, and soon . . . once you are prepared." She moved to the door and pulled it open, then motioned out in the hallway adjacent to Tsabrak's quarters. In came Gromph, and Tsabrak bowed before the archmage. As he rose, Gromph's companion entered the room, and Tsabrak's eyes went wide.

He did well not to scream out, which was the expected reaction of anyone when an illithid walked into his bedroom.

"You're a blessed one, Tsabrak," Matron Mother Quenthel explained. "You will do your family great honor. I expect that you will return to this city of Q'Xorlarrin and be awarded a place of high honor—perhaps even as Archmage of Q'Xorlarrin, yes?" She looked to her brother slyly. "A rival to Gromph?"

The old Baenre wizard scoffed at the absurd notion, and only because he understood the truth of this new incarnation of Quenthel did he resist the urge to magically melt Tsabrak before her then and there, just to prove a point.

"Methil will show you the way, and will instruct you how to enact the spell," Gromph explained to Tsabrak.

"Spell?"

"The Darkening," Matron Mother Quenthel said. "You are preparing the greatest battlefield of this age, for the glory to the Spider Queen." She nodded, then turned on her heel and left, but tarried long enough in the hallway to hear the first delicious screams of Tsabrak as the illithid sent its tentacles into his brain. Methil wouldn't truly hurt him, she knew—indeed, far from it!—but none could feel that intimate intrusion without a bit of screaming, after all.

Her soldiers and scouts had spied out every corner of the Q'Xorlarrin complex, and Matron Zeerith's children had done an impressive job of preparing the substructure of this ancient dwarven homeland to serve as a proper drow outpost—they would call it a city, but of course Matron Mother Quenthel would never let it rise to quite that level, that it might rival Menzoberranzan.

She didn't knock on the next door, but pushed right through, to find Saribel Xorlarrin, a minor priestess by all accounts, but one that Tiago had inexplicably decided to take as a wife.

Saribel stared at her in puzzlement for just a moment, then cried out "Matron Mother!" and fell to her knees.

"Get up, child," Matron Mother Quenthel said.

As Saribel rose, Quenthel cupped her chin and forced her head up as well, that she could look her in the eye.

"I am returning to Menzoberranzan with my entourage," the matron mother explained. "I will leave only a few behind, including the illithid, who works with your uncle, Tsabrak. The creature is of no concern to you or any others."

"Yes, Matron Mother," Saribel replied, her eyes instinctively lowering.

Matron Mother Quenthel grabbed her more roughly and forced her to look up once more. "Tsabrak has work to do," she explained. "He will not be impeded. When he returns to the east, he will take as many of your contingent as he pleases. If he instructs any to join him, your sister or brother or even your mother, if Matron Zeerith is here before he departs, then so be it. His word will be followed."

"Yes, Matron Mother, I will go if ordered . . ."

"Not you," Matron Mother Quenthel sternly corrected. "No, you will gather Tiago and return to me in Menzoberranzan. Where is he?"

"He is out of the complex, on the surface with Ravel and others."

"I know that, you simpleton. Where have they gone?"

Saribel blinked repeatedly and seemed as if she was looking for an escape.

"Dear child," Quenthel said, and her tone made it a clear threat.

"They had word of enemies," Saribel blurted, "in a small city of humans and dwarves, not far. They have gone to eradicate . . ."

The matron mother blew an exaggerated sigh. "Impulsive children," she said. "When they return, you will gather up Tiago and return to me at House Baenre, immediately."

"Yes Matron Mother, but I am . . . I was left here to prepare the way for Matron Zeerith."

"You will gather up Tiago and return to me at House Baenre, immediately," Matron Mother Quenthel repeated slowly and evenly, her tone showing no room for debate.

"Yes, Matron Mother."

"Do not expect to return here," Quenthel Baenre warned. "Ever."

Saribel withered under those words and Quenthel's continuing glare, but she didn't dare argue.

"Fear not, child," Matron Mother Quenthel added with her knowing grin. "You will find a place of honor in a fine House of Menzoberranzan and that is no small thing. Perhaps you will one day sit on the Ruling Council." Even as she spoke the words, Quenthel thought them ridiculous, for Saribel Xorlarrin was hardly worthy of her surname. Even Matron Zeerith had little to say about Saribel that was not rife with derision. But still, Quenthel thought, perhaps having such a stooge on the Ruling Council would secure her a second vote on any issue she wanted. Her smile turned genuine for just a moment before she reminded herself that she was getting way out in front here. Too many things still had to be accomplished before any of this would come to fruition, with the first battle of words no doubt looming.

She had a surprising announcement to make, after all, when next the Ruling Council was joined, and even her allies at the table might take exception.

But she was moving along the path beautifully, Matron Mother Quenthel Baenre believed. With the addition of High Priestess Minolin Fey to the Baenre ranks, and Gromph's coming child, House Fey-Branche had been secured as an ally. The avatar of Lolth had confirmed the alliance, clearly, and the Fey-Branche family would never dare go against so obvious an imprimatur!

And now Quenthel found herself on the verge of diffusing the predicted battle between Andzrel and Tiago, to the satisfaction of both, and to the benefit, ultimately, of House Baenre.

She heard the continuing screams of Tsabrak Xorlarrin echoing down the hall when she left Saribel's chamber. She remembered when she had screamed like that, when Methil's tentacles had wriggled up her nose and into her brain.

If only she had understood then, as she did now, the beauty Methil had been imparting to her, the understanding of the millennia, the wisdom of her great mother, the clear vision of Lady Lolth's grand scheme!

Quenthel would welcome another intimate intrusion by the illithid if such a gain was to be found again. She suspected that Tsabrak would feel the same.

He was learning the spell now, perhaps the greatest spell a drow would cast, at least since Matron Mother Yvonnel Baenre had created the tentacles that had grabbed House Oblodra and torn it from its stone roots to drop the whole of the place into the Clawrift.

"The Darkening," she whispered as she moved along, and she wished that she could go all the way out to the east with Tsabrak to witness the beauteous spectacle!

She had only one more visit to make before heading home to Menzoberranzan, and she waited patiently in the hall, enjoying the music of the screams for just a short while until Gromph came out of Tsabrak's room, Methil close behind.

"Tsabrak is prepared?" she asked.

"Almost," the archmage answered. "He will scream again, but at least now he has come to understand that there is indeed a reason. Still, we will find some pleasure in his pain."

Quenthel smirked at her brother, who was indeed, she knew, finding great pleasure in tormenting Tsabrak. As much as Gromph tried to deny it, Quenthel suspected that there was a bit of trepidation and even envy within him regarding Tsabrak.

Or perhaps she just hoped there was.

The trio went to Berellip Xorlarrin's room, collected the high priestess, and traveled to the Forge, where goblins scrambled all around to supply the drow craftsmen as they worked their magic.

"I have heard much of this place," the matron mother said to Berellip. "Blacksmith Gol'fanin has told me that there is no forge upon Toril to exceed the heat and power of this one."

"He does not exaggerate," Berellip assured her, and she waved her arm out at the great Forge of Gauntlgrym, set in the middle of the long and narrow chamber.

"It is an oven. I do not need to view an oven," Matron Mother Quenthel said with a derisive chortle that set Berellip back on her heels.

"Show us the source of the power within those furnaces," Gromph explained, and the Xorlarrin priestess nodded excitedly and hustled to a small mithral door set back behind the main forge, halfway along the room's long side wall. Beyond it lay a narrow tunnel that had once been sealed with several doors, it seemed.

"Portals designed by dwarves to keep all others out," Berellip explained as they passed through one empty jamb where a door had been removed.

The air grew humid, then steamy; they could hear the sound of falling water, and an angry hissing noise in response. The tunnel wound for many paces before ending at another door, this one slightly ajar. Berellip pushed it open and led them through, spilling out into an oblong chamber.

A chamber that was alive with the power of the elements.

The chamber was cut, wall-to-wall, by a very deep pit, into which a perpetual waterfall poured from the ceiling.

"Do you feel it, Archmage?" Matron Mother Quenthel said, and she closed her eyes and moved forward, basking in the power of the primordial. With Gromph beside her, she moved to the edge of the pit and looked down at the bared power of Gauntlgrym, and even for the Matron Mother of Menzoberranzan, who knew best the beauty and grandeur of the City of Spiders, and even for the Archmage of Menzoberranzan, who had walked the planes, such a sight as this surely stole their breath.

They could not see the walls of the pit, for they were obscured by a spinning vortex of water, living water elementals forming the shaft prison for the beast far, far below. Through that spray and mist it loomed, the fire primordial, a living beast older than the dragons, older than the gods, perhaps.

NIGHT OF THE HUNTER

It was trapped but it was not still. Nay, the bubbling lake of lava popped and spat forth its fire and magma, vomiting them upward to fall against the watery wall of the spinning vortex, the endless battle between fire and water.

The two Baenres stepped back from the ledge and turned to look upon a beaming Berellip.

"This is . . ." the matron mother started to say, glancing around and shaking her head as if in disgust, which stole more than a bit of Berellip's bluster.

The matron mother stared her in the eye. "Why have you not prepared this room?"

"M-matron Mother?" Berellip stammered, hardly able to grasp the dangled concept. "The room is functional. Perfectly so. The forges . . ."

"Functional?" Matron Mother Quenthel snapped incredulously, and Gromph gave a little laugh. "This is not *functional!*" she insisted, spitting the last word as if it rang out as a tremendous insult to her sensibilities. "This is majesty! This is glory! This place, that beast, the elementals trapping it, are the reason Lolth has allowed your departure from Menzoberranzan. Do you not recognize that, priestess?"

"Yes, Matron Mother, of course."

"Then why have you not prepared this room?" the matron mother emphatically demanded.

Berellip's lips moved, but she said nothing, so at a loss as to even know where to begin.

Quenthel pushed past her impatiently, moving out to the center of the flat stone area and surveying the room.

"That tunnel?" she asked, pointing to a second exit from the place, just down the wall from the door through which they had entered. She could see that it was a natural tunnel, perhaps a lava tube, burned out from the stone. "Where does it lead?"

"To a back corridor, Matron Mother," Berellip answered.

"Seal it where it joins the outer corridor," Quenthel instructed Gromph, who nodded and started across the way.

"I will put up a wall of iron, but it may be dispelled," he informed her.

"Seal it," she said again. "And then the Xorlarrin craftsmen will construct more permanent walls to support your magical construct."

"This place!" Quenthel exclaimed, and then she began to dance, slowly turning, and she began to sing, an ancient song of the founding of Menzoberranzan for the glory of the Spider Queen.

Her twirls became more enhanced and rapid, her spidery gown flowing out wide from her slender form, and from that gown dropped small spiders, living spiders, that scurried away from her as if they knew their task.

For indeed they did. The song of consecration had brought them to life from the magical garments of the Matron Mother of Menzoberranzan, and that song told them.

Gromph came back out of the tunnel a short while later, his wall constructed to seal off the far end. Quenthel continued her song and dance. Spiders ran all around the ledge and up the walls, many already trailing their filaments.

Quenthel twirled around and then stopped abruptly, dramatically, her grasping hands cupping at the front of her shoulders, at green, spider-shaped brooches she wore. She tore them free of her gown, her song becoming a powerful chant and plea to the Spider Queen, and she threw those brooches out to the floor before her, where they landed and skidded and animated.

And grew.

"This is the chapel of Q'Xorlarrin!" the matron mother declared to Berellip, and now the jade spiders were the size of ponies, then the size of horses, then the size of umber hulks. One moved to stand beside the door through which they had entered, the other to flank the tunnel Gromph had sealed.

And there they froze in place, perfectly still, guardian statues.

"Matron Mother, we are blessed by your generosity!" Berellip said and she threw herself to the floor before Quenthel Baenre.

Quenthel ignored her and once more scanned the chamber, smiling as she saw the webs coming into being, the thousand little spiders working their magic.

"There is a chamber across the pit," Gromph informed her, and he led her gaze to the far end of the room.

"What is in there?" Quenthel demanded of Berellip.

"The lever of magic," she answered. "It controls the water to feed the elementals to hold the primordial, so Ravel has told me."

"A simple lever?" Quenthel asked, turning to Gromph.

"Simple to a dwarf of noble Delzoun blood, so Jarlaxle has told me," the archmage answered. "Impossible for any others."

"And such a dwarf might pull that lever to free the beast," Quenthel reasoned.

"Such was nearly the destruction of Gauntlgrym," Gromph explained, "The volcano that alerted us to this place many years ago."

"But if a dwarf king found the hallowed Forge under the control of the drow . . ." Quenthel remarked.

Gromph led her down the way to stand opposite the chamber, then enacted a magical doorway, a dimensional warp, that the two of them and Methil could step across.

"A simple lever," Quenthel said when they moved under a low archway into the antechamber.

"Let me complicate it, then," the archmage offered. He moved back under the archway and began casting a powerful spell, calling to the water.

When he came back into the antechamber, he led a large, flowing, humanoid construct created entirely of water.

"A proper guard, against any and all who would come in here," Gromph explained. "Except, of course, those who wear the insignia of House Baenre."

The matron mother nodded her appreciation.

Gromph signed his fingers at his illithid companion, and the mind flayer's tentacles began to wave and waggle around.

"Mark it?" Quenthel asked, having read his hand signal to Methil.

"When we decide to return here, would there be a better place to arrive?" Gromph replied, and Quenthel understood then that the archmage and his mind flayer had just magically attuned to this particular room for purposes of teleportation, both magical and psionic.

When that was finished, Gromph moved back under the archway and reconstructed his dimension door and followed Quenthel back to the ledge across the way.

"The Chapel of Q'Xorlarrin," she repeated to Berellip. "And that tunnel, I think, would suit well your matron as her private quarters."

"Yes, Matron Mother."

"Consecrate this ground with the blood of slaves," Quenthel instructed. "Feed the primordial beast with the flesh of our enemies."

"Yes, Matron Mother," Berellip eagerly replied.

So eagerly, Matron Mother Quenthel thought. On impulse, Quenthel lifted her arms out wide, tilted her head back, and closed her eyes.

"Lift your scourge," she told Berellip.

"Matron Mother?" the priestess replied with a clear tremor in her voice.

"It is fitting that my blood is first to seal the chapel. Lift your scourge!"

With trembling hands, Berellip complied. She didn't snap her snake-headed whip at the matron mother, but she didn't have to, for it was an instrument of Lady Lolth's wrath, and the snakes understood their purpose here.

They lashed and tore at Quenthel's skin, and she reveled in the glory of Lolth as her blood dripped to the stones. She began to twirl and to dance, and Berellip kept pace, her four serpents biting again and again.

After many steps and much blood it ended, and the matron mother cast a spell of healing to close her wounds, regain her strength, and neutralize the poison of Berellip's vipers.

Then she took her own five-headed instrument from her belt. Now it was Berellip's turn to dance for the Spider Queen.

Some time later, Quenthel, Gromph, and Methil left Berellip lying on the floor of the primordial chamber in a pool of her own blood. Dazed and disoriented, the priestess would surely die if she could not find the clarity to collect her thoughts and her powers enough to heal herself from the venom of Quenthel's vicious serpents.

In that tragic event, the matron mother figured, it would be the will of Lolth, and Matron Zeerith would have no one to blame but herself for raising such impotent daughters.

CHAPTER 12

NETS AND WEBS

Artemis Entreri twisted and turned, trying to upright himself before his descent. He had no idea what had hit him, and everyone around him, but only that they were all flying now, bounced a dozen feet into the air by the rolling ground.

He came around and saw his opponent similarly reacting. He glanced at the globe of darkness, behind him and to the side, and noted Brother Afafrenfère bouncing down then lying still along the ground beside the darkness globe now, and twisted around, having landed awkwardly.

This fight was over. He had no chance. He might defeat this noble drow of House Baenre, but to what end?

So he half-turned in his descent and landed with his legs already moving, sprinting back for the building down and to the right of the burning Stonecutter's Solace. He waved his heavy cloak out behind him as a shield against the hand crossbow bolts. He heard Tiago Baenre's protest.

"Coward!" the drow cried.

Entreri ignored him and sprinted around the edge of the building, sheathing his weapons as he went. He leaped and caught a handhold, and with exceptional strength and agility, spun himself up and over, throwing his legs above him and onto the low roof. He rolled over and came up in a crouch.

And saw again Tiago Baenre, floating in the air just beyond the roof's edge.

With an evil grin, the drow banged his sword against that translucent shield and stepped onto the roof. He lifted his blade in salute, bidding Entreri to come on.

The assassin glanced around, seeking an escape route. He could run, perhaps, moving to the lower sections of the city—surely the pursuit would become distracted by the many other targets . . .

Entreri shook the thoughts from his mind and focused instead on this one drow stalking him.

With a shrug, he drew his weapons and charged.

They came together in a blur of movement, turning and leaping out to either side, diving back in. Sword and shield met sword and dagger, blades ever turning and re-angling, particularly from Entreri who took great care not to let either of his weapons become entangled again in the web-like properties of that strange shield.

The combatants turned and rolled as readily as their weapons, each seeking an advantageous angle, for they were surely well-matched here.

Other dark elves rose up as spectators, levitating around the roof line. Somehow that spurred Entreri on, and he began to drop his trailing foot back just a bit more with each riposte and each turn. He wanted to win now, even at the cost of his own life. So be it, he thought, as long as he could bring this one, this Baenre, down before him.

But he was running out of time as Tiago's allies positioned around them, and as this young drow warrior, superbly skilled and trained, matched his every move. Entreri dropped his foot back just a bit more as he spun out to the left, coming around with a backhand that Tiago ably ducked.

And in came Tiago, clearly understanding Entreri's desire to flee. The jeweled dagger flashed, taking aside the drow's sword thrust, but that thrust was merely a feint, Entreri realized, and he leaped up as the real attack, a sidelong slash of that shield, cut in at his knees.

He went up in a turn, and kicked out, but pulled short on the kick, his own feint, and let his leg fling out to the side as Tiago's sword vainly tried to catch up. And around went the leaping Entreri, and now his right leg came around instead in a circle kick, and the drow could not recover before getting Entreri's boot slammed into his face.

Tiago staggered backward. "Oh clever!" he yelled, his voice slurred as he spat blood.

"Get used to it," Entreri growled and came on. He pulled up short, though, and twisted around to avoid a hand crossbow bolt, diving in over Tiago's right shoulder and flying for his face. A click from the other side had him turning fast back the other way, and the second dart skipped past.

And in came Tiago with a shield rush, bulling toward him, and the drow's sword flashed out beside the blocker.

Entreri hit it with his own blade, and stabbed in behind it, and just over Tiago's shield, with his deadly dagger.

The drow ducked the thrust and lifted his shield to lift Entreri's arm, and the assassin felt the buckler grabbing at him, pulling at his clothes with its web-like stickiness. So Entreri didn't fight it, and instead pressed ahead, pressed into the shield and bulled into Tiago, driving him back and standing tall to drive him down.

The bite of a hand crossbow dart got him in that leading left shoulder. A second grazed his face, and as he fell down atop Tiago in a heap, he saw the other dark elves moving for the roof to intervene. More than spectators after all, he realized, and knew he was doomed.

He tried for the kill, desperately wanting to see Tiago's last breath before he breathed his own, but even caught by the sudden reversal and the surprisingly aggressive move, the drow noble proved up to the task of defending, keeping Entreri's dagger arm stuck and up too high, and working his sword in tight against Entreri's at the proper angle to keep the blades out to the side.

Entreri couldn't gain any leverage here, and he felt the drow noble wriggling out from under him even as he felt the drow poison seeping into his body.

Never in her experience had Dahlia felt the sheer power and magical strength contained with Ravel Xorlarrin's lightning web. It floated down over her and her son, chasing her to the ground, it seemed, as she transformed back from her cloak's crow form. Immediately, she drew forth her flail, slapping it together and straightening the whole in a single motion to have the fully reconstituted Kozah's Needle in hand, and she prodded up the end of that staff to catch the center of the descending lightning web.

"Fly away!" she heard Effron cry to her, and there was great fear in his voice, she knew, and she understood as soon as her staff touched the drow dweomer. The energy of the gathered storm crackled within her—her hair flew wildly.

The web descended, sparking and exploding, shaking the ground. Teeth chattering, unable to speak, Dahlia tried to cry out to Effron to take her hand, hoping that somehow Kozah's Needle would shield them both. She barely managed to glance his way out of the corner of her eye, and saw that he was a charred thing already, sinking to the ground.

And the explosions roared on all around her, the ground shaking, like a prolonged peal of thunder reflecting back and forth off canyon walls, and hardly dissipating.

More energy flooded into the staff, arcing around its length, stinging her hands, reaching into her. She felt her heart pounding. Her temples throbbed, the world seemed to go dark, black splotches racing across her vision.

But she held on, because to let go was to be consumed, to melt, as Effron had.

Effron! Her son!

Rage drove her back against the mounting force, a scream of denial deep in her mind. She clenched her jaw tightly to stop from cracking her chattering teeth, or biting off her own tongue.

And then it was done. The lightning web folded up, swirling above her once more as it seemed to be sucked into the end of her mighty staff. She couldn't contain the power; she felt as if the metal staff would simply explode, or if it did not, as if the sheer power of the drow magic would consume her.

She half-turned, half-fell, and in that movement saw Ambergris lying off to the side, propped on one elbow, staring at her dumbfounded, and had Dahlia been able to see her reflection in the eyes of that dwarf, she would have understood, for she seemed more a creature of lightning then than anything resembling an elf, with powerful arcs of magical energy streaming along her sides and limbs.

And Dahlia saw the female drider, staring back at her, lifting a club as if to throw it at her.

Dahlia threw first, desperately, Kozah's Needle flying like a spear.

It went in short, landing at the drider's spidery legs, but it didn't matter. The blast launched the abomination into the air, and sent a shock wave through the ground that made the street seem as malleable as a pool of water.

Ambergris went flying. The porch of the building rolled and buckled, and then the building itself collapsed as the wave rolled under it.

Dahlia felt herself lifted into the air. She saw the drider descending as she rose, legs curling under it as if melting under the sheer heat of the blast, face locked in the mask of a dying scream.

Out rolled the wave, up the hill to scatter the drow wizards and throw Entreri and Tiago into the air as they battled on the street before Stonecutter's Solace. It rolled across the street to send Yerrininae bouncing—and screaming all the while for his beloved Flavvar.

Dahlia came down awkwardly, twisting her ankles and knee, then falling hard to her face in the road. She managed to prop herself up enough to see Ambergris sitting in the road, dazed and battered. And it was Amber's expression of sudden shock and terror that told Dahlia that the other drider, the huge male, had come up behind her—an instant before she felt a blinding explosion around her head and went flying away into the darkness.

The sheerest denial drove Artemis Entreri. Up on the rooftop, turning and twisting with Tiago Baenre, stuck to the drow noble's shield, the wider world spun around. And in that panorama, Entreri saw Dahlia fall. The elf woman lay in the street before the towering drider.

Ambergris would fare no better, the assassin knew in that instant. The dwarf sat there, clearly dazed, the monstrous abomination closing in.

And so denial and anger drove Entreri. He managed to plant his feet and regain a measure of balance, and with a defiant roar, he rose quickly, taking Tiago with him, and spun around powerfully, throwing the drow aside. The stubborn shield let him go then and he staggered behind the falling Tiago.

But he caught himself quickly and reversed direction, sprinting for the far end of the rooftop.

Another dart hit him, then another, then a barrage, sticking him and stinging him and filling him with poison. His arms felt heavy, his vision and other senses suddenly dull, and he knew the drow noble would be close behind.

He dived down to the edge of the rooftop, or perhaps he fell, for his legs grew numb beneath him. He reached over, making as if to pull himself forward to drop to the ground.

But that wasn't the point. He hadn't run off with any thought of escaping, because he knew that he couldn't possibly escape.

But his dagger could.

He reached under the eaves of the roof, hooking his arm down and around, and tucked his dagger neatly in place, and then he did pull himself over and simply let go, crashing down to the ground.

He rose stubbornly and staggered away, cutting between other buildings, around corners, the drow's taunting laughter following him every step. Finally, thinking that he had done enough to throw them off the track of his prized weapon, Entreri stopped and turned to face the pursuit of Tiago Baenre.

The assassin was falling into darkness before the drow noble even caught up to him, the drow poison taking his strength and sensibilities.

He heard Tiago Baenre call to him—by name!—and that seemed a curious thing, a ridiculous thing, but he couldn't quite figure out why.

Dahlia felt the heat all around her, and the constant ring of metal on metal. She sensed that she was standing, but couldn't be certain, and she couldn't understand how that might be in any case, for she had no strength in her legs.

She felt something pressing against her cheek, like the flat of a sword blade, perhaps.

The elf woman opened her eyes and recognized the place at once, or at least realized that she knew this place, though she couldn't quite sort it out. She remembered the explosion in the street, Kozah's Needle releasing a tremendous burst of magical lightning. She saw again the drider female, curling up in charred death.

She winced as she remembered the explosion in her own head, then wailed loudly as she thought of Effron, her son, melting beside her. She had tried to save him, but to no avail.

"Welcome back," she heard, a familiar voice that brought Dahlia more fully into the present and the scene around her.

Never lifting her check from the metal strap on which it rested, she glanced to the side at the speaker, Artemis Entreri.

He was hanging in a metal cage, almost a coffin of banded straps, it seemed, pressing him tightly, holding him upright.

As was Dahlia's own cage.

"Caught again," she heard Entreri say, his voice hopeless and helpless, too far removed from caring to express any real concern.

They were in Gauntlgrym, Dahlia realized, in the Forge itself, strung up just a few feet from the floor. Goblin slaves moved around the various forges, carting wheelbarrows of scrap metal, carrying solid bars yet to be worked, while drow craftsmen stood by the trays and anvils, going about their work.

Dahlia tried to turn to face Entreri, but so tightly was she held in the cage that she really couldn't manage it. Her effort did cause the cage to swing and rotate just a bit, though, and before it turned back, she noted a third cage in the line, beyond Entreri's.

"Effron," she whispered, hoping against reality.

"Afafrenfere," Entreri corrected. "Though I expect that he's already long dead. He hasn't moved or made a sound in the hours I've been awake."

"They brought him here," Dahlia argued.

"To torment us, no doubt," said Entreri, and he finished with a grunt when a drow moved up behind his hanging cage and prodded him with a hot poker shoved between the slats. That same drow walked over to Dahlia's prison as well, and very casually laid the poker against her ankle.

How she screamed.

And none in the room, not goblin or drow, seemed to care.

When the pain had ended, she glanced back at Entreri, and managed to swing her cage once more.

He just shook his head.

He had been in a situation akin to this before, Dahlia recalled, a prisoner of the drow in their dark city of Menzoberranzan. He had told her some of the tale, and had hinted at parts far worse. He had told her that he would rather be dead than fall into the clutches of the dark elves ever again.

Dahlia could only wince as she considered that ominous warning, for she was an elf, the ultimate enemy of the drow.

She would be tortured to death, she knew, and likely her torment would last for years.

The four heads of Berellip Xorlarrin's whip rose and struck at the form in the cage, biting deeply into the legs of the victim, tearing his skin, but alas, Afafrenfere did not stir.

"Your friend is dead," Berellip announced to Entreri and Dahlia, walking over to stand where they both could see her. "He is the fortunate one."

She looked up at Entreri and grinned wickedly. "Bregan D'aerthe?" she said. "Do you have any more lies to add to your tale? It was they, these allies you falsely claimed, who informed us of your return."

Entreri didn't answer.

"We will learn where you have been these last twenty years, do not doubt," she said. "And then you will die. How that will happen is somewhat to your choosing. Tell me where Drizzt Do'Urden is hiding."

"I don't know," Entreri answered, and he glanced to the side as a pair of male dark elves moved up to Afafrenfere's cage, one fumbling with a ring of keys as if to remove the corpse.

The Xorlarrin high priestess laughed at him. "So be it," she said, then waved off the two male attendants. "Leave him! Let them bask in his stench, to remind them that they, too, will soon begin to rot."

Berellip turned to Dahlia. "Where are the rest of your companions?"

The elf woman steeled her gaze and tightened her jaw, and again, the drow priestess laughed, mirthlessly and wickedly, taking pleasure in pain and nothing more. Berellip turned and motioned to an attendant, who rushed forward bearing a basket, which he handed to the priestess.

Berellip upended it, and a blackened and misshapen head tumbled out to land on the floor. It didn't roll or bounce, but landed with a splat and seemed to flatten out a bit, liquid oozing from it.

"Your son, I believe," Berellip said, and despite her determination to give these wretched creatures no satisfaction, Dahlia screamed.

She could not believe how badly it hurt, seeing this child she had long thought dead by her own hands now truly dead before her. And so she cried and she hated the world all the more.

And the many drow in the Forge paused in their work to laugh at her.

<hr />

The forges did not go quiet, and when the drow craftsmen tired, other dark elves replaced them at their work.

Artemis Entreri hung there, half-conscious, half-asleep, exhausted and hungry, as the hours slid past. He was long past being bothered by the heat, or by anything. The drow going about their business, the goblins running to and fro . . . none of it meant anything to him any longer.

In the cage to his left, Afafrenfere hung limply.

To Entreri's right, Dahlia cried, softly now as exhaustion stole her volume.

That sound alone truly hurt him. He could accept his own fate—he figured he'd find a way to die soon enough and so be it—but for some reason he hadn't yet figured out, Dahlia's fate touched him profoundly, and painfully.

He wanted to go to her. He wanted to hug her and talk her through this newest violation. He wanted to get out of his cage if for no better reason than to dispose of that blackened, misshapen skull, to get it out of Dahlia's sight, to bring her some relief, perhaps, from the agony.

Many times did he reach out for the elf woman, his hand almost getting to touch her when she one time reached back.

But clever were the drow, of course, experts in torture and imparting hopelessness.

Their fingers could almost touch.

Her sobs whispered in his ear and echoed in his heart.

Jarlaxle had done this, he believed. Berellip had mentioned Bregan D'aerthe. Jarlaxle had once again sacrificed Entreri for his own gain.

But it made no sense to Entreri. Jarlaxle had rescued him from the curse of the medusa in the Shadowfell. To what end, then? That, and this?

He cursed the drow mercenary under his breath anyway, and glanced back at Dahlia.

All that he wanted was to go to her and try to help.

His feelings, so foreign, surprised him.

CHAPTER 13

THE COLD NIGHT FOG

I HAVEN'T EVEN ASKED HOW YOU FEEL," CATTI-BRIE SAID TO DRIZZT. They sat on some rocks at the edge of their encampment on a starlit night, the southern breeze warm for the season.

"About?"

"All of it," the woman said. "The turn of events, the return of—"

"How could I be anything but thrilled?" Drizzt asked and he took his wife's hand.

"But surely it is overwhelming. Have you even come to the point where any of this seems real?"

Drizzt gave a helpless little laugh. "Perhaps I am too busy basking in the joy of it all to care. I admit that there have been some fears—didn't Wulfgar tell us tales of grand deception along these same lines during his captivity with Errtu?"

"Is it all just a dream, then?" Catti-brie asked. "A grand deception?"

"No," Drizzt answered without hesitation. "Or if it is, I don't care!" he looked over at Catti-brie, to see her leaning back from him, her expression curious.

"Perception is reality," Drizzt explained. "My reality now is joyous. A welcome reprieve." He laughed again and leaned in to kiss the woman.

"So it is real," Catti-brie agreed. "But is it truly joyous to you?"

"Do you doubt my love?"

"No, of course not! But how overwhelming this must be. For the rest of us, returning was a choice, and for me and Regis particularly, our lives did not move on from that night in Mithral Hall when Mielikki took us away to heal our broken minds. The movement of time for us has been insignificant compared to the century of life without us that you have known, and even through the last two decades, we walked in our new life with the single purpose of rejoining as the Companions of the Hall. We knew what to expect—indeed, we strove for exactly this—but for you, it is a surprise, a dramatic bend in a road."

"The most welcomed surprise any person has ever known, no doubt," said Drizzt.

"Are you sure?"

He put his arm around her and pulled her back in close, side-against-side. "I have spent a century missing—all of you, but you most of all."

"That pains me," she said quietly, but Drizzt dismissed it with a determined shake of his head.

"No," he told her. "No. Your memory was sustenance and surely no burden." He gave a little chuckle and kissed her on the cheek to preface his next comment. "I tried to forget you."

"You make me feel so loved," she teased.

"Truly," he said in all seriousness. "When I battled orcs beside Innovindil, when I thought you, all of you, were dead, her counsel to me was straightforward. Live your life in the shorter spans of time of human lifetimes, she told me. To be an elf is to know and accept loss. And so I tried, and so, to this day, I failed. I tried to forget you, and yet I could not. You were there with me every day. I blocked you out and denied you. But alas."

He paused and kissed her again. "I have known another lover, but I have not known love again. Perhaps it was Mielikki, reaching into my heart and whispering to me that you would return to me . . ."

"You don't believe that."

"No, I don't," he admitted. "What, then? Perhaps we two were just fortunate to truly find love, and a bond that outlived our mortal bodies?"

"Fortunate, or cursed?" Catti-brie asked with a wry grin. "Were you not lonely?"

"No," Drizzt answered, again with surety and no hesitation. "I was lonely only when I denied you. I was lonely when I was with Dahlia, who I could not, could never, love. I was never lonely when the ghost of Catti-brie walked beside me, and the smiles I have known over the last century have ever been in connection with you." He glanced back over his shoulder, to look where Wulfgar, Regis, and Bruenor were exchanging tales of their adventures of the last two decades. Drizzt's expression grew curious when Wulfgar set a bucket of water down in front of the halfling, who shoved his head into it.

"Or in connection with them," Drizzt added with a smirk.

Catti-brie squeezed his hand tightly. "There is something strange with Regis," she said.

"Something that should concern us?"

"No, nothing like that. He had told me that he is as comfortable in the water as in the air, almost. Watch. He will keep his head in the water in the pail for a very long time—longer than the rest of us could hold our breaths if we followed one after the other into a second pail beside him."

Drizzt did watch. Regis kept his head submerged, but kept snapping his fingers, as if to keep time, perhaps, or just to let the others know that he was all right. Drizzt looked at Bruenor, standing over the halfling with hands on hips. The dwarf glanced back at Drizzt and shook his head in disbelief.

Many more heartbeats passed and still Regis remained underwater, snapping his fingers, seemingly without a care.

"Ain't right," Bruenor said.

"Was his father a fish?" Wulfgar asked.

"His mother, so he said."

"A fish?"

"Not a fish, but some ancestor . . . a *gensee* or somethin' like that."

After what seemed an eternity, Regis finally surfaced, and came up with a smile, hardly gasping or distressed.

"Genasi," Catti-brie said quietly to Drizzt as they turned back to the open night sky and the rolling terrain of the Crags before them. "He has genasi blood, so he believes."

"I don't even know what that means."

"Planetouched," Catti-brie explained. "Genasi are genies of varying elements, and rumored to reproduce with humans. I have never heard of a genasi-halfling offspring, but it is possible."

"Of the five of us, Regis seems the most profoundly changed, and not just physically," Drizzt said.

"Perhaps. Not as many years have passed for us as for you, but we have all been touched, profoundly, do not doubt. But doubt neither that he is Regis, the same halfling you once knew and loved."

"I speak of changes in outlook, and perhaps purpose, but not in character. Not so much."

"Is that your confidence or your hope?"

"Both!" Drizzt exclaimed and they both laughed.

"We've passed through death itself," said Catti-brie, as if that would explain everything.

Drizzt leaned back and put on a more serious expression. "I would think that such an experience would make you more averse to the possibility."

"Possibility?"

"Of death again. But yet you, all four, walk willingly into danger. We are chasing a vampire, and in a very dark place."

"And then to war, it would seem, and yes, willingly."

"Happily? Happily to your death?"

"No, of course not. Happily to adventure, and to whatever awaits us."

A cold chill came over them then, as if the wind had shifted to blow down from the snow-capped mountains in the north, and Catti-brie pulled Drizzt closer, and shivered just a bit.

A fog came up before them, and Drizzt looked at it curiously. The weather shift seemed abrupt indeed—how much warmth had simply fled the air?—but there was no snow, and no water that he knew of, so what had brought forth the fog?

The cold fog, he realized as it drifted closer.

The cold, dead fog.

"Always got a tale, don't ye, Rumblebelly?" Bruenor said with a laugh when the halfling finally resurfaced from the water bucket. "Can't ever be nothing regular about ye, eh?"

"I live to entertain," the halfling said with a polite and exaggerated bow, and as he rose, he shook his head vigorously, drying himself as a dog might, and splashing Bruenor in the process.

"Brr," he said as he did, feeling a bit chilly and attributing it to the bucket of water.

But Wulfgar, too, stood up and rubbed his bare arms and took a deep breath—a breath that showed in the air.

"Getting cold," Bruenor agreed.

Regis started to answer, but when he looked at the dwarf, or rather, looked past the dwarf, the words caught in his throat.

He saw the fog.

He knew this particular fog.

"What other tales ye got to entertain us then, Rumblebelly?" Bruenor asked with a wide smile. "Part fish, part bird? Can ye fly, too?"

Oh, Regis did indeed have a tale for him, but the halfling wasn't confident that Bruenor would find it entertaining. And Regis wished he was a bird, truly, that he could fly far, far away!

"Run," he said, his voice barely more than a whisper. "Oh, run."

"Eh?" Bruenor asked, not catching on.

Regis continued to look past the dwarf, and he shook his head slowly in denial as the fog behind the dwarf began to coalesce and take the distinctive form of a tall, emaciated man.

"Oh, run!" Regis cried out, falling back a step. "Bruenor! Behind you!"

Wulfgar rushed past the halfling, between Regis and Bruenor, roaring to his god. "Tempus!" he cried and he pulled Aegis-fang over his shoulder and let fly the warhammer in one motion. The missile spun right over the dwarf's head, for the barbarian had used the horn on one side of Bruenor's helmet and the horn stub on the other side to line up his throw.

"Hey, now!" Bruenor shouted in surprise, diving down. He came up and looked back just in time to see the hammer slam into the leering humanoid figure moving toward him through a ghostly fog. That fog intensified, as if flying out of the creature itself, when the warhammer hit.

If the creature had felt that hit at all, it didn't show it. It was as if it had become something less than substantial to accept the blow, the warhammer powering right through it, hardly slowly. The fog coalesced once more, the creature reforming as soon as the threat had passed.

"Rumblebelly, what do ye know?" Bruenor asked, backstepping toward the other two and veering to the side, where his axe rested against a stone.

"Ebonsoul," Regis stammered. "The lich."

The horrid creature drifted in, eyes shining with inner, demonic fire. Its emaciated, rotting face twisted and turned, shapeshifting, it seemed.

Wulfgar's hammer returned to his grasp. Bruenor grabbed up his axe and ran beside the man. Regis inched forward on the other side of Wulfgar, and all three stared, gawking, at Ebonsoul, all three unable to break the trance.

NIGHT OF THE HUNTER

All three horrified and transfixed.

This was the power of the mighty lich. It went beyond the normal, gruesome realm one might expect from an undead monstrosity. Ebonsoul's terror transcended garishness, and focused to the deepest fears of any mortal creature, to the most primal fear of death. In the lich's rotting face, an onlooker saw himself. Undeniably so. To gaze upon Ebonsoul was to peer into your own grave, to see your own inevitably rotting corpse, to see the worms burrowing into your eyes, wriggled into your brain.

That was the horror.

Regis could only think of poor Pericolo Topolino, sitting in his chair, scared, quite literally, to death. He recalled how the Grandfather's hair had turned white from terror. The aging halfling had looked beyond the grave, and like any mortal creature, had not relished the image and the implications.

Regis could truly understand now the formidable weapon of Ebonsoul.

He could understand the power of it, but understood, too, that he was not nearly as susceptible to it as Pericolo had been. Nor were his companions, for like him, Bruenor and Wulfgar had already passed through death. Bruenor had even looked upon his own rotted corpse in a cairn in Gauntlgrym, as Regis knew that his former body lay rotting under rocks in Mithral Hall, and Wulfgar's bones lay windblown on the tundra of Icewind Dale.

"Come on, then, ye rotten beastie," Bruenor taunted, and Wulfgar slapped the returned Aegis-fang across his open palm.

Ebonsoul stopped and stood up straight and tall, his thin arms lifting out to his sides, sleeves drooping wide to the ground, and crackles of lightning showing around his skeletal fingers.

"He's got tricks!" Regis yelled.

Bruenor leaped forward and Wulfgar lifted his warhammer to throw again, but both stopped as a black form flew in from the left side, crashing into the lich. Again the fog exploded from the undead monster, but not enough this time, and Guenhwyvar's pounce—of course it was Guenhwyvar—drove Ebonsoul hard to the side.

From the darkness behind came Drizzt, weapons in hand, pressing hard on the creature.

But Ebonsoul was gone then, just an intangible fog, and it swept as if driven by a hurricane in a sudden burst that landed the lich right beside Wulfgar. The barbarian and both flanking him cried out in surprise as Ebonsoul instantly reconstituted, his bony hand sweeping in to slap at Wulfgar.

Lightning crackled as the blow connected and the barbarian was flying then, lifted from the ground and thrown over Regis. He landed right at the edge of the encampment and pitched over a log he had earlier placed across two stones as a bench seat.

Across swept Bruenor's axe in response, but the lich was fog once more, and Bruenor overbalanced and stumbled forward when he hit nothing tangible. And then Bruenor went down hard as Guenhwyvar flew in through the fog and collided with him.

Regis saw the incorporeal lich coming for him. He called upon his ring, warp stepping just as Ebonsoul reformed, and now it was the lich's swing that hit nothing but air and with the halfling turning around behind him to stab Ebonsoul with his own dagger.

The halfling felt the press for a bit and knew he had stung the creature, at least, but that solidity melted quickly, as did Ebonsoul.

Now the fog blew away to the halfling's left, across the camp for the charging drow. Regis called out a warning, but Drizzt was already moving in any case. The drow ranger leaped into the air in a great spin, scimitars flashing out left and right, front and back, and repeatedly in a wild blur.

Ebonsoul came back to corporeal form before the drow, and those scimitars dug in, slashing repeatedly at reaching arms and at the robed torso.

But the lich accepted the blows in exchange for his own, an open hand that slammed into Drizzt and staggered him backward, and it was all the clearly dazed drow could do to hang onto his blades. He recovered quickly and fell into a defensive posture as the lich advanced.

And Drizzt dived, rolling as far aside as he could as a ball of fire appeared in the air above the undead beast, erupting into a line of fire that raced down hungrily upon the lich. Again Ebonsoul became a fog cloud, reforming almost immediately just to the side, and spinning around. Wisps of smoke rose from the creature's robes as it turned toward Regis and Bruenor, and toward Wulfgar, who was coming back into the firelight, staggering somewhat but ready once more for battle.

A forked lightning bolt reached out at the trio, and they scrambled and dived, cried out in stinging pain, and spun down to the ground.

Through the blinding flash came Guenhwyvar once again. From the side came another barrage of magic, arcane this time, as magical missiles swarmed into the firelight and stung at Ebonsoul. Only then did the lich seem to realize the presence of a sixth companion, a robed woman standing off in the darkness to the side of the encampment.

Ebonsoul melted to fog and rushed away from the springing panther, and Guenhwyvar burst through the insubstantial curtain and landed far beyond the spot, digging in her claws and chewing up the ground as she tried to quickly turn around.

"Me girl!" Bruenor yelled in warning.

Catti-brie knew Ebonsoul was coming.

She called to her goddess and brought forth a brilliant light all around her, then saw the incoming rush of fog and lifted her hands to meet it, thumbs touching, fingers fanned horizontally, greeting the reforming Ebonsoul with a fan of flames.

But the lich hissed through the magical fire and swatted Catti-brie aside, sending her into a roll. She came around with a spell on her lips, but was relieved when Wulfgar's hammer took Ebonsoul on the side of the head, staggering him. The huge barbarian charged in behind the throw, Bruenor and Regis close behind. And on came Drizzt from across the camp, blades rolling eagerly.

Ebonsoul was fog, then reformed, and Wulfgar went flying even as he caught his returned hammer.

Then to fog again went the lich, in a frenzy now, becoming corporeal in front of Regis, and dematerializing almost immediately as the halfling dived away and Bruenor turned in.

Lightning crackled around Catti-brie's fingers, but she didn't dare let loose the stroke of magic, for the lich was all around, near one companion, then another.

She thought she had a shot, but Ebonsoul swirled into fog once more and swept around a startled Bruenor, becoming solid behind the dwarf.

Bruenor grunted and rushed at Catti-brie as a clawed hand raked his back, and a thrust open hand crunched into the back of his neck and sent him flying forward and to the ground.

Catti-brie dismissed her spell, the crackling lightning dissipating around her. She searched her thoughts and recounted her spells and focused her attention at last upon a ring on her finger.

Drizzt came at the lich, blades whirling. But faster still was Ebonsoul, just a fog again, then reforming out to the side.

Drizzt turned to pursue, but found a stroke of black lightning instead, slamming him in the chest and throwing him backward, eating at his very life force. He still watched Ebonsoul, the lich becoming fog, the fog exploding all around as Guenhwyvar leaped through harmlessly.

Back and forth went the fog, darting all around the encampment, the lich reforming and striking, going away once more to strike again at a different target.

The four friends and Guenhwyvar tried to formulate some defensive posture, but Regis went flying, and then Wulfgar grunted and was driven to his knees, and Guenhwyvar roared in frustration again and again, always a heartbeat too late to the spot to rake at the undead monster.

And the companions were taking serious hits now, bruised and battered and bloody, and their occasional hits on the frenzied lich seemed to show little effect.

"Elf, take me left!" Bruenor ordered, right as Ebonsoul appeared behind him and whacked him across the head as he tried to turn, staggering him to the side.

Drizzt rushed in, magical anklets speeding him, but he had to turn aside, indeed dive aside, to avoid getting swatted by an outraged Wulfgar, who swung mightily at the lich. But alas, Ebonsoul was already gone.

They couldn't match the speed and power of this one, Drizzt knew. They all knew it, and it seemed more likely that they'd inadvertently kill each other before ever landing any solid blows on the monster. Out in the darkness, Drizzt heard Catti-brie chanting in an arcane language he did not know.

"Scatter!" Regis ordered. "We cannot beat him!"

But Drizzt didn't run, and he went at the fog, meeting Ebonsoul as the lich became corporeal, attacking furiously if futilely, but determined to keep the creature occupied, determined to give Catti-brie the time she needed.

"Drizzt, no!" he heard Regis cry out, and the words distorted in Drizzt's ears as he pitched through the air, swatted hard by Ebonsoul.

The fog pursued.

The lich returned right in front of the flight of Wulfgar's hammer, a desperate throw that would only narrowly miss Drizzt. Guenhwyvar soared in beside Aegis-fang, but again Ebonsoul became fog, hammer and panther flying through, and the fog rushed for Regis then, and the blood drained from the halfling's face as Ebonsoul came up fearlessly before him, and surely the halfling saw his doom in the monster's fiery eyes.

He stabbed out with his rapier desperately and repeatedly, and knew he was doing little damage, his pointed blade barely digging in. Ebonsoul ignored it, not even bothering to dematerialize, but instead determinedly reaching his clawed hands for the halfling thief.

"Come to me, little pirate," the lich said in a vocal tremor that shivered Regis's bones, and Regis nearly fainted away, and Drizzt cried out from far behind, and Bruenor, still on his knees to the halfling's left, called out for his doomed halfling friend.

As he swooned, Regis barely registered the distortion that came into Ebonsoul's watery voice, and it took him heartbeats to realize the visual weirdness as well, as the lich's face seemed to elongate as if it was being pulled backward like soft dough or Sword Coast taffy.

Ebonsoul reached for him, but the moving hands seemed to be getting no nearer.

And the lich was pulled back and stretched. Ebonsoul's expression became one of puzzlement, and the lich became a fog, as if trying to escape.

But the fog offered no escape, not this time, and it was pulled fast back the way it had come, rushing past the charging Wulfgar, past Drizzt, and out into the darkness.

Silence fell over the camp.

Guenhwyvar paced warily, turning tight circles. The four friends looked to each other, at a loss.

"Me girl," Bruenor at last breathed.

And as if on cue, into the firelight walked Catti-brie, one hand clenched in a fist and held tight against her breast, her other hand up and out before her, holding aloft a large gemstone.

"What did you do?" Drizzt asked.

"We could not beat it," Catti-brie answered in a whisper. "I had to."

"She caught it!" Bruenor howled, and he scrambled to his feet. "In the gem! Oh, good girl!"

"Catti?" Drizzt asked.

She looked up at him, and seemed as if waking from a trance. She guided his gaze to the phylactery and nodded.

"That was the spell for Pwent," Wulfgar interjected. "The spell the Harpells put in the ring."

"What'd'ye do, girl?" Bruenor asked, suddenly near panic.

"Saved us, likely," Drizzt answered. He turned to Catti-brie. "But what now? Back to Longsaddle?"

The woman considered the words for a long while, then shook her head. "On our way," she answered. "The lich is caught, his soul trapped within the phylactery. Ebonsoul will bother us no more."

"But you used the spell stored in the ring," Bruenor and Regis said in unison.

"And I have a scroll from the Harpells replicating the magic," Catti-brie answered.

"Ain't yer prison full?" asked Bruenor.

"That spell is beyond you, so you said," Drizzt added.

"I have performed it once, through the ring," Catti-brie answered. "I will find the power again. And the phylactery . . . we will find another. Or we can go back, if you choose, but didn't you say when we set the camp that we are close to Gauntlgrym's entrance?"

"Aye, we'll make the rocky dell soon after sunrise," the dwarf confirmed.

Catti-brie shrugged and looked to Drizzt, and the drow took the cue to glance at each of his companions.

"To Gauntlgrym, then?" he said. "Though I fear we'll have to destroy our old friend Thibbledorf Pwent where he resides instead of bringing him forth to accept the resurrection and true and clean death dealt by a high priest."

By the time he had finished talking, Catti-brie stood before him, blue mist snaking out of her wide sleeves, and she reached out to him with healing magic, soothing the bruises and cuts inflicted by Ebonsoul. She made her way around the four, casting warmth and healing.

It was a night of uneasy sleep for all of them, after that horrifying encounter, but they were out before the dawn anyway, and into the rocky dell soon after, as Bruenor had predicted. With the sun still high in the sky, they entered the tunnels and began their descent into Gauntlgrym.

CHAPTER 14

SO MANY MOVING PARTS

THE BAENRE ENTOURAGE MADE ITS WAY THROUGH THE TUNNELS OF the Underdark, but not directly back to Menzoberranzan as they had planned. On the matron mother's order, they moved out to the east, escorting Tsabrak on the first leg of his most-important mission.

The matron mother was not among the contingent when they set their daily camp, of course. Gromph had created an extradimensional mansion where the selected nobles of House Baenre could relax without threat. The illithid went to that refuge as well, and Tsabrak, too, had been given a room of his own. He was too important now to risk.

"I would have thought you more agitated," Quenthel said to her brother Gromph, sitting with him beside a glowing wall of artwork, whose colors shifted through the spectrum in a most pleasing display. Gromph created this distraction each night, to sit and enjoy a fine wine or brandy. This was no surprise to his sister. He did the same thing in Menzoberranzan. But she was a bit surprised at how content he seemed, and how peaceful the artwork appeared.

The old wizard looked at her curiously. "I am sure that the longer you intrude in my private quarters, the more agitated I will become," he replied and lifted his snifter of brandy in toast. "As pleases you, of course."

"We will leave Tsabrak soon," Quenthel announced. "He will finish this journey alone."

"The sooner I am away from the ambitious and sniveling Xorlarrin, the better."

"Then you are bothered," the matron mother said with a sly smile.

187

"Not in the least."

"Truly? Dear brother, does the coming rise in Tsabrak's stature not evoke a bit of fear, at least? Might it be time for a new archmage in the City of Spiders?"

"Replaced by a Xorlarrin, whose family has departed Menzoberranzan?" Gromph said rather incredulously.

"Would the elevation of Tsabrak not serve as a strong tie between Menzoberranzan and the fledgling outpost the Xorlarrins have created?"

Gromph laughed aloud. "Ah, dear sis—Matron Mother," he said, shaking his head as if it should be obvious. "Why should I fear this movement of Lady Lolth? Do I not have more to gain than you? Than any of the matriarchs? The Spider Queen seeks Mystra's realm, and of Lady Lolth's current ranks, that realm is better served by trained males, and best served by me."

"Or by Tsabrak!" Quenthel snapped back, her clear agitation showing the old mage that his reasoning had crawled under her skin.

"The illithid's tentacles will not find my brain," Gromph assured her. "Nor do I wish to cast this spell. It will not be Gromph channeling Lady Lolth under the open sky of the Silver Marches, and that, I assure you, is to Gromph's liking."

"Were Lolth to hear that—"

"She surely will!" Gromph interrupted. "I have just told it to her primary voice upon Toril. Willingly."

"And you do not fear her wrath?"

The archmage shrugged and took another drink. "I do as Lolth has instructed me. I do not try to hide from her, for what would be the point? She knew of my . . . feelings toward you when you were Quenthel—when you were *merely* Quenthel."

"How you plotted with Minolin Fey, you mean," Matron Mother Quenthel retorted. The archmage merely shrugged and didn't even try to hide his smile.

"And Lolth did not approve," Gromph said, "because she had other plans for you—plans that I executed upon her command. I am a loyal servant, and please, for both our sakes, do not ever confuse my apparent lack of ambition with anything more than greater ambitions I concoct on my own."

"What does that even mean?"

"It means, Matron Mother, that the Archmage of Menzoberranzan is Gromph, who has outlived all of his contemporaries. Those who think me old and near dead will find the grave before me, do not doubt, and any who try to usurp me will need more than a single spell imparted through El-Viddenvelp to do so, even if that spell is inspired by the Spider Queen."

The way he emphasized the illithid gave Matron Mother Quenthel pause. "Methil is your creature, so you believe."

"Prove me wrong."

"Methil was Yvonnel's advisor."

"The illithid is no longer controllable enough to serve in such a role."

"But he serves you?"

The archmage tipped his glass at his sister and made no move to disavow her of that notion.

"And Gromph serves the matron mother," she said with determination.

"Of course."

Matron Mother Quenthel left the archmage's chamber soon after, feeling a bit unsteady on her feet. Gromph's insistence that he had more to gain than she did echoed in her thoughts. She went to her own room and sat in the darkness, seeking the memories of her dead mother, seeking the insight she would need.

Quenthel Baenre had never recognized the relationship between the genders in Menzoberranzan as anything more than mistress and servant, and so Gromph's straightforwardness and cavalier, even imperious attitude threw her off-balance. But in the secrets of Yvonnel, the current Matron Mother Baenre again found her answers, and through those memories, Quenthel came to understand that, for many males and certainly Gromph, that matriarchal arrangement was less severe and formal than she had been raised to believe.

The Spider Queen valued her priestesses above all, there could be no doubt, and for the majority of Menzoberranzan's males, life was as it appeared. But there were exceptions: the Xorlarrin male wizards, the Barrison Del'Armgo warriors, Gromph Baenre, even Jarlaxle.

These individuals and groups simply did not fit the paradigm.

The matron mother came out of her meditation amused by the irony. With her increased stature and knowledge and power had come as well, that very night, a measure of sincere humility.

The archmage, her brother, was yet another of her weapons, and he was a weapon to be treasured . . . and respected.

He wasn't strong enough to stand by the time his captors collected him from his cage. They dragged him from the Forge to a side chamber bedecked in tapestries, rugs, and plush pillows. High Priestess Berellip Xorlarrin lounged there in luxury.

The two drow males unceremoniously dropped Entreri face-down on the floor, bowed to the priestess, and quickly departed, closing the door behind them.

When he realized that he was alone with the priestess, Artemis Entreri wondered if he could summon just enough strength to get his fingers around her throat.

"So we meet again, and again in my city," Berellip said to him.

He just lay there, unmoving.

"Get up!' she ordered, and when he did not move, the priestess threw a jug of water his way. It hit the floor before him and shattered, showering him with ceramic shards and splashing him with magically cold water. Despite his stubbornness, Entreri couldn't help but lick up a bit of that nourishing liquid. How good it felt on his parched lips and throat! His captors had been giving him food and water, but just enough to keep him alive.

The drow were so good at this cruel game.

Berellip's next move came as more of a surprise to the assassin, as she walked over to him and put her hand on his head, chanting quietly. A wave of magical energy rolled over him, bringing warmth and nourishment. He felt the strength returning to his limbs and the clarity returning to his mind.

"Get up," she said again, quietly and more threateningly this time.

Entreri propped himself on his elbows, then rolled back to a kneeling position, his joints stiff from standing motionless while propped in the metal cage, aching with every movement.

"A clever lie you told when last we met," Berellip said.

Entreri stared at her unblinking.

"Bregan D'aerthe, you said," she reminded him. "But it was not true."

"I spent many years beside Jarlaxle," Entreri said, his voice cracking and barely getting past his broken lips.

"Jarlaxle is irrelevant," Berellip said, and with a tone of authority that had Entreri thinking she knew something he did not.

"You remain alive for one reason—or perhaps for two," she went on. "The choice is yours."

"I am teeming with options," he whispered with sarcasm.

"One of your band was missing," Berellip said. "Where is he?"

"The dwarf is a woman, not a man," Entreri answered innocently.

"Not her!" the priestess snapped back, and she slapped Entreri across the face. "Where is he?"

Entreri held up his hands and wore a puzzled expression. "Two dead, two in cages, the dwarf absent."

"The sixth of your troupe."

"We are five."

"The drow," Berellip said. "Where is Drizzt Do'Urden?"

"Him again?" Entreri quipped.

"It is the last time I will ask you, while you live, I assure you," she replied. "But do not doubt that I can inquire of your corpse!"

"He is long dead," Entreri answered, "in a crevice in a glacier, far to the north. A decade and more now . . ."

The way he had answered, so casually and without any hesitation, clearly put the priestess off her guard. Her shoulders sagged a bit and she fell back a step.

"You dare lie to me?" she asked, her hand going to her snake-headed whip. She tried to sound confident, but her initial reaction had already surrendered her inner feelings, and the perceptive Entreri knew that his lie had struck her profoundly.

"You will tell us everything we wish to know," Berellip said.

"About Drizzt Do'Urden? Why would I not? I was never fond of the fool."

"Yet you saved him with your lie when last we met!"

"I saved myself," Entreri replied. His voice was growing a bit stronger now. "Would you expect anything less? And my tale was effective, you must admit, because only around the edges was it false. You knew me as Jarlaxle's companion, back in Menzoberranzan . . ."

"Are you half-elf? What magic keeps you alive? That was more than a hundred years ago, yet you appear as a human of perhaps forty years."

Entreri shrugged and laughed. "I am no elf. And the magic? I thought I knew, but alas, I was surely wrong."

"Then how are you alive?"

"You should ask Jarlaxle. Likely he knows more about it than I."

Berellip came forward then, smiling wickedly. She put her hand out to cup Entreri's chin and forced him to look up at her. "Once you pleased me," she said. "Perhaps again."

He didn't respond, and did well to keep the hatred out of his expression. But Berellip took a step back from him, walking away, then swung around suddenly, snake whip in hand.

And she beat him—oh how she beat him!—the serpents gashing his flesh, spilling poison into his veins. It went on for a long, long while, and Entreri was left squirming on the floor.

Several drow males appeared then, out of nowhere, as if they had been in the room all along, hidden under a dweomer of mass invisibility, perhaps. Two grabbed him by the ankles and dragged him away. He realized that much at least, as the whip's poison drove deeper into his sensibilities, pushing him farther from reality.

By the time he opened his eyes again, brought back to consciousness by the pinging of smithy hammers, he was back in his hanging cage, Dahlia sobbing quietly and pitifully off to his right, Afafrenfere slumped within the iron bands in a cage to his left.

The battered assassin nodded as he took in the scene. The drow priestess had just made a mistake, he knew.

She had given him purpose. He had no hope of leaving this place alive, unless it was to be dragged to Menzoberranzan as a slave once more.

But now he was determined to see at least one of these drow dead before him.

"Little Doe, oh my dear child," Tos'un said when he was at last reunited with Doum'wielle in the lower corridors of the Underdark. The Baenre entourage had broken away from Tsabrak, returning home to Menzoberranzan.

"What have you led me into?" Doum'wielle asked, her voice and expression a combination of terror, shock, and dismay.

That sad look and inflection wounded Tos'un more than he ever could have imagined. He was the son of House Barrison Del'Armgo, after all, a drow noble warrior of high standing among the ranks of the Second

House of Menzoberranzan, and perhaps the greatest warrior garrison of any drow House in the world.

Why did he care about his daughter, any more than the glory or trouble she would bring to him?

"What did you expect?" he asked rather callously. "Did I not teach you enough about the ways of the drow? Did growing up among our weakling cousins make you, too, weak?"

"Father . . ."

"Silence!" he cried and he slapped her across the face. "Are you drow or are you *darthiir*?" he demanded, using the drow term for the surface elves, and it was not a word spoken with any warmth at all.

"If I am *darthiir*, then I am dead," Doum'wielle replied.

"If you are *darthiir*, then you will beg for death," Tos'un was quick to clarify. "Do you think that Matron Mother Quenthel, or any of them, or even I, would suffer you to live—"

"Did you love my mother?"

"Love," the drow spat with open contempt. The question struck deeper than Tos'un would admit—even than he would dare admit to himself!—for yes, he had known love with Sinnafein. And yes, his time among the elves of the Moonwood was at first out of convenience, and for simple survival, but it had become more than that as the years had drifted past.

But for it to remain more than that now meant certain doom, Tos'un Armgo knew, both for himself and for his daughter.

"Love is reserved for the goddess," he instructed. "Your mother was my captor and nothing more. I took carnal pleasure from her as I could, and from that pleasure were you and your brother born. I could not leave her and her foul *darthiir* tribe, on my very life. But now, you have led me . . . home."

Doum'wielle stood perfectly still for a long while, digesting those words and the clear, callous spirit in which they had been offered. Her gaze lowered to Tos'un's hip.

"Give me my sword," she instructed.

"The matron mother told me to carry it."

Doum'wielle stared at him hatefully, imperiously. Tos'un could see the struggle within her, as clear as the one she had fought when trying to dominate Khazid'hea. Now she was trying to dominate her *darthiir* side, the soft elven weakness of Sinnafein's heritage and the environment of the Moonwood. She had to win this fight, Tos'un knew, and had to win it decisively and quickly, or she would become fodder for the torturers of Menzoberranzan, and perhaps would find continuing life as an eight-legged abomination.

"The sword is mine, fairly earned in blood," she said.

"As soon as the matron mother wills it, I will return it to you."

He noted Doum'wielle's blanch, and noted, too, that she was looking past him suddenly, and Tos'un spun around to find Matron Mother Quenthel standing right behind him.

"When we return to the east, should I allow Tos'un Armgo to lead the attack upon the Moonwood?" Matron Mother Quenthel asked with a sly grin.

"Allow me," Doum'wielle interjected, "that I might use the battle to purge myself of the weakness of my mother's heritage!"

"Doe, your place!" Tos'un warned, but Matron Mother Quenthel was laughing then, and seemed quite pleased.

"Give this child her sword back," she instructed and both Tos'un and Doum'wielle stared at her incredulously.

"At once!" Quenthel demanded, and Tos'un quickly unfastened his sword belt and handed it over to his daughter. As Doum'wielle strapped it around her waist, the matron mother moved very close to her.

"That was my brother's sword," she said quietly. "Sword of the great Dantrag Baenre, the greatest weapons master of his time." As she finished, she turned slyly upon Tos'un, as if daring him to disagree, for it was a source of great pride among House Barrison Del'Armgo to name the legendary Uthegental as the greatest weapons master of that era. Indeed, the rivalry between Uthegental and Dantrag had elicited whispers and argument in every corner of Menzoberranzan for centuries.

Tos'un, of course, did not openly challenge her assertion.

"Do you think it fitting that the sword of Dantrag hangs on the hip of an Armgo?" Matron Mother Quenthel pressed, and Tos'un swallowed hard.

"No, Matron Mother," he said quietly, and Doum'wielle whispered her agreement.

"Nor do I, of course," Matron Mother Quenthel said. "But it will be fitting when our Houses are joined anew in common cause. Walk with pride and consequence, both of you, for you are the ambassadors of the

Second House of Menzoberranzan, who will lead Baenre and Barrison Del'Armgo to a place of greater understanding."

"Matron Mother?" Tos'un heard himself saying as he tried to sort through that startling declaration. Lost within the wide web Matron Mother Quenthel had just cast was the reality that she was apparently now accepting not only Tos'un but Doum'wielle, a half-drow, half-*darthiir* in to her grand plans.

With a superior laugh, Matron Mother Quenthel spun around and walked away, rejoining Andzrel and the Baenre entourage as she took her place on her floating magical disc.

"Father?" Doum'wielle asked skeptically.

But Tos'un could only shake his head in confusion.

"It is a Baenre blade," Andzrel complained to Gromph as the two continued along to the east with Tsabrak's group. "To give it to a son of House Barrison Del'Armgo—"

"Is the matron mother's choice," Gromph coolly interrupted. He looked down on the weapons master. The two were not close and had never been, but their relationship had only deteriorated since Andzrel had learned that Gromph had played a role in helping Ravel Xorlarrin find the ancient dwarven homeland of Gauntlgrym, and that Gromph had been instrumental in making certain that Tiago Baenre, Andzrel's rival for the coveted weapons master rank, had represented House Baenre on that successful mission.

The old archmage looked at Andzrel with a mixture of pity and disgust, his expression purposely conveying both. "There are many moving parts," he said. "The matron mother sees them and puts them into proper play, and she does not yet see many others."

"But you do?" Andzrel asked with a derisive chortle.

"Why, yes," Gromph matter-of-factly answered.

"Do enlighten me."

"Hardly," Gromph replied. "Your ignorance amuses me. I will offer you this, however: Tiago will not challenge you as Weapons Master of House Baenre."

That startling revelation set Andzrel back on his heels, for he knew that Matron Mother Quenthel had instructed Saribel Xorlarrin to return to Menzoberranzan with Tiago posthaste. Andzrel had assumed that the brash young warrior, grandson of the famed Dantrag and armed with a new, and by all accounts fabulous shield and sword, would make his play for House weapons master quickly.

"He will remain with the Xorlarrins?"

"No."

Andzrel looked at the cryptic old mage curiously.

"Too many moving parts for you to comprehend," Gromph explained. "Tiago will be well-rewarded, but not as the Weapons Master of House Baenre, a position that is far too mundane at this time to waste his talents upon."

The clever insult elicited a wince from Andzrel, but just a small one, and one that could not hold against the obvious relief Gromph's news had brought.

And that had ever been this one's limitation, Gromph recognized clearly at that moment. Andzrel was thrilled at the prospect of not having to go against Tiago, a fight he knew he could not win, but so focused was this small-minded warrior on the issue at hand that he could never see the larger picture and, of course, the bigger threat to his position. Quenthel's own son, Aumon Baenre, would soon enough graduate from Melee-Magthere, and at the top of his class, of course, and the matron mother surely intended that he would soon thereafter become the Weapons Master of House Baenre. Tiago had never been seriously considered for that position by Matron Mother Quenthel and certainly wouldn't be now that Quenthel had rightly and properly assumed the mantle as Matron Mother Baenre, in heart, in mind, and in cunning.

No, she had other plans for Tiago and his new bride Saribel, Gromph knew, and those plans would include a more important position for Tiago.

Because unlike Andzrel, Tiago understood something more than the martial arts.

Tiago knew how to play the game of intrigue.

"Count yourself fortunate," Gromph said at length, "for you are to witness the Darkening, and it will be a glorious sight."

Andzrel looked at him curiously. "Are you not planning to see Tsabrak through to the surface?"

"No," Gromph answered, and he glanced back and waved to his mind flayer companion to catch up. "I have been out scouting this very morning. This is the final run to the surface, a few tendays hence, and the way is clear, and so I am done my duty here to Tsabrak. Stay with him and keep him safe—it should be an easy enough task."

He began to cast a spell, tracing the outline of a doorway into the air. "You are home to Menzoberranzan, then?"

"In time," was all that Gromph would answer, and he waved the illithid into the portal before him, then nodded to the weapons master and stepped through, coming out into the small antechamber in the primordial room he had previously marked for just this purpose. The huge water elemental remained in there, at its guard, and it rose up menacingly before recognizing the archmage and melting back away.

Gromph created a dimensional door that he and Methil might cross the pit, then led the mind flayer into the bending, narrow tunnel that would take them to the Forge, the ping of hammers echoed off the stones to guide their way

They crossed the Forge, drawing a few stares from goblin and drow alike, though of course none dared to hinder their passage in any way. Gromph noted the cages hanging, but took little interest in them at that time.

They exited into a large corridor lined with magnificent dwarf statues, and even though he hated the bearded folk profoundly, Gromph could appreciate the craftsmanship, and thought it a good thing that the Xorlarrin force had not desecrated these remnants of another age. He was heading for Berellip's chambers, but Gromph paused at a door along the way and listened with growing amusement. Without bothering to knock, the archmage cast a spell of opening and the door swung in, revealing a very surprised trio of dark elves.

Gromph swept into the room, Methil right behind. He found it curious that the highest-ranking of the three within, Saribel Xorlarrin, was the one who showed him the most deference, stepping back and politely bowing.

Yet the other two, her upstart and ambitious brother Ravel, along with the ever-upstart Tiago, seemed too agitated at the moment to even properly acknowledge the great presence of the Archmage of Menzoberranzan.

"I have been recalled to Menzoberranzan!" Tiago growled.

"The matron mother has use for you."

"But no, Archmage, it cannot be!" the young warrior shouted, and he slapped his hands together in frustration.

"We are so close now," Ravel explained. "We have captured his friends and dragged them here. They will tell us, and then the wayward rogue will be ours!"

"The wayward rogue? Drizzt Do'Urden again?"

"Yes!" the two young drow answered in unison.

Gromph wasn't sure where to take this. The matron mother had set many plans in motion, in Menzoberranzan and in the surface region known as the Silver Marches, and Gromph doubted that those plans included a showdown between Tiago and Drizzt, particularly at this delicate time.

"Take me to these captives," he decided, and shortly after, the five stood before the hanging cages in the great Forge of Gauntlgrym.

After a telepathic conference with the mind flayer, Gromph ordered Dahlia to be taken down, but the whole time, he continued to look at Entreri.

"Jarlaxle's old friend," he said to Tiago and Ravel, standing beside him. "A formidable warrior, as I recall."

"Not so formidable," Tiago replied.

Gromph turned to regard the vain young drow. The archmage wore a slight grin then, which Tiago did not understand, for Gromph was picturing this young warrior in combat with Drizzt Do'Urden, and expecting that Tiago would learn a bit of humility at the end of that one's curved blades.

Gromph turned his attention to Dahlia, who seemed as if she would simply fall over were it not for the two drow guards holding her up.

"Take her to a room where I might be alone with her," the archmage instructed and Dahlia was hustled away. "Well, not alone," Gromph corrected, looking at his illithid companion.

"What do you intend to do?" Tiago asked.

Gromph looked at him incredulously, letting him know how ridiculous it was for him to even question the archmage in such a manner. "Did you intend to torture her?" Gromph asked. "And this other one? Would you wound them and sting them until they told you what you desired to know?"

"The thought had crossed my mind," said Tiago.

"Then let it serve as a perfect illustration of the limitations of Tiago," Gromph said with a snort. "And of anyone who favors the blade over the greater powers."

Soon after, the stone walls of lower Gauntlgrym echoed with the horrified screams of poor Dahlia as Methil El-Viddenvelp intruded into her mind.

"You dare to spy upon the archmage?" Saribel asked Ravel from another room, where the Xorlarrin wizard had cast spells to magically and covertly intrude upon the interrogation of Dahlia.

"Silence," Tiago said to the priestess. "Let him do his work."

"It is the Archmage of Menzoberranzan!" Saribel argued. "If he detects—"

"Would you have us simply leave, as the matron mother instructed? Should I abandon this quest when the treasure is so near at hand?"

"When disaster is near at hand, you mean, if you intend to go against—"

"On the side of a mountain in Icewind Dale," Ravel interrupted and the other two turned to regard him. He seemed to be looking off into the empty distance, and Tiago and Saribel understood that the mage's senses were indeed far away: in the other room with Gromph, the illithid, and Dahlia.

"The Battlehammer dwarves," Ravel said. "She thinks Drizzt is with the Battlehammer dwarves under the mountain in Icewind Dale."

"We know the tunnels to take us there," Saribel whispered eagerly.

"It is not so far," Tiago added. "We can get there and be done with our task, then return triumphant to Menzoberranzan within any reasonable timeframe—reasonable even to the matron mother."

The door opened and Tiago and Saribel nearly fell over in surprise, although Ravel, who was not really there, continued his work. Great relief flooded through the young drow couple to see that it was Berellip come calling, and not some ally of Gromph.

"Icewind Dale, to the north," Tiago said to her, moving fast to shut the door behind her as she entered. "Dahlia reveals the way to Gromph's ugly pet."

Berellip looked from Tiago to Ravel curiously. "You are spying on the archmage?" she said with a gasp.

"Nay, we are done spying on the archmage," Ravel answered before Tiago could, the mage coming back from his clairvoyance and clairaudience dweomers. "And it was a fruitful exercise indeed."

"Gromph will destroy you with a snap of his fingers," Berellip warned.

"To what end?" Ravel asked, at the very same moment as Tiago insisted, "Not when I walk into Menzoberranzan with the head of Drizzt Do'Urden."

"You have found him?" Berellip asked, and suddenly she seemed interested. She moved in close, sitting opposite Saribel at the room's small table.

"When is your Matron Zeerith due to arrive?" Tiago asked.

"Two tendays, perhaps three."

Tiago grinned and turned to Ravel, who was similarly beaming. "Plenty of time," the wizard agreed.

Gromph Baenre and Methil learned much more from Dahlia that day than Ravel and the others had discerned, not that those lesser drow would have understood the startling revelations anyway. Gromph wasn't even certain that he understood it all, but in the greater context of the events all around them—the coming Darkening; the war Matron Mother Quenthel was determined to wage; a war for the glory of Lolth and the widening of her realm of influence to the sphere of the arcane; a war to wound the rogue Do'Urden and by extension, the goddess who had stood by him to pull him from Lolth's clutches—the important role of this miserable *darthiir* known as Dahlia had truly surprised him.

Gromph was not one to be surprised easily.

He left Gauntlgrym that day, with a word of warning to Tiago to be quick to Matron Mother Quenthel's call, and another warning to him to keep the woman Dahlia alive. Unbeknownst to the Xorlarrins other than Berellip, whom he swore to secrecy, Gromph did not take his companion mind flayer with him. Methil still had work to do here.

Gromph did not expect to see Tiago marching back into the Baenre compound anytime soon, for of course the archmage had recognized that the sneaky little Ravel Xorlarrin had spied upon him and likely knew some of what Dahlia had divulged regarding the last place she had seen Drizzt Do'Urden. Almost certainly, Ravel was even then plotting with Tiago to go and confront the rogue.

So be it, Gromph decided, for this was not his play, but the game of Lolth and of Matron Mother Quenthel. He would play his role as directed, and nothing more.

He was barely back in his chambers in Sorcere, Dahlia barely back in her hanging cage in the Forge of Gauntlgrym, when the Xorlarrin strike force, led by Tiago, Ravel, Jearth, and Saribel, set out on the hunt through the tunnels to the north.

PART THREE

THE RHYME OF HISTORY

Even in this crazy world, where magic runs in wild cycles and wilder circles, where orcs appear suddenly by the tens of thousands and pirates become kings, there are moments of clarity and predictability, where the patterns align into expected outcomes. These I call the rhymes of history.

Regis came to us just ahead of pursuit, a dangerous foe indeed. The rhyme of history, the comfort of predictability!

He is very different in this second life, this halfling friend of ours. Determined, skilled, practiced with the blade, Regis has lived his second life with purpose and focused on a clear goal. And when the lich arrived at our encampment that dark night in the wilderlands of the Crags, Regis did not flee. Nay, he called out for us to flee while he continued to try to battle the fearsome monster.

But for all of those alterations, the whole of the experience rang with the comfort of familiarity.

The rhyme of history.

I have heard this truth of reasoning beings mentioned often, particularly among the elves, and most particularly among the eldest of the elves, who have seen the sunrise and sunset of several centuries. Little surprises them, even the tumultuous events like the Time of Troubles and the Spellplague, for they have heard the rhyme many times. And this expected reality is so, particularly concerning the rise and fall of kingdoms and empires. They follow a course, an optimistic climb, an ascent through the glories of possibility. Sometimes they get there, sparkling jewels in periods of near perfection—the height of Myth Drannor, the glory of Waterdeep, and yes, I would include the rebirth of Clan Battlehammer in Mithral Hall. This is the promise and the hope.

But the cycle wheels along and far too often, the fall is as predictable as the rise.

Is it the ambition or the weakness of sentient races, I wonder, that leads to this cycle, this rise and fall, of cultures and kingdoms? So many begin beneficent and with grand hopes. A new way, a new day, a bright sunrise, and a thousand other hopeful clichés . . .

And each and every one, it seems, falls to stagnation, and in that stagnation evil men rise, through greed or lust for power. Like canker buds, they find their way in any government, slipping through seams in the well-intended laws, coaxing the codes to their advantage, finding their treasures and securing their well-being at the expense of all others, and ever blaming the helpless, who have no voice and no recourse. To the laborers they cry, "Beware the leech!" and the leech is the infirm, the elderly, the downtrodden.

So do they deflect and distort reality itself to secure their wares, and yet, they are never secure, for this is the truest rhyme of history, that when the theft is complete, so will the whole collapse, and in that collapse will fall the downtrodden and the nobility alike.

And the misery and pain will feast in the fields and in the sea and in the forest, in the laborers and the farmers, the fishermen and the hunters, and in those who sow and those who eat.

For the rhyme of history is a sullen one, I fear, ringing as a klaxon of warning, and fading fast into distant memory, and even to fable, while the new cankers burst from their pods and feast.

It need not be like this, but too often it is. It was my hope for something new and better, and something lasting, that led to the Treaty of Garumn's Gorge, a path I am coming to lament.

And so I should be despondent.

But, nay, far from it, for I have witnessed divine justice now, and am blessed in the glories of those things most valuable: the truest friends and family anyone could know. With open eyes and open hearts we go, the Companions of the Hall, and well aware of the rhyme of history, and determined that those sad notes will give way to triumphant bars and soothing melodies of hope and justice.

The world is chaos, but we are order.

The world is shadow, but we are determined to shine as light.

Once, not long ago, I had to coax my former companions to good deeds and selfless acts; now I am surrounded by those who drive me to the same.

For even the too-often dark truth of the rhyme of history cannot overwhelm the unceasing optimism that there is something more and better, a community for all, where the meek need not fear the strong.

We'll find our way, and those lesser rhymes will find discordant notes, as with this lich Regis dragged upon us, this Ebonsoul creature who thought himself beyond us.

For this was part of the play, and a part expected had we looked more carefully at our halfling friend, had we remembered the truth of Rumblebelly—that same Regis who brought upon us one day long past the darkness that once was Artemis Entreri (once was, I say!).

And so we now look more carefully as we tread, for with Regis, there is something about him—an aura, a mannerism, perhaps, or a willingness to take a chance, often foolishly?—that throws a tow-rope to trouble.

So be it; perhaps, as the old saying goes, that is part of his charm.

He drags the shark to its doom, I say.

—Drizzt Do'Urden

CHAPTER 15

THE HOME OF HOMES

WELL, ELF, IF YE GOT ANY IDEAS, NOW'D BE THE TIME TO SPIT 'EM OUT," Bruenor said to Drizzt as they stepped out of the mushroom cap boat onto the small muddy beach before the underground castle wall and open doorway of Gauntlgrym. The whole of this large cavern was dimly lit by natural lichen, and around the makeshift boat, even more so by a minor light spell Catti-brie had cast on a small stone that she had picked up before entering the long tunnel leading to this place.

Wulfgar held the craft steady with one strong arm, using his other as a railing to help his companions clamber out. As Bruenor moved to the front lip of the raft, the huge man easily lifted him over the remaining splash of water and deposited him on dry ground.

Shaking his hairy head, Bruenor glanced back at him. "As strong as ye was last time," the dwarf muttered.

"When I saw Pwent, in a cave long ago, he was rational," Drizzt replied to the dwarf. "Perhaps there remains enough of Thibbledorf Pwent for us to coax him along to a priest that will alleviate his pain."

"Ain't so sure o' that," said Bruenor. "Pwent was back and forth when I seen him, cheerin' and snarlin', sometimes the friend, sometimes the monster. He was keeping control, out o' respect for me and the throne I'm guessin', but just barely."

"I have the scroll," Catti-brie said as she, too, came onto the beach, guided and lifted by Wulfgar's strong hand. "And Regis gave me this." She held up a small sapphire.

"Not much of a prison, compared to the one ye caught the lich in," said Bruenor.

"Will it work?" Drizzt asked.

"It's the best I have," Regis answered, pushing aside Wulfgar's offered hand and hopping easily from the boat. He brushed the sand and water from his fine clothing, straightening his trousers as he went.

"Then if it needs to do, it needs to do," Bruenor decided.

The four continued to chatter as they moved along, but Wulfgar, taking up the rear, didn't join in, and hardly listened. With his great strength, he dragged the giant mushroom cap raft from the water and up onto the beach, then hustled to catch up to his companions as they entered the grand upper hall of Gauntlgrym.

This place was not designed like Mithral Hall, Wulfgar noted immediately, for its first room was huge indeed, unlike the myriad tunnels that led to any significant chambers in Mithral Hall. Conversely, Drizzt had described this first hall as the crowning jewel of Gauntlgrym's upper levels. Despite those obvious differences in architecture, the barbarian couldn't escape the sense of déjà vu, a feeling as strong as any memory that he had been an actor in this play before. He remembered vividly that long-ago day when the troupe had first entered Mithral Hall, when Bruenor had gone home.

Wulfgar felt a twinge at the back of his knee, a pain of memory alone, he knew, for the troll's clawed hand that had dug in there in that previous adventure had done so in an entirely different body.

But this place smelled the same to him, as if the ghosts of dead dwarves left a tangible scent, and his mind danced back across the decades and to that other place and time and body, even.

He shook the memories away, tuning back into the situation around him. Drizzt, Catti-brie, and Regis stood by the wall of the chamber just to the right of the door. Catti-brie had cast a greater magical light, illuminating the area more brightly, and Wulfgar noted an emaciated corpse, a woman's shriveled body, stripped naked and brutally torn.

Catti-brie blessed it and sprinkled some holy water upon it, and only in witnessing that did Wulfgar remember Bruenor's tale of his visit here, and the gruesome fate of the dwarf's companions. Catti-brie was making sure that this one never could rise in undeath, it seemed, though many months had passed since the drow vampires had slain her.

Wulfgar's gaze went to Bruenor, the dwarf moving slowly, almost as if in a trance, toward the great throne on the raised dais perhaps a score of long strides from the front wall. With a last glance at the other three and a cursory scan of the large chamber, the barbarian hustled to join his adoptive father.

"The Throne o' the Dwarven Gods," Bruenor explained when Wulfgar arrived. The dwarf was rubbing the burnished arm of the magnificent seat, stroking it as if it was a living being. "Thrice have I sat on it, twice to my blessing and once to be thrown aside."

"Thrown aside?"

"Aye," Bruenor admitted, looking back at him. "When I was thinkin' of abandoning our quest and puttin' aside me oath to me girl's goddess. I wasn't heading for Icewind Dale, boy, but heading home."

"Abandoning Drizzt, you mean," Wulfgar said as the other three walked up.

"Aye," Bruenor said. "I forgot me word and convinced meself that I was thinkin' right in turning aside the quest. 'For Mithral Hall,' I told meself! Bah, but didn't that chair there tell me different!"

"The throne rejected you?" Catti-brie asked.

"Throwed me across the room!" Bruenor exclaimed. "Aye. Throwed me and reminded me o' me place and me heart."

"Take your place upon it now," Wulfgar prompted, and Bruenor looked at him curiously.

"You believe your path to be true, to Pwent and then to your home," Wulfgar explained. "Do you hold doubt?"

"Not a bit," Bruenor replied without hesitation.

Wulfgar motioned to the throne.

"Are ye asking me to bother me gods so that I'm thinking I'm doing what's right?" Bruenor asked. "Ain't that supposed to be me own heart tellin' me?"

Wulfgar smiled, not disagreeing, but he motioned to the chair once more, for he could tell that Bruenor was more than a little curious.

With a great "harrumph," the dwarf swung around and hopped up onto the throne. He settled back almost immediately, and closed his gray eyes, and wore an expression of complete serenity.

Regis nudged Catti-brie, and when she turned to him, she saw that he was holding aloft another vial of holy water. "A dead halfling and a dead man, and a few slain drow vampires," he reminded her. "We've work yet to do."

"And all stripped naked," the woman agreed. "This place was looted after the fight."

That brought a large and audible swallow from Bruenor, who hopped down quickly. "Aye, and me grave and Pwent's grave sit just on th'other side of the throne," Bruenor told them, already heading that way. He stopped short as he came around the throne to views the cairns, however, and shakily stated, "Bless that old body o' mine, girl! I beg ye."

On that, Wulfgar moved around the chair to see the two cairns, both disturbed, obviously. He moved to the nearest, and grandest—Bruenor's own—and fell to his knees. He began arranging the bones back in order, but he looked back, and couldn't help but wince.

"What'd'ye know?" a concerned Bruenor asked. He hustled up to stand over the open cairn, then spun away with a snarl and stomped back to the throne.

The skull was missing, as well as the thick femurs.

Wulfgar went back to his work settling the remaining bones, then began replacing the stones. He felt a hand on his shoulder and glanced up to see Drizzt, smiling and nodding.

"Am I burying the past or securing the present?" Wulfgar asked.

"Or neither?" Drizzt asked back.

"Or merely honoring my father," Wulfgar agreed and went back to his task.

Drizzt moved beside him and similarly dropped to his knees, beginning his work reconstructing the broken cairn of Thibbledorf Pwent, though that grave was, of course, quite empty.

"Feelin' strange to see it again, even though I'm knowin' in me head the truth of it all," Bruenor admitted, walking up between the two of them. "That's me own body there—don't know that I'll ever get past that one bit o' truth!"

He growled. "What's left of it, I mean," he added.

Wulfgar glanced back at his adoptive father, and had never seen the dwarf so clearly flustered before. He thought of his own former body, turned to bone now out on the open tundra, no doubt, and wondered what he might think if he happened upon it. He made a mental note to do just that, to find the evidence of his former life and properly inter it.

Then he went back to his work on Bruenor's skeleton and cairn, gently and lovingly.

"You looked at peace on the throne," Wulfgar said absently as he went about his task.

"Aye, and ye named it right, boy," Bruenor replied, though he still held a bit of consternation and irritation in his tone. "Me course is right and the gods agree. I could feel it, sittin' there, I tell ye."

"And it didn't throw you across the room," the barbarian quipped.

Bruenor put his hand on Wulfgar's shoulder in response, and dropped his other hand on Drizzt's shoulder. "Me course was for me friends," he said quietly. "As a dwarf's road has to be."

They got the cairns back together, Catti-brie finished blessing the corpses strewn around the room, and then went to the graves to properly consecrate them.

"Put a glyph on it, too," Bruenor bade her. "That way when them thieves come back, they'll put their own bones next to what's left o' mine!"

Catti-brie bent low and kissed him on the cheek. "Probably just an animal," she said. "It is the way of things."

"Better be," Bruenor muttered, and Catti-brie began her prayer.

"So where do we go from here?" Regis asked when that was done, the day slipping past.

They all looked to Bruenor, who simply shrugged. "I didn't go deeper," he admitted. "Pwent and his beasties came to me last time, but not now, seems. Might be that we're showing respect, though—last time, he come to me to protect the graves."

"That's a good sign," Regis remarked.

"Aye, but like I told ye, up and down with him, edge of control," said Bruenor. "And it don't seem like he come back to protect the graves again after I met with him, since me bones were taken."

"I've been lower into the complex," said Drizzt. "All the way to the Forge, and to the primordial pit that fires it."

"Had to bring that up, eh?" Bruenor quipped with a snort.

"I have been back since that ill-fated journey," Drizzt clarified. "I know the way."

"Drow down there, lots o' them," said Bruenor. "Pwent told me so."

Drizzt nodded. "We go slowly and carefully, one room, one corridor at a time."

"Our light will serve as a beacon for drow eyes," Regis remarked, and he looked to Catti-brie, as did the others.

"I have nothing else to offer," the woman said. "You do not need it, nor certainly do Bruenor or Drizzt, but Wulfgar and I . . ."

"I will take the lead, far in advance," said Drizzt. "With Bruenor second and you three in a group behind." He pulled out his onyx panther figurine and called to Guenhwyvar. "Bring forth some light, as dim as you can, and shield it. Guen will stay with you. Be at ease."

The panther came in and the party started off, Drizzt taking the point position, far in the lead. He moved down one of the hallways leading from the grand entry hall, silent as a shadow, his lithe form pressed against every cranny and jag, and was out of sight before he moved out of range of Catti-brie's minor candle spell.

Melkatka was not a noble of House Xorlarrin, but this particularly cruel drow had garnered great favor among the noble family. Jearth, the House weapons master, knew his name and spoke to him with clear interest, and spoke of him often, from what he had heard of those other male warriors higher up than he among the family ranks.

It was his cruelty that so impressed, he knew. He was an instrument for them, and in a role he cherished. The whip he now brandished was not snake-headed, of course, for those were reserved for the high priestesses of Lolth, but it was a vicious scourge nonetheless, with several barbed hooks along its twin lashes.

Melkatka liked the feel of the weapon, and loved the opportunity now presented to him to put it to prolonged use. This art was a balancing act, he understood, and a delicious one at that.

The whip rolled up over his shoulder and snapped out, and the tough little dwarf yelped despite herself.

"Faster!" Melkatka shouted at her, and he cracked the whip again, this time drawing a line of blood behind the dwarf's right ear, and indeed nearly removing the ear in the process! She started to shriek, but bit it back, and fell to the side to one knee, growling against the bite.

A balancing act, Melkatka reminded himself. He couldn't disable these pitiful captives; they were needed for the mines! Indeed, they had only been kept alive for this very purpose.

The drow guard snapped the whip three times in rapid succession, cracking the air above the dwarf's head. "To work!" he ordered.

The dwarf looked back at him hatefully, and he relished the baleful stare. She tried to talk, to curse him no doubt, but all that came out of her mouth was garbled nonsense and putrid greenish-white foam. She was a spellcaster, this one, a cleric, and the dark elves knew how to deal with such creatures. For she had been cursed by the high priestesses, by Berellip Xorlarrin herself, and anytime the dwarf tried to formulate a word, her mouth was filled with the putrid, vomit-inducing poison.

She doubled over, spitting furiously to clear the choking, wretched foam. Then she staggered and fell to the ground, and Melkatka put his whip to use once more, coaxing her back to her feet, and back to the pick and stone.

The drow torturer was quite pleased with himself when he heard the ring of that pick against the rock wall once more, the tap-tapping mixing in with the cacophony of other mining implements ringing in these tunnels far below the Forge of Gauntlgrym.

Several new slaves had been brought in from the coastal city the Xorlarrins had raided, to join in with the goblin laborers. The drow craftsmen needed metal, lots of metal, for the hungry forges, and mithral could be found here, along with several other minerals, even adamantine. Work continued furiously along the lower chambers of Gauntlgrym, as the drow craftsmen fashioned doors and stairways and barricades—not with the finest metals, though, for those were reserved for armor and weapons. They were building a drow city here, and one settled around a primordial forge, one capable of fashioning the most wondrous weapons and armor. Melkatka fantasized about being awarded a new sword and mail shirt, and the hope drove his arm back and forward yet again, cracking his whip one more time at the poor little dwarf, who just grunted and dug her pick hard into the stone wall.

"Are they so sturdy that they do not even feel the blows, or so stupid that they do not understand that they are supposed to cry out?" another of the drow guards asked, coming over to join the expert torturer.

"A bit of both, perhaps, but no matter," Melkatka replied. "Tough hide will strip away with enough beating, and cry out or not, doubt not that she feels the bite of the whip."

The two shared a laugh at the dwarf's expense, but their titters died away quickly as they both noted a curious creature fluttering toward them:

a large bat—curious because they had not noticed any bats in this part of the complex before. And they were too deep for such creatures as the one approaching, for this one seemed the normal type of cave bat, if quite large, and not one of the types commonly found in the deeper Underdark.

It came toward them in a haphazard flutter, bouncing back and forth across the wide tunnel. Melkatka raised his whip while his companion drew out his twin swords.

The bat pulled up short, still a dozen strides away, then rolled over weirdly in mid-air, and strangely elongated as it came out of its somersault, growing legs, it seemed, that reached for the ground.

Then it was no bat, but a dwarf, dirty and stout, wrapped in ridged armor and with the most absurd helmet spike protruding from the top of his metal helm almost half again his height!

He landed with his feet wide apart, hands on his hips.

"Another slave!" Melkatka's companion said, then repeated the words in the common language of the surface, which most dwarves would surely understand.

"Nah," the dwarf replied and began a steady approach. "I thinked yerself might be making for a good slave," he quipped, throwing the drow's words back at him. "But I seen what ye did to the girl there, and so now I'm thinking not."

Melkatka raised his whip, while cleverly pulling out his hand crossbow with his free hand, and firing off his dart just as his companion dropped a globe of darkness upon the newcomer. Lightning quick, the drow torturer dropped his hand crossbow to the length of its tether and drew out his own sword.

His companion moved to the side, both dark elves intent upon the area of magical darkness.

Many heartbeats passed.

"He is down," Melkatka's companion said. "Well shot, brother!"

The two glanced at each other, then watched together the hand crossbow bolt that came spinning between them—from behind.

Melkatka started to swing around when the heavy gauntlet of the dwarf, who had somehow slipped out of the darkness and arrived behind them, backhanded him across the side of his ribs and sent him flying. He accepted the blow and turned and leaped with it, touching down lightly and quick-stepping to hold his balance, thinking to rush right back in at the surprising enemy. Indeed, he even managed a step that way.

But he was too focused on the newcomer, unaware that he had landed near the female slave. He did realize his error, but only for the instant until the blinding white flash of a miner's pick driving through his skull dissipated into the absolute darkness of a sudden and brutal death.

Amber Gristle O'Maul shook the embedded pick all around, not to extract it, but simply to feel its end mashing around inside her torturer's skull. She watched across the way as she did, to see the remaining drow battling furiously with the strange dwarf battlerager—for of course she recognized this furious fighter as a battlerager—who had come onto the scene.

Drow swords worked brilliantly—of course they did!—cutting in side to side against lifted blocking arms. And fine indeed was that ridged armor, Amber realized, for the dwarf's arms remained intact against solid hits from those magnificent drow blades!

The dwarf kept advancing, steadily and unbothered. Around went the drow swords, one coming in again from outside in, the other retracting and stabbing straight ahead.

And the dwarf became as insubstantial as fog, the stabbing sword hitting nothing tangible. With a yelp of surprise, the drow wisely turned and fled, but he had only gone a few strides when the dwarf reconstituted, just to the side as the fleeing drow passed, and despite the drow's quick turn and dodge, swords slashing in a frenzy, the dwarf came on with a barrage of punches. His short legs pumped furiously, driving him against the drow, driving the drow against the far wall.

The drow tried to scamper out to the side one way, then the other, but the dwarf cut him off expertly. No novice, this!

The drow struck out ferociously, one sword blocked by a grabbing hand that slid down the blade to cup the drow's hand, and with a deft twist of his wrist, the dwarf turned his hand over and slid his gauntlet spike into the drow's wrist and forearm.

The other sword got through, a solid slash atop the dwarf's shoulder, but if the battlerager was at all wounded, he didn't show it.

Nay, he just kept boring in, and when the drow retracted, he grabbed that arm.

The drow tried to hold him back, and tried to get away, but the dwarf methodically lowered his head and slowly pushed in. The helmet spike went against the drow's fine armor, and how the dark elf squirmed.

"No! No!" he pleaded.

The dwarf offered a soft whisper of "Shhh," in reply, his powerful legs continuing to drive him forward.

The drow went into a frenzy, dropping his swords and pulling his hands free to pound at the dwarf. But the dwarf bored in, the helmet spike finally pressing through fine drow armor.

The drow gasped and grunted, squirmed and continued to flail, but ever slower as the helmet spike slid into his chest and stabbed at his heart.

The spike was against the wall then, fully through the poor victim, but the dwarf kept methodically driving onward.

The drow fell limp and the dwarf finally came back from the wall, standing straight and with the slain dark elf bobbing weirdly, impaled atop his helm. Blood spewed freely from the impaled corpse, showering the dwarf.

Amber nodded eagerly at him, but her smile disappeared when the dwarf heaved the drow up, pressing him off the spike, and lifted his face to bask in—nay, to drink!—the pouring blood.

A long while later, he dropped the corpse to the ground, grabbed the drow by the hair, and dragged him along as he came toward Amber. She shook her head and tried to speak, which of course just filled her mouth with wretched foam.

"But aren't ye a lovely sight," the battlerager said when he stood before her, and he dropped the dead and drained drow fully to the stone and reached a bloody hand up as if to stroke Amber's face. She recoiled instinctively, only then fully grasping what it was that stood before her: an undead monstrosity, a vampire.

She tried to speak again, to ask him who he was, and simply spat out a line of wretched foam. How she hated these dark elves! And she almost wanted this undead creature to kill her then and there.

"Pleasant little lovely," the vampire said with a puzzled look and a mocking snort. He looked at her shackles. "I'd break ye free, but them drow'd get ye and blame ye for their dead." He paused, as if another thought had suddenly come to him, and the look that came over his face chilled Amber to the bone. "Might be another way, eh?"

His hand came up again, tenderly—and so discordant that movement rang to Amber, for the gauntlet was still liberally dripping the blood of his dark elf victim. She shuddered and shrank back, shaking her head and pleading with him with little mewling sounds.

The battlerager paused, his hand hovering near to her, his expression shifting through a myriad of emotions, from eagerness to puzzlement, to consternation and ending with a little, feral growl.

Amber sucked in her breath, swallowed a bunch of the putrid magical foam in the process, and vomited all over the ground between herself and the vampire.

"I'm lookin' that wretched to ye, eh?" the undead dwarf roared, and he lifted his hand as if to strike.

But he pulled back, shaking his head, muttering to himself.

Fighting his urges and his hunger, Amber realized.

And then something else came over him, and he looked off into the distance, up the tunnel and higher. He muttered something that sounded like, "The graves!" And he stomped his heavy boot. "Ah, ye thieving dogs! Ye let him be! Me king!"

He had gone mad, clearly, and Amber believed her life to be at its end, believed that this vicious creature would then tear her apart.

But he didn't. He ran off up the tunnel, but skidded to a stop and came running back the other way. Down went one spiked fist, driving hard into a drow corpse, and down hard went the other hand on the second corpse, like a gaffe hook pulling a fish up the side of a boat. A drow corpse tucked under each arm, the dwarf ran away, down the tunnel.

He came back a short while later, and Amber knew it was him, although he was in the form of a flapping bat then, and he went right past her without a notice, back the other way.

He had moved the bodies so that she could not be blamed for the murders, she realized.

The captured dwarf cleric fell back against the wall, overwhelmed and terrified. She slid down to the floor and sat there, crying. Spewing foam with every chortle, cursing the dark elves and cursing life itself.

And, at times at least, savoring the revenge, feeling again her pick inside her torturer's skull, with that thought in mind, she began digging that pick into the sandier areas of her limited run, obscuring the blood and brain matter.

NIGHT OF THE HUNTER

The three friends and Guenhwyvar, moving along at the back of the procession, turned a corner into a wide, straight corridor lined with doors on either side.

"Slow," Regis whispered, for with his lowlight vision, the halfling could see Bruenor down at the other end of the corridor, just out of their light radius, where this passage ended in a sharp right turn. The dwarf crouched and looked back, his hand held up to his approaching friends.

Regis looked to Catti-brie and Wulfgar and whispered, "Wait." He noted that Catti-brie had already stopped, and was already nodding her agreement. She had one hand on Guenhwyvar, and could clearly feel the tenseness within the panther. Guenhwyvar sensed something nearby, some enemy likely, Regis could see and Catti-brie could feel.

After a few heartbeats, they started off again slowly, moving toward Bruenor, who was still some twenty strides away. Once more, though, Regis held out his arm to stop the others as Bruenor swung around, coming fully into their corridor and throwing his back to the wall at the corner. Up came his axe, clutched tightly diagonally across his chest, the many-notched head resting on the front of his left shoulder.

He glanced back at his friends and smiled, then whipped around in perfect timing, his battle-axe sweeping across to cut down the first of the monsters charging out of the side corridor.

"Goblins!" Regis cried, recognizing the diminutive monster as it pitched over backward under the weight of Bruenor's blow, big flat feet shooting forward from under it.

Catti-brie slapped at Guenhwyvar's flank and the panther leaped away, brushing hard against Wulfgar, who had already started his charge. Wulfgar staggered under the weight of the collision, but stumbled forward anyway, right past a door on the left-hand side of the corridor.

And that door flew open behind him, and out poured more goblins, two abreast, war-whooping and waving their crude weapons. Another door down the corridor, just in front of the barbarian, burst open and still more poured out, shouting even louder.

Regis leaped past Catti-brie, landing solidly with a powerful step and thrust, his rapier stabbing the throat of the nearest creature. Up came his second hand, hand crossbow drawn, and he let fly into the face of the second goblin in the front ranks. The monster shrieked and grabbed at the quarrel, stumbling aside, then getting thrown aside by the one behind it as it pushed through to stab at the halfling with its spear.

But Regis already had his dirk in hand, and he caught the thrusting spear between its main blade and one of the side catch-blades.

"Aside!" Catti-brie ordered.

With a twist of his wrist, Regis snapped the end off of the crude spear. He feigned a counter, but complied with Catti-brie instead, enacting his prism ring magic and warp-stepping to his right, farther down the corridor, leaving the opening for his magic-using companion.

Up came Catti-brie's hands, thumbs touching, fingers fanned, and a wave of flames flew from her fingertips, engulfing the goblin clutching at its stabbed throat and the spear-wielder beside it, and the two behind them as well.

And in came Regis from the side, rapier plunging home once and again to finish off the burning creature in the second rank, then going out a third time with brilliant speed, catching the nearest goblin in the third rank before it ever even realized that he was there.

And Catti-brie was casting again, he heard, and a quick glance at her told him to hold the line back from her.

At the other end of the hall, Bruenor chopped down a second goblin, then blew aside a third and fourth in a single sidelong sweep. Four down already, squirming and dying, but the wild-eyed dwarf was far from sated, for behind those front ranks came larger creatures: hobgoblins and bugbears.

Bruenor Battlehammer hated nothing more than smelly bugbears!

But he hated the one coming in at him even more in that moment when it blocked his axe swing and countered with a heavy blow of its makeshift club—a club that looked very much like the thick thigh bone of a sturdy dwarf.

Bruenor accepted the hit, the bone slamming against his one-horned helm. In exchange he bored in on the creature and caught a handhold of its hide jerkin. It hadn't been a fair trade, of course, as the dwarf's ears were surely ringing, but he had to grapple this one and had to pull it back. For in flew Guenhwyvar, right behind the bugbear as the dwarf tugged it forward.

"Ah, no ye don't!" he said to the creature and to Guenhwyvar, warding her away from this one. He spun around and heaved the bugbear the other way across the hall. "Ye're mine, ye dog!"

The bugbear, much taller and twice as heavy as Bruenor, hadn't gone far, of course, and it howled and leaped for him, more than eager to grant him that wish.

Bruenor met the charge with his own fury, launching a series of short and powerful chops to drive his enemy back against the wall, his focus entirely on the bugbear, entirely on its weapon, entirely on his own decomposed leg.

And that was his mistake, he suddenly realized, for while he couldn't help but hear the cries and roars of Guenhwyvar's fury behind him, a second bugbear had slipped past the panther.

And now its spear slipped through a seam in Bruenor's armor, biting into the dwarf's back.

Wulfgar fully recovered from the brush of the leaping panther and turned his attention on the hobgoblins and bugbears spilling out into the corridor from the door in front of him.

He tried to make sense of the chaotic scene, but a couple of things struck him as curious. First, several of these goblinkin were not dressed in the typical hides or smelly sackcloth one might expect of such creatures, nor even in pilfered leather armor. No, they wore the fine dress of the dark elves, the smooth shirts and flowing capes and even the fabulous armor.

But even with that oddity clear to see, their demeanor seemed even more curious to Wulfgar. They had not burst out, as had the others, to leap into battle, it seemed, but rather to flee.

And so the first in line, a thick-chested hobgoblin of around Wulfgar's own height, seemed hardly even aware of the barbarian's presence and made a last-moment, too-late attempt to block the heavy swing of Aegis-fang, the warhammer shattering its ribs and blasting its breath away, and blasting the hobgoblin away to the ground.

A second nearby brute lifted its club to strike, but Wulfgar was too close and caught it by the arm with his free hand. He shoved it away and yanked it back, and then brutally a second time, and then a third, and in this last collision, the barbarian snapped his forehead into the hobgoblin's face, splattering its nose.

He hit the dazed creature with a second and third head butt, then threw it down to the floor before him, right in the path of a closing bugbear, which stumbled and lurched forward, putting its face right in the path of a swinging Aegis-fang.

Wulfgar leaped and called out to his god, landing with a determined stomp of his boot onto the struggling hobgoblin's neck. The mighty barbarian reached for his silver horn, thinking of summoning reinforcements from the halls of his warrior god. He held back, though, when he at last realized the reason for the commotion with this group. In the room through the open door, more monsters battled, though most seemed to want only to flee.

And in their midst swirled the scimitar dance the barbarian knew all too well, the brilliant spin of a martial display he had not witnessed in more than a century. Drizzt worked around a growing pool of blood, slicing through ranks of goblins, hobgoblins, and bugbears with wild abandon.

Wulfgar reminded himself to focus on his own pressing needs, and almost too late as a bugbear leaped in at him, sword raised above its head.

He thrust out Aegis-fang straight ahead, spear-like, with both hands, the heavy hammerhead thumping into the bugbear with jarring force. Not enough to stop the creature, but enough to buy Wulfgar the time he needed.

The barbarian dropped his shoulder and drove forward, under the cut of the sword, and as the bugbear tried to regain its interrupted momentum, it pitched right over the bent-over man.

Or would have, except that Wulfgar dropped his hammer and grabbed the tumbling beast as he came up fast, lifting the bugbear right over his head. He turned and flung it into the opposite wall of the corridor, into another door, actually, which exploded under the weight of the impact, leaving the bugbear sprawled in a tumble of broken wood.

The barbarian swung around. A pair of goblins leaped in at him, their spears thrusting, for now he appeared unarmed. Behind them stood another bugbear.

And in the room beyond, Drizzt fought one against ten, and any momentum the drow had gained with his obvious surprise assault seemed gone by then.

"Drizzt!" Wulfgar started to cry out, but his voice and his vision was stolen by a sudden flash of fiery light and a burst of heat that had him and everyone else in the corridor recoiling in shock.

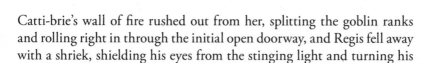

Catti-brie's wall of fire rushed out from her, splitting the goblin ranks and rolling right in through the initial open doorway, and Regis fell away with a shriek, shielding his eyes from the stinging light and turning his face from the heat of the roaring flames.

Inside the room, he heard the squeals of the goblins, agonized and terrified. Confident that Catti-brie had this area well in hand, the halfling stumbled farther along to join up with Wulfgar.

As his sensibilities returned, the halfling came to see his choice as a fortunate one. Wulfgar was in trouble.

Two goblins assailed him, and one had stabbed its spear right into the barbarian's huge left forearm. Grimacing against the pain, denying it, it seemed, Wulfgar used that arm as a shield, forcing the spear to stay out wide, while he fought off the second creature with Aegis-fang.

And directly behind that goblin, the bugbear lifted a club that looked to Regis very much like one of the missing femurs.

"Wulfgar!" Regis cried, charging ahead. A small snake appeared in the halfling's hand, and he flung it over the head of the nearest goblin and onto the chest of the tall bugbear. The serpent rushed up around the bugbear's throat, and before the tall and hairy goblinkin had even managed its swing, that leering, undead specter appeared over its shoulder, tugging it backward and to the floor.

Regis continued his charge, coming in fast against the nearest goblin, turning it aside from the speared barbarian with a series of powerful rapier thrusts.

The goblin parried and tried to counter, but Regis lifted its spear up high with his now two-bladed dirk, and rolled his opposite shoulder underneath the lifting weapon, rapier driving up at an angle, through the creature's diaphragm and into its lung and heart.

At the same time, Wulfgar turned to the side and rolled his left arm around the spear so that he could grasp its bloody shaft. Grimacing harder against the pain, the barbarian roared and swung around, using the spear as his lever to swing the goblin back behind him and send it slamming into the far wall. It crumbled to the floor.

Wulfgar didn't even bother to extract the spear at that moment, instead turning with the throw. Aegis-fang returned to his grasp as he turned, and he rolled the warhammer up high over his shoulder. The goblin popped up just as the overhead chop descended, the warhammer hitting the creature on top of the head with a sickening splat of bone and brain, the force driving its head right down into the cradle of its collarbones. Weirdly, the goblin sunk down on shivering legs, the blow so heavy that it tore one of its knees out of joint, and the energy rolled all the way down to the floor and back up again, the goblin bouncing right from the ground. It landed on its feet and somehow held that posture for a few heartbeats before tumbling over, quite destroyed.

"Behind me, Regis!" Wulfgar ordered, spinning around to face the open doorway once more, and the dark elf battling within.

Regis understood the command as a bugbear pulled itself from the pile of a shattered door, and the halfling was there in the blink of an eye, rapier jabbing at the hulking goblinkin.

"Down!" Wulfgar shouted to Drizzt, and he launched Aegis-fang as he yelled, aiming right for the back of his drow friend's head.

"Me leg!" the furious dwarf screamed over and over, bashing the pinned bugbear with his shield and short-chopping his axe all around the creature. He even stomped on its bare foot with his heavy boot—anything to inflict pain on this ugly beast that has dared to raid his grave.

He tried to ignore the burning pain in his back all the while, but futilely as the bugbear behind him drove its spear in farther.

Around swung the dwarf, suddenly and ferociously, so powerfully that his turn yanked the spear from the bugbear's grasp. The creature was still reaching for the weapon as Bruenor came around fully, rolling under and low with his shoulder, then springing up with a great uppercut of his axe that drove the blade up into the bugbear's groin.

And Bruenor growled, ignoring the fiery pain, denying it completely as every muscle in his body tightened with rage. He felt the strength of Clangeddin Silverbeard coursing through his powerful limbs. Up rose his axe, through the bugbear's pelvis, tearing skin and shattering bone. Then up went the bugbear as Bruenor drove on. Clangeddin roared inside the dwarf as the dwarf roared in defiance. Up and around went Bruenor, lifting the bugbear right over his shoulder and heaving it forward at the end of his axe to crash into the bone-wielder as that battered goblinkin tried to come forward once more to attack.

And in flew the dwarf behind the bugbear, leaping high, axe spinning up higher, to come down with a devastating blow that nearly chopped the spear-wielder in half.

Again and again, Bruenor's axe went up high and came thundering down into the bugbear tangle, severing limbs and gashing torsos, so that is was soon impossible to tell where one bugbear ended and another began.

The dwarf heard a roar behind him, but didn't turn, for he knew that call, Guenhwyvar's call, and it seemed to him one of power and victory.

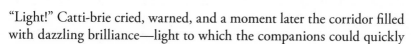

"Light!" Catti-brie cried, warned, and a moment later the corridor filled with dazzling brilliance—light to which the companions could quickly adjust but that put the goblinkin at a serious disadvantage.

Regis was about to call on his dirk for the second snake, but the rising bugbear grimaced against the brilliance and threw its arm up instinctively to shield its eyes.

In went the halfling's rapier, a series of sudden and powerful thrusts that dotted the bugbear's drow clothing with spots of blood.

Regis didn't need his second snake.

And as he continued his barrage of blows, easily finding holes in the bugbear's defensive shifts, scoring a hit with almost every thrust, he became convinced that he would never need such a trick facing up squarely against a monster such as this.

He thought of Donnola Topolino then, and their endless hours of training, as he marveled as his own precision and speed.

He thought more of Donnola, of their lovemaking and bond, and the notion that she was away from him stung him and angered him.

And the bugbear felt his wrath, one poke at a time.

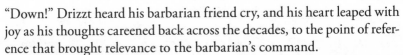

"Down!" Drizzt heard his barbarian friend cry, and his heart leaped with joy as his thoughts careened back across the decades, to the point of reference that brought relevance to the barbarian's command.

Fully trusting Wulfgar, Drizzt flung himself backward and to the ground. He hadn't even yet landed, the two bugbears in front of him rushing in to take advantage, when magnificent Aegis-fang flew fast above him, taking one of the surprised bugbears right in the chest and blowing it away.

Drizzt's shoulder-blades touched the floor, but up he came as if in a full rebound, his muscles working in beautiful concert to throw himself back up to face the remaining monster, and with his scimitars already leveled for the quick kill.

Down spun that bugbear, struck a dozen times, as the drow twirled off to his left, launching a wild flurry designed simply to keep the creatures there back from him, to buy him time. He noted a couple of clear openings in the meager defenses presented against his flashing routine, but he held back, confident that the odds were about to turn in his favor. With a knowing grin, Drizzt spun back around to his right, similarly driving back the monsters on that flank.

Even as he turned to face the new group, a goblin came flying past him, flailing wildly in mid-air. It clipped the weapon of the hobgoblin immediately facing Drizzt before bouncing far aside, and Drizzt used that distraction to suddenly step ahead with a killing thrust.

He retracted his bloody blade and launched it out behind him, then followed the backhand by turning with it, going around the other way once more, batting aside the spear and sword of a hobgoblin and bugbear, leaping above the spear thrust of a goblin, then managing to re-align his left-hand blade as he descended to slash a downward chop across that goblin's face.

He landed lightly and continued his turn, back the other way, to intercept prodding weapons.

And to smile as his old friend, his dependable battle partner, as Wulfgar charged in at the line. The hobgoblin down at that end turned to meet the barbarian, and saw its advantage.

And Drizzt smiled all the wider, knowing the deception all too well, and he continued his turn once more. Before he even came around to face the remaining hobgoblin and bugbear on that flank, he heard a heavy splat and the grunt of a dying hobgoblin behind him.

Aegis-fang had returned to Wulfgar's grasp. Drizzt had anticipated that, and the hobgoblin had not.

Drizzt could only imagine the stupid look upon the creature's face when it suddenly realized, as doom descended, that the huge man held his mighty weapon once more.

He felt Wulfgar behind him then, back-to-back, and this time he met his enemies full on and without regard for what was behind him. He parried the sword and spear with dazzling efficiency, his left-hand scimitar, Twinkle, rolling over the hobgoblin's spear once and then again, angling and turning on the second circuit so that Drizzt had the spear caught under one expanse of the scimitar's crosspiece and the in-turned bend of the weapon's curving blade.

At the same time, so independently that the drow might have been two separate fighters, Drizzt lifted Icingdeath at just the right angle to slide the bugbear's downward chop out to the side, and before the creature could retract and attack again, the drow quick-stabbed Icingdeath straight out.

It wasn't a heavy blow, of course, just a flick of the wrist, but the precision of the strike needed little weight behind it as it took the bugbear in the eye. The beast howled and fell back, leaving its poor hobgoblin companion straight up against Drizzt.

The hobgoblin roared and tugged mightily, but it needn't have, for Drizzt gave a subtle twist that released the spear even as the creature began its pull. And so the hobgoblin overbalanced and stumbled backward, and Drizzt closed fast with a leap, scimitars dancing and whipping around.

The drow landed and darted behind the hobgoblin, passing it on the left and going right behind, and before the creature could even react to the blinding dash, the drow came back around the other side, spinning into position right where he had been standing before the beast in the first place.

The hobgoblin stared at him incredulously, curiously, then its look grew even more puzzled as the truth began to dawn, apparently.

"Yes, you really are dead," Drizzt explained, and down sank the dying hobgoblin, stabbed and cut a dozen times.

The drow glanced back to see a goblin go flying at the end of a mighty swing of Aegis-fang. With a grin, Drizzt focused his attention on the remaining bugbear.

Still holding its bleeding eye, the beast turned and fled through a side door, and as it opened the portal and rushed through, Drizzt saw another bugbear, this one holding a curious item.

"The skull!" he yelled, pointing a blade at the heavy door as it slammed shut. The drow darted ahead and threw himself against the door, but it did not budge.

"Wulfgar!" he called, bouncing off and turning to face his friend.

Regis entered the room then, diving to the side to avoid getting bowled over by Guenhwyvar, who came in roaring.

Across the other way, Wulfgar let fly his warhammer at a retreating hobgoblin, catching it in the back of the head and pitching it headlong into the wall. In his other arm, the barbarian choked a second missile, a living missile, and he spun on Drizzt and lifted the kicking goblin up high.

Two running steps built momentum at the door and Wulfgar heaved the creature into it.

The iron-banded wood groaned under the heavy hit, but the door proved the stronger, and the broken goblin crumbled down at its base.

"Better key coming!" shouted Bruenor as he, too, ran into the room.

"Your skull is . . . !" Drizzt started to yell at him, but the dwarf cut him short with, "I heared ye, elf!"

Bruenor leaped into the air near Wulfgar, who half-caught and half-redirected him, putting his own strength behind the dwarf's momentum.

Bruenor tucked his shoulder tightly under his shield as he collided with the door, and this time, the portal exploded inward, the dwarf bouncing through, and bouncing right back to his feet to drive forward powerfully into two very surprised bugbears.

Drizzt started for the opening, but in the mere heartbeats it took him to arrive, all that remained standing within the room was Bruenor Battlehammer.

Drizzt skidded to a stop and grimaced. His friend's back was soaked in blood, and not the blood spraying about him as he repeatedly chopped his axe upon one or the other of the destroyed bugbears.

The drow looked to Wulfgar with concern, and only then realized that the barbarian, too, had not escaped the fight unscathed, and indeed had a piece of a broken spear sticking out of his left forearm, which, like Bruenor's back, was covered in blood.

"Where is Catti-brie?" he asked, and the words had barely left his mouth when a stroke of lightning flashed in the corridor beyond, the thunderous retort reverberating off the stones.

Right behind that blast came Catti-brie, calmly entering, seeming perfectly composed, and with strands of bluish mist curling out of her sleeves and around her arms. She looked past the three to the broken doorway and to Bruenor, coming back out of the side room, and holding a skull up before his eyes.

"An old friend," the dwarf said, somewhat sheepishly, although he tried to cover that with a snicker. Clearly, though, Bruenor was more shaken than he was trying to let on as he stared into the empty sockets that once held his own eyes.

Catti-brie beat Drizzt to his side, and began casting a healing spell immediately after glancing over the dwarf's shoulder to take a closer look at his wound. The dwarf grimaced in pain as she put her hand up against that deep gash, and against the remaining piece of spear that was stuck there, but he gradually unwound from that tightness as the waves of soothing magic brushed through him.

"Better?" Catti-brie asked.

"Ah, aye, hands o' magic," Bruenor breathed, and his eyes went wide and Drizzt gasped as Catti-brie brought her hand back over his shoulder, holding the large spear tip that had been sunk into his back.

"You'll need more spells on that wound," she said.

"Do 'em on our way back to me grave, then," Bruenor said.

"And Wulfgar, too," Drizzt added. "You three return to the cairn. Regis, Guen, and I will remain here so we don't lose any of the ground we have gained."

Bruenor and his adopted children set off immediately, skull and femurs in hand.

"We should scout out the area," Drizzt remarked.

Regis had other ideas, however. He reached into his magical pouch of holding and brought forth a large multi-layered and pocketed bag. He put it gently on the floor and began unwrapping it, revealing the pieces of his portable alchemy lab. He opened a large book, then, flipped to a marked page.

"That lichen," he said, looking up from the picture in the book to a patch of mossy green fungus at the base of the room's wall. "You go and scout and keep Guenhwyvar as relay. If you find any more of the lichen, gather it."

"For?"

"Many things, and probably many more I haven't yet discovered," Regis answered. He reached into one pocket and pulled forth a vial filled with a bluish liquid. "And here," he said, offering it to Drizzt.

The drow took it, looking at his halfling friend curiously.

"A potion of healing," Regis explained. "Good to have until Catti-brie is back, at least."

Drizzt nodded and started away.

"Fire protection," Regis said suddenly, turning him back. "The lichen, I mean. I think I can use it to finish a potion of fire protection, and if I'm to be marching beside Catti-brie, that is something I desire! She seems to favor the flame!"

Drizzt smiled and nodded, his hand going to Icingdeath, which similarly protected him, and his thoughts going to the ring he had given to Catti-brie that afforded her the same. He was thinking about the longer term implications, fitting pieces of the greater puzzle together to find even more harmony and power within the group.

He glanced one last time at Regis, who had buried his nose in his alchemy book and who was, obviously, musing along the same lines.

"Allow me," Wulfgar said.

Bruenor, still holding the skull, looked at him and hesitated.

"Please," Wulfgar added.

"Are ye sad that ye weren't there to bury yer Da the first time?" Bruenor asked with a wry smile as he handed the skull over.

"Just respect," Wulfgar explained. "Respect owed to you." He knelt beside the cairn and gently moved aside the stones.

"It is . . . sobering," Catti-brie said, standing back with Bruenor. She draped her arm across the dwarf's sturdy shoulders. "I wonder how I will feel when I return to Mithral Hall and look upon my own grave."

"Sobering?" Bruenor replied with a snort. "Feeling more like I could use me a bit o' the gutbuster!" He put his arm around his daughter's waist and pulled her closer.

Wulfgar put the femurs back in place first, then tenderly placed the skull. Before he replaced the stones, he stood at the foot of the grave, where Catti-brie and Bruenor joined him. As the woman consecrated the grave, Wulfgar and Bruenor lowered their eyes.

It proved a cathartic moment for this unusual family. They did not bury their past there, just their past differences, Wulfgar most of all.

When Catti-brie finished her chant, he pulled the woman close in a tight hug. "Ever have I loved you," he said, but there was no tension there in his voice or between them. "And now I am glad to be back beside you, both of you."

"I didn't think you'd leave Iruladoon to return to Toril," Catti-brie said.

"Nor did I," Wulfgar replied. "Curiously, I have not regretted my choice for a moment of the last twenty-one years. This is my adventure, my journey, my place."

"Will you tell me about your wife and children in time?" Catti-brie asked, and Wulfgar smiled wide and nodded eagerly.

"Two lives," he said as if he could not believe his good fortune. "Or three, as I consider the two sides of my previous existence."

"Nah, just the one," Bruenor decided. He stepped away from his children to the grave and kicked at one of the stones. He looked back at the pair, nodding as if in epiphany.

"What's in here's what's countin'," he said, poking a stubby finger against his chest, over his heart. "Not what's in there," he finished, pointing to the cairn.

The other two, who had passed through death, who also wore their second mortal bodies, could not argue that fine point.

CHAPTER 16

RESILIENCE

The DIMINUTIVE TIEFLING WARLOCK STRODE ANGRILY ALONG THE devastated section of Port Llast, his dead arm swinging behind him, his bone staff tucked up under his other arm. Often he used that staff for support, but not now, not with his blood on fire with anger.

They had taken his mother, if she was even still alive.

They had destroyed his band of companions, his band of friends. Some of the citizens had seen Afafrenfere down and dead. Some had seen Artemis Entreri dragged away. And Amber, too, poor Amber, hoisted upside down by her feet and jostled around like a plaything at the end of an enormous drider's ugly arm.

And Dahlia had been beaten—Effron had seen that with his own eyes. When the lightning net had descended, so had Effron descended, reverting to wraith form and slipping into a crack between the cobblestones, rushing down and along the ground, then up between the planks of a nearby building. Fortunately, he had gone to the opposite side of the avenue from where Dahlia's magical weapon had redirected the lightning web energy, and how proud the young warlock had been to witness his mother enacting such a mighty blast as that!

But he had witnessed the savage retribution of the male drider as well, and even in his two-dimensional form, the tiefling warlock felt his breath leaving him as that monster battered Dahlia about the head, laying her low.

And now she was gone. They were all gone, and Effron found himself alone.

He thought of the Shadowfell and Draygo Quick, once his mentor in what was once his home, but dismissed the thought with an angry shake of his head and a mutter of curses that had the many citizens moving about the disaster area looking at him curiously, as if he had surely lost his mind.

They were not far off in their estimation of his emotional stability, he realized as he took note of them.

Effron was indeed nearly insane with anger and frustration, and sheer hopelessness. He was alone now, two decades removed from his time—was Draygo Quick even still alive? And how far had the Shadowfell receded from the shores of Toril? Effron doubted he could even shadowstep back to that dark place, but he doubted even more that he wanted to.

Likely, he was an outlaw there, and would not survive for long.

He came up before the smoldering rubble of Stonecutter's Solace, the inn a complete ruin from the magical fires and thunderous lightning of the dark elves' assault. Many had died in there; almost a dozen bodies had been pulled out at last count.

All around him, the folk of Port Llast vowed that they would rebuild. These were hardy folk, resilient and stubborn, and their words gave Effron some comfort.

He could go his way now, he realized, free to roam as he saw fit, free to build a new life. He was a warlock of no small power, after all, and powerfully outfitted. With the bone staff he had taken from the skull lord in the Shadowfell, he could raise an army of undead to do his bidding, if it came to that.

"On my own," he said aloud, trying to bolster his own resolve.

But the words rang hollow, and their echoes were not welcomed in his thoughts, he found to his surprise.

"No," he said. "No."

He would go and find his mother. It would take him years, perhaps, but that was his place now, that was his guiding mission. He would find Dahlia and hopefully the others of their band, and he would destroy their captors.

Or he would die trying.

That last thought surprised him, but mostly because that last thought did not bother him. If he died trying to save Dahlia, then so be it.

"So be it," he said aloud.

"So be what?" asked a man near to him, and he turned to see that fellow and a companion regarding him curiously. "First the damned sea devils, now the drow! Is Port Llast cursed, do you think?"

The twisted warlock brought his staff out before him and tapped it hard against the cobblestones, feeling its resonating power, feeling his own inner strength.

"The world is a dangerous place," Effron said. "And that danger comes in all manners and enemies. Would you go to Waterdeep to be cut down by a highwayman's knife in an alleyway? Would you go to Baldur's Gate and be dragged off on a slaver's boat? Or would you build again, here in Port Llast, and be ready next time should these drow dogs return?"

"Well said, young one," the man's companion said with a courteous bow.

Effron nodded and walked away.

Yes, he decided, he would go and rescue his mother.

But of course, he had no idea where to start.

"You do not seem overly bothered by this turn of events," Jarlaxle castigated Kimmuriel when the psionicist at last arrived to his call in the empty back chambers of House Do'Urden.

The psionicist shrugged as if it hardly mattered. "Did you not expect that this would happen someday?"

"I expected that things would continue to progress, and splendidly, as they were."

"And you were miserable," Kimmuriel replied. "A most miserable clerk."

Jarlaxle was starting to answer before Kimmuriel had even finished, but he bit back his response as he more fully realized the prescience of the psionicist's remarks.

"Even that was better than this," he said in exasperation instead. "Show some respect, Houseless rogue, for you are in the presence of the Captain of the Guard of Daermon N'a'shezbaernon, more commonly known as House Do'Urden. Impressive, yes?"

"I am brimming with humility," Kimmuriel dryly replied.

"The returning army of House Baenre will enter the city this day," Jarlaxle explained. "And dear Matron Mother Quenthel has acquired a most interesting pair."

"The son of House Barrison Del'Armgo and his half-*darthiir* daughter, yes," Kimmuriel agreed.

Jarlaxle looked at him, shook his head, and blew an exasperated sigh. Just once he would like to surprise Kimmuriel with some bit of information!

"She will use this retrieved Armgo to strengthen the bond between House Baenre and Matron Mez'Barris Armgo, no doubt. Or she will find a way to twist the young Armgo's situation to her advantage over Mez'Barris. Either way, she is determined to strengthen her hold on the whole of the city."

"Matron Mother Quenthel has grown," Kimmuriel remarked.

"Yes, she has grown tremendously somehow— through the use of an illithid, I believe, though my information is far from complete. Gromph drags Methil El-Viddenvelp along behind him."

"Matron Mez'Barris hates Matron Mother Quenthel profoundly," Kimmuriel replied, and he did not seem surprised by Jarlaxle's information. "As much as she hates anyone alive."

"She is a matron of a powerful House," Jarlaxle reminded. "Her personal vendetta matters not. She will choose pragmatism over anger."

Kimmuriel nodded, hardly disagreeing. "There is one who hates the Matron Mother of House Baenre even more," he remarked. "One who long ago abandoned any thought of anything other than revenge."

Jarlaxle looked at him curiously.

"My mother," Kimmuriel explained.

"K'yorl? She fell into the Claw—"

"She was taken from House Oblodra before the wrath of Lolth destroyed the structure and given to a great demon as a slave."

Jarlaxle's expression did not change—this was all new information to him.

"Errtu the balor," Kimmuriel explained. "K'yorl Odran is its plaything, but she cares not. All that enters her mind for these many decades is her hatred of Matron Mother Yvonnel Baenre and Yvonnel's children, including the new matron mother. She is single-minded, I assure you."

"You speak as if you have met with her."

"In my own manner," Kimmuriel admitted. "There is more to this tale. Matron Mez'Barris entered into a conspiracy to release K'yorl upon the city, upon House Baenre, specifically. Archmage Gromph was part of that conspiracy, along with a high priestess of another House."

"Minolin Fey, no doubt," Jarlaxle reasoned. He considered the current situation and realized that the matron mother had severed that conspiracy rather neatly. He looked at Kimmuriel, still confused about how his compatriot could be in the know regarding so much interesting subterfuge of the spider's web that was Menzoberranzan, but then, suddenly, it all sorted out to him, and very neatly.

"So, Methil El-Viddenvelp is not as damaged as he seems to be," Jarlaxle said with a wry grin. "Not so damaged that the mind flayer cannot contact its hive-mind, perhaps."

Kimmuriel nodded in deference to the fine reasoning.

"So Quenthel is now more akin to Yvonnel, and far more formidable," Jarlaxle remarked. "And I am the captain of the Do'Urden garrison." He shook his head and snickered at the sound of that, repeating, "The Do'Urden garrison."

"Soon to be a noble House, seated on the council, no doubt," Kimmuriel reasoned.

"Replacing Xorlarrin, I expect," said Jarlaxle.

"And what is the place of Bregan D'aerthe in all of this?" asked Kimmuriel, but Jarlaxle could tell from the psionicist's expression and demeanor that he already had the answer, whatever Jarlaxle might offer.

"We will find our opportunity, and our way," Jarlaxle assured him. "There is a war coming—somewhere. There can be no other explanation for the machinations of the matron mother. She brings all others close now, and holds them fast as her collective thrall."

"She thickens her armor indeed," Kimmuriel agreed.

"There will be seams in that armor," Jarlaxle stated rather determinedly before he could catch himself.

Kimmuriel offered a wry smile at his outburst.

"I did not build Bregan D'aerthe to see it turned into a faction of the House Baenre garrison," Jarlaxle explained. He hesitated then, thinking that he would be wise to temper his words. But as he considered it, it didn't really matter, for Kimmuriel could read his thoughts as easily as listen to his words, even if the magical eyepatch prevented psionic intrusion. So flustered was Jarlaxle at that time that he was wearing his emotions openly.

"I will do as the matron mother commanded, for now," he told his co-leader. "But this is a temporary arrangement. I did not escape this wretched hole in the ground only to be pulled back in at the whim of my foolish sis—of the matron mother."

"Sister," Kimmuriel added. "And no, this is not a desirable detour for Bregan D'aerthe."

"So let us find the seams in my dear sister's armor," Jarlaxle offered.

"Mez'Barris Armgo already has discerned one," Kimmuriel replied.

"K'yorl?"

"Indeed. It was a Baenre, Tiago, who last slew and thus banished Errtu, and the balor will hold no love for that House."

Jarlaxle's smile widened so much that the psionicist apparently felt compelled to add, "Patience."

But of course, Jarlaxle thought, but did not say. He wanted Luskan back. He wanted Bregan D'aerthe back.

He wanted to see the stars once more.

And so he would, even if it had to be over his sister Quenthel's dead body.

CHAPTER 17

THE ORDER WITHIN THE CHAOS

THE EIGHT RULING MATRONS OF MENZOBERRANZAN GATHERED AROUND the spider-shaped table in the secret council chamber, with Matron Mother Quenthel Baenre and Matron Mez'Barris Armgo taking their seats at the ends of the longest arms of the arachnid.

Between them sat an empty chair, one that seven of the ruling matrons expected would be filled in short order.

But Matron Mother Quenthel knew better.

This council had been long-awaited, and indeed had been delayed longer than many had expected. Nearly all of House Xorlarrin was gone from the city now, and a few of the ruling matrons were surprised to see Zeerith Q'Xorlarrin in attendance and seated in the chair of the Third House to the right of Matron Mother Quenthel. Rumors had filtered throughout the city that Zeerith had already departed.

No matter, though, they all whispered, for surely this was the day of Zeerith's formal withdrawal from the Ruling Council and House Xorlarrin's formal withdrawal from Menzoberranzan. Their settlement in the dwarven complex once known as Gauntlgrym was going splendidly, by all accounts. Several Houses had already set up trading arrangements with the Xorlarrins, and indeed, some fine armor and weapons had already begun to flow back to Menzoberranzan, crafted in the primordial forge.

After the many obligatory prayers to the Spider Queen, led by High Priestess Sos'Umptu Baenre, Matron Mother Quenthel called the chamber to order.

Surprisingly, though, Sos'Umptu did not depart, as was the custom. She moved to the chair between the matron mother and Matron Mez'Barris and calmly sat down, a movement that clearly did not sit well with the Matron of House Barrison Del'Armgo, who squirmed in her seat and openly glowered at the Baenre high priestess, and then at Matron Mother Quenthel as well.

"You know why we are gathered," the matron mother began. "Matron Zeerith Q'Xorlarrin's expedition to the rediscovered dwarven mines has been quite successful and fruitful. By the will of Lolth, and as previously discussed in this very hall, it is time for us to rebuild that which was lost in the decades of tumult, in the War of the Spider Queen and the devastations of the Spellplague."

She looked to Zeerith and bade her to speak.

"The city of Q'Xorlarrin is prepared," the old matron said as she stood. "We secure the halls and the magical Forge of the dwarves is fired once more, its flames the hot breath of a captured primordial."

The declaration, though it was not news to anyone in the room, of course, brought a round of applause.

"Q'Xorlarrin is not an independent entity," Matron Mother Quenthel interrupted, stifling those cheers and drawing surprised glances from a few of the others, though the still-standing Matron Zeerith's expression did not change. All of this had been long-ago decided, in private, between the two, the others soon realized.

"You have your city, as you desired, Matron Zeerith," the matron mother explained. "And your autonomy—to a point."

Matron Mother Quenthel patted her hand in the air, bidding Zeerith to sit down, and when she had, the matron mother continued, "Q'Xorlarrin is a sister to Menzoberranzan, and will pay a tithe, mostly in the form of armor and weapons, machines of war, and the like. In its daily routines, Q'Xorlarrin is Matron Zeerith's own to rule, as she sees fit. But know this, my old rival, my old friend, my old enemy: In a time of need, Menzoberranzan will call upon you, and you will answer as we desire. In a time of war, your soldiers will march to the call, and under the banner of Menzoberranzan, and under the command of the Baenre garrison. Your prayers to Lady Lolth will confirm these truths. Are we agreed?"

Matron Zeerith nodded. "My family is humbled by the great respect and opportunity Lady Lolth has offered us. Q'Xorlarrin stands with Menzoberranzan, in peace and in war."

"You are our eyes to the World Above, and the implements of your master smiths will sound gloriously throughout the tunnels of the Underdark," Matron Mez'Barris added, and everyone in the room knew that she had done so merely to interject her voice into a discussion so clearly dominated by Matron Mother Quenthel.

These events were moving along without Mez'Barris's consent, without her opinion, even.

"Is it your decision to remove yourself to your settlement at this time?" Matron Mother Quenthel asked Matron Zeerith.

"Yes," she answered. "I will depart Menzoberranzan within the tenday."

"And so your seat?"

Matron Zeerith took a deep breath, glanced across the way to Matron Mez'Barris's left, at Matron Vadalma Tlabbar of the Fourth House, Faen Tlabbar, and Zeerith's most-hated rival. Then she turned to her own right, to Matron Miz'ri Mizzrym of the Fifth House, another hated rival. Zeerith stepped behind the chair and pushed it into the table, signaling that she was done.

"Be gone," Matron Mother Quenthel told her coldly. "No more is this your place."

Without a bow, without a salute, without a word, Matron Zeerith Q'Xorlarrin left the Ruling Council.

The other remaining matrons stared at Matron Mother Quenthel for guidance, and Quenthel understood their anticipation. Was she commanding ascent, where each would step up one rank to replace the vacated third seat? Or was she to leave it open, inviting someone, anyone, to try for the rank, which would likely result in a House war?

Or a third option, perhaps, a blend of orderly ascent and enjoyable chaos.

"Matron Vadalma," Matron Mother Quenthel said to the woman at Mez'Barris's right, and the matron mother indicated the open chair.

Vadalma Tlabbar rose and paced the long way around the table, so as to not walk behind her superiors, Baenre and Armgo. With a superior look to the others in the room, she pulled back Zeerith's seat and took her place as the Matron of the Third House of Menzoberranzan.

"Matron Miz'ri," Matron Mother Quenthel bade, and Miz'ri reversed Vadalma's course, taking Vadalma's former seat and rank.

And so it went for the next three, each matron ascending to the seat in the position immediately above their previous station, an orderly advancement for the fourth through eighth ranked Houses, elevating them to the third through seventh positions. When they were done, the seat diagonally across the table from the matron mother was left open.

Matron Mother Quenthel said nothing for a long while, letting the others consider the possibilities.

"Matron Prae'anelle Duskryn?" Matron Mez'Barris finally asked, referring to the Matron of House Duskryn, currently the Ninth House of Menzoberranzan.

"If Duskryn is awarded the Eighth House, who here believes that it will be a lasting arrangement?" Matron Mother Quenthel said with a wicked little laugh, and the other matrons joined in, for her words rang of truth. House Hunzrin was currently ranked eleventh in the city, but it was commonly conceded that Hunzrin could defeat any of the lesser Houses with ease, and likely a few of the ruling Houses as well. And particularly so with the new city of Q'Xorlarrin established, for House Hunzrin was a powerful economic force in Menzoberranzan, and with many channels outside the city, spiderwebbing out into the wider Underdark and even to the surface. Many in Menzoberranzan had been expecting House Hunzrin to make a move on the Ruling Council for years now, and only the web of alliances among the various other eight Houses had kept Matron Shakti Hunzrin's hand at bay.

House Duskryn had no such tight ties, and would easily be picked off by House Hunzrin should Duskryn be elevated to the Ruling Council, everyone seated at that table believed.

"House Duskryn is Ninth, and Matron Prae'anelle is prepared to take her rightful seat," Mez'Barris pressed.

Of course she did, Matron Mother Quenthel understood, for House Duskryn was a devout and fairly isolated clan, with few allies to protect it from House Hunzrin, and House Hunzrin's closest ally within the city was Mez'Barris's own House Barrison Del'Armgo. Both Shakti and Mez'Barris had one thing in common: their hatred for House Baenre. If Duskryn was given the title as Eighth House, Mez'Barris would force Shakti's hand from her preferred subterfuge and into a straightforward attack to land her on the Ruling Council.

"Matron Prae'anelle will find her seat accordingly," the matron mother explained, "as soon as there is an opening."

Mez'Barris began to ask the obvious question then, and some of the others shifted uncomfortably in their seats at the unexpected proclamation, but the matron mother turned to her left and nodded, and Sos'Umptu rose from the chair and marched around the table—pointedly behind Matron Mez'Barris—and took the vacant seat for the Eighth House.

"House Baenre will hold two places on the Ruling Council? This is your design?" an astonished Mez'Barris remarked.

"No," the matron mother curtly answered. "Sos'Umptu is no longer of House Baenre."

"Who has she joined? Will she begin her own? If so, the rank is far lower, by precedent!"

"By the will of Lolth, Daermon N'a'shezbaernon is hereby reconstituted," the matron mother declared.

"Daermon . . ." Mez'Barris echoed, hardly able to get the name out of her mouth.

"The cursed House Do'Urden?" scoffed Matron Zhindia Melarn, the youngest drow on the Ruling Council, and easily the most fanatical and rigid in her devotion to Lolth. "Apostasy!"

"Go and pray, Matron," the matron mother coolly replied to Zhindia. "When you are done, you will select your words more carefully."

"There is no precedent for this," Matron Mez'Barris added.

"There has been no time like this before now," the matron mother replied. "You have all heard rumors of Tsabrak Xorlarrin's journey to the east. The whispers are true—he goes with the blessing of Lolth, and empowered in her great spell, the Darkening. We will wage war in the east, on the surface, by the Spider Queen's demand, and we will wage that war in the name of House Do'Urden."

She paused for a moment to let that sink in around the table.

"Sos'Umptu, Mistress of Sorcere, High Priestess of the Fane of the Goddess, hereby relinquishes her position as First Priestess of House Baenre, to assume the seat as Matron of House Do'Urden."

Even House Baenre's allied matrons ruffled a bit at this seemingly obvious power play.

"It is a temporary appointment," the matron mother assured them. "In a House that will be formed through a cooperation of the other ruling Houses. Her patron, for example . . ."

She paused and glanced at a door at the side of the room, and opened it with a shouted command word.

Into the chamber limped a male drow of middle age. He measured his steps and kept his gaze to the floor as he moved to sit at the chair Sos'Umptu had vacated.

"To let a male in here!" Zhindia Melarn said, and spat.

"Are we agreed, Matron Mez'Barris?" the matron mother said, noting with an open grin the curious way in which the Matron of Barrison Del'Armgo stared at the unexpected newcomer.

"Do you not recognize your own son?"

"Tos'un," Mez'Barris breathed, and she turned a sharp eye upon Matron Mother Quenthel. But Quenthel matched her glare, and with a wicked grin that Mez'Barris could only take as a thinly veiled threat. There was something here, Quenthel's look clearly told Mez'Barris, that could embarrass the Second Matron of Menzoberranzan and her family.

"Are we agreed, Matron Mez'Barris?" the matron mother repeated.

"I will pray," was all that Matron Mez'Barris would concede at that point.

"Yes, do," said the matron mother. "All of you. I will accept your accolades when Lady Lolth has informed you that I am performing her will."

With that, she clapped her hands sharply, bringing the meeting of the Ruling Council to an abrupt end.

The six non–Baenre matrons hustled from the room, whispering in small groups regarding the startling turn of events. Quenthel noted that Zhindia Melarn only remained away from Mez'Barris's side until they reached the door. Quenthel knew those two would confer at length about this. Now they understood why Bregan D'aerthe patrolled the corridors of the former House Do'Urden.

Now they would complain, but they would take it no farther than that. Not at present, at least, with the Darkening imminent, as well as the war it portended. And not until Matron Mez'Barris came to fully understand the implications of the unexpected return of Tos'un Armgo, her son.

House Barrison Del'Armgo was not brimming with allies, after all, and a major embarrassment could bring the rest of the city storming their gates.

"It played as you anticipated?" Gromph asked the matron mother when she went to him in his room at House Baenre.

"Of course."

"I would have enjoyed witnessing the expression borne by Matron Mez'Barris when her long-lost child entered the chamber."

"You revisited Q'Xorlarrin?"

"I did," Gromph replied, though he left out any details, particularly his rather startling revelations concerning the surface elf, Dahlia.

"Tiago has returned with you?"

"No, but he will be along presently, I am confident, along with Saribel Xorlarrin, who will be his bride."

"Good, he has much to do."

"As Weapons Master of House Do'Urden, no doubt," Gromph remarked, and the matron mother looked at him curiously, then suspiciously, for she had not divulged that little bit of information to him.

"Logic could steer you no other way," the archmage remarked. "Aumon of your seed will supplant Andzrel in the hierarchy of House Baenre, of course, and I doubt you allowed Tiago those fabulous and ancient items forged by Gol'fanin that he might serve as a guard captain or some other meaningless position."

"Well-reasoned," the matron mother said, but her expression revealed that she still thought it too fine a guess.

"And the House Do'Urden wizard?" Gromph asked innocently.

"You tell me."

"Not Gromph, surely!" the archmage said. "I find my platter quite filled enough."

Matron Mother Quenthel stared at him, unblinking.

"Tsabrak Xorlarrin," Gromph answered, nodding with clear resignation at the inevitableness of the choice.

"He of the Blessing of Lolth," the matron mother replied.

"You hinted that he would be the Archmage of Q'Xorlarrin," Gromph reminded.

"A necessary tease. I will not afford Matron Zeerith any hopes that she can break fully free of us." The matron mother paused there and eyed Gromph slyly. "Does it concern you that Tsabrak will return to Menzoberranzan so soon after finding such glory in the eyes of the Spider Queen?"

"Lolth is a spider," the archmage quipped. "Her eyes can be filled with many such glories, all at the same time."

He wasn't sure, but it didn't seem to Gromph as if his sister was amused.

"I have already told you of my concerns for Tsabrak," Gromph said more seriously. "And those concerns are . . . none."

"We shall see," said the matron mother as she took her leave. "We shall see."

Gromph wore a grave expression—until he magically shut the door behind his sister. He'd allow her the illusion of an upper hand.

He could afford to, for she clearly had not sorted out that Methil El-Viddenvelp was not only imparting memories to her but was discerning her intent and feeding it back to Gromph. In essence, crafty old Gromph was using the mind flayer in the same way Yvonnel had used Methil to gain an upper hand in the chamber of the Ruling Council.

Quenthel was sharper than she had been before the interactions with the illithid, perhaps, and surely far more knowledgeable about the ways of Lolth's world.

But thus far, at least, she was no Yvonnel. Not yet.

After the ease with which Quenthel had dominated and manipulated Minolin Fey and Gromph at House Fey-Branche in the Festival of the Founding, Gromph Baenre found himself quite glad of that.

CHAPTER 18

A SLIGHT TASTE OF REVENGE

Hanging in his iron cage, Artemis Entreri didn't know what to make of any of it. Something had happened to Dahlia, obviously. Something awful, something perpetrated by that horrid mind flayer.

She wasn't crying about Effron. She wasn't tight with anger or pacing with excessive anxiety and frustration. She wasn't speaking, not even to answer Artemis Entreri's soft calls. She wasn't looking at him, or at anything, it seemed.

She was just sitting there, uncaged, unguarded, broken. She had one shackle around her ankle, chained to a metal ball, but it hardly seemed as if her captors needed it.

"Dahlia!" he called again, as loudly as he dared. He really didn't want to give any of the dark elves moving around the Forge any excuse to walk over and beat him some more—not that they really needed an excuse; many paused to and from their respective forges to stick him with a small knife, or a heated poker, or to toss some hot ash up toward his face, just to see him try reflexively and futilely to turn away.

The woman made no movement to indicate that she had heard him, or that she even cared to listen, in any case.

She was broken, perhaps beyond repair, he realized, and he couldn't deny, as much as he wanted to, that the thought of Dahlia's grim fate gnawed at him.

Gnawed at him and tugged at his heartstrings, more than he ever could have imagined.

Knowing where this would inevitably lead, Entreri tried to block out the train of thought, but he could not.

In his memories, he saw Calihye again, and he imagined her in Dahlia's place. She, too, had been taken by the dark elves, by Jarlaxle's band of Bregan D'aerthe.

Taken from him.

Had he really loved Calihye? To this day, he wondered, and for this man, who for most of his life was certain that love did not exist, the conundrum truly echoed through his thoughts. Perhaps he had loved Calihye, perhaps not, but surely his relationship with her was the closest he had ever come to knowing love.

Until now? Until Dahlia?

Entreri stared down at her from his cage.

This could not stand.

Very slowly and deliberately, Entreri manipulated his shoulders, twisting and turning and flexing the powerful muscles along his side until his left shoulder blade had moved downward, in effect shortening his arm. More turning and twisting and stretching at last brought his left hand into view.

He noted his exceptionally long thumbnail. He kept it that way on purpose.

He grimaced with the last painful twist, turning his arm practically out of socket so that he could turn it in around the outside of the cage and bring that fingernail to his mouth.

He sucked that thumb for some time, softening the nail with his spit, then he bit and slowly peeled, taking the top of the fingernail in one long strip.

Activity in the room forced him to twist the arm aside before he could put that nail back into his hand, so he used his tongue to tuck it deep to the side of his lower gum, out of sight and leaving his tongue clear in case he needed to speak.

Out of the tunnel that led to the primordial pit floated High Priestess Berellip, sitting comfortably on a magically glowing summoned disc. Entreri thought that surely meant he was in for another round of torture. But that diminished quickly when more notable drow came out of the tunnel right behind Berellip, including Tiago Baenre and the other Xorlarrin priestess in the second rank, followed closely by the House wizard and weapons master, the priestess upon a similar floating disc, the males all riding battle lizards.

And many others followed, all outfitted for battle, clearly, and with a contingent of driders bringing up the back of the long line.

Entreri considered their course, and traced them back to the chamber that had become, he had heard in whispers, the chapel of this new drow settlement. They had come forth with Lolth's blessing, then, and had come forth prepared to go to war.

They were marching out of Gauntlgrym again, Entreri realized, as they had gone to Port Llast. More prisoners, more slaves, more dead, more blood. It was the drow way.

They came very near to his cage and to Dahlia, and Berellip halted the march with an upraised hand and guided her disc to the side, hovering near the broken elf woman.

"*Darthiir*," she said with a sneer and shake of her head. "Know that I would pull your limbs off on the rack, were it my choice. And I would keep you alive and find more ways to wound you. I would give you hope, and then I would feed you to Yerrininae, and I would watch with joy the unspeakable things he would do to you for killing his beloved Flavvar."

"Priestess," Jearth dared to interrupt, and Berellip turned a sharp stare upon him. She didn't look at him for long, though, Entreri noted, but settled her glower at the male sitting beside her sister, the warrior Entreri knew to be Tiago Baenre.

A large bit of bluster left Berellip's features as she matched stares with the noble of House Baenre.

The archmage had told her to leave Dahlia alone, Entreri realized from that silent exchange. From his time in Menzoberranzan, Entreri knew well that few would dare cross Gromph Baenre. Even Jarlaxle offered that dangerous wizard more than a bit of deference. Despite the tight press of the cage, Entreri managed to cock his head to the side just a bit with curiosity. The archmage and House Baenre were protecting Dahlia?

The second disc floated closer to him.

"You should force Yerrininae to come with us," the younger Xorlarrin priestess said to Berellip.

"He is grieving—I did not know that driders were possessed of such emotions," Berellip answered.

"He hates the *darthiir* above all others."

"He will not disobey me," Berellip assured her. "Go now, to the glory of Q'Xorlarrin. Return to me with the head of Drizzt Do'Urden."

Him again!

After the initial shock, Entreri found an epiphany: none of this was coincidence. He and his friends had not been misfortunate in being in Port Llast when the drow had attacked. Nay, the drow had attacked *because* he and his friends had been in Port Llast. They were still obsessed with Drizzt, after all these years. Were they keeping Dahlia alive as bait, then?

That thought hit Entreri almost humorously as he recalled the last bloody meeting between Dahlia and Drizzt.

Almost humorously, for in his current predicament, he really couldn't find humor in much of anything.

Below him, Berellip waved her sister back to Tiago's side, then motioned for the procession to be on its way. The force moved by swiftly and steadily, exiting the Forge in short order.

Entreri hung motionless and expressionless, trying not to stare too intently at Berellip and Dahlia, trying to seem as if he was far beyond any concerns of the world about him, too walled up within his own pain and misery. Indeed, he showed no interest at all, and showed himself to be too beaten and broken to even care.

But he cared indeed. By his estimation, well over half of the Xorlarrin garrison had just departed the complex, and with all of the nobles save Berellip, a good portion of the goblinkin slave force and many of the monstrous driders with them.

He would get his chance.

***

The Forge lay quiet, the stillness interrupted only by the occasional ping of the hammer of the lone drow blacksmith still at work and the snorts and chortles of sleeping slaves.

Dahlia, too, was fast asleep, lying on the stone floor right in front of Entreri's cage.

The assassin used her as his focus, staring at her, thinking of what these wretched dark elves had done to her, and what they would likely do to her going forward.

He focused on that as his one hand reached up and worked deliberately, fingernail in hand, on the tumblers within the cage's lock. Entreri had contorted himself enough to stick a finger from his other hand into his ear, blocking the sound, while he rested his open ear against the same metal bar that ran up to the lock.

He heard and felt the subtle vibration as a tumbler clicked.

Nothing mattered to him beyond that sound, then. With perfect concentration, the skilled assassin tuned all of his senses to his work, feeling and learning the intricate mechanism, listening for the tell-tale sounds.

A second tumbler was soon defeated.

Entreri fell deeper into his trance, blocking out all distractions. Pure focus.

Click went the third, then the fourth.

And then came an unexpected sound indeed as the lock opened and the leaning assassin inadvertently pressed the door open, just a bit, just enough to set off a lightning glyph that crackled about him, stinging him painfully and alerting those in the room.

He dropped his arms and hung there, seeming unconscious, but still the drow blacksmith approached, hot poker in hand. The drow called out as he did, and another pair of dark elves ran into the room from the corridor beyond, rushing to join their kin.

They came up to Entreri, glancing about nervously.

The cage door moved imperceptibly and another shock rattled the assassin. He groaned and lolled his head to the side.

He understood the drow language enough to recognize the obvious question, and he did well to hide his smile at the answer.

"His weight has loosened the door enough to set off Priestess Berellip's traps!"

Entreri unclenched his muscles enough for his weight to shift the door the tiniest bit yet again, to jolt him with magical lightning yet again.

He groaned.

The dark elves laughed.

The two guards were still laughing when they went back to their posts. The blacksmith was still laughing when he lifted his hammer once again.

Entreri let the cage shock him again, and several more times after that, at varying intervals, and for varying periods of time, sometimes through several painful heartbeats.

The blacksmith stopped even looking back his way.

The cage sounded again, for a long while, then fell silent as Entreri, on the floor, quietly closed the door.

Dahlia sprawled before him, and how he wanted to go to her! He slithered off into the shadows instead, crawling by the sleeping goblins, where he appropriated a long shovel.

Like a whisper of wind he moved, forge to forge, shadow to shadow, pile to pile. None were better at hearing the quiet than the drow, but none were better at being the quiet than Artemis Entreri.

He came up behind the drow craftsman, leaning the shovel diagonally against the tray of the workplace. In one fluid movement, Entreri stepped up beside his intended victim, lifted the hot poker, and brought it in against the drow's belly. The shocked blacksmith instinctively threw his hips back, and Entreri helped him avoid the press of the poker by grabbing the hair at the back of the drow's head and driving forward with all his strength. Already bending forward to avoid the poker, the surprised blacksmith offered little resistance as Entreri slammed his face down on the edge of the metal tray in front of him.

Up came the dazed and bleeding dark elf to Entreri's strong pull, and down he went again, even harder.

Entreri kicked down hard on the leaning shovel, cracking the handle in half, and before the broken top piece could fall, he snatched it out of the air with his free hand.

The drow craftsman finally reoriented himself enough to start to call out, but around came Entreri's arm and makeshift weapon, the now sharp end of the broken handle stabbing up under the drow's jaw and stealing his words in a gurgle of erupting blood.

A third face slam had the craftsman falling limp, barely conscious. Still holding him fast by the hair, Entreri set down the spear and drove his free hand up against the drow's crotch. With the strength of a warrior, muscles hardened by decades of fighting, Entreri hoisted his victim from the ground and tossed him into the oven, feeding the forge with drow flesh.

Primordial fire ate the poor drow immediately, consuming flesh and charring bones before he could even truly cry out.

Still, the dying dark elf issued enough of a sound to remind Entreri that he had to move fast. He slid the halves of the broken shovel back together, using the splinters of the wood to make the piece appear whole at a cursory glance. He noted a narrow nail on the tray and collected it, thinking it a far better lockpick than a thumbnail, after all. Then he quickly dabbled some ash on the floor at the base of the forge and rushed off into the shadows, crossing by the sleeping goblins just long enough to replace the shovel among their utensils.

Back at his cage, he accepted another painful sting of the lightning glyph as he swung the door open and leaped back into place, then shut the door with his arms and shoulders positioned carefully to make it look as if it had never opened. He twisted around and reached up, using his new and better lockpick to engage one of the tumblers before setting it into his mouth, tight beside his gums.

The assassin fully relaxed and fell back into place. He leaned his face on the iron band and cried out suddenly, sharply, and very briefly, just enough to stir the goblins and to alert the guards outside the room.

And then he appeared to be, to all who might look, no more alive than the monk in the cage beside him, hanging limply against the press of the cage.

Just a heartbeat later, Entreri noted one goblin standing and looking around curiously. The creature kicked another nearby sleeper, and so on down the line until several were up and about, scratching their ugly heads and pointing to the still-fired forge, where the drow had been at work.

The group moved there, filling the ash Entreri had sprinkled with their footprints, and looked all around until one of them noted the charred remains inside the oven. Then how they jumped, falling all over each other to get away from the murder scene.

They scrambled and went for their tools, makeshift weapons to use against whatever intruder had murdered the drow craftsman.

In came the dark elf guards at the sound of the commotion, and when shown the murder scene, they called in many more.

Watching through one half-closed eye, Artemis Entreri enjoyed the spectacle indeed as the drow demanded answers from the goblins. He had only one moment of fear, when the goblins pointed to Dahlia, gibbering that she must be the culprit.

It was precisely that moment, however, when one of the ugly little creatures lifted the shovel Entreri had borrowed. It noted the stains on the handle only then, and when it moved to inspect the blood, the shovel fell in half, revealing the makeshift spear.

Leaving the goblin holding the murder weapon.

And with goblin footprints all around the ash near the crime scene.

The goblins kept pointing at Dahlia, who seemed unaware of anything going on around her, but the dark elves ignored them.

And beat them, and stabbed them, and threw them into the oven, one by one.

Entreri did well to keep a wry smile off his face as he watched the unfolding massacre. It had been a good night's work.

"Take her and flee!" Entreri heard a drow call out to another.

The assassin's thoughts whirled, for they were speaking of Dahlia, obviously, and the nearest two drow, a male soldier and a priestess, rushed for her. Entreri rolled his lockpick around in his mouth, thinking he might need to put it to quick use. Something was happening, some excitement, some tension.

Might he use this sudden distraction to break free and be away?

He looked at Dahlia and winced. She seemed hardly aware of the rising tensions. She just sat there, her expression void. He didn't think he could convince her to flee beside him, and if he had to drag her along, he knew he could never escape the drow.

His eyes scanned upward to the approaching dark elves, and he steeled his resolve. Perhaps he wouldn't escape, but he'd surely take a few drow to the grave beside him.

His confusion increased a moment later, when the source of the tumult came into view, in the form of a huge drider.

"You are supposed to be with Priestess Saribel!" one drow screamed at him.

"Silence!" the drider—Entreri had heard this one called Yerrininae before—growled back. "Where is the vile *darthiir*?"

"She is not your concern!" said the priestess then standing over Dahlia. "On the word of Priestess Berellip!"

Obviously spotting Dahlia, the drider approached, eight spider legs scratching the stone floor, a heavy mace swinging easily at the end of one of his huge, muscled arms.

Entreri knew that mace, Skullcrusher, was the weapon of Ambergris, and he allowed himself just a heartbeat of grief at the loss of the fine dwarf.

Just a heartbeat, though, as he tried to sort out his movements. He would exit that cage and rush to the nearest forge to secure a weapon, then . . .

"Yerrininae!" he heard, and he knew the voice.

As did the drider, obviously, for the behemoth stopped and swung around to face the speaker, Priestess Berellip, as she rushed to stand before him—before him and between him and the captive Dahlia.

"The *darthiir* lives at the suffrage of Archmage Gromph," Berellip said. Yerrininae offered a low growl in response.

"You know what he will do to you," Berellip warned, and when Yerrininae continued to lean forward aggressively, she added, "You have met his companion!"

It struck Entreri profoundly that the mere mention of a mind flayer could so diminish a creature as obviously powerful as this one. The drider backed off, the blood draining from its drow face.

"I have not forgotten you, murderess!" the drider roared at Dahlia, and it lifted its club, and as Berellip yelled for him to halt, Yerrininae swung anyway.

But not at Dahlia.

Skullcrusher slammed the side of Entreri's cage with bone-rattling force, stinging the surprised man profoundly and sending his prison into a wild, spinning swing. Before Entreri could even register the hit—and the sheer power of it awed him—the cage was struck again.

And Berellip was cheering, along with all the other drow and goblins in the room.

"Take this one out, that I might feast upon his beating heart before the eyes of the *darthiir*!" the vile drider begged.

"Do not kill him," Berellip intervened. "Not yet."

"I will pull off his arms, then, and just eat those!"

Berellip began to laugh, and Entreri thought the hour of his doom was surely upon him, and once more his thoughts began focusing on how he could cause the most devastation before his inevitable demise.

"I do want his arms intact," Berellip replied to Yerrininae. "Maybe just one leg . . ."

And Dahlia began to laugh.

Entreri looked at her incredulously as each spin of his cage flashed her into his view, and he noted that he wasn't the only one gawking at her.

"Yes, a leg," Dahlia said giddily. "Like a farmer's plucked chicken!"

A long while passed and the cage settled back to its original position, leaving Entreri to stare at Dahlia, and at the stupefied Yerrininae, who stood perfectly still, mace held sidelong as if he meant to hit the cage again.

"Well, that is an interesting turn," Berellip whispered.

"I promise you that I will avenge Flavvar," the drider said, moving its sneering face very close to Dahlia, who stared back at him blankly, as if she had no idea what he might be speaking of.

Berellip motioned to the drow soldier and priestess who had been first on the scene. "Take her," she instructed, and her fingers flashed some message to them that Entreri could not make out, likely the location she had in mind.

The assassin did share a parting gaze with Dahlia, but he could not tell if her expression was one of sympathy, antipathy, or utter disinterest.

The dark elves hustled her away, the male carting the metal ball, the female all but holding up the unsteady Dahlia, and Berellip waved the other onlookers back to their duties.

"If it was my choice . . ." she lamented to Yerrininae.

The drider nodded and turned its angry glare back over Entreri.

"One more," Berellip offered, and the drider took up Skullcrusher in both arms and rattled Entreri's cage, and rattled Entreri's bones. The assassin had been hit by the club of a giant before, almost squarely, but this was something even beyond that experience.

By the time the cage had stopped its wild swings and spins, Berellip and Yerrininae had moved away.

The cage settled fully again, but Entreri could not.

His side ached, his hips seemed as if on fire, and he could only hope that there were no serious wounds.

He would have to get out of this cage very soon.

CHAPTER 19

HALF A MONSTER

"Too much!" Regis lamented. In the commotion, he had inadvertently dumped the whole vial onto the mithral head of Aegis-fang.

"Too much?" Wulfgar asked frantically when the room's opposite door banged open, a host of goblinkin appearing.

"Just throw it!" the halfling cried, and Wulfgar was already moving to do just that.

"Tempus!" the barbarian bellowed, spinning the warhammer end-over-end at the far wall, the open door, and the bugbear standing within its frame.

The hammer struck with the power of an Elminster-inspired evocation, the halfling's bath of oil of impact exploding in a great and concussive fireball. The bugbear flew away, as did its companions huddling in the shadows behind it, as did the door itself, blown from its hinges to somersault off to the side of the room, trailing flames with every bouncing tumble.

The door frame collapsed, stone crumbling and bouncing down. The floor groaned, the ceiling groaned.

"Get out!" Regis cried, pushing Wulfgar back to the door through which they had entered.

"My hammer!" he yelled back, and on cue, Aegis-fang reappeared in his grasp, undamaged, indeed unmarked, by the blast.

Out into the hall the pair scrambled, the room collapsing behind them with a thunderous tremor and roar, and blasts of dust and small stones flying to pelt them.

"What did you do?" a startled Wulfgar asked.

"I want to make crossbow bolts like the ones Cadderly used to use," Regis explained. "Do you recall? They would collapse on themselves as they hit . . ."

Wulfgar just sighed, for before he could answer, a door farther along the corridor burst open and more goblins spilled out. Side-by-side, Wulfgar and Regis met their charge, the barbarian a half-step before the halfling, sweeping monsters aside with every great swipe of Aegis-fang, while Regis darted in behind each stroke, his rapier flashing against the disoriented and staggering goblins.

Three were down, then five, and when a hobgoblin in the third rank began barking orders, Regis warp-stepped to its side and promptly silenced it.

Recognizing the maneuver, Wulfgar pushed on before the halfling had even reappeared, and as soon as Regis struck, his rapier sliding under the side of the hobgoblin's skull, the barbarian caught the halfling by the shoulder and hauled him back.

He needn't have bothered. Their leader so abruptly cut down, the smaller goblins scattered, falling all over each other to be away from the murderous duo. Some fled back through the door, while others ran farther down the corridor, only to be met by Drizzt and Bruenor coming back the other way, rounding from the left where this corridor ended in a T junction.

Caught between two powerful pairs, the goblins scrambled for the lone open door, creating a tight grouping in the hall before it.

A ball of flame appeared in the air, roiling for just a heartbeat before suddenly striking a line of killing blaze down in the midst of that group.

And on came Wulfgar and Regis from the south, and on came Bruenor and Drizzt, Catti-brie right behind them, from the north, the vice closing.

The goblins dying.

"What was that explosion?" Drizzt asked when they had joined together once more.

Wulfgar looked to Regis, who shrugged and replied, "Oil of impact. A healthy batch."

"Ye shook the place to its roots," Bruenor said, trying to sound stern, but unable to hide his grin. "Ye wantin' to tell everythin' in the place where we be?"

Somewhere back behind them, Guenhwyvar roared.

Drizzt motioned for Wulfgar and Regis to chase the goblins that had retreated through the door, then he and the other two sprinted back to the end of the corridor and disappeared to the right.

"Once I didn't hit hard enough, and now, I fear, I hit too hard," Regis lamented.

"Too hard?" Wulfgar laughed. "No such thing, my friend. No such thing!" And off they went, side-by-side, a rambling catastrophe.

"Ye sure we're meetin' up with 'em, then?" Bruenor asked, and he lifted his axe up high, tucked his shoulder under his buckler, and charged at the next door in line.

"The two courses are side-by-side runs to the same corridor," Drizzt assured him, and up came Taulmaril.

"Now, girl!" Bruenor roared, and even as he finished, the lightning bolt sizzled past him, cracking into the ancient wood, followed immediately by Drizzt's lightning arrow, similarly driving against the door's planks.

Bruenor hit the portal right behind the bolts, axe splintering wood and his lowered shoulder pounding through. He crashed down to the floor, by design, and the two enemies in the room, a pair of hobgoblins, eagerly leaped at the prone form.

Guenhwyvar leaped over him first, though, flying through the broken portal, touching down in the room just long enough to spring again into the face of one of the hobgoblins, sending it flying backward.

The other hobgoblin made the mistake of glancing back at its tumbling friend. It turned back just in time to see another enemy leap in over the dwarf, just in time to see the deadly drow touch down just a stride away, just in time to see a pair of magnificent scimitar cutting an X before its eyes, cutting an X across its face.

"I'm callin' half that kill as me own!" Bruenor roared, running past Drizzt and sending a backhand chop into the hobgoblin's side for good measure. He rambled up to the door directly across the room and kicked it open, revealing a long corridor, lined on the right side by a multitude of doors.

"Not liking that!" Bruenor declared. He glanced back to see Catti-brie close behind. She took a quick survey of the corridor, then began spellcasting, and Bruenor moved aside.

A wall of fire reached out from her, rushing down the corridor, splitting it down the middle. The flames roiled and roared, but all seemed to be biting out to the right, toward the doors.

"Stay left," she explained.

Bruenor started in hesitantly, for even though the magical flames of the wall were directional, burning away from him, he couldn't deny the heat.

"Liked ye better with the damned bow," he muttered, sliding along the wall as quickly as he could.

The group eased its way along. At least one door did open, and a goblin shrieked and fell back when faced with Catti-brie's fiery wall.

Drizzt turned and fired off a series of arrows into the roiling flames in the direction of the sound, and from a distant cry, it seemed clear that at least one had gone through the open door and struck home.

They reached the far end of the corridor, which forked right and turned left, and paused there, turning back.

Catti-brie dropped her wall of fire, and sure enough, stubborn goblinkin came rushing out, though many foolishly turning the other way, back the way the companions had come.

Drizzt put some shots down the corridor and Guenhwyvar roared.

Goblins turned and goblins died, Taulmaril's arrows driving through them two or three at a time.

Some came on into the fury of Guenhwyvar and Bruenor, but most scrambled back into the side rooms. One goblin almost got a stab at Bruenor with its spear before Drizzt blew it dead and to the ground.

Almost.

Aegis-fang spun end-over-end, blasted through the bugbear's shield and struck it dead, simply dead.

"Lots of fighting to the side," Regis called to his companion.

Wulfgar nodded, for he, too, could hear the lightning strokes, and the roar of Guenhwyvar and of magical fires.

Drizzt had anticipated that his course would be through more populated areas of the goblin nest, which was why he kept the bulk of the force beside him. For Wulfgar and Regis, the run had been much clearer, with only a few enemies here and there, and most of those more intent on running away than in coming in to fight.

The pair weaved around the dead bugbear, Aegis-fang returning to Wulfgar's hand. Under an archway, they came into a wide corridor, running diagonally back behind them to the left, or forward to the right, toward their friends.

They went right, trotting along, but a portion of the right-hand wall ahead of them slid aside and out scrambled a group of hobgoblins.

Wulfgar wasted no time in sending Aegis-fang flying devastatingly into their midst.

"Let them come to us," Regis bade him, and he glanced at his halfling companion to see Regis with his hand crossbow leveled.

The hobgoblins regrouped and charged, the nearest catching a quarrel in the face. Regis dropped his bow and lifted a ceramic jar from his pouch.

"Let them come to us," he reiterated, and he held his throw a bit longer, then flung the jug. It smashed to the floor at the feet of the charging monsters. Shards and liquid burst forth, splattering the stone and the feet of the hobgoblins.

And that liquid, Regis's next trick, slicked the floor as surely as water thrown on stones on an Icewind Dale's winter night. Like floating seaweed in an irresistible wave, the hobgoblins pitched and crashed, tangled into each other, and spilled to the floor.

Wulfgar went up to the edge of the greasy splash and pounded down at the tangle with heavy hits of Aegis-fang, the warhammer shattering shields and bones, crushing through feeble hobgoblin armor.

Regis rushed up beside him and seemed to simply disappear, warp-stepping across the slippery splash zone, stepping back securely and stabbing ahead before the surprised hobgoblins in the back of the tangle even realized he was there.

He scored a series of hits, most on one unfortunate creature that spun down spurting blood from a dozen holes.

The remaining creatures ran off, and Regis turned to follow.

He thought his friends had joined him when he saw that group of hobgoblins collectively shudder, one monster flying up to crunch heavily into the wall, another sailing back the way it had come, bowling aside its companions to fall in the middle of the corridor, only a few strides down from Regis, where it convulsed and twitched in its death throes.

With a glance back, confident that Wulfgar had the tangled enemies caught in the grease trap well in hand, Regis started along, taking only a couple of steps before he spotted the devastating dwarf among the hobgoblins.

"Bruenor!" he called, but even as he spoke the name, he realized that it was not Bruenor.

It was Thibbledorf Pwent.

The bone in Bruenor's finger was surely broken, the digit sticking out at an odd angle.

"Clench your teeth," Catti-brie instructed, and when the dwarf bit down, she popped the finger back into place, then immediately cast a minor healing spell, the blue mist of her magic rolling out of her sleeve and wrapping around the tough dwarf's hand.

"My magic is nearly exhausted this day," she told Bruenor and Drizzt. "Both arcane and divine."

"Bah, but we got along in the last life without it, and so we'll do again," Bruenor replied.

In response, Catti-brie pressed just a bit on the wound she had healed in the dwarf's back, where Bruenor had previously caught the bugbear's spear. Bruenor grimaced and winced and pulled away, then glared at the girl, silently admitting that her point had been made.

"Give her the bow, elf." Bruenor suggested.

Drizzt nodded and reached out with Taulmaril, but the woman recoiled.

"I don't even know if I can wield it anymore," she said. "I have never shot a bow in this new life. I have not trained my body . . ."

"Ye'll get it back, then," Bruenor insisted and he pulled the bow from Drizzt's hand and gave it over to Catti-brie.

"I've some tricks left with my magic," Catti-brie said, taking the weapon tentatively, and then slinging the offered quiver over her shoulder.

"Well use 'em as ye can, and use the bow when ye can't," said Bruenor, settling it, and the dwarf started off once more, shaking out his hand, then taking up his axe.

Drizzt looked to Catti-brie questioningly, and the woman just shrugged in reply. The drow pointed to the room's door, broken in and hanging by one hinge.

Catti-brie lifted Taulmaril and set an arrow, leveling the bow. She took a deep breath to steady herself as she drew back, but then eased the string back to resting and offered a plaintive look at the drow.

"Go ahead," Drizzt coaxed. "You have an unlimited supply of arrows."

Catti-brie closed her eyes and drew back once more, took a deep breath and held it, set her sights, and let fly. The lightning arrow shot off, the bright streak lighting the room with its flash, and hit the door dead center, splintering the wood.

"Well then, lookin' to me like y'ain't lost a thing!" Bruenor cheered, and again he started off. "Right in the heart, as the bow's name says!"

Drizzt, too, smiled and congratulated the woman, albeit silently.

Catti-brie just returned that look and nodded. She didn't bother mentioning to either of her companions that she had aimed for the hinge, not the center.

Before they had even exited the room's far door, the trio heard the sound of renewed fighting echoing along the corridors and knew that their companions had engaged goblins once more.

Guenhwyvar, who had gone out the other way in pursuit of one fleeing goblin, apparently heard it, too. The cat bounded back into the room and leaped over the dwarf to take the lead.

Regis grimaced in revulsion as he watched as Pwent bit out the throat of a hobgoblin. The dwarf glanced up at him, smiled weirdly, and tossed the convulsing monster aside—with ease.

With such ease! Pwent had hardly swung his arm out, it seemed, and just that one arm, yet the hobgoblin, thick and heavy, flew across the corridor to crunch into the wall with bone-shattering impact.

"Well met, Thibbledorf Pwent!" Regis announced as enthusiastically as he could manage past the lump of fear welling in his throat.

" 'Ere, ye little rat thief," the dwarf muttered, stalking forward slowly, casually even.

"Pwent, it's me!" Regis cried. "Don't you know me?"

"Oh, I'm knowin' ye," the dwarf said, but Regis got the feeling that the dwarf was not specifically referring to Regis, who was, of course, long-dead in Pwent's thoughts.

The vampire walked forward. Regis lifted his rapier.

"Pwent!" he cried. "It's me, Regis!"

He almost finished stating his name when the undead dwarf rushed up suddenly, so suddenly, seeming almost to warp-step himself, much as the specter of Ebonsoul had done. Regis cried out and dived aside, and still got clipped by a swinging arm and sent tumbling. As he fell aside, Regis reached back with his dirk hand to fend the dwarf away, but the dwarf's spiked gauntlet dug a line across the back of that hand, and the halfling retracted with a yelp.

He pulled himself to his knees and wheeled back as quickly as he could, turning some semblance of a defensive posture at the closing Pwent—though what he might do against one so powerful and heavily armored as this, he did not know!

Pwent leaped at him, fangs bared, fists punching in from out wide, and Regis cried out, thinking himself surely doomed.

But Pwent never got there, intercepted in mid-leap by a spinning warhammer that drove him aside and sent him staggering back down the corridor. He turned immediately, though, his hateful gaze still focused squarely on Regis, and with a feral growl that froze the marrow in Regis's bones, he charged.

The halfling yelped again and flung his remaining snake at the vampire. The living garrote did its magic, racing up and around the dwarf's neck, and the sneering undead specter's face appeared over Pwent's shoulder, tugging hard.

But the vampire didn't draw breath. The vampire didn't even seem to notice.

Again the halfling was saved by a missile, this time a living one, as Wulfgar leaped past Regis to crash heavily into Pwent. The dwarf tried to hit him with a left hook, but Wulfgar caught him by the arm, then grabbed Pwent's right arm as well, holding and twisting.

The two powerful combatants locked and strained. At first Pwent, with the lower center, seemed to gain the upper hand, with Wulfgar sliding backward under the dwarf's ferocious press.

Wulfgar growled his god's name and drove on with renewed strength, halting the momentum.

Pwent twisted to the side and Wulfgar had to turn with him, struggling to hang on as the dwarf tried to pull away.

But then Wulfgar leaped the same way as the pull, and Pwent overbalanced. Wulfgar let go of the dwarf's left arm and chopped a short right cross into the dwarf's face, but then grabbed back quickly before the dwarf could counter with a left.

Regis wanted to cheer that strike, but like the garrote tugging around his neck, Pwent didn't seem the least bit hurt or stunned or slowed. And it was Wulfgar showing the cost of their struggle, Regis saw, for the barbarian's hands dripped blood, his flesh tearing against the dwarf's ridged arm plates.

Pwent ducked his head, dipping his helmet spike, and bore forward, and Wulfgar barely avoided getting stabbed in the face. Then he, too, bowed forward, tucking his head against the dwarf's helm to maintain the clench.

He had to keep Pwent in his grasp, he knew.

"Pwent! Thibbledorf Pwent! It's Regis and Wulfgar! You know us!" the halfling cried, trying to reason with the snarling vampire. He rose as he shouted and ran around to the side, and when Pwent didn't react at all to his call, Regis grimaced and stabbed hard.

The vampire howled, in pain or in anger, and went into a wild struggle, arms flailing, head whipping around. Wulfgar tried to hold on, tried to stay too close for Pwent to cause any real damage.

"Stab him!" the barbarian cried, his last word cut short as the dwarf managed to get his helm away from Wulfgar's head just enough to butt it back in hard to the side, cracking against Wulfgar's jaw.

Regis stuck Pwent again, but the dwarf growled it away and whipped around, sending Wulfgar skidding across between himself and the halfling to crash across Regis's arms and drive him back. Wulfgar was out of the way immediately, but not of his own accord, for while the clench was tiring him, the vampire knew no such limitations. Suddenly Wulfgar went flying back the other way, Pwent turning to slam him hard into the wall, and then out Wulfgar flew back again, the furious dwarf throwing him at Regis.

Regis reflexively ducked and Wulfgar crashed into the wall behind him.

"Pwent!" came another shout, this time from Bruenor, who appeared farther along the corridor. "Ye know me, Pwent! Ye gived me back me helm!"

That gave the vampire pause, and so did Guenhwyvar, leaping over Bruenor and charging right in.

But Pwent became a cloud of gas and the panther skidded through, right past Regis, and Wulfgar behind him.

The gas reformed almost immediately, but now Drizzt came in, rushing past Bruenor. "I left you in a cave, brave friend!" the drow cried.

"Aye, and ye're a fool for it!" the vampire shouted back, and he threw himself at the drow, a barrage of punches meeting a flurry of scimitar parries.

"Pwent!" Bruenor screamed.

Finally it seemed to get through to the vampire, a bit at least, and he abruptly disengaged from Drizzt and stepped back past Regis, who held his strike.

But Wulfgar did not. Aegis-fang back in his hand, the barbarian cried out and swept the weapon across, smashing Pwent in the chest and sending him skidding farther along. Wulfgar jumped out into the center of the corridor and pulled Regis defensively behind him.

Then Drizzt rushed up, shoulder-to-shoulder with the barbarian.

"Pwent, ye know us," Bruenor said, rushing up beside Regis and behind Drizzt. "We come to help ye."

The vampire growled.

Behind the vampire, Guenhwyvar growled.

"Pwent, my old friend, remember the fight in the primordial pit," Drizzt coaxed. "You saved us that day. You saved all in the region from another cataclysm."

The vampire looked at him, clearly struggling, memories battling demons within.

"Aye, and I damned meself," he replied, his voice shaking with every syllable.

"In the cave," Drizzt said. "The sun."

"Couldn't . . ." Pwent answered weakly, and he trembled, his eyes darting all around. He was thinking of escaping, they all realized, but only for a moment before he grunted and stood straight once more, glaring at them hatefully—and also, strangely, plaintively.

"Finish me, then!" he roared and he came forward a step as if to renew the fighting.

But he stopped short, a curious expression on his dead face. He looked at the companions, then past the companions, and shook his head.

That distant look made them all glance back, to see Catti-brie standing down the hall, one hand extended, palm up, balancing a sapphire as the woman, scroll in hand, continued a soft arcane chant.

"No!" Pwent growled, and it seemed as if he tried to come forward then, but could not, locked in place by the mounting dweomer of Catti-brie. "No, ye dogs!"

He leaned forward then, toward their line, and he seemed to elongate, then to become something less than substantial. And he floated past them suddenly and swiftly, stretched and insubstantial, flowing into Catti-brie's waiting phylactery.

"Ye got him, girl!" Bruenor cried, starting her way, but he stopped even as he turned.

Catti-brie trembled and shook her head as if something were very wrong.

With only that unclear warning, the gemstone exploded into a million pieces, the concussion sending Catti-brie flying backward and flinging dust and pellets around the corridor.

And there, where Catti-brie had been, where the gem had been, stood a very shaken Thibbledorf Pwent.

"They got prisoners," he said to Bruenor, fighting every word. "Entreri's caught in the Forge. And more there beside him, and a lady dwarf in the mines . . ."

He stalked about a step to the left and back to the right, then dived back with startling speed and grabbed up the dazed Catti-brie by the throat.

"Could'o' killed ye," he whispered to her, and he dropped her there and leaped away, becoming a bat before he ever landed. He fluttered off the way he had come.

Catti-brie pulled herself to her feet and reached up to pat at the blood on her face—blood from the cuts of a dozen shards of the burst gemstone.

"Me girl!" Bruenor said, rushing up to her, as did the others.

"I'm all right," she assured them, her gaze turning in the direction of Pwent's retreat. "The gem was not sufficient to hold him."

"He's a monster," Regis whispered, the halfling thoroughly shaken by what he had seen in Pwent's dead eyes.

"Half of one, perhaps," Catti-brie replied, and the fact that she was still alive and could reply bolstered her argument.

"Half and more, and the bad part's gaining," Bruenor lamented. "Wilder than I seen him in the throne room them months ago."

"The curse," Catti-brie agreed. "He cannot withstand it."

"They," Drizzt whispered, and all turned to him at that unexpected word.

"Pwent said they've got prisoners," the drow explained to their curious expressions.

"The drow got the Forge, then, from what he said and what we're knowin'," Bruenor agreed. "And we might be needin' to go through them to get to Pwent again."

"And to free Entreri," said Drizzt. "I'll not leave him to the dark elves."

"Yeah," Bruenor replied, hands on hips. "Figured ye'd say as much. Durn elf."

"We go through them, then," said Wulfgar.

"Think we might be warnin' them drow that they'll get some more o' their kin and make it more of a fight?" Bruenor said to Drizzt. "Might only be a few hunnerd o' them to fight."

Drizzt looked around at the others, all of them nodding and smiling and eager to go—even Regis.

So be it.

PART 4

THE CALL OF THE HERO

Words blurted out in fast reaction so oft ring true.

They flow from the heart, and give voice to raw emotions before the speaker can thoughtfully intervene, out of tact or fear. Before the natural guards arise to self-censor, to protect the speaker from embarrassment or retribution. Before the polite filters catch the words to protect the sensibilities of others, to veil the sharp truth before it can stab.

Bruenor calls this fast reaction "chewing from yer gut."

We all do it. Most try not to do it, audibly at least, and in matters of tact and etiquette, that is a good thing.

But sometimes chewing from your gut can serve as an epiphany, an admission of sorts to that which is actually in your heart, despite the reservations one might have gained among polite company.

So it was that day in the chambers of upper Gauntlgrym when I said that I would not leave Entreri to his drow captors. I did not doubt my course from the moment Thibbledorf Pwent revealed the situation to me. I would go to find Artemis Entreri, and I would free him—and the others, if they, too, had been taken.

It was that simple.

And yet, when I look back on that moment, there was nothing simple about it at all. Indeed, I find my resolution and determination truly surprising, and for two very different reasons.

First, as my own words rang in my ears, they revealed to me something I had not admitted: that I cared for Artemis Entreri. It wasn't just convenience that had kept me beside him, nor my own loneliness, nor my flawed desire to bring him and the others to the path of righteousness. It was because I cared, and not just for Dahlia but for Entreri as well.

I have many times circled around this realization through the years. When I learned that Artemis Entreri had become friends with Jarlaxle, I hoped that Jarlaxle would lead the man from his personal demons. I wished Entreri well, meaning that I hoped he would find a better life and a better way. That thought has often flitted about my consciousness, a quiet hope.

But still this particular instance of chewing from my gut surprised me on this matter because of the depth it revealed of my feelings for the man.

I had my friends with me, after all, the Companions of the Hall, the group of my dearest friends, yea, my family, the only family I had ever known. My chewed-from-the-gut proclamation that I was going after Entreri was much more than a personal declaration, because of course these beloved companions would go along with me. Presumably, it follows that I was willing to put my dearest friends, even Catti-brie, into such obvious and dire jeopardy for the sake of Artemis Entreri!

That, I think, is no small thing, and looking at it in retrospect reveals to me much more than my desire to free Artemis Entreri.

When I first ventured to Icewind Dale, those around me thought me a bit reckless. Even Bruenor, who leaped onto a shadow dragon's back with a keg of flaming oil strapped to his own back, often shook his head and muttered "durned elf" at my battle antics!

I fought as if I had nothing to lose, because in my heart and mind, I had nothing to lose. But then, so suddenly, I learned that I had so much to lose, in these friends I had come to know and love, in this woman who would be my wife.

This is not a new revelation—indeed, I have spent the better part of a century seeking freedom from these self-imposed restraints, and indeed, I thought I had found such freedom when Bruenor, the last of my companions, passed on to Dwarfhome. Even in my great lament at his passing, I felt as if I was finally free.

And then my friends, my family—my constraints?—returned to me. What did it mean? Surely I was glad, thrilled, overjoyed, but was I doomed to return to that place of caution I had known before?

But in that simple chew-from-the-gut moment, my insistence that I, that we, would go and free Entreri and the others, no matter the odds, I knew without doubt that my beloved friends had not brought my emotional shackles back with them. Perhaps it was their transformation, their literal passage through death, which had bolstered my own faith and resolve and willingness to engage the adventure. Perhaps this courage stemmed from my growing acceptance that these friends had been lost to me, and so I had not reclaimed the fear that they could be lost to me.

More likely, it was something more, something rooted in the twining of my core beliefs. In the course of events, you do what you think is right and proper, and hold faith that such a course will lead to good ends. To believe less . . . if this is what I truly hold in my heart and proclaim, then what a coward I would be to deny such a course out of fear, any fear, even fear for the safety of my beloved companions.

I spoke purely on reflex to the news of Entreri's capture, spouting the course I knew to be correct, but when I went back and examined that moment, I discovered much more about myself indeed.

And much more about my friends, for the second revelation in that moment came with their response. They did not hesitate in the least, and indeed were eager for the fight—as eager as I. Even within Regis, there was no fear. This was the course, the correct path, and so we would walk it.

And so we did. I have not walked this lightly in decades, since long before Catti-brie was first lost to me in the advent of the Spellplague. So many times have I strived for this freedom, wandering from Mithral Hall with Catti-brie after its reclamation, time and again resolving to find joy.

But this was different. This wasn't a considered thought, a spoken determination or pledge. This was what I have been seeking, come full circle from the time when Wulfgar and I entered the lair of the verbeeg named Biggrin. This choice was without a second thought—there was a problem and so we would go and fix it, and we would go brimming with confidence in ourselves, with faith in each other.

"Think we might be warnin' them drow that they'll get some more o' their kin and make it more of a fight?" Bruenor had joked, but it almost didn't seem like a joke at the time.

Because we knew in our hearts that we'd prove victorious.

Because no other outcome was acceptable.

It was just that simple.

Yet these were dark elves on the road ahead, a sizable number, and a band that had already managed to somehow defeat and capture Artemis Entreri and the others, and so as we began our steps, doubts crept in.

Not doubts regarding our chosen course, but doubts about whether or not we could succeed.

And doubts regarding how high the price might prove.

But this is our way.

This is our creed.

This is the mantra of the Companions of the Hall.

It can be no other way.

And since we knew our course to be true, doubts could not equal regret.

No matter the price.

—Drizzt Do'Urden

CHAPTER 20

WHEN THE DROW CAME

Vein's going dead," a dirty dwarf miner by the name of Minto Silverhammer, who claimed bloodlines from both the Battlehammer and Silverstream family trees, remarked to his fellow workers as he emerged from a side tunnel in the deepest reaches of the mines beneath Kelvin's Cairn. "Hearin' echoes when I tap at it, so I'm not to go much deeper afore I'm breakin' into new tunnels."

"Hold yer pick, then," said Junkular Stonebreaker, the team boss, a heavyset dwarf of many winters.

"We'll have a light load o' metal then, eh Junky?" the miner replied, using the boss's more common nickname.

"Better that than an open run to the Underdark," said Bellows, one of the other miners, and to accentuate his point, he leaned back on the heavy metal door that had been recently constructed to block off the main tunnel to the deeper and more expansive corridors and caverns beyond.

"How 'bout a closed run, then?" said yet another, and the group murmured and nodded.

This had been a long-running debate among the dwarves of Icewind Dale, Stokely Silverstream's boys, with a constant side implication hanging over it: Gauntlgrym.

They knew where it was, they had been there, but that ancient and hallowed homeland remained out of their grasp. Paradoxically, the journey to Gauntlgrym inspired new caution under Kelvin's Cairn. Now Stokely and his boys had first-hand knowledge of the profound dangers lurking just outside their domain, including the devil-worshiping zealots they had

267

found in Gauntlgrym, and including, if reports—and now King Bruenor and Drizzt—were to be believed, that a sizable number of dark elves had filtered into the region.

"We'll scout out beyond yer wall," Junky assured Minto. "And get new doors in place if they're needed. And once we got it secured, know that I'll make sure yerself gets the breakthrough chop to the new veins."

"Bah!" snorted Bellows, still leaning against the iron door, and now shifting back and forth to scratch his back on one of the huge hinges that kept the portal securely in place.

The others began to chuckle, knowing well that this would soon devolve into an argument. Breaking through a wall to another vein was considered a point of high honor, after all.

"I telled ye a tenday ago that there be another tunnel just behind that vein!" Bellows predictably complained to Junky and Minto. "I'll flip a gold piece against Minto for the first chop, if ye want, but—"

His rant, and the corresponding chuckles, ended abruptly with the sharp crackle of energy, a single pop that straightened Bellows where he stood and painted his face with an incredulous expression.

Then came a second, louder pop, followed by a resounding and continuous crackle, like the cacophony of a multitude of fireworks released into the air after the explosion of the main rocket. Poor Bellows flew forward, trailing smoke.

The others watched his flight in stupor, then collectively looked back to the iron door just in time to see blue fingers of crackling magical energy crawling all around it, popping and singeing and cutting lines in the iron.

"Suren to blow!" Minto cried, grabbing Junky and pulling him into the side corridor as the other dwarves scrambled.

The tunnel shook with a tremendous explosion, and Minto watched in shock as the heavy door, as thick as a strong dwarf's chest, went soaring past the opening of the side tunnel, clouds of dust and splinters of stone chasing it in its flight. He heard the grunt of a companion who had fled straight back along the main corridor as the door caught up to him, and a second grunt as the door crashed down—upon poor Bellows, it seemed.

Out rushed Minto and Junky, side by side, and they didn't turn for Bellows, but for the now-opened corridor, knowing that an enemy was upon them.

NIGHT OF THE HUNTER

How they gulped when they realized that enemy to be an army of dark elves.

"Cave collapse?" a miner in an adjacent tunnel breathlessly asked his digging buddy, for the ground had shaken under their feet.

The two rushed out of their dig together, to find other dwarves coming out of side tunnels and into the main corridor, all looking wide-eyed, which seemed wider, given that their faces were all covered in dark dirt and torch smoke, and all looking to each other for answers.

Another blast reverberated around them, and the group turned as one to a perpendicular main corridor.

"Collapse!" one yelled, and they all started running—not away from the suspected area, but toward it, toward their fellow dwarves. Picks in hand, torches in hand, the gang rumbled down the side corridor. They all knew these reaches of the mines as well as they knew their own homes above, and knew, too, that they had friends in that adjacent tunnel. Several began to call out for Junky.

Still convinced it was a collapse, the dwarves were ready to dig. As they neared the parallel main corridor, though, the flash of a lightning bolt stole that idea as surely as it stole the darkness, and then the dwarves knew the truth.

And then the dwarves were as ready to fight, whatever enemy had come, as fully as they had been ready to dig.

Ravel Xorlarrin grinned wickedly as the door blew asunder, yet another victim of the spell of his own creation he called the lightning web. Through this spell, he and his fellow wizards had joined their lightning energy together into one deadly stroke that obliterated the formidable barrier.

None of them, not even Archmage Gromph had he been there, could have sundered that iron door with a single bolt. But with their energies combined, the lightning web had blown it from its jamb and sent it flying down the corridor behind it, chasing the scurrying dwarves.

And that sight turned Ravel's grin into open laughter.

269

In went the goblin shock troops, crossing over the blasted portal to engage the few dwarves that stood to muster a defense.

Ravel looked to Tiago, who nodded, and in response, in went the next magical barrage, a volley of fireballs falling over dwarf and goblin alike, and when the burst of flame and smoke cleared, the line of tough dwarves had held, though shakily, but no goblins remained alive.

Ravel put a lightning bolt into the center of the dwarf line, and more pointedly, a bolt that pressed through and reached back from that point as one fleeing dwarf sprinted away down the corridor.

Tiago kicked his lizard mount into a charge, Jearth Xorlarrin at his side, a host of running warriors at their back. As they neared the portal, Tiago and Jearth broke left and right, rolling their mounts up the side walls and slowing, allowing the drow warriors to pass them by and engage the dwarves.

The forces came together just inside the blasted door with a thunderous ring of metal on metal, roaring dwarves, and stomping boots. These were drow warriors, supremely skilled and trained and outfitted. They were used to winning such fights, and used to winning them in short order.

But their opponents were dwarves of Clan Battlehammer and of Icewind Dale, hardened by the stones they mined, by the endless cold winds of the dale, and by many years of desperate fighting against all sorts of powerful enemies, from white worms to orcs to the ever-present tundra yetis. Many drow swords and spears found their marks in those early moments of battle, but no one strike felled a Battlehammer dwarf defending his home.

"Flight! Flight!" the drow group commander yelled back to Tiago and Jearth, telling them that that runner was still on his way for reinforcements.

The two shared a nod and sent their mounts away, riding up to the ceiling, sticky feet holding fast. Side-by-side they charged out over the battle line. They spotted the fleeing dwarf immediately, far down the corridor, and made for him, but up came a line of dwarf shovels and picks to stab at them and engage them before they had even crossed over the combatants.

Tiago cut in front of Jearth, his shield spinning out to its full size as he swept it across, his sword going out the other way to deflect the remaining weapons.

"Go!" he ordered his companion, and Jearth rushed past the Baenre noble, and beyond the fighting dwarves and drow.

Jearth spurred his lizard mount into an awkward, upside-down gallop, easily outdistancing the few pursuing dwarves, and quickly closing in on the one who had fled.

Never slowing, riding easily though he was hanging upside down from the ceiling, Jearth pulled a barbed javelin from a long quiver behind his saddle and quickly fastened a cord to the catch-weapon's end loop. He leveled his arm to throw, taking a moment to remember that down was up and up was down, so that to account for the natural fall of the thrown weapon he had to, from his perspective, aim lower.

He reached back to throw the missile, but found himself distracted by other missiles—a barrage of spinning missiles, and a volley thrown at him.

Jearth's sprint brought him right past a side tunnel at the same moment that a host of dwarves had reached the same juncture, and the bearded folk wasted no time in launching their mining picks the drow's way. Some bounced aside harmlessly, skipping off the uneven ceiling, while others battered both the rider and his lizard, mostly to minimal effect.

But one pick turned around perfectly to stab its tip deeply into the lizard's rear flank, into the thigh of its back leg.

The wounded beast stopped its run and wriggled around, battling the determined tug of Jearth. The lizard's rear right leg detached from the ceiling, waving around in the air as it tried to dislodge the pick, and it even tried to turn around to bite at the pained area.

Jearth fought hard to keep his mount straight and to keep it moving, realizing all the while that it was probably not a good idea to idly hang there with a mob of angry dwarves closing in.

He had to leap free of the saddle, he realized, but too late, as another mining pick spun in, barely missing him as he ducked back from it.

Missing him, but hitting his mount, and more specifically, hitting one of the straps securing Jearth's saddle, and as that strap severed, Jearth's right leg came free, too suddenly for him to adjust himself properly to cleanly fall free.

Instead, he just fell, or half-fell, from the saddle, hanging awkwardly, his left foot twisted and thus locked into place, holding him there, inverted and staring into the eyes of charging dwarves.

With a shake of his head and a sigh, the inverted drow drew out his swords.

Back at the furious battle line, still on the ceiling and batting aside the reaching picks and shovels of the dwarves, Tiago managed a glance down the corridor. He saw Jearth's weapons working brilliantly, fending off dwarves from all angles. The Weapons Master of House Xorlarrin parried a mining pick with one blade while cutting a dwarf's throat with his other. Jearth got that second blade back in close to his own torso in time to meet the heavy swing of a hammer, and used that push to go into a spin—a spin, Tiago realized in just that heartbeat—that would help him free his trapped foot.

He saw Jearth fall, but it was a good thing, the drow dropping from the ceiling and flipping over as he went to land lightly on his feet before the press of the dwarf miners.

Tiago smiled and nodded as he faded back behind the drow line, confident that Jearth would dispatch the group, or at least hold them at bay, until this line could be breached and the foot soldiers could run to his aid.

To facilitate that point, the Baenre noble rode back down to the floor and drove his mount between a pair of drow infantry, shoving them aside that he could join in the fight properly. His lizard pressed ahead, maw snapping, and Tiago had to pull it back just a bit as it tried to pursue those dwarves as they fell back.

The lizard, like all of Tiago's mounts, was superbly trained, though, and pulling it back for Tiago meant nothing more than a clicking sound and a proper press of his left heel, leaving his arms free.

He swept his shield across at the dwarf to his left, and before the blocker had gone fully past the intended target, the dwarf eager to come in at him behind the swipe, Tiago called upon that shield to diminish in size. It did so instantly, rolling in on itself, and thus allowing the drow to strike first with his sword, to stab his fine blade out at the unsuspecting dwarf from under the edge of the diminishing shield.

He pulled the bloodied blade back in and cut it across to the right, rolling it over a swinging pick. He turned the sword back the other way brilliantly, and with enough leverage and strength to send that pick flying away. Hardly pausing to admire the flight of the weapon, Tiago plunged his sword straight ahead, straight into the dwarf's chest.

He prodded his lizard mount into a charge then, but rolled off the lizard's back as it leaped away—rolled off with a complete somersault that landed him back on his feet and moving forward, throwing himself with glee into the midst of battle.

Better armed, better armored, better trained, the drow had clearly turned the tide of battle. One-against-one, few warriors in the Realms could match a dark elf, but even among the ranks of these elite warriors, Tiago Baenre stood tall. His blade and shield worked in a concerted blur, sweeping and stabbing, blocking and parrying. His fight was not straight-line, moving ahead, but became a dance all around, the drow commoners gladly surrendering ground as he crossed before them, the dwarves wishing they had!

The fight in that corridor had already favored the dark elves, but with Tiago among them, the fight became a rout and the dwarven line quickly shattered.

Tiago brought his shield up fast to catch a chop of a dwarf's pick, and he enacted the magic of the shield, whose name was Spiderweb, to hold the weapon fast as he pulled it out to the side. The movement invited the dwarf to press in, and so the bearded fellow complied, leading with a fist.

But Tiago was ahead of his move, and that punching fist met the tip of a fine weapon, a sword that cut through gauntlet and knuckles, and drove up through the dwarf's wrist and split the bone of the dwarf's forearm.

The dwarf howled—oh, how he screamed!—and Tiago pressed out fast with the shield, freeing the pick before retracting his arm. In the same movement, the drow warrior turned his sword down and under with a sharp jerk, tearing it free of the muscled arm and shooting it ahead only briefly before turning his shoulders to retract the sword and throw the shield out before him, to bull ahead over the dwarf as the poor fool fell backward and to the ground.

But fell without a scream, for that quick strike of the sword had taken out its throat.

Crossing over the falling Battlehammer, Tiago broke free, leading the way, his wicked smile wide indeed.

He saw Jearth, battling far ahead. Up came the weapons master's blade, shining with dwarf blood, and down it went, repeatedly.

But only one blade, Tiago realized even as he eagerly started forward. Only one blade!

And one of Jearth's arms hung limply at the weapons master's side!

One blade against a horde of dwarves pressing in from every angle. Jearth spun and struck, leaped aside and darted ahead, then back, brilliant in every movement.

But the dwarf net closed, a relentless barrage of picks and fists.

"To me!" Tiago called to the warriors, now all in a full charge to get to Jearth's side.

A charge that would not arrive in time, he realized.

"Ravel!" he cried to the mage behind him as he saw Jearth pulled down in the teeming mass of dwarf muscle.

On they charged, and the mage's spell flew over them in the form of an amorphous green glob. It soared into the midst of Jearth's desperate fight and exploded into a cloud of virescent gas, the stench rolling back to make Tiago crinkle his nose in disgust. He could hardly see the tangle ahead through the ugly fog, and even the sound of the fight seemed to diminish, dulled by the thick haze.

And hopefully, he thought, the fight had diminished, the combatants crippled by the stinking cloud.

But then out of the fog came some of those fighters, a line of angry dwarves, spitting and snorting, but hardly slowed, it seemed, by the nauseating fumes.

"Jearth," Tiago mouthed in shock as he drove into their ranks.

Those dwarves fought valiantly, but like their comrades at the blown door, they could not win out against the superior force that had come to their tunnels. Several drow died in that corridor, but three times the number of gallant Battlehammer dwarves met their end there, and a similar number were taken as prisoners.

Tiago Baenre could not consider it a victory, though, because the fight for Kelvin's Cairn had just begun, because at least one dwarf had escaped the assault to run ahead to warn his bearded kin.

And because Jearth, Weapons Master of House Xorlarrin, Tiago's friend and companion, lay bloodied in the corridor before him.

Tiago watched intently as the priestess Saribel rushed to Jearth and began frantically calling upon the powers of Lolth to heal the fallen warrior.

But to no avail.

Jearth Xorlarrin, Tiago's most trusted companion among the ranks of the rival House, lay dead.

"You should not have let him run ahead alone!" Ravel scolded when Saribel stood up from the dead Xorlarrin noble and shook her head.

Tiago's threatening stare reminded the wizard that he was scolding a Baenre, and one that could cut him into pieces.

"What fool would cast such a cloud of noxious fumes over a bevy of dwarves?" Tiago retorted. "Their food and drink is fouler than your pathetic spell! Likely you crippled Jearth and no others—or was that your intent all along?"

Ravel found himself back on his heels at that outrageous accusation—for was it so outrageous that it would not bring the wrath of Matron Zeerith upon him?

"In the opening salvoes," Saribel said with great remorse, drawing the attention of both. The priestess shook her head. "We must finish this fight in our favor to atone for the loss. Berellip will not be pleased. Matron Zeerith will not be pleased."

"Unless we return with a gaggle of slaves to work our mines," Tiago said, and he motioned for driders to come forth with their shackles to gather and secure the captives. "And with the head of Drizzt Do'Urden. Come," he said to Saribel, to Ravel, and loudly enough to include all the others, "let us avenge the death of Jearth."

"With all speed," Ravel agreed. "Before a formal defense can be put in place." The mage cast a spell then, creating a floating wizard eye, which he sent off down the side passage.

Others of Ravel's wizardly contingent did likewise, their magic vision spreading out among the corridors, showing them the way.

CHAPTER 21

A PILE OF NIGHTCRAWLERS

"WHERE IS YOUR PET?" QUENTHEL ASKED GROMPH WHEN SHE FOUND him in his private quarters in House Baenre.

The archmage chuckled at the characterization of the illithid. "Methil remains in Q'Xorlarrin."

Quenthel took her seat opposite him, and she seemed far from pleased at the news. "Still?" she asked sourly.

"I can recall him at any time," Gromph explained. "And he is constantly in my mind, communicating. Physical distance matters little to an illithid."

"Tsabrak is off to the east," the matron mother said. "Matron Zeerith has not yet departed for Q'Xorlarrin. I do not trust her daughter Berellip . . ."

"Berellip is of no concern. To me, to you, or to Methil, surely."

"Then why have you left the mind flayer behind?"

"We found . . . an instrument," Gromph explained, a grin undeniably spreading across his face.

Matron Mother Quenthel looked at him curiously, and seemed not pleased by his cryptic response. "An instrument?"

Gromph nodded. "So it would seem."

"An instrument to further the aims of the Spider Queen?"

"Or one that was already used in that capacity," said Gromph.

"Do tell," Quenthel remarked.

"This is yet another of many moving parts," Gromph replied. "Perhaps. Or perhaps not. It is astounding, is it not, how so many things have come full circle, to land back before us at this critical time?"

The matron mother seemed initially as if she would shriek in rage at the continuing evasiveness of the archmage, but Quenthel, instead of bluntly verbally lashing out, paused and tilted her head.

She was honestly considering the words, Gromph recognized, and he saw that as further evidence of the progress his once immature and weakling sister continued to make. Methil's work implanting Yvonnel's memories continued to amaze.

"The son of Barrison Del'Armgo returned to us at precisely this time," Gromph explained, "and bearing the sword of our slain brother, no less! Slain by the hand of the same heretic who once murdered you."

Quenthel's eyes narrowed, but she was not angry with him, Gromph knew.

"The same rogue who brought the recent scream from Lady Lolth, and to whom you have now properly and cleverly reacted by reconstituting his damned House."

"A rogue known to Jarlaxle," Quenthel agreed. "Who is surely now caught in the web of Drizzt."

"You will force alliance from Matron Mez'Barris through manipulation of Tos'un, no doubt, as you glue the bondage of Matron Zeerith through Tsabrak and Saribel. And really, is there anything more facilitating than war to bring all of the Houses into line?"

"And now another instrument, so you say," Quenthel prompted.

"So many seeming coincidences!" Gromph replied with dramatic flair. "That Jarlaxle brought to me the head of our dead mother, and that Methil El-Viddenvelp returned to haunt the caverns just outside of our home, that he and Yvonnel the Eternal could so aid us in this time of great upheaval. Are these fortuitous and random events? Or have the gods, or has Lady Lolth, so cleverly planned for this time of the Sundering?"

"It is enough to make you wish that you were more devout, I expect," Matron Mother Quenthel said slyly.

Gromph laughed. "Devout enough, it would seem, given my current role in the Spider Queen's spinning web."

Quenthel conceded that point with a nod. "And now another instrument, so you say," she prompted again, a bit less patiently this time.

"Perhaps."

"Do tell."

Gromph stared at her for a few moments, then shook his head. "When I am certain," he answered, and Quenthel scowled.

"There are too many moving parts in this great clockwork," the archmage explained. "You need not bother with this other potential cogwheel at this time."

"It is not your place to determine what I should or should not bother with," the matron mother warned.

But Gromph merely smiled. "My play parallels your own," he informed her, "as it was in the tunnels outside the city, when I took you to Methil. Go and pray, I beg, and you will see that my decision serves Lady Lolth best. You have a dangerous rival to coerce to your side, a House to reconstruct and a war to prepare, do you not? If this instrument I have found is deemed suitable for your needs, then I will reveal it to you, and indeed, trouble you with it. If not, then better that you are not distracted."

"You hide this from me for my own good?"

"I hide nothing. I will not distract you until I am sure that the distraction is worthy of your time and thought."

He watched his sister closely as he spoke the words, thinking of how Quenthel would handle such a retort as compared to the expected reaction he would have received from Yvonnel.

And indeed, Quenthel seemed to be working her way through an internal struggle at that moment, though she did well to keep her expression calm. Her long pause was telling, though.

"A parallel play to a common goal, then," she said at length, and rose to leave. "You will inform me when the illithid returns."

Gromph nodded and his sister—no, he couldn't think of her as such at that moment, for indeed, she had answered as wise Yvonnel would have—and the Matron Mother of Menzoberranzan left his chamber.

The intrusion of the tentacles did not disgust her as much, her revulsion diminishing with each session—sessions that were fast becoming commonplace, though Dahlia truly had little notion of the passing of time.

She knew this place, she thought, as memories of the swirling sounds of the water elementals and the subtle thrum of the fire primordial in the pit before her brought her back to the days of Sylora Salm and the destruction of Neverwinter.

She couldn't quite sort it out.

She knew the chamber was different, too, and she noted the many drow craftsmen and goblin workers rushing around, carrying metal. A ladder? A railing?

Directly before her came a grinding sound of stone sliding on stone as the many goblin workers fitted the marble top of . . .

Of what? A sarcophagus? An altar? A sacrificial table, perhaps? It was a smooth black stone, she noted, shot with red veins, like blood.

Yes, like blood.

Fleeting images, many of Dahlia's memories, some of things she did not understand, crossed her mind as the room before her faded away, and she could not honestly recognize what the illithid was taking from her, or what it was offering to her.

It was all a blur, and the throbbing pain of Methil's work could not be denied.

She heard herself screaming, but that, too, seemed distant, as if she was hearing the screams of some other woman in some other room being violated to the core of her very identity.

She tried to thrash around, but the spiders had done their work well and the filaments held her in place, standing there, arms out wide as if staked.

Helpless.

At some point, she lost consciousness, overwhelmed by the intrusion, the horror, the confusion.

"There!" Regis said triumphantly, holding forth a small piece of pottery he had created, like a tiny soup bowl.

Wulfgar stared at the item for a few moments, then let his gaze drift past it to the elaborate set-up of smoking vials, metal tubing, and a small fire pit. Then he looked to Regis, his expression blank.

"Magnificent, is it not?" the halfling teased.

"It is not," Wulfgar remarked. "I have seen old women fire clay with half the trouble, to create bowls one might actually use."

"Ah, because you do not understand. This is no ordinary pot."

"Perhaps for a chipmunk."

Regis sighed and returned the stare, and Wulfgar merely shrugged.

Sitting at the side of the small room, Catti-brie gave a little chuckle, enjoying their banter.

"Come and see," Regis bade her.

"See what?" Wulfgar asked him. "All this effort for a chipmunk bowl?"

"On what item did you place your enchantment of light?" the halfling asked when Catti-brie had come over. After the goblin fight, the woman had lit up the area with a great light spell, and kept it with them now, in this room, allowing Regis to more easily practice his alchemy.

"My ring," she explained, holding up her hand to show the ruby band Drizzt had given to her.

"Place it on the table," Regis instructed, and Catti-brie pulled off the band and set it down.

"Notice that the light is not blocked by the table," Regis explained. The others knew that, of course, but they reflexively looked down at the floor beneath the table. There was a bit of a shadow, but not much, for such was the dweomer of magical light spells that they didn't actually emanate from the target source, but rather, they encompassed an area.

"Of course," Catti-brie said.

Regis's smile went wide at that prompt and he upended the small bowl and placed it over the ring. The room was still lit, but the bowl remained dark, clearly blocking the magical light.

"Like the hood of a lantern!" Regis announced.

Catti-brie was nodding, obviously trying to sort through the implications and possibilities, though Wulfgar seemed at a loss.

"How did you do that?" Catti-brie asked.

"The lichen," Regis explained. "I noticed when harvesting it that it emanated its own light, of course, but was not translucent to the light, any light, even yours. I've read about this," he explained and nodded to his alchemy book, "but I didn't think I could properly distill the essence."

"A trick, but to what end?" asked Wulfgar.

Smiling even wider, Regis scooped up a second tiny ceramic bowl, then gathered the first and the ring it held and put the two together, forming a ball. The room darkened a bit, but the magic still leaked through the seam of the two joined cups. Regis moved to a tray at his still, and dipped his finger in some of the material that had not yet hardened. He held up his finger for the others to see, showing them the dark brown stain of the material there, then ran it along the seam between the halves of the ball, smearing it with his concoction.

The room darkened immediately, and would have been pitch black except for the small flame of the still and a bit of greenish-white light from the glowing lichen along the edge of the room.

"You blocked the light," Wulfgar remarked, his tone showing him to be thoroughly unimpressed.

"No," Catti-brie corrected, her voice filled with awe. "You blocked the magic."

"Yes," Regis replied.

"What does that mean?" Wulfgar asked at the same time.

"When I wore that ring, if I put my hand under the folds of my robes, the light around us would not have diminished," Catti-brie explained. "It would take a thick wall of dense material to truly defeat magical light, yet Regis has done it with a small piece of ceramic."

In the dim light, Regis noted Wulfgar's conciliatory shrug, but the barbarian still wasn't quite catching on here as to how powerful a tool Regis had just crafted, as was obvious when Wulfgar pointedly asked, "To what end?"

"The ceramic is brittle," Regis explained. "What do you think might happen if I threw the ball against the stone floor, or wall?"

Wulfgar paused for a few heartbeats, then laughed. "I think our enemies would be surprised."

"Particularly drow enemies," Regis remarked, "who prefer the darkness."

"What ho!" came a cry as the door banged open and torchlight flooded the room. Under that orange flicker loomed the shadowy and scowling face of Bruenor Battlehammer, battle-axe up and ready for a fight.

"Bruenor!" Regis and Catti-brie called together to calm him.

"We thought you were in trouble," came a whispered explanation in the voice of Drizzt who was, somehow, standing right among the trio.

And all three nearly jumped out of their boots.

"The absence of light," Drizzt explained. "I thought the drow had come and countered your spell."

Regis crushed the ceramic ball in his hand and the room brightened immediately.

"Our halfling friend has created valuable tools for us as we travel deeper," Catti-brie explained, taking the ring back from Regis and slipping it on her hand.

"Several, I hope," Regis agreed. "If you can cast the spells."

"Tomorrow," Catti-brie promised.

"And antivenin," Regis added, moving to his still. "I have become quite adept at making it since I brew poisons for my hand crossbow and often prick my fingers on the darts. I cannot tell you how many times I have fallen into a deep slumber when I should have been working!"

"Aye, and he's thinkin' we're to be surprised by that," Bruenor dryly replied.

Regis gave him a smirk, then held up one of a handful of glass vials, each filled with a milky liquid. "Specifically to counter the drow poison," he explained. "If we draw near to them, drink one of these and you should fend the insidious sleep of their hand crossbow quarrels for half the day."

"Good," Drizzt congratulated. "And we will draw near to them, I expect. Bruenor and I went all the way to the great stair—it is down, but that should not prove too great a challenge." He glanced to Catti-brie, who returned his look with an assuring nod.

"The better news is that the room below was empty," Drizzt went on. "Gauntlgrym is not as thick with drow as we feared, it would seem."

"But if that is so, then perhaps they have gone with their prisoners," Wulfgar remarked.

"Let us take our rest and take it quickly," Drizzt said, and he didn't add, but they all knew and feared that they might be traveling deeper into the Underdark in pursuit of the dark elves.

Dahlia awakened many hours later to discover that she was lying once more before the three hanging cages in the hot Forge. She glanced over at dead Brother Afafrenfere, and felt only a fleeting moment of pity.

She turned her head to regard Artemis Entreri, hanging limply within his cage, his face pressed against the bar. Was he, too, dead? A stab of fear struck her.

Yes, fear, and that instinctive reaction reminded Dahlia of who she was, triggered the identity she had known as her own. With great effort, she forced herself to a sitting position, and she sighed in relief as Entreri opened his eyes to consider her.

But like her pity for the monk, it was a fleeting blip of consciousness, for other thoughts crowded in at her then, and a sly smile came over her as she thought about how delicious it would be to gather up a hot poker and stick Entreri with it.

That image jolted her and her smile disappeared, replaced by a scowl that was not aimed at Entreri, but at herself. She felt overbalanced, overwhelmed, as if her true thoughts were a single worm in a pile of slithering nightcrawlers, all crowding in to gain supremacy in her thoughts.

"Dahlia?" Entreri asked in a voice that was too firm for one who had been left hanging for this long—but that was too fine a point for battered Dahlia to register.

"Have you gained their confidence, then?" Entreri asked, and motioned to Dahlia's legs, neither of which was chained to a metal ball any longer.

But Dahlia had no idea what he might be referring to.

"They are not many now," Entreri whispered.

"You believe you can escape?" Dahlia said back at him with a little smirk.

"We," he corrected.

"No, we cannot," she stated simply.

"It's worth the chance," he prodded. "Better they catch us and kill us than . . ." He paused and looked up, then leaned in tight, like dead weight pressing limply against the bars.

The mithral door leading to the primordial chamber opened and Priestess Berellip entered the Forge, her focus immediately falling on Dahlia, and thus, on him. She moved up to the drow craftsman at the Great Forge of Gauntlgrym and struck up a conversation, but she kept glancing over at Entreri and Dahlia.

"We have to try," Entreri whispered to the elf woman, though he never changed his position.

But Dahlia shrugged, unable to wrap her thoughts around his suggestion, unable to even comprehend such a thing as leaving.

She understood what he was saying, and one worm among the pile of nightcrawlers in her mind thought his advice to be correct. That one worm became harder and harder to find in the teeming mass, though, as the intrusions of illithid conjured other memories, painted other images, and offered other temptations.

Dahlia laughed and simply turned away.

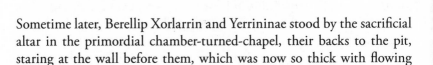

Sometime later, Berellip Xorlarrin and Yerrininae stood by the sacrificial altar in the primordial chamber-turned-chapel, their backs to the pit, staring at the wall before them, which was now so thick with flowing veils of webbing that the stones could no longer be seen.

To either side of that web-wall stood the large jade spiders, the web anchors, the sentries of the two exits, one beside the corridor to the Forge, the other beside the now-closed tunnel that would serve as Matron Zeerith's private chambers.

The entry of that second tunnel could not even be seen now, so blocked was it by thick webbing.

Berellip glanced to her left, past Zeerith's chamber, and to the walkway that had been rebuilt to the anteroom across the primordial pit. Water poured down around it from the continuing magic that secured the primordial, and steam rose up from below, so that she could only catch glimpses of the glistening metal.

The priestess turned a bit more, straining her neck, looking across the way to that anteroom where Methil El-Viddenvelp meditated and where a large water elemental guarded the lever—and likely guarded, too, the illithid, since both creatures were allied with Gromph Baenre.

"Ravel will soon turn for home," Berellip told the drider, changing the subject in her thoughts because she didn't want to remind herself too often that the conniving Baenres had such ready access to this most holy place.

"Successful in his hunt?"

Berellip's pause had the angry drider narrowing his eyes threateningly. "Tiago Baenre's obsession with the rogue has cost me greatly," he reminded.

"This is not about you, aberration," a strange voice, watery but undeniably female, answered, and both Berellip and Yerrininae turned fast at the unexpected sound to see the webs in front of Matron Zeerith's chambers turning around as if unwinding, like Tiago's rotating shield, except that their movement drew the circular strands together at the web's perimeter, opening a portal through which walked a most beautiful and quite naked drow female.

NIGHT OF THE HUNTER

"If you speak again, I will cast you into the primordial's maw," the drow woman warned.

And Yerrininae obeyed, because he knew, as did Berellip, that this was no mere drow but a handmaiden of Lolth, a yochlol come unbidden to their House chapel.

Berellip fell to her knees, dropped her face into her palms, and began to pray. The huge drider beside her squatted so that his bulbous spider body went flat to the floor, and he similarly lowered his gaze. He did not pray, though. Driders were not allowed to pray.

"Rise," the handmaiden commanded Berellip, and she did, and quickly, and awkwardly and she felt quite the fool as she nearly pitched over the edge of the stone altar in front of her.

The handmaiden made no note of it, and wasn't even looking at her, she realized as she noted the beautiful drow turning all about, nodding slowly and approvingly it seemed.

"Where is the staff?" she asked, turning back around to face the priestess.

Berellip looked at her in puzzlement.

"The *darthiir*'s weapon," the handmaiden clarified impatiently.

"I-in my chambers," Berellip stammered, truly at a loss, for how could the handmaiden know about that curious quarterstaff?

The handmaiden nodded and slowly turned around in a movement that reminded Berellip that the creature's true form more resembled a half-melted, legless candle than this exquisite woman standing before her. The handmaiden lifted one arm out toward the antechamber across the chasm, though it was not visible through the fog and raining water.

"It is time," she said, her voice drifting around, filling the room, and she walked back to the tunnel-like room, through the opening in the web, which immediately began to rotate once more, the other way this time, sealing the entrance behind her.

Fetch, came the notion in Berellip's head, and in the drider's as well, and both knew what it meant, strangely, and both were moving, and swiftly, before the mind flayer had even crossed the bridge to the main chapel.

Dahlia thrashed in her sleep, groaning and tearing at the few clothes she still wore. Her shirt hung in tatters, the smooth and white skin of her legs showed in many places through the tears in her pants, and she had lost her boots—or her tormentors had taken them from her.

Entreri watched it all with true sympathy, sharing Dahlia's pain—or trying to, for he could not imagine what horrors the dark elves might be inflicting upon her to elicit the distant and profound screams he had heard her cry.

He was going to have to leave her, he realized.

No, he was going to have to kill her, for her own sake. He had been given only meager scraps to eat, and his strength would not hold for much longer. He couldn't wait, and he could not hope to get through to Dahlia. He would escape, that very day when the forges burned low.

He looked at Dahlia, realizing how hard it would be to take her life no matter the justification, no matter that it was for her benefit.

A loud banging sound drew his attention away from the sleeping elf woman, to the small door in the middle of the room, the entryway to the primordial chamber. A group of drow worked there, goblins rushing to and fro to their calls, putting the finishing touches on a new archway they had fashioned to further strengthen the mithral door.

One drow crafter, a priestess, Entreri believed, had sculpted a drider-like relief that was now being applied to the smooth door. The black adamantine stood out in stark contrast to the shining silvery mithral.

The mark of the drow on the home of the dwarves.

A moment later, the female and others rushed aside as the door banged open, and Entreri watched with hatred as the huge spidery legs of the great drider led Yerrininae's way out of the tunnel. He came through stooped low, so tall was he and so out of place in a tunnel made for dwarves, and when he straightened up in the Forge, it seemed to Entreri like a demon raising up from the Abyss.

A great, black abomination of a demon, both beautiful and ugly.

With Ambergris's mace set easily over one shoulder, Yerrininae came straight for Entreri's cage, and the assassin tried to appear unconscious, but also braced himself, expecting a rude greeting. One eye barely opened, Entreri noted Berellip also rushing from the tunnel, running across the Forge toward her private quarters.

"Wake up, little *darthiir*," Yerrininae said when he loomed over Dahlia, and he announced his arrival by using Entreri and his cage like a bell.

Fighting for breath as he spun, the assassin was sure that the hit had broken more than one rib.

He came winding around and saw Yerrininae reaching down to hoist Dahlia by her braided hair.

He came around again to see Dahlia half-standing, lurched over awkwardly, kept up only by the drider's grasp on her hair.

He came around a third time to see Dahlia struggling, grabbing at the drider's hand, trying to pull free. As he continued his spin away, Entreri heard the woman gasp in pain, and saw her straighten as Yerrininae brutally yanked her upright.

He came around once again just as Dahlia went flying to the floor as the hulking beast backhanded her across the face.

"No!" Entreri cried out despite himself.

A mace stabbed against the cage, stopping the spin.

"It lives!" the drider said, clearly elated.

The crushing blow of the heavy mace stole Entreri's breath, and before he could begin to collect his thoughts, Yerrininae hit him again.

The goblins cheered, and the drider pounded home another devastating strike.

The drow in the Forge stopped their work and similarly began to prod the drider on.

Entreri felt the metal cage cave in against his leg, which also buckled under the weight of the next agonizing blow.

The dark elves cheered, the goblins howled with sadistic glee.

"Drider!" came a cry, a voice that seemed so distant that Entreri couldn't begin to comprehend it.

The cheering stopped immediately, the only sound the fire of the furnaces and the creaking of the chain holding Entreri's wildly swinging cage.

But the assassin didn't hear any of that, nor did he register Dahlia's cry as Yerrininae yanked her up to her feet once more and dragged her across the room.

A long while later, Entreri's senses returned. He tasted blood. He felt burning pain when he tried to draw breath, and knew that one of his legs would hardly support him.

He couldn't hope to escape now, he came to realize.

And Dahlia was gone, and unless they returned her to the floor in front of him, he couldn't hope to end her misery, either.

Dahlia stood tall, with her arms straight out to the side and with a thousand spiders crawling all around her.

She knew this all too well.

But something was different this time, Dahlia sensed, though she couldn't quite sort it out. She could feel the filaments winding around her, binding her to the web wall behind her, holding up her outstretched arms.

Those arms were straighter than before, perfectly outright, and she could not bend them at all. That was the difference. The drow had put a pole across her shoulders.

No, not a pole, Dahlia then realized, to her shock. It was Kozah's Needle, her staff.

They had armed her!

For a moment, she thought that a grave mistake by her captors, thought that she could tear free of the webs and attack this Xorlarrin priestess standing before her.

But no, she could not, she then came to understand, as the strands pulled against her, pulled her to her tip-toes, then lifted her off the ground altogether.

She hung there, swaying.

The spiders continued their work, covering her with webs.

The illithid approached her, tentacles waggling.

Her screams began anew.

A long while later, she hung limply and knew no more.

She is yours now, Methil El-Viddenvelp telepathically imparted to Berellip. He methodically turned and walked off to the side, to the walkway that would take him to the antechamber across the gorge. *A fitting ornament to complete your chapel,* Methil's watery voice said in Berellip's mind, and in the minds of all the others in the room.

A wry grin spread on Berellip's face as the spiders continued their work, cocooning Dahlia. They busily crawled across her face, weaving their filament strands.

Dahlia opened her blue eyes, wide with shock. Under the mask, her face contorted in a hopeless, muffled scream.

Berellip stared at her unblinking. It would not do to laugh aloud, the priestess understood as the solemn ceremony neared its end. With a look to the great jade spiders on either end, Berellip sharply clapped her hands, and those magical arachnids began drawing in the strands, which reached up and looped over an unseen beam amidst the cobwebs, and the cocooned Dahlia began to lift higher.

She went up at a slight angle, leaning forward as she came against the web wall.

Against and into the web wall she went, just an outline then.

Just an ornament in the Q'Xorlarrin chapel, a tortured and imprisoned *darthiir* forever to look down at the sacrificial altar.

"In this place, eternally in death, may you witness the sacrifice of many of your foul kind," Berellip prayed.

Dahlia couldn't hear her.

Dahlia couldn't hear anything.

CHAPTER 22

STOKELY'S STAND

WE HAVE KILLED A SCORE AND CAPTURED A DOZEN," TIAGO LAMENTED. "They are not easily taken alive," Ravel Xorlarrin replied. "Our poison hardly slows them and they will fight even when grievously wounded. Foul dwarves."

"We came for slaves, but find corpses instead!" Tiago fumed.

"We came for Drizzt," Ravel reminded him.

"Who is likely long gone now that word has passed ahead."

The wizard gave a little laugh and Tiago glared at him murderously.

"Drizzt Do'Urden would not flee, by any accounts of his reputation," Ravel wisely explained, easing the sudden tension a bit. "Nay, he is up there with the dwarf leader, this Stokely creature, whose name is the last word uttered by the dwarves as they fall."

Ravel wisely left off the rest of his thought: that Drizzt had not been here since long before the attack. He had interrogated a few of the dwarf prisoners and as far as he could tell, they were not lying when they had divulged the news of Drizzt's departure. But Tiago didn't need to know that little tidbit, he thought, for without the coveted prize, the impulsive young Baenre would likely call off the attack and head back for Q'Xorlarrin.

That would not be a good choice, Ravel believed. They had lost several drow and a drider, and Matron Zeerith would not be pleased with that price for the gain of a few slaves. Even more important, they had lost Jearth, the Weapons Master of House Xorlarrin, the head of the Xorlarrin garrison, and one of Zeerith's favored minions.

If they returned now with this meager offering of slaves, Matron Zeerith would be outraged. She couldn't fault or punish Tiago, of course, given his nobility and protectors. And since Saribel was now to be his wife and had been ordered to return with him to Menzoberranzan by Matron Mother Quenthel herself, Matron Zeerith likely wouldn't exact any punishment upon Saribel, either. The only other targets upon whom Ravel could deflect the responsibility, Berellip and Yerrininae, had remained in Q'Xorlarrin.

That left Ravel to feel the weight of Matron Zeerith's anger.

They, indeed he, needed more slaves and a greater victory to present to Matron Zeerith to overcome her inevitable anger over losing Jearth.

"We press on," Ravel advised. "There is greater treasure to be found among the higher levels of this complex."

"Treasure and slaves, let us hope," Tiago started to say, but did not finish, for halfway through his sentence, the corridor began to shake and rumble, dust and stones falling from the ceiling. It became so violent that at one point, Ravel began casting a contingency spell to transport him far away. The shaking stopped before he cast the spell, though, and he and Tiago both understood that some other nearby tunnel had likely collapsed.

Side-by-side, Tiago on his subterranean lizard and Ravel on a created floating disc, the two nobles moved ahead to join up with their defensive line, but they were met after only a few steps by a frantic young drow female.

"The ceiling has fallen upon them!" she cried, pointing frantically to a side tunnel, and one with a cloud of dust and debris billowing out. "Oh, these devil dwarves!"

The noble drow picked up their pace and swept into the side tunnel, crossing just a short distance before coming to the intersection with a tunnel that ran parallel to the one in which they had been standing. Piles of rock blocked their way, and a swarm of dark elves and goblins dug at the stones frantically.

Ravel tapped Tiago on the shoulder and guided his glance across the way, to where a drider leg protruded from the collapsed mound, twitching in the crushed creature's death throes.

"How many?" Tiago yelled at the dark elves scrambling around the rubble.

"Several at least, Lord Baenre," one answered.

"A trio of driders," another added.

"And a host of goblin fodder," said a third from far across the way.

"Rigged to collapse," Ravel remarked. "This is a formidable enemy, and they know we've come now. We will battle for every room and corridor."

"No," Tiago replied. "Find a way. You and your mages. Find a way. We must be done with this, and quickly."

Ravel started to argue, but remembered his own predicament here and knew that Tiago's advice was doubly important for his own standing, and perhaps for his own health. He went to confer with the wizards he had brought along on this expedition.

Within an hour, a dozen magical constructs, disembodied giant eyeballs, floated along the corridors of the dwarven complex, as the drow mages took a full reconnoiter of the complex.

They had come in here without proper respect for the dwarves' resilience and readiness, but they would not make that mistake again.

"Word's out to Lonelywood," a dwarf runner reported to Stokely Silverstream. "Her boats're out, though, and it'll be a bit to bring 'em back in."

"Same with other lake towns," another dwarf remarked.

"It's all on Bryn Shander," Stokely told them, and they nodded their agreement. Bryn Shander wasn't built on the banks of any of the lakes and so her garrison was always at the ready. Still, it would be many hours before any sizable force of reinforcements could arrive.

"We'll need to hold stronger, then hold strong some more when them Bryn Shander boys get here," Stokely explained. "The boys from the lakes'll be coming in later, and here's hopin' that them boys out in Easthaven can find a barbarian tribe or two to tow along for the fight."

"Heigh-ho to that!" a dwarf cheered.

"Not takin' much to convince a barbarian to fight, eh?" said another. "That's why I'm liking them tall boys!"

Many fists began to pump at that proclamation, and Stokely even offered a nod of encouragement. The battle had started as a rout that morning, but the heroic run of Junky and the brave sacrifices of those dwarves who stood behind him and held back the drow line had given the dwarves a fighting chance.

These were Battlehammers, and to a dwarf they had seen years of combat. Construction of the bulk of the tunnels of the complex had been overseen by King Bruenor himself, along with his most trusted and veteran shield dwarves, and so had been built for defense above all else.

The drow had come on quickly, but Stokely's boys had been ready to meet that charge, and more important, Stokely's tunnels had been ready to drop in the face of that advance.

"We keep 'em locked down below and we'll turn 'em back, don't ye doubt," he told the dwarves around him.

"Aye, and might that we then chase 'em back, all the way to Gauntlgrym!" said another. "Huzzah!"

"Huzzah!" cheered the others, and Stokely nodded.

And then five of the dwarves near the wall to Stokely's left fell away suddenly, as the floor beneath their feet simply vanished.

And the wall across the room disappeared and huge javelins came flying into the gathering, and huge driders charged in behind the volley, a horde of goblins close behind.

"Breach!" Stokely and several others all cried out together, and the dwarves began to scramble, forming defensive lines. The room's conventional doors banged open and more Battlehammers charged into the fray.

The audience chamber's walls echoed with the cries of battle, the ring of metal on metal.

Stokely ran to the unexpected pit and slid down to his knees beside its edge, other dwarves joining him, including several with ropes and grapnels. The sheer walls—so sheer and smooth it was as if the stone had simply vanished—fell away for more than twenty feet, to a lower tunnel running beneath the audience chamber, and there lay the broken dwarves, two looking dead, two crawling, and one pulling himself back to his feet, having survived the fall.

Stokely started to call down to him, but the poor fellow began to jerk this way and that, and it took a moment for Stokely to register that the dwarf was being hit with missiles, hand crossbow bolts, likely.

A brilliant flash of sizzling light defeated Stokely's next attempt to call out, as a lightning bolt stole the darkness. And when it passed, only one dwarf was still trying to crawl, and none were standing.

Over went the ropes, dwarves leaping onto them to rappel down to their kin. Stokely, too, took a rope in hand.

"No, no!" cried another dwarf, a priestess named Brimble who was one of Stokely's most trusted advisers. Stokely paused and looked to her for an explanation, while others began their descent.

"It is a magical passwall!" Brimble cried. "They can dispel—"

Before she even finished, Stokely felt the weight of the rope disappear, and as he stumbled back a step, overbalanced by the suddenly diminished weight. He looked to the pit that wasn't a pit any longer, but simply the floor, as it had been.

And dwarves had started down there!

Several of those brave dwarves lay on the floor now right near to Stokely, having been ejected from the tunnel that was not a tunnel.

"Where's McGrits? He was on the rope ahead o' me!" one cried, leaping up to his feet, and two others expressed similar concerns for dwarves ahead on their respective ropes, as well.

"In the tunnel below, then," Brimble replied.

Stokely threw down his rope and drew out his battle-axe from over his shoulder. "Plenty to hit here, then!" he cried, and led the charge into the side of the drider-goblin line.

More dwarves poured in from the side tunnels.

But so, too, came the drow, and the dwarves hacking through the goblin ranks soon found more formidable foes, quicker and more deadly, and far more skilled with the blade.

The advance bogged down, the lines dissipated, and the room became a tumble of confusion, with battles in every corner.

"A blade wins a duel, but magic wins a battle," Ravel said to Tiago as they neared the battle.

"How long will our tunnel remain?" Tiago asked.

"The better part of the night, unless we choose to remove it," the confident mage replied.

No sooner had the words left his mouth, though, than the last expanse of that magically created tunnel became stone once more, and in the corridor not far from the two drow nobles, several other drow, ejected by the lapsing magic, pulled themselves to their feet.

Tiago turned a scowl on his companion.

"They have priests," Ravel explained, and calmly, as if this was a not-unexpected complication. "To more conventional tunnels, then. We have scouted them extensively and will find our way."

His calm was not persuasive, though, and Tiago continued to scowl as he swung his lizard mount around and waved for the others to follow him, and quickly.

Ravel called ahead to a pair of his fellow wizards, and they ran off, leading the way and motioning for the main drow contingent to follow. Ravel and his magical peers had indeed scouted the tunnels in this part of the dwarven complex and could make their way to the throne room through more conventional routes.

"We will get there," the brash Xorlarrin wizard told Tiago. What he didn't add, however, was that it would take some time—likely more time than those forces caught in the throne room could afford.

Tiago's returning look, however, showed that he saw right through that phony confidence. A dozen drow, a handful of driders, and a few score of goblins had gotten into the throne room, the main dwarf stronghold, before the passwall tunnel had been dispelled. A powerful force by most standards, but they were up against the bulk of the fierce dwarves of the complex, and were without magical aid.

The young Baenre warrior was trained enough and seasoned enough to understand what they'd likely find when they reached that stronghold.

Tiago grimaced and cursed the clever dwarves when the ground rumbled in the distance, as more rigged tunnels collapsed.

The dozen-and-two goblins fleeing the battle, which had become a rout, almost made it out of the room. But as they finally breached the door, they found not an open corridor waiting for them but a quartet of grim-faced dwarves, holding firm in the narrow exit, two abreast and two deep.

The lead goblins hesitated, but their frantic kin pushed them ahead, and even when they were dead, one skull split by a battle-axe, the other crushed by a warhammer, those leading goblins remained upright, pinned between the crush of their desperate kin and the braced shields of the sturdy dwarves.

"Can't hold 'em!" warned Tregor Hornbruck, a yellow-bearded shield dwarf in the front rank. He lowered his shoulder some more, and managed a weak swing of his heavy hammer, but had to retract it immediately to doubly brace the shield against the press. He was the largest and strongest dwarf under Kelvin's Cairn, so those words struck an alarm indeed.

The corridor widened just beyond the door, and if the goblins got through that bottleneck, they'd swarm.

His companion beside him grunted, too strained to even articulate his concern.

To the surprise of Tregor and his struggling sidekick, the two in the second rank didn't press in more tightly, but suddenly ran off.

"Hey, now!" Tregor roared at them, and the other dwarf grunted again. A goblin spear propped in between the shields then, nicking Tregor's shoulder, and the sting just made him set himself more firmly and push back with all his considerable strength.

"Back!" came the call behind him, and the two returned, and Tregor understood when black-shafted pole arms prodded out beside him, stabbing past the dead goblins to weaken the press behind.

"Well-thinked!" Tregor congratulated, for just back of their position stood some stone statues, and the artists had completed the sentry sculptures with actual pole arms, albeit of simple iron instead of prized mithral or adamantine.

Despite the desperate situation, Tregor couldn't help but chuckle when the pole arm stabbed past him again and he noted a stone hand, broken off at the wrist, still grasping the iron shaft.

The goblins came on again, more furiously, and the shield dwarves began to slide once more, and the pair behind them stabbed with abandon, trying to break the press.

They could not, though, despite the goblin blood pooling on the floor, and for a brief moment, the four thought their position surely lost.

But then the press disappeared, and the four soon realized it to be the last desperate move of the fleeing goblins as Stokely and his boys caught up to them inside the room.

"Well fought," Stokely congratulated when the last of the wretched goblins breathed its last.

Tregor looked past him into the throne room to note the carnage. It was hard to visually separate the bodies enough to determine where one torn corpse ended and the next began, so tight had been the fighting. Despite that chaos, the young warrior dwarf noted many of his kin among the piles of dead.

"The drow have gained this level, and own everything below it," Brimble said, running up to Stokely.

"Where're they coming up?" Stokely asked.

"East stair, but . . ." Brimble replied, and she ended there, and with a bit of a sigh, reminding Stokely of the pit that had appeared in the throne room. With their passwall spells and other magic, was there really a line of battle to be drawn?

Stokely looked to Tregor and his three companions, then glanced down the tunnel behind them, which led to the uppermost area of the complex and the outer door. "What word?" he asked hopefully.

"Bryn Shander's hours away," Tregor grimly reported. "If the folk're even comin', I mean."

"Three hours o' sunlight left," Brimble reminded him, and in looking at her plaintive expression, both Stokely and Tregor understood her intent.

"Nah!" Tregor boomed, and those around him, catching on, began to shake their heads.

But Stokely Silverstream looked back into the throne room, where at least a score of his kin lay dead. And several more had fallen through the vanished floor, surely dead or captured. They had fought terrifically, by any measure, and the goblins lay dead by the dozen, and a few monstrous driders dominated the scene, upturned and with their ugly spider legs curled upward. And drow had died, but Stokely had seen those fights, and indeed had been in one of them.

It took two of his boys to kill every drow, it seemed, and even then, it would not be an easy fight.

"Call in every outpost, gather 'em all!" he called out to all around. "We'll make for the daylight in the dale, and them damned drow won't follow!"

Not a dwarf moved, but many sets of disappointed eyes stared back at him. He had just called for them to abandon their home, something no dwarf was ever wont to do.

"We'll be back!" Stokely promised. "And we'll have the garrisons of the towns and a horde o' barbarians aside us! Don't ye doubt!"

Several dwarves began to nod.

"Now get ye going!" Stokely ordered, and that broke the trance, and all began to scramble.

But then the darkness came, blinding them all, and even the lightning bolts sizzling through the magical blackness and the brilliant, flaming bursts of fireballs could not be seen.

But surely felt.

Stokely Silverstream and Brimble staggered into a side room to catch their breath.

"Junky's down," Brimble said. She leaned on a chair by the door off the main corridor, while Stokely raced across the room to a second door. He cracked it open.

"Way's clear," he said, turning back to face her. "This'd be a better run to the front door." Even as he spoke the words, they stung him profoundly. His group had been routed and scattered in and about the throne room, overwhelmed by the dark elven magic and spinning blades in the darkness.

Now it was every dwarf for himself, something no clan leader ever wanted to face.

He knew Brimble's words to be true. Junky and some others had been catching up, but, alas, they hadn't made it. Now the best Stokely could hope for was to get out of the complex and round up some reinforcements to try to take it back.

But even that didn't exactly inspire, for how many of his dwarves would be left to inhabit the place?

Yes, it seemed to Stokely Silverstream in that dark moment that the centuries-long domain of Clan Battlehammer in Icewind Dale had come to its end.

"Come on, then," he called.

Brimble just stared at him, unblinking.

"Lass?" he asked and took a step toward her.

He stopped fast when a pair of dark elves pushed in through the door behind Brimble, a male and a female, both superbly outfitted, particularly the male, whose sword and shield both glistened, nearly translucent, and seemed as if they had captured the very stars within their depths.

"Where will you run, dwarf?" the male drow asked, stepping past Brimble without a care, and only then did Stokely fully appreciate that his dear cleric friend had fallen victim to a spell she often used, and was magically, fully, held in place.

The drow warrior lifted his sword out to the side, in line with poor Brimble's throat. "Run, then," he bade Stokely. "She will feel the pain, I assure you, and she will die slowly."

"Save yourself—perhaps you will get away," said the female, moving up to cruelly stroke Brimble's hair. Her command of the surface language was not so strong, and her accent thick, so that it took Stokely a few heartbeats to decipher her words.

"But you will know that you fled and left your friend to die," the male added, "until the darkness of death mercifully releases you from your private torment."

Stokely Silverstream turned back from the door and banged his axe against his shield. "Come on, then," he bade the drow warrior as he stepped back toward the middle of the room. "Or are ye too a'feared to fight me alone?"

"I?" the drow asked, moving forward to meet the challenge. "Do you not know who I am, dwarf?"

Stokely leaped ahead, axe swinging as he went for the quick kill—which would be his only chance to save Brimble and hustle her away, obviously.

The drow's shield seemed to roll around, and each circuit made it larger, and though Stokely had aimed to drop his axe over the top of the blocker, by the time it connected, the shield was large enough to fully defeat the attack.

Stokely fell off to that side, his right, and tucked his own shield in tight to block the stab of the drow's sword.

The fine magical blade cut right through a wooden plank, but the adamantine bands of the shield held—just barely, Stokely realized as he disengaged and glanced down. One of the bands had been cut halfway across.

"I have killed a balor at the gates of the city," the drow boasted, just as Stokely began his next advance. "Is the name of Tiago so quickly forgotten?"

That stopped the dwarf in his tracks.

"Yes, dwarf," the drow went on. "Tiago, friend of Drizzt."

"No friend of Drizzt!" the dwarf declared. "Drizzt is friend to Clan Bat—nay, Drizzt is *of* Clan Battlehammer!"

In he charged, axe swinging and chopping wildly as he moved through his best attack routines. At one point, he cut his weapon viciously across, and let himself get pulled in the wake. He came around with his shield angled sidelong to strike at the drow if he tried to advance behind the axe cut, then came all the way around, ready to strike again.

But the drow was gone, and Stokely wisely threw himself forward, barely avoiding the stabbing sword.

"Nay, foolish dwarf," said the drow who had been quick enough to get out to the side halfway through Stokely's pirouette. "Drizzt is of House Do'Urden, ever of House Do'Urden, ever of Menzoberranzan!"

And now the drow came on, pressing the attack, his sword stabbing forward in rapid succession as he powerfully advanced.

Stokely could only hope his shield would hold as he blocked the repeated thrusts and stepped back furiously. Finally he caught his balance enough to counter, and out went his axe with all his considerable strength behind it. It creased into the drow's shield, but to Stokely, it seemed more like he had struck a feather mattress, for the blow did not sound or feel sharp, but muted.

He couldn't begin to fathom the material of that shield, and his confusion became even more complete when he tried to pull the blade back but found it stuck fast.

He hesitated, staring blankly.

A drow sword slashed against his extended elbow, and Stokely let go of his weapon and retracted the torn arm.

On came the drow and up went Stokely's shield, and the dwarf's mind whirled as he considered how he might retrieve his axe, still stuck fast to that curious shield, or wondered where he might flee to gain another weapon—perhaps he could pull Brimble's mace from her frozen hand.

Or perhaps, he quickly understood, he could do no such thing.

The drow came on with such a fury that Stokely could not dodge left or right, or even retreat after the few steps he took that put his back up against the room's wall. And there, trapped, he tried to cover, but this one was too proficient, too skilled, and too well-armed.

Stokely blocked a series of sudden, powerful thrusts that cracked and flecked the wood of his shield, and a pair of heavy downward chops that creased the adamantine ring that bound the materials in place. Another thrust got through the breaking blocker and severed one of the arm straps that secured it to Stokely's forearm, and cut a nice line in the dwarf's sleeve and skin as well!

The shield fell to pieces. Stokely threw it at the drow, and threw himself at the drow behind it.

He felt the burning explosion of the sword slash across his face in mid-leap, and reached out as he descended, determined to grab hold of the drow.

But Tiago was already off to the side, and Stokely landed and staggered and groped at the empty air.

The next explosion knocked the dwarf's helm free, and cracked the back of his skull, adding to the angle of his forward lean and to his momentum, and he pitched headlong to the stone floor, pitched headlong into darkness.

And so the Battle of Kelvin's Cairn did end, and Tiago Baenre could rightfully claim victory.

But it was a hollow cheer, the noble drow knew as his kin began looting and rounding up the new-found slaves, for Drizzt Do'Urden was nowhere to be found.

And Jearth Xorlarrin, Weapons Master of Q'Xorlarrin, remained very much dead.

CHAPTER 23

THE DELICATE BALANCE

The grin on Gromph Baenre's face did little to calm the Armgo nobles standing around the throne of Matron Mez'Barris.

"The husband of Minolin Fey graces us with his presence," High Priestess Taayrul announced to her Matron, and Gromph understood that the sleight had certainly been practiced by Taayrul and approved by Mez'Barris. Taayrul was a sniveling little witch, after all, and would never expose herself to the wrath of Gromph without her powerful mother's blessing, and indeed, demand.

"By the determination of Lady Lolth herself," Gromph replied, and lightly, as if taking the insult without a care. "I would be a poor servant to ignore the Spider Queen's direct command, and a fool to ignore her determination that my child will be favored."

"Child?" Matron Mez'Barris asked.

Gromph merely smiled wider.

"Then you will elevate Minolin Fey to Matron of House Baenre, perhaps," Mez'Barris pressed. "Now that your sister Sos'Umptu has moved on to serve in House Do'Urden, the path to ascent seems rather simple."

"The path to ascent would go through Matron Mother Quenthel," Gromph replied. "Hardly simple, for there is no more difficult path to walk in all of Menzoberranzan."

"Difficult, yes, but we have a way."

Gromph matched the matron's sly look with a smirk and chuckle, which had the ever-wary Priestess Taayrul staring hard at him, and across from her, Weapons Master Malagdorl, an impulsive oaf, even took a threatening step Gromph's way, his hand going to his sword hilt.

"You have already had this discussion with Priestess Minolin," Gromph said.

"Are we to pretend that our many plans never happened?"

"That would be wise, yes."

"Or perhaps I will go to Matron Mother Quenthel and tell her of your designs against her," Matron Mez'Barris warned.

"Yes, let us go forthwith," Gromph casually replied, and that had the nobles of Barrison Del'Armgo whispering and looking at him curiously. "Or better, perhaps . . ." The archmage paused and began some spellcasting.

Malagdorl drew his weapon, Taayrul began to pray and Matron Mez'Barris leaped from her chair at the affront. To enter the audience chamber of a rival House and cast a spell unbidden by, and in the presence of, the matron . . .

Gromph paused and looked at Mez'Barris incredulously. He shifted his gaze just a bit to the side, to Malagdorl, and the archmage's smile reappeared, and this time it was one threatening a sudden and brutal death.

"You don't need to be so on edge, Matron of Barrison Del'Armgo," Gromph assured her. "Though if your weapons master advances another stride, you will need to replace him."

Matron Mez'Barris glared at her impetuous son and hissed at him until he moved back beside the throne and sheathed his great sword.

"This is a time of unity," Gromph explained. "View every step the matron mother has recently taken through that prism, and you will see the reasoning of her design."

"Will House Melarn agree with that assessment?"

"House Melarn?" Gromph asked innocently, and Mez'Barris narrowed her eyes. She wanted to call him out, the archmage knew, but she could not. If she elaborated on the affront to House Melarn, she would, at the same time, be admitting that House Melarn had put those soldiers and driders into the abandoned and sequestered House Do'Urden in clear violation of the orders of the Ruling Council.

She would even be hinting at her own complicity in creating the garrison the Baenre's had cleared from that restricted House, for surely there were Barrison Del'Armgo soldiers among that garrison. Such open secrets could never be admitted, even if all knew the truth.

"The Melarni ascend to the Sixth House with the departure of the Xorlarrins," Gromph replied. "That will satisfy eager Matron Zhindia."

"They are more powerful than Houses ranked higher, and they are more devout," Mez'Barris reminded him.

"If Matron Zhindia is as devout as you claim—and I do not dispute that," he quickly added, seeing Mez'Barris's scowl, "then she will know that the Spider Queen will not sanction any inter-House warfare at this time. Indeed, should she move against Fey-Branche, she will find Houses Mizzrym and Faen Tlabbar allied with her enemy."

The matron scowled more profoundly, clearly anticipating Gromph's next remark.

"And all of them allied with House Baenre," he stated. "Our entire might will turn against House Melarn, and destroy Zhindia's family as fully as Matron Mother Yvonnel destroyed House Oblodra in the Time of Troubles. Do not doubt that the Spider Queen would favor this."

"Have you come here to threaten—"

"Quite the opposite, Matron." Gromph cut her short and offered a bow as he spoke. When he came up, he lifted his arms in the same pose as when he was spellcasting earlier. He froze there and looked to Matron Mez'Barris for permission to continue.

Malagdorl was already leaning forward again, his face a scowl, and how Gromph wanted to simply make him vanish, to obliterate him to nothingness.

The archmage remembered that he was an ambassador here and settled for the fantasy of melting the impudent weapons master.

Matron Mez'Barris held up her hand to hold Malagdorl back, then motioned for Gromph to continue.

The archmage began to chant softly. His fingers glowed with black energy and he drew a doorway in front of him, trailing lines of blackness as substantial as if he had been painting on a canvas.

The completed lines shimmered and sparked and bled blackness within the square Gromph had drawn, until the whole shimmered like a curtain, a black portal.

Mez'Barris and her children and all the Armgo guards stood ready, many glancing around as if expecting an open portal to the Abyss itself, as if expecting a horde of demons to come roaring into their audience chamber.

But it was no horde, just a solitary figure, and that figure was not demonic, but was, rather, a drow, a female drow: the Matron Mother of Menzoberranzan.

In glancing around, it occurred to perceptive Gromph that the nobles of this Second House looking at the spectacle of Matron Mother Quenthel would have been less shocked if it had been the demon horde instead.

"Matron Mez'Barris, am I welcomed in your home this day?" the matron mother asked.

The Matron of Barrison Del'Armgo stared at her arch-rival, not knowing what to make of any of this. She swallowed hard as her gaze slipped to the portal, still shimmering, still open. Her expression revealed her fear: Was there a Baenre army ready to pour through at the matron mother's command?

"Of course, Matron Mother, if you come in the name of the Spider Queen," Mez'Barris properly replied.

"I am the Matron Mother of Menzoberranzan," Quenthel imperiously replied. "Where I go, so goes the Spider Queen, in name and in heart."

"Y-yes, Matron Mother," Mez'Barris replied, stammering just a bit in surprise, and she wisely lowered her gaze.

Quenthel's assertion of power had hit the perfect tone, Gromph understood, and he did well to hide his grin.

"There is no threat here, Matron of Barrison Del'Armgo," the matron mother said. "I am here in solidarity and alliance. We look outward now—the Spider Queen will not accept intrigue among her matrons. Not now. You are under House Baenre's protection."

Gromph held his breath at that explosive remark, and he saw the expressions of Mez'Barris and her two children tightening immediately, yet again.

"We do not need Baenre's protection," the proud Mez'Barris retorted, but Quenthel went on undeterred.

"And House Baenre is under yours," she said, stealing her counterpart's bluster.

Indeed, Matron Mez'Barris stammered indecipherably for a few moments.

Now Gromph did smile, and almost chuckled. Quenthel was playing her. She had moved Mez'Barris to a place of pride and stolen it away with her own humility in the course of two simple sentences!

"We go to war, Matron Mez'Barris," the matron mother said, squaring her shoulders to reflect the gravity of the declaration. "Tsabrak Xorlarrin prepares the battlefield, and House Do'Urden will lead the march from Menzoberranzan and Q'Xorlarrin."

"Your mother went this way before," Matron Mez'Barris warned.

"I am painfully aware of that," the matron mother replied, the personal reference a reminder that she, Quenthel, had been slain on that very adventure.

"Your mother sent forth the greatest army Menzoberranzan has dispatched in the modern age, and we returned wounded, one and all."

"A mistake that will not be replayed," Quenthel assured her. "Our force will be modest this time, for no great drow army is needed in the coming battle."

Mez'Barris and the others looked at her curiously. "What goal . . . ?" Mez'Barris started to ask.

"We have a vast army already assembled and awaiting our lead," the matron mother explained. "A kingdom of orcs, entrenched upon the land, that will sweep down upon the peoples of the cities and citadels in the region known as the Silver Marches. Woe to the dwarves in the mines who turned us back a century ago, and woe upon their fellows in two nearby citadels as well. Woe to the *darthiir*, the elves in the Moonwood, and woe to the great cities of Sundabar and Silverymoon."

"Grand claims."

"An army of tens of thousands, perhaps hundreds of thousands," Quenthel told her. "An army that was put in place for just this day. An army waiting for us to come and prod it forward."

"And so we will march," Mez'Barris said. "A collection of all the Houses, or of Do'Urden alone?"

"House Do'Urden is a creation of the Spider Queen's bite," the matron mother explained. "For Lady Lolth, this action is personal, a stab at the heart of a fellow goddess. All the Houses will send representatives. I would expect proud Barrison Del'Armgo to complement the warrior ranks. That is at your discretion, of course, though I tell you openly that House Baenre will be well-represented."

"By Sos'Umptu, who will lead this force," Mez'Barris reasoned, but Quenthel shook her head.

"Sos'Umptu will not go," the matron mother said firmly. "She leads House Do'Urden in the interim only, directing Bregan D'aerthe in their work to reclaim the House. We will determine suitable leaders for this force we send, but among them . . ." She paused and smiled.

Gromph liked that touch, noting that she had Mez'Barris leaning forward in her throne.

"The orcs will carry the fight to the peoples of the Silver Marches and they will be led by . . ."

Again she paused, holding the thought for many heartbeats. Her delay soon had Mez'Barris's two children leaning forward eagerly.

"By the son of Barrison Del'Armgo," the matron mother finished.

"Malagdorl?" Matron Mez'Barris incredulously replied.

"By Tos'un Armgo," Quenthel corrected, "wielding the sword of Dantrag Baenre, marching in the name of Daermon N'a'shezbaernon, House Do'Urden. We will wreak carnage upon the Silver Marches from behind a throng of orcs. We will repay them for our defeat that century and more ago, and we will ruin the name of the apostate Drizzt, to Lolth's glory."

"Drizzt?" Mez'Barris echoed incredulously. "I care not for Drizzt Do'Urden!"

"But the Spider Queen does, and so you shall," the matron mother replied. "Go and pray and seek guidance, you and Taayrul and all the priestesses of your House. You will see. We are called now, there is no doubt."

Mez'Barris and her daughter exchanged concerned looks, but Quenthel had them, Gromph knew, and he nodded, silently congratulating his sister, who did indeed seem more like his mother.

"There is no intrigue now among us," Matron Mother Quenthel said with a snap of finality that brooked no debate. "This is not the time."

"And so House Baenre gains two seats on the council!" Mez'Barris reminded, a flash of anger in her red eyes.

"No," the matron mother replied. "Sos'Umptu will not remain as Matron of House Do'Urden."

"Then who?"

"We will know," was all that Matron Mother Quenthel would offer.

"But still, House Do'Urden is the matron mother's creation, and so to the matron mother's control," Mez'Barris reasoned.

"If the son of Barrison Del'Armgo performs well, then perhaps Matron Mez'Barris, too, will find alliance in the reconstituted House Do'Urden—if Matron Mez'Barris is wise enough to properly support the quest of Lolth, of course. Perhaps then we will both have gained a second voice on the council."

With that tempting tidbit, the matron mother bowed and stepped through Gromph's portal. The archmage lingered in the audience chamber for a few moments, weighing the expressions and reactions of the Armgos.

I will not forget our conspiracy, or your weakness in seeing it through to fruition, Mez'Barris warned him, using her silent handcant instead of speaking aloud in case Quenthel could hear her on the other side of that magical door.

"Go find a handmaiden and discuss the matter," Gromph replied. "You will learn wisdom in my . . . weakness, and humility to temper your dangerous pride."

He bowed and stepped through, and the magical door disappeared.

"We'll not hold Luskan for long if you insist on keeping such a sizable force here in Menzoberranzan," Jarlaxle dared to say to Matron Mother Quenthel when she and Gromph paid him a visit in the Do'Urden compound.

"Beniago has the city well in hand," the matron mother replied. "Tiago is not far away, and the Xorlarrins will march to his call."

"Tiago is on his way back here, so it is said, although he seems to be taking his time about it," Jarlaxle replied, rather slyly, tipping his hand that he might know more than his counterparts regarding the movements of the brash young warrior.

Which he did not.

"And are the Xorlarrins not foremost in your plans to march to the east?" Jarlaxle went on. "Surely you will include Matron Zeerith's garrison among your army."

Jarlaxle noted Gromph's angry scowl. The archmage, standing behind the matron mother, even offered Jarlaxle a disgusted shake of his head to warn him away from this line of questioning.

Because he had called Quenthel's bluff, Jarlaxle realized. Keeping him and Bregan D'aerthe bottled up here at House Do'Urden would certainly leave their well-constructed network in Luskan too weak to resist any pushback from the more conventional forces up there; the other high captains would move on Ship Kurth if they thought they could be rid of Beniago, and more than that, if they thought they could grab their city back from Jarlaxle's hold.

"I have less than four hundred soldiers," Jarlaxle elaborated. "In total. More than a hundred are out and about the Underdark and the surface, as scouts and emissaries. You have more than two-thirds of the remaining garrison here."

Gromph held his breath, as if he expected their sister to lash out at Jarlaxle, the mercenary leader realized, but Quenthel took a long pause and seemed to be seriously considering Jarlaxle's words.

"That leaves Beniago with less than a hundred to hold our place among a city of thousands—and thousands of veteran pirates and scalawags," Jarlaxle said.

"It is said that one drow warrior is worth a hundred enemies," Quenthel replied.

"Many things are said. Few are true," Jarlaxle dared to press. "Whatever the demands of Lady Lolth in the east, it would not be wise to lose Luskan in our pursuit of her favor. This is our trade route to the surface, and has already brought great wealth and power to Menzoberranzan, including strange and mighty artifacts from the Empire of Netheril. And it is a trade route, though going straight through Q'Xorlarrin, which is solidly controlled by House Baenre."

"Neither you nor Beniago seem eager to claim that family name," Quenthel reminded him.

"Would you have us do so?" Jarlaxle asked innocently, knowing the answer, and Quenthel had to concede the point. "Through Luskan, through my organization, you will track the trading, and ultimately control the power, of Q'Xorlarrin."

"You overestimate your importance to me."

"Matron Shakti Hunzrin would disagree," Jarlaxle replied without hesitation, referring to the Matron of the Eleventh House. Even though she was not on the Ruling Council, Shakti Hunzrin carried an inordinate amount of power, because House Hunzrin was among the greatest economic forces in the city, thanks to an elaborate trade network spidering out far beyond Menzoberranzan's borders.

Matron Mother Quenthel turned and glanced at Gromph, who shrugged almost apologetically before nodding his agreement with Jarlaxle.

"You have secured the alliance with House Barrison Del'Armgo," Gromph reasoned. "Matron Mez'Barris is fully within your web. Given our stated alliance to House Do'Urden, none will dare move on House

Do'Urden at this time without Barrison Del'Armgo's nod, which Matron Mez'Barris will not dare give."

Quenthel settled comfortably then, mulling it over.

"May I return to Luskan?" Jarlaxle asked after a short silence.

"No," the matron mother sharply replied, and then more calmly, "No, but you may return half your foot soldiers from House Do'Urden back to Beniago's command."

"I am to join in the procession to the east, then," Jarlaxle said with enough of a sigh to show that he would consider that a tedious task indeed.

"No," Quenthel said flatly.

Her answer surprised the mercenary. From everything she had said, and everything he had heard elsewhere, the work in the east would be that of diplomacy more than combat, after all. And who better for that task than Jarlaxle?

"It will not be a large force that we send to the east," the matron mother explained, but perceptive Jarlaxle heard something else in her dodge, something personal regarding him, he suspected. "Our posture there is as advisors, directing the orc thousands. I'll not repeat Yvonnel's mistake. Win or lose in the Silver Marches, the price will not be high to Menzoberranzan."

"You are stirring a wasp's nest," Jarlaxle warned.

"And letting the wasps bite where they may," Quenthel agreed.

Jarlaxle mulled that over for a bit. The idea that Menzoberranzan would start a war and care so little about the outcome did not seem correct to him. Not at all.

He considered his surroundings, and considered the target. He spent a long while studying Quenthel.

Was this about Drizzt? Drizzt had once killed Quenthel, after all, and quite painfully.

"House Do'Urden will lead the fight in the east, but you will remain right here, by my side and at my call," Quenthel said flatly.

Because of his relationship with Drizzt, Jarlaxle understood, but did not dare say.

The mercenary bowed, recognizing the meeting to be at its end.

"So the march against the Silver Marches will be led by Tos'un, the Patron of House Do'Urden," Gromph said to Quenthel when they were back in his quarters at House Baenre. "And by Tiago, Weapons Master of House Baenre."

"Well reasoned," Quenthel replied. "And where is the prideful whelp?"

"He will be along," Gromph assured her. "Will you send Sos'Umptu to the east?" he asked, eager to change the subject, for he did not want to fill the volatile Quenthel in on Tiago's excursion to Icewind Dale.

"Mez'Barris already asked as much."

"Tell me personally," Gromph bade her.

"No," she answered after pausing for a moment to take a close measure of Gromph. "Priestess Saribel will serve."

"How many of our House will go?"

"Few," Quenthel replied. "The city will send perhaps a hundred warriors in total, with a score of that number from House Barrison Del'Armgo and the rest of the ranks filled with weapons masters of lesser Houses, eager to make their reputation. The contingent of priestesses, again from lesser Houses, will serve Saribel, and Q'Xorlarrin will supply the contingent of wizards—all of them, save one."

"Me," the archmage remarked, and he made sure he didn't sound enthusiastic about the possibility.

"Nay, your lackey," Quenthel corrected to his surprise and delight. "Whoever you decide that to be. Your duty is simple, my Archmage: You keep a direct line open to Tiago's fortress in the east, wherever he makes it. We would converse with him regularly on the prosecution of the war, and we will go to him with a sizable force if necessary, or recall him if prudent. I'll not lose Tiago in this excursion."

"Because he will help House Do'Urden rise to legitimate promise, affording you a second vote on the Ruling Council at your will," Gromph replied.

"After our glory in the east, House Do'Urden will ascend in rank, favored by Lolth," Quenthel agreed, and Gromph understood then that Quenthel was determined about two things in the east: that Tiago would not fall and that Tos'un Armgo would.

He saluted his clever sister with a bow.

CHAPTER 24

THE FIGHTER BESIDE YOU

Iᴺ ʟɪꜰᴇ, ꜱᴛᴇᴀʟᴛʜ ʜᴀᴅ ɴᴇᴠᴇʀ ʙᴇᴇɴ Tʜɪʙʙʟᴇᴅᴏʀꜰ Pᴡᴇɴᴛ'ꜱ ɢʀᴇᴀᴛᴇꜱᴛ strength. Quite the contrary, the ferocious battlerager usually took great pride in announcing his presence to his enemies long before battle was joined, even if that meant a few arrows or spears flying his way during his inevitable charge.

Not so in death, however, for Pwent's vampirism afforded him a congruence with the shadows that he could use as a great advantage, along with a lightness to his step enhanced by his coexistence within two forms, solid and gaseous, and two planes of existence. He was hunting among and against the dark elves, the masters of darkness, the silent killers, whose domain was the eternal night of the Underdark, and so the vampire had honed his craft to perfection now, so he believed. He wove around the drow and the goblins and the half-drow, half-spider abominations with impunity. They couldn't find him, couldn't begin to even sense him, save the shivers that coursed their spines from the chill of his proximity or the tiny hairs standing along their arms or at the back of their necks as he passed just below their conscious senses.

Pwent had murdered a score of drow, and taken nearly half of those as undead minions, and he had feasted liberally on the blood of goblin slaves many times.

Yes, this was his domain now, for none alive knew the ways of Gauntlgrym better than he. Every corridor, every broken crack, both from the sheer age of the complex and from the volcanic eruption when the primordial had found a decade of freedom, was known to him.

Never was he out of place here, for this was his place. He fancied himself the Steward of Gauntlgrym, the protector of the dwarven homeland.

He knew that to be half of his existence, at least, even while he hated the other half, the darker half, the half that could turn him against even Bruenor, his king of old.

He wanted to suppress that darkness now, he reminded himself as he crouched at the corner of a four-way intersection. His king was close, he knew, along with the others, and they, too, were friends of Gauntlgrym, though he knew not how or why or where he had once known them, if he had at all.

"Me king," he silently mouthed, but he ended with a sneer, and it was all he could do to stop that twisted scowl from becoming an audible, feral snarl.

He couldn't take a deep breath, of course, since he no longer drew breath, but Pwent settled himself more comfortably on his feet, as if allowing the gaseous aspects of his form to solidify. He eagerly rolled his fingers together, his ridged and spiked gauntlets squeaking slightly with the rub.

He knew where they were and understood where he could set an ambush with his dead drow minions.

"Me king," he mouthed again, pointedly reminding himself that he didn't want to set an ambush.

Or did he?

He glanced back, thinking how clever it would be to summon his undead drow minions, and he noted movement as he turned just slightly, just out of the corner of his eye, and so close that he knew he could be struck before he could react.

How had the dark elves gotten so close? What scout was this?

He turned around to face the would-be assassin and allowed a growl to escape his lips, and moved as if to pounce.

But he did not, for Drizzt Do'Urden stepped out before him.

Pwent eyed him carefully, shocked that he had gotten so close so easily, so invisibly, so silently. The dark elf ranger hadn't drawn his scimitars, the magical blades resting comfortably at his hips.

The vampire's roving eye met Drizzt's gaze and Pwent let another soft growl escape his lips.

"I left you in a cave," Drizzt said. "As a friend. In trust."

"Then yerself's a fool," the dwarf replied.

"Am I? The Thibbledorf Pwent I once knew was no coward."

As the insult registered, Pwent threw himself at the drow.

Out came Drizzt's blades in a flash, cutting and stabbing, it seemed, before they had even lifted from their respective scabbards. Despite his rage, despite his condition, Pwent surely felt the bite, and that sting slowed him, but only for a moment as he reset his feet, roared, and leaped ahead.

But leaped to the side of his intended target, he realized to his surprise, and it took him a moment to understand that his aim had indeed been true, but that Drizzt had moved aside, so quickly and effortlessly.

The scimitars slashed hard at Pwent as he tried to slow and turn, driving him along. He stumbled as he disengaged, and swung around, ready to lower his head and charge back to impale the fool, but Drizzt was already there with him, beside him, hacking away, driving Pwent back down to the side.

His defensive movements couldn't catch up to the barrage; everywhere he managed a swing, Drizzt was already gone, the scimitars ringing in against him from another angle.

Finally, the vampire leaped and twirled around, roaring and landing solidly, feet wide apart, arms swinging in left and right.

But Drizzt was already far away from him, standing comfortably, blades swinging easily.

"Must it be like this, my old friend?" Drizzt asked.

Pwent turned half-gaseous, leaving a trail of swirling fog, so swift was his sudden charge in that curious ghost step of the greater undead. But Drizzt had seen it before, both from Pwent and from Ebonsoul, and the drow appropriately dodged aside and even managed to meet Pwent's return to his full corporeal form with another stinging stab of a curving blade.

Then off Drizzt scampered, to the side once more, and an angry Pwent turned to face him.

"Ye're not hurtin' me, elf," the vampire growled. "And yerself's sure to get tired, but not for me, no." He wore a wicked grin and came forward menacingly.

"I never knew you to be a coward," Drizzt stated flatly.

Pwent pulled up short. "Eh?"

"I left you in a cave, awaiting the sun," Drizzt explained. "I trusted that you, that the Thibbledorf Pwent I knew, would prove strong enough and courageous enough to meet his better fate with his eyes open. But no, you disappoint me, my old friend. In death, you are nowhere near the dwarf you were in life."

"Bah, but what're ye knowin'?" Pwent snapped back. "I found me way and found me place."

"A place to agree with the principles of who and what you once were?"

"Aye."

"Protector of Gauntlgrym, then?" asked Drizzt.

"Aye!" Pwent said with great exuberance. "Steward!"

"And defender of the grave of King Bruenor?"

"Aye, and ye're knowin' as much!"

"And so you attack me? An ally to your beloved king?"

"Get out!" Pwent roared and took another step forward.

"Because you're hungry," Drizzt said, and he sheathed his scimitars. That motion froze Pwent in place once more and he stared at the drow, clearly at a loss. "I'm tryin', elf," he managed to mouth.

"We're going for Entreri and the others."

"Lots o' drow," the dwarf vampire warned. "But there are ways to get in."

"You know these ways?"

"Aye."

"Then help us," Drizzt offered.

Pwent trembled; his face twitched and twisted, upper lip raising in a snarl to reveal his long canine teeth. "I . . . meself . . . I, I can't be with ye, or near ye," he said in a pleading tone. "The smell . . ."

"Smell?"

The vampire growled.

"Pwent!" Drizzt said sharply.

"Yer blood!" Pwent explained. "Ah, but the sweetest o' smells."

"Then go ahead of us!" Drizzt said, his voice raising in a bit of desperation and his hands going to his blade hilts again, as he clearly saw that Pwent was about to throw himself into battle once more.

"Go ahead and mark the way for us!" Drizzt continued. "Scrape the wall at every intersection! Lead us to the drow, to Entreri and Dahlia and the others!"

"Girl's gone," Pwent managed to grumble. "Drow killed her to death, I'm guessin'. Fed her to the spiders . . ."

Drizzt felt an enormous lump in his throat, but he managed to say, "Lead us," right before the area lit up with the magic of an enchanted light.

Pwent went into his half-gaseous, half-corporeal swift step once more, rushing at Drizzt so quickly that the drow could not react and thought himself surely doomed.

But the vampire went right past him, hustling away down the corridor and around a bend, and a moment later, Drizzt heard Bruenor call out, "Elf?"

And a moment after that, Drizzt heard a metallic scrape against the stone wall from the other direction, and knew that Pwent was guiding them.

"I envy you," Artemis Entreri said to Brother Afafrenfere, who hung motionless beside him.

Despite his words, though, the assassin could not bring himself to join Afafrenfere in the long sleep of death. He could have easily accomplished that end if he truly so desired. He could pick the lock and hold the door just a bit open and let the lightning magic of the glyph eat him. Or he could just sneak out and murder another drow, take his weapons and battle until they overwhelmed him. Yes, that would be a fitting end, he thought.

Several times, Entreri told himself to do it.

Several times, he lifted his hand and the small metal scrap he had secured near the cage's lock.

But every time, the hand came back down.

Dahlia was out there somewhere, and she needed him to find a way, Entreri told himself. He couldn't give up. Not yet.

Even as he tried to convince himself of that, though, his hand drifted back up toward the lock. What did it matter? Dahlia wouldn't even talk to him—how could he begin to convince her to leave even if he discovered the impossible and found a way to facilitate such an escape?

But no, he decided. There was no way. So he'd get out and find a weapon and kill a few drow and be done with it all. His hand actually made it to the lock this time and he had just slipped the metal scrap in when a sudden noise made him instinctively retract.

He looked out across the way, to see the great drider, Yerrininae, rushing along, his eight legs scraping loudly against the stone floor. He carried Skullcrusher in one hand, his great trident in the other. A trio of driders followed him along the opposite wall of the long and narrow room, moving past the portal to the primordial chamber, the now-ornate mithral door with its new adamantine border, then past Entreri's position. They paused to confer with some drow, blacksmiths and guards, the great drider issuing orders, it seemed.

The driders moved on, turning out of the last side corridor exiting the room, diagonally and far to Entreri's right. That tunnel ran behind the primordial chamber, he knew, and to the outer tunnels of this low level. In the Forge, the dark elves scurried about, motioning to goblins who rushed to close the forge oven doors and smother the open fires.

The room darkened, then grew blacker still as dark elves cast their magical darkness where the hot orange light slipped through the creases about an oven door.

"Dahlia?" Entreri asked quietly, wondering if perhaps she had somehow managed to escape.

He heard a sound, a scuffle, off the other way, back toward the near end of the room. He craned his neck to see, but it was too dark. He heard a goblin shriek, and with such terror that it surely startled the assassin.

The ugly little creature came by him then, very near, near enough for him to make it out, and to note the drow draped around it, tearing at it, biting at it.

Biting? Entreri couldn't make sense of it, but there it was, right in front of him.

More noise erupted back from where the two had come, the sound of fighting, of goblins crying out in fear, of dark elves calling out for help and damning their enemies. Had the goblins revolted, Entreri wondered?

But only briefly, for there came a cry, a dwarven cry, and it was followed almost immediately by the scream of a dark elf, one quickly muffled.

Another pair of combatants rolled past Entreri, actually banging against his cage and sending him into a swing. His hand went up immediately to the lock, thinking that he might have to quickly get free here, but he froze in amazement as he noted the combatants, a pair of dark elves. And one seemed unarmed, while the other slashed at her wildly.

Again and again, the fine sword struck, drawing deep gashes. But the victim didn't seem to care. She just grabbed at him and bit at him, her hands raking deep wounds in the male's face. He hacked mightily, frantically, and an arm fell to the floor, but still she came on, throwing herself over him and bearing him down and biting hard at his face as they rolled away into the darkness.

Entreri didn't know what to do, or what might be going on around him. It made no sense.

A bright light exploded back the other way, past the Great Forge that centered the chamber, filling that far area of the room with its brilliant shine. The dark elves in that illuminated region threw their hands over their eyes and fell back—one waved her hands in spell-casting, squinting with every word, clearly stung by the light. Her darkness spell countered the brightness, but only briefly as another burst of light appeared.

The drow female fell back, and was assailed by an attack that Artemis Entreri surely recognized, as the sizzling, blue-white streak of a lightning arrow chased her back into the shadows, and stole those shadows with a flash as it blasted into the drow and sent her flying away.

Another arrow flew off, and Entreri anticipated it and so could follow it to its source. He noted the archer in the form of a drow crouched near the mithral door. For a brief instant, Artemis Entreri wondered how he might have possibly gotten there in the midst of his wary and deadly enemies. But the assassin dismissed that question before it could even register, for he knew this drow, Drizzt Do'Urden, the Hunter, and with that recognition, the assassin could not be surprised.

Another burst of light erupted, and this time Entreri managed to better note the attackers: a dwarf, a halfling, and a giant of a man, forming a wall before an auburn-haired woman who twirled in spell-casting movements, her white gown and black shawl flying out with each turn like ghostly wisps of a partly ethereal form. Blue-glowing mist swirled out of the voluminous sleeves of her gown, curling around her arms like some physical manifestation of the magical energies she collected around her.

"No," Entreri breathed as all three raised their hands and threw forth some small objects, tiny stones, they seemed. But no, they were ceramic balls, which broke open when they crashed down, freeing more globes of magical light to fill the room.

"It cannot be," Entreri mouthed silently.

A pea-sized lick of flame flew from the woman's hand off to the side of the room, where it exploded into a tremendous fireball, immolating a group of goblins and sending a couple of dark elves running off into the small bits of remaining darkness, covering their heads and diving into rolls and frantically patting at the biting flames.

And on came the invading foursome, their determined advance led by a sudden barrage of lightning arrows that tore through the defensive line being formed to block them.

They were using the light as the dark elves might use the darkness, Entreri realized, blinding their foes as surely as a drow's darkness dweomer would steal the sight from a surface dweller.

And this small group was not alone in the fight, obviously, for back the other way, a wilder battle had joined, drow against drow, goblin against drow, and with a single dwarf thrashing furiously among the wild tumult, a dwarf wearing a huge head spike and gauntlet spikes and spiked armor all around, a dwarf covered in blood and reveling in it.

Back the other way, the cry of "Tempus!" echoed off the stones and the forges, and a spinning warhammer sent a dark elf flying, dead long before she hit the ground.

"It cannot be," Artemis Entreri whispered again, now watching as the warrior trio met their foes.

A great horn sounded, melodic and rumbling, harmonic and cold, as if it had bellowed from the very halls of a barbarian god.

"It cannot be," he said a third time, and then came the rumbling growl of a giant hunting cat and he knew that it was indeed.

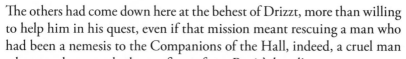

The others had come down here at the behest of Drizzt, more than willing to help him in his quest, even if that mission meant rescuing a man who had been a nemesis to the Companions of the Hall, indeed, a cruel man who once long ago had cut a finger from Regis's hand!

Yet Regis was here in the line, fighting bravely, for the sake of Artemis Entreri, for the responsibility of his friendship to Drizzt.

Bruenor did not miss the significance of that, reinforcing the bond of this troupe, the true measure of friendship. He thought himself a fool once more for ever thinking of abandoning his oath to go to Kelvin's Cairn on the appointed night, and he was glad to be here for the Companions of the Hall, for his dear friend Drizzt.

But there was indeed another reason, another impetus, powering the dwarf ahead, and he centered the line between Wulfgar and Regis and drove them on furiously, his many-notched axe cracking through goblin shields and goblin skulls, tossing aside the fodder that he could catch up to the dark elves who had taken this place.

This was Gauntlgrym, the ancient home of the Delzoun dwarves. These were the forges, particularly the Great Forge, which had brought Bruenor's people wealth and commerce and high reputation.

The damned drow did not belong here!

Bruenor felt the spirits of the dwarven gods within him, the wisdom of Moradin, the strength of Clangeddin, the secrets of Dumathoin. In his last battle in this place, he had become as those gods and had battled a pit fiend, among the mightiest devils of the Nine Hells, a great monstrosity that should have been far above his ability. But he had won. With the wisdom, the strength, and the secrets, he had overcome that foe, and so it would be now, he decided flatly.

A goblin came up before him and up went his axe, and up went the goblin's shield.

The power of Clangeddin flowed through Bruenor's arms as he brought that axe down, and though the goblin's shield, forged in this very room, held firm, the sheer weight of the blow stunned the creature and drove it to its knees.

And Regis was there suddenly, beside Bruenor, stabbing the goblin through the ear.

Bruenor kicked the dying creature aside and charged at a pair of dark elves.

A hammer flew in over him, a magical arrow shot in from the side and a barrage of bolts of magical energy swerved around the dwarf's stout frame and stabbed ahead at his enemies to lead him in.

"Bah!" he snorted in disappointment, with one drow struck dead by Wulfgar's hammer, the other hustling back the other way, calling goblins in around her to defend her limping retreat.

"Bah!" Bruenor shouted again, swatting aside a pair of goblins. "Ye're stealing all me fun!" His axe cut deep into the side of one goblin and drove the victim hard into the other, knocking it aside. Still focused on the dwarf, that goblin squeaked in surprise when it found the waiting grasp of Wulfgar, who hoisted the flailing creature up above his head and launched it hard into the side of the nearest forge.

"Get me something big to hit!" Bruenor cried, and no sooner had he spoken the words than it seemed as if his wish would be granted, as a quartet of monstrous driders came onto the battlefield. They seemed to want nothing to do with Pwent and his vampire minions, and rushed past that skirmish, heading straight for the Companions of the Hall.

"Well now!" Bruenor said, enthusiastically.

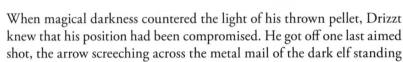

When magical darkness countered the light of his thrown pellet, Drizzt knew that his position had been compromised. He got off one last aimed shot, the arrow screeching across the metal mail of the dark elf standing before Bruenor, then turned to the middle of the battlefield, the drow and goblin position between Pwent's force and the advancing companions, and let fly a barrage of bolts, one after another.

He took no pause to aim, though more than one goblin and even another drow went down under his explosive assault. He was more interested in causing confusion, preventing any coordinated movements by the enemy.

Somewhere in the background of the thunderous battle sounds, the ranger heard the click of hand crossbows and he reflexively covered, and just in time against a concerted volley aimed his way.

Still, Drizzt felt the sting of a quarrel, then another, and a third, finding seams in his armor and crouch to bite at his flesh. The wounds were not serious, nor, Drizzt hoped, would be the poison.

He silently thanked Regis when his arms did not go heavy. The halfling had given them all potions to drink before entering this room, magical elixirs that would counter drow poison, so Regis believed, and so they all had hoped.

Drizzt broke from his crouch and came up strong, scimitars flashing into his hands to meet the charge of a pair of dark elves, and he felt no sluggishness, no weight of sleep poison at all, as his blades worked in and out, ringing with parries against all four swords that came in at him.

He ducked fast before he had even disengaged to avoid a javelin flying between his foes and straight for his face.

"Guen!" he called as that drow woman behind the fray lifted another javelin his way.

Her arm went back to throw, but did not come forward. Nay, it went fast to the side instead, as she went fast to the side instead, buried under the raking claws of six hundred pounds of fighting panther.

Drizzt had no time to watch that show, his scimitars snapping all around, working across before him and back out wide on sudden backhands. He tried to take a measure of his opponents, to see which was the weaker, the more vulnerable. But these drow were not strangers to battle, he soon realized, and had fought side-by-side before, likely many times, and it was all Drizzt could do to keep them at bay.

He needed help to break away, he realized, and he looked to Guenhwyvar and started to call out for her to be quick to his side.

But then he saw the driders, one in particular rushing for Guenhwyvar, and his call transformed into one of warning.

The chamber door banged open, startling the drow females inside. As one they jumped and turned around, spells already begun, but they saw that it was one of their own, the priestess they had sent scouting. "The Forge, lady!" that young drow cried to Berellip.

Berellip Xorlarrin chewed her lip and silently cursed her ambitious brother and that fool Tiago. They had taken too many on their hunt. They had left Q'Xorlarrin vulnerable.

"Gather the guards from the mines and all the goblin workers," she ordered. "Where is Yerrininae?"

"He has gone to the fight with his driders," the young priestess reported, and Berellip nodded.

Berellip started to respond, ready to order her sisters into a proper fighting group that they could charge in to support their allies. But before she could even get started, she noted the young cleric's lips moving, as if she were struggling to convey something.

"What is it?" she demanded.

"The rogue," the young priestess explained. "It is Drizzt Do'Urden, come to Q'Xorlarrin!"

Berellip's eyes went wide as she sucked in her breath, nearly knocked from her feet by the startling news. She looked around at her sister priestesses and saw them equally at a loss.

She could claim the prize, she dared to think, and would not Tiago Baenre suffer then for his choice of Saribel?

"Gather the guards!" she started to yell, but a sharp intrusion stung her brain, a watery voice sounding in her thoughts.

They are beyond you, the voice warned, and Berellip looked all around in confusion. *Do not engage the rogue, daughter of House Xorlarrin. He is beyond you.*

"Methil," Berellip whispered.

"Lady?" the young priestess and another of the clerics asked in unison.

Berellip blinked repeatedly, trying to focus on the room once more. She wanted to argue with the illithid, but had no idea of how to even return his communication—and it was him, she knew, and his warning echoed in her thoughts.

"We go," Berellip said to the others.

"To war!" one cried.

"No!" Berellip cut her short. She turned to the oldest and most powerful of the bunch. "Gather back whatever of our soldiers you can find," she ordered, and to the others, she said, "To the mines, all of us. To the mines and below."

"You are fleeing the apostate?" one priestess dared to argue.

But at the same time in Berellip's head, the illithid's watery voice warned, *They will win the room before you arrive. They are beyond you.*

"He has come alone?" Berellip asked the young priestess, her voice halting as she considered Methil's assertions.

She shook her head. "With—with allies," she stammered. "And Mistress, our missing kin are there in the battle, fighting on the side of Drizzt!" She lowered her voice. "They are undead, Mistress, and being led by a vampire dwarf who controls them."

Berellip silently cursed her brother and Tiago again, although it occurred to her that perhaps the hunting army had indeed come upon Drizzt and had been defeated. Had the rogue arrived in Q'Xorlarrin through Tiago's march? It was too much for her to comprehend, and she could not make sense of it without more information, clearly.

And whether that was the case or not, Berellip's duty now was to the city, to the Xorlarrin forces still within Q'Xorlarrin. What would be left of her family if she stayed and fought, and lost, as the illithid had assured her would be the case? What would Matron Zeerith find upon her arrival to the lost chambers, to the ruin of all her dreams?

Berellip sucked in her breath hard. If she went to the battle and lost, Matron Zeerith would likely walk right into a trap!

Nay, she had to survive, had to warn Matron Zeerith, had to warn Menzoberranzan.

"To the mines," Berellip said again, and she swiftly led the way out of her private chambers.

Madness, Entreri thought, looking left at the advancing companions and the drider trio rushing to intercept them.

But even that word seemed too trite somehow, somehow unworthy of the chaos to the assassin's left, where drow undead battle living drow and goblins, and where that wild dwarf—it was Bruenor's former shield-dwarf, Entreri believed—continued to wash in the blood of enemies.

And if that weren't enough to scramble Entreri's sensibilities, out of the air, from a cloud of smoke that rolled in the reverberations of the winding horn, appeared a contingent of new warriors, barbarian warriors, leaping down or falling down from above, to hit the floor running into battle.

Any battle, it seemed.

They each carried a pair of hand axes, and put them to use wherever they could, whether on a goblin or a drow—alive or dead—it seemed not to matter.

Berserkers, Entreri realized, and perhaps they had come from Warrior's Rest, indeed.

The assassin didn't know whether to hang there and let it all play out or find a way to join in the melee. He brought his metal scrap up to the lock and slipped it in, easily managing the tumblers. But when the cage was unlocked, he held it tightly closed, still unsure of his course and not wanting to get stung by Berellip's lightning glyph.

His leg and his ribs ached from the beating the drider had put upon him. He put more weight on that particularly injured leg, ensuring that it would hold his weight. Then he settled his thoughts and reached into his warrior core, determined to ignore the pain if the need arose.

He watched the unwinding battle and waited and figured he'd sort it out.

And indeed he did, almost immediately, when he saw Drizzt in trouble across the way, squared up against a pair of skilled drow warriors, and more so when he saw a third enemy approaching him, swords in hand.

"To the lower tunnels!" he heard a fourth dark elf call to that one, and the swordsman nodded but did not veer to follow.

Nay, that third drow came for Entreri, his hands wringing eagerly around his weapon hilts, his intent clear in his red eyes.

Entreri set his cage to swinging.

"They'll not have you, *iblith*!" the drow said, rushing in fast to stab at him. He thrust his sword through the bands of metal, or tried to, but Entreri deftly rotated the hanging and swinging cage so that as the sword came through, the band of metal went against it and turned it.

And at that same moment, Entreri opened the cage, back across from the thrusting sword, and threw himself backward and up. The lightning glyph charged into him, but he was expecting it, and used to it, though his foe was not.

Indeed, as that shock went up the blade of the sword, to the hilt and into the grasping hand, the drow yelped in pain and surprise and dropped the weapon.

And around came the cage in its swing, its door, arcing with lightning magic, opened like a biting maw.

The drow was too quick for that, though, and he fell back, but first fell down to the floor to retrieve his blade.

Except that his blade was not there.

And the swinging, sparking cage was empty.

Down low, caught by utter surprise, and against Artemis Entreri, the drow had no chance. He managed to block the first stab, even to deflect the second, and he almost got his legs back under him to stand.

Almost.

He felt the blood fountaining from his collar, felt the human pull the second sword from his grasp, felt the stone floor, which suddenly seemed so cold.

So cold.

Wulfgar tangled with a horde of goblins, several bloodthirsty enemies leaping all over each other to get at him.

Regis faced just one opponent, but he would have gladly traded places with his large friend. For this was a drow, a dark elf warrior, supremely armed and armored and trained, and it only took the halfling the first exchange—his rapier thrust easily knocked aside and his dirk barely clipping the thrusting sword in time to move it aside of his face—for him to realize that he was sorely overmatched.

On came the drow with a dazzling flourish, and Regis retreated fast and thought to simply warp-step as the first movement in a full retreat!

But no, a snake was in his hand, re-grown on the dagger, and as the drow pursued, the halfling threw it at him. Up it crawled, the leering spectral face appeared, and the charging drow's feet came out from under him as he was yanked backward.

"Heigh-ho!" Regis cheered and leaped ahead to stab at him, but he skidded to a fast stop as the drow twisted around and stabbed back over his shoulder into that leering face, which disappeared in a heartbeat.

Still twisting and rolling, the formidable drow was back on his feet before Regis had taken another step.

"Wulfgar!" Regis cried, throwing the second snake, and again the drow was tugged back, and again he stabbed and broke free and came back up.

And charged, and Regis shot him in the face with his hand crossbow.

The drow staggered forward, Regis fell to the ground, and a great sweep of Aegis-fang swept the air above him and sent the dark elf spinning away.

"Well fought!" Wulfgar congratulated.

Regis nodded as he stood once more, not disagreeing, but surely glad that he was surrounded by such fine allies . . . and carrying such unusual and powerful toys.

And doubly glad when he saw the next enemies charging fast into the fray, a trio of horrid abominations, huge half-spiders that the halfling knew were far beyond him, with or without his toys.

The drow battled wildly, stabbing up with her knife, but Guenhwyvar caught her arms in curling claws and held her firmly as the panther's back claws went into a swift rake. One feline foot caught hold and the sheer power of the cat pulled the drow from her defensive curl. Fine armor, this one wore, but the claws caught hold repeatedly and tore at the supporting leather straps, loosening the various mail pieces and allowing Guenhwyvar's next rake to take a bit more flesh.

The drow tried hard to break free, throwing herself to the side, and Guenhwyvar did retract the claws of one paw.

If the drow thought it a small victory, the hope was short-lived, though, as that paw came down upon her face, claws extending, hooking.

A heavy blow struck Guenhwyvar in the flank, throwing the cat around sideways. She went with the weight of it, roaring in pain and anger, and tugged her claw free, taking the drow's face with it. Before she had even settled, Guenhwyvar slashed across, snapping the long spear that had embedded in her flank, and sprang away fearlessly, flying into the torso of the intervening drider.

The creature closed up to accept the hit and brought its half spear in to batter the cat.

The panther drove on, kicking and clawing and biting, her maw always snapping for the drider's face, forcing it back, back, until Guenhwyvar could scale a bit higher and drive a bit harder, and the tangled combatants rolled over in a thrashing heap.

The drider cried out for help, but no goblins would go near this deadly cat, and suddenly there seemed to be few dark elves around.

The drider cried out again, but found that it was yelling right into Guenhwyvar's mouth as the panther bit down powerfully upon its face.

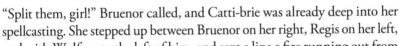

"Split them, girl!" Bruenor called, and Catti-brie was already deep into her spellcasting. She stepped up between Bruenor on her right, Regis on her left, and with Wulfgar to the left of him, and sent a line a fire running out from her extended hands, right at the drider in the middle of the approaching trio.

The targeted drider screeched and tried to go to its right, for the fury of the wall of fire burned out the other way, but just as the spidery creature came free of the blinding flames, Aegis-fang crashed against it, jolting it and stunning it and driving it back the other way, back into the conflagration.

Catti-brie fell back and moved behind Bruenor as he broke out to the side, and she began casting immediately.

On came the drider on that side, the hot side, of the fire wall, and out charged Bruenor to meet it. The dwarf slid in low on his knees, under the creature's stabbing long spear, and he cracked his axe against the hard exoskeleton of the monster's front leg.

Up came his foaming-mug buckler, turning aside another spear stab, and Bruenor hit it again.

Then the dwarf leaped back, blinded and surprised as a lightning bolt sizzled over his head, slamming his opponent and staggering the drider backward.

Catti-brie had forked that bolt, Bruenor realized, for behind his opponent came the middle drider, batting at the stubborn flames that curled and ate its skin. The force of the lightning bolt jolted the distracted creature backward, its trailing legs collapsing, and down it went, halfway to the floor, the hungry flames still biting.

Bruenor put his feet under him and reversed his momentum, thinking to charge right back in. He felt Catti-brie's hand on his shoulder, though, and heard the woman casting another spell.

Then he felt light on his feet—so light! And Catti-brie easily lifted him into the air and threw him like a living missile, the levitating, floating dwarf soaring in at the still-staggering drider.

Now Bruenor was up close, above the spidery body, and too near for the drider to properly bring its spear to bear.

The abomination bit at him instead, but tasted only the edge of a sturdy buckler, followed quickly by the notched head of Bruenor's swinging axe.

Across the flame wall came the largest of the three abominations, a heavy mace in one hand, huge trident lifted in the other. Ignoring the small halfling, the monstrous creature veered for Wulfgar, who was apparently unarmed, stabbing with its trident.

The barbarian dodged back, then dived and tried to roll away, but down came the trident, diving into and through his boot, into and through his foot!

He growled in pain and tried to twist around as the spider legs came over him, as the heavy mace lifted above him.

And as Regis flew in from the side, leaping and shooting his hand crossbow, and not with a poison-coated bolt this time, for he doubted that any poison would affect this abomination. He used his prototype dart, from Cadderly's old design, with a tiny vial of oil of impact set in its center within collapsible bars.

The dart hit, to little effect, then crushed in on itself, smashing the vial. The oil of impact exploded and the drider staggered. But the dart didn't have quite the effect Regis had hoped, startling the drider more than hurting it, for the explosion was not properly shaped, and the bulk of its force came back the other way, throwing the back end of the broken quarrel across the room the other way.

Regis didn't slow—Wulfgar couldn't afford any hesitation on the halfling's part. He leaped at the drider and lived up to his nickname of Spider, scrambling up the leg to stab at the drow torso with his fine rapier.

This time he did hurt the creature, he learned, and painfully, as the drider yelped and let go of the trident pinning Wulfgar, freeing up its hands so that it could slap Regis aside.

The halfling flew back and tumbled when he landed, avoiding serious injury, and as he came around, he thought to put his feet back under him and charge right back in. That thought flew away, however, for the drider proved much quicker than he had anticipated, and before he ever got back to his feet, Regis found the monstrous beast towering over him, front four legs lifted as it reared, rising up to gain more momentum for a two-handed crushing chop of that huge mace.

Down it came, and Regis fainted away before it ever hit him.

Mercifully.

They came in at him left and right simultaneously, each with two swords leading the way. Worse, the drow on Drizzt's right stabbed and slashed alternately, while the one to his left sent his swords into a rolling motion.

Drizzt's hands worked independently, vertical parries to his left, alternate blocks to his right. Every hit of metal on metal rang out as a testament to the skill of Drizzt Do'Urden, for these were no novice fighters before him, and a duo of dark elves who had obviously battled side-by-side many times in the past.

But Drizzt wasn't gaining any ground here, and it was all he could manage simply to keep those deadly blades away. He looked to his friends for help, but saw the fire wall and the monstrous driders. He looked to Guenhwyvar, but she, too, was locked in mortal combat, a broken spear hanging from her flank, a drider battling her mightily.

Over rolled the blades of the dark elf to Drizzt's left, but out of the roll came one thrust low, and Drizzt had to lurch and slap Twinkle down low to deflect the cunning attack. And in that lurch, he found an insurmountable disadvantage to the right, as that warrior stabbed low, forcing a similar downward block, then double-thrust, one blade high, one blade low.

Too fast.

Drizzt had no way to block.

He could only dodge, but in the tight press, that meant one option alone, and he threw himself into a back flip, knowing his enemies would pursue, doubting that his position would be any better when he landed than when he had leaped.

And worse, and he knew himself doomed, his leap took him over a third warrior, one that had come skidding in at his back.

Drizzt landed with a flourish, blades spinning in wide circles, expecting six swords rushing in at him.

But no, he found none, for it was no drow he had somersaulted but a human, and one wielding two drow swords, and doing so with the skill of any weapons master who had ever graduated from Melee-Magthere, and doing so with the skill of Drizzt himself!

"Quick, fool!" Artemis Entreri yelled at him as the assassin took Drizzt's place between the dark elf warriors.

Drizzt leaped ahead, spinning sidelong, yelling "Right!" and at precisely the correct moment, Entreri spun to his left to face up against that drow, while Drizzt rolled in at his back to meet the other.

Now the parries included counters, clever ripostes as Drizzt and Entreri, mirror images of each other, found an easy rhythm against the skilled drow warriors. In separate fights, one-against-one, either of these skilled Xorlarrins might have held firm for some time against either of these opponents, and so of course, they both assumed that with their practiced teamwork, they would still win the day.

They both assumed wrong.

Drizzt and Entreri had not battled together nearly as often as their opponents, but it didn't matter. Not with these two, so perfectly matched, each with so great an understanding of the other.

Drizzt went into a sudden charge, Twinkle and Icingdeath slashing in a powerful flurry that drove his opponent back. But Drizzt did not follow for long, cutting into a sudden back-step and throwing himself down and around.

Entreri felt the motion as Drizzt moved from his back, and listened carefully for the sudden return. When it came, the assassin struck hard to keep his enemy engaged, then leaped up high, legs flying out to either side. He waited for Drizzt to slide through, before snapping himself around in mid-air to meet the rush of the warrior Drizzt had driven off.

And by that time, though it was only a heartbeat, both of Drizzt's blades had thrust in beneath the attempted block of the surprised dark elf who had been battling Entreri, whose eyes had lifted with Entreri's jump, and who had not even noted the sliding charge of Drizzt until it was far too late.

Drizzt retracted his bloody blades, tucked one leg in tight in his slide and propelled himself up and around in a spin, a backhand slash of Twinkle cutting down the wounded drow.

By the time Drizzt came around, he found the other enemy in full flight, running fast from Entreri, who did not pursue. That drow danced and leaped among the carnage, heading for the doorway in the far corner of the room.

He made it more than halfway, quickstepping past fallen kin, fallen goblins, and the torn bodies of dark elf vampire minions, before a powerful and squat form appeared out of nowhere, flying against him and throwing him crashing to the floor.

Holding fast to his victim, Thibbledorf Pwent began to shake and thrash, his ridged armor tearing the drow to pieces.

Drizzt spun back the other way, toward the wall of fire and the Companions of the Hall. He couldn't see Bruenor or Catti-brie, or two of the trio of driders that had gone against them. The wall of flames obscured that fight. But he did see Regis, lying on the floor, covering up pathetically as the rearing drider came down, the huge mace—the mace of Ambergris, Drizzt realized!—crashing down in a surely killing blow.

"Regis!" Drizzt cried out desperately.

* * *

Above the hiss of the fires, above the ring of swords, above the cries of the wounded, above the growls of Pwent's undead, came the thunder as Aegis-fang swept up to meet the downward chop of Skullcrusher. Both Wulfgar and Yerrininae roared as their weapons collided, the cries and the crash blending together in a sound of pure power that reverberated off the Forge walls.

Intent on protecting Regis, who was not moving and was not even conscious, Wulfgar tried to skip out to the side, but the fierce drider stopped him with a planted leg and cleverly stabbed in with Skullcrusher. Wulfgar managed to sweep his warhammer vertically to turn the mace aside, but he sucked in his breath as he realized the stab to be a ruse, a way for Wulfgar to help the drider properly angle his weapon for another strike at Regis.

Wulfgar threw Aegis-fang at the beast. He couldn't get any weight behind the throw to hurt the drider, so he used it as a distraction, a way to slow the strike at Regis, and he launched himself out, catching Skullcrusher's handle just above the drider's grip.

The barbarian's muscles corded and strained against the powerful abomination, and a lesser man would have simply tumbled down atop Regis behind the mace's descent.

But Wulfgar held on, and when Yerrininae jerked the mace back, the barbarian was ready, rolling around and leaping up, crashing against the drider's drow torso.

Face-to-face the mighty warriors clenched and struggled.

Yerrininae bit down hard on Wulfgar's left shoulder, digging in, and Wulfgar felt poison coming from that abomination's deadly bite.

Regis's potion had saved him again, he knew.

The duo wrestled and twisted. The drider lifted a spider leg and Wulfgar realized that it meant to stomp Regis. With a great, desperate twist, Wulfgar yanked the drider aside and the two nearly tumbled into the wall of fire.

Yerrininae bit down harder and pushed ahead, bending Wulfgar backward. The barbarian wedged the fingers of his free right hand in against the drider's cheek.

Wulfgar tightened the muscles of his chest and shoulder, growling back against the bite, hardening the drider's target and so weakening the drider's hold.

The two stumbled around on eight spidery legs—they seemed like bipedal combatants fighting atop a giant spider. Back and forth they went, sometimes touching the wall, sometimes hovering dangerously around Regis.

Wulfgar slipped his little finger into the drider's eye and pressed on, and Yerrininae had to relent.

"Tempus!" the barbarian roared, as much to infuse himself with heightened anger as to call to his god. He pushed out with all his strength, driving Yerrininae's head to his left, the drider's free hand tugging at his wrist.

Wulfgar let go of the face suddenly, snapping his arm back with the tug and at the same time replacing it with his left hand, clamping fully on Yerrininae's face. The barbarian rolled his shoulders forward and bulled ahead and down.

The fire wall fell away then, showing the two dead driders on the other side, with Bruenor atop one, staring back slack-jawed at the titanic battle between Wulfgar and Yerrininae. Catti-brie watched, too, as did Drizzt and Entreri, all four stunned to inaction by the spectacle.

Wulfgar bulled and pushed, his muscles standing taut. Huge Yerrininae pushed back, cords of sinewy muscles straining and glistening with sweat.

The drider stumbled backward and nearly toppled, but kicked its rear legs out and planted them firmly.

Yerrininae had made a mistake. He should have rolled over.

He was locked in place, unable to give, forced to hold back Wulfgar's push, which he could not. He bent over backward and the barbarian plowed on, driving his left hand forward, bending Yerrininae's head back.

Down Wulfgar jerked with all his strength, and then again when Yerrininae stopped his press. And a third time and again after that, and the drider could not retreat and could not hold.

Again the barbarian bulled and now Yerrininae did give way, not by backing and not by rolling, but simply because Yerrininae's muscle and bone could not resist the press.

The crack of Yerrininae's shattering backbone sounded as loudly as the crash of Aegis-fang against Skullcrusher.

Wulfgar pushed once more, but it was done and he was done, his rage and stamina exhausted. He fell back and stumbled off the drider, who still stood on planted spidery legs, drow torso bobbing weirdly, fully broken.

The Forge was quiet then, and eerily so.

CHAPTER 25

THE CALL OF AN OLDER GOD

THE COMPANIONS AND ENTRERI WERE NOT THE ONLY ONES REMAINING in the room. Pwent was there, though only a few of his drow minions remained standing. Another crawled weirdly around the floor, relieved of its legs and one arm by drow swordsmen.

And a trio of summoned berserkers remained. The shocking sound and effect of the titanic struggle between Wulfgar and the drider gave them pause, but the berserkers had come in to the call of the horn for one reason alone: to fight against the enemies of the one who blew the horn.

The surreal stillness shattered as the berserkers threw themselves into battle against the undead, and Thibbledorf Pwent, a battlerager in heart and soul, was more than happy to engage.

He met the charge of a berserker, lowering his head at the last moment to drive his helmet spike right through the reckless fool. He snapped up straight as the spike plunged through, and held his hands out wide, laughing maniacally as if in expectation of a shower of blood.

But these manifestations didn't bleed, and the corporeal form exploded into sweeping dust when Pwent struck the mortal blow, leaving the vampire standing alone, confused and hungry.

And angry.

He leaped to the side and dispatched a second berserker, even as his minions pulled down a third, tearing at flesh, then swiping futilely at flying dust.

"Pwent, no!" Drizzt screamed from the side of the room as the four undead charged at the foursome across the way, Pwent leading the way to Wulfgar, it seemed.

And over on that side, Wulfgar was clearly no less angry. He stood beside the broken drider, blood running freely down his muscular chest, leaning uneasily on his stabbed foot, and with every vampiric strike on one of Tempus's warriors, he growled and limped forward.

"No, boy!" Drizzt heard Bruenor warn.

"Go," Entreri told him, and shoved Drizzt into pursuit, and ran for Pwent right alongside him.

Then came the roar of "Tempus!" and Aegis-fang spun out from Wulfgar's hands, flying into the approaching Pwent. The dwarf didn't dematerialize at all, but took the ringing blow, one that sent him staggering and skidding backward several strides, one that actually seemed to hurt him.

Catti-brie moved up beside Wulfgar and held forth her hand, invoking the glory of Mielikki, the very name manifesting itself as a bright light upon the woman. The vampire minions staggered and turned away, hunched and cowering.

But not Pwent.

He focused on Wulfgar, seemingly oblivious to Drizzt and Entreri as they closed in fast from behind. Not fast enough, however, for the vampire executed that curious and devastating ghost-step to bring himself right in front of the man, fog trailing and swirling as he became solid once more, holding fast for just an instant before leaping onto Wulfgar, who caught the force fully and went flying away in a clench with the dwarf.

Pwent began to thrash and shake, but the sheer strength of Wulfgar matched the dwarf and kept him from ripping Wulfgar apart with his ridged armor. They rolled and struggled mightily, Bruenor trying vainly to intercede, Catti-brie beginning yet another spell.

On one roll, Pwent put his stout legs under him and regained his footing, driving Wulfgar back. But Wulfgar, as in his previous existence, was possessed of fine agility for one so large and he turned his torso and also got his feet planted, and so Pwent's drive actually brought the barbarian upright as well.

Pwent tried to punch, but Wulfgar held him by the wrists. They struggled and twisted, the dwarf suddenly lowering his head to line up his helmet spike.

Wulfgar had to grab it to twist it aside, and he tried to twist further, to throw the dwarf off him.

R.A. SALVATORE

He wasn't fast enough, though, as Pwent's freed hand immediately pounded against the barbarian's massive chest, the gauntlet spike tearing through flesh and rib and lung alike, and Wulfgar went staggering back and to the ground.

"Pwent!" Bruenor screamed, finally catching up and throwing himself against the dwarf.

Pwent bounced aside and turned, ready to leap back in. He paused, though, and stood there staring at Bruenor, confused, trembling.

"Me king," he said, his voice thick with sorrow, and he lowered his gaze in shame.

"Get aside, ye fool! By Moradin's word, get aside!" Bruenor roared.

Pwent looked up at him and nodded. "Me king," he said reverently, and seemed fully in control once more, and full of remorse and shame.

Drizzt and Entreri came running up, swords in hand, and skidded to a stop behind Bruenor, who lifted his hand to halt them.

"Ye do what I'm tellin' ye, and ye do not-a-thing more," the dwarf king said to Pwent, who nodded obediently.

But that nod transformed into a curious expression, then one that included a bit of pain, it seemed, and Pwent's eyes led all to the right, to the fallen Wulfgar and to Catti-brie standing over him, holding a curious object and chanting an arcane poem.

"Girl?" Bruenor asked at the same time Pwent yelled, "No!" and leaped for the woman.

And again, this seemed a curious, supernatural stride, one elongated and too swift, and one full of spinning wisps of foggy trails.

But Pwent didn't materialize from that step as before, and indeed became wholly insubstantial, mist or fog or dust, perhaps, right before all of it swept into the object Catti-brie held before her: Wulfgar's horn.

The silver horn shuddered with the vampire dwarf's entrance, and a strange low note came forth, spraying the dust of captured ancients, and ten berserkers appeared in the room before Catti-brie. They all looked around curiously, confused, and they all blew away to dust, then to nothingness altogether.

"Girl, what'd'ye do?" Bruenor asked, running up.

Already bathed in her ghostly blue mist, Catti-brie tossed him the horn and fell over Wulfgar, casting once more. Blue tendrils snaked out of her sleeves and rolled down over the prone form, warm healing to wash over the badly wounded Wulfgar.

"Girl?" Bruenor asked breathlessly a few moments later, Drizzt flanking him. Just to the side of them, Entreri helped Regis back to his feet, and they, too, looked on.

Catti-brie looked up and smiled, and below her, Wulfgar matter-of-factly remarked, "Ouch," then with great difficulty propped himself up on his elbows.

Drizzt took the horn from Bruenor and held it up to examine it, and noted a crack running along its side.

"Ye breaked it, girl," Bruenor remarked when Drizzt pointed it out.

"It will hold him."

"I had him back to his senses," Bruenor protested. "We ain't done yet!"

"No, but Pwent is," Catti-brie said, rising and coming over to take back the horn. She slung it over her shoulder, shaking her head to deny any forthcoming protests from the dwarf.

"We came for Pwent and we got him," Regis interjected. He looked at the man standing beside him and added, "We came for Entreri and we got him."

Entreri looked down at him curiously. "Who are you?" he asked, and in response, Regis held up his hand with the missing finger, a digit removed in the trauma of his near-catastrophic birth, but so eerily similar to the wound Entreri had put upon him in his previous existence.

Entreri turned his confused expression to Drizzt, who merely answered, "Are you really surprised by anything anymore?"

The assassin shrugged and glanced back the other way, where the vampire minions huddled together at the far end of the room, cowering from Catti-brie's powerful invocation. He nodded to Drizzt and started off to dispose of them, but it was Regis who led the way.

"Ye sure it'll hold him, then?" Bruenor quietly asked Catti-brie when the trio had gone off.

The woman inspected the horn and nodded.

Bruenor sighed.

"It is best," Catti-brie said. "Pwent can't control himself—not for long, and not for much longer at all. It's a curse full of great powers, and surely not a blessing. We'll find him his rest, the proper rest for Thibbledorf Pwent."

"Ah, but I loved the dirty brawler."

"And Moradin will enjoy him at the great feast," Catti-brie replied, managing a smile, and Bruenor nodded again.

"Ouch," Wulfgar said again from beside them, and with great effort, he rolled around and managed to sit up.

Bruenor pulled one of Regis's healing potions from his belt, but Wulfgar waved him away. "We may need it later," he said, his voice still a bit breathless.

They sent Regis to finish off the crawling beast, then Drizzt and Entreri waded into the trio of cowering undead with wild abandon, blades hacking the creatures apart before they ever knew they were being attacked.

"Is it really them?" Entreri asked quietly, and Drizzt nodded.

"Where is Dahlia?" Drizzt asked as they approached the hanging cages.

Entreri shook his head. "I haven't seen her in more than a day—perhaps longer. I have little sense of the passage of time down here."

"Effron?"

Entreri shook his head, and pointed to lead Drizzt's gaze to the misshapen pile of splattered skull.

Drizzt gasped and averted his eyes.

"They tormented her with that, your fine kin," Entreri said. "The sight of it . . . of him, broke her and left her vulnerable."

Drizzt sighed. He could only imagine the pain such a loss would have inflicted on fragile Dahlia, and so soon after she had come to reconcile with her son, both in his forgiveness of her and her own forgiveness of herself. Effron had allowed Dahlia to come to terms with her own dark past, and had given her hope for the future.

And there it lay, splattered on the floor.

"How long since your capture, do you think?" Drizzt asked, needing to shift the subject.

"Several days—less than a tenday, I believe. They took us in Port Llast, and laid waste to much of the place."

Drizzt looked around, his expression curious. "Not so many dark elves," he remarked.

"Because Tiago led them off," Entreri replied, "with an army at his heels—looking for you, I expect. That seems to be the driving desire in his life."

Entreri climbed up the side of Afafrenfere's cage and picked the lock quickly, then dropped down to help the drow ease the monk to the floor. Fortunately, this cage hadn't been glyphed like Entreri's.

"We'll throw him in the primordial pit," Entreri offered. "So they can't raise him and torment—"

"No," came an interruption, a weak and parched whisper—from Afafrenfere!

Entreri jumped back and nearly jumped out of his boots, staring wide-eyed.

"We thought you were dead," Drizzt cried.

"For all the days we've been here!" Entreri added.

The monk stiffly moved up to one elbow, swallowing repeatedly. "Fortunately," he said, his voice a thin whisper, "so did our captors."

"How?" Entreri cried. "What?"

"He faked his death," Regis announced, rushing over to join them, having finally dispatched the crawling monstrosity. "Convincingly! He is a monk, after all."

"Repeatedly," Afafrenfere confirmed. "Whenever anyone was about."

"You could have let me know," said Entreri. "For all the days I hung beside you."

"That the illithid might draw it from your thoughts?"

"You're lucky we didn't just leave you here," Entreri grumped.

Afafrenfere started to rise and Drizzt and Entreri moved fast to help him up, but they found immediately that they would have to fully support him if he was to remain upright. They eased him to a sitting position instead, and Drizzt called out to Catti-brie.

"Now what?" Entreri asked Drizzt when the group, now seven strong, was all together.

"We should make for the exit quickly," Catti-brie said, and nodded at Wulfgar and Afafrenfere, both sitting propped against the wall, both weak and weary and in no condition for another fight anytime soon.

But Drizzt answered by bringing forth the mace the largest of the driders had carried. "Amber is down here," he said. "And Dahlia, likely."

"Likely both dead or taken away by those who fled," Entreri answered.

"Like Effron? So we should leave?" Drizzt asked, and it seemed more an accusation than an honest question.

"No," Entreri answered. "You and I should go and find them. And quickly."

Drizzt looked to Catti-brie, who nodded.

"Not without meself, ye don't," Bruenor grumbled.

"Or me," said Regis.

"Aye," Entreri sarcastically replied. "Because it would do well to leave our injured with the woman alone, to face the drow should they return through another course."

Bruenor made a noise that sounded remarkably like a growl.

But Entreri ignored him. "Stealth," he said to Drizzt.

"I'm as quiet as any," Regis protested.

"And speed," Entreri added without missing a breath. He turned to Regis. "Then keep a silent watch," he said and started off. Or tried to, but by that point, his adrenalin had played out and his knee buckled. He pulled himself straight immediately and stood very still, as if willing away the pain.

A tap on his side brought Entreri from his self-imposed meditation to find Regis standing beside him, holding forth a small potion bottle.

"Healing," the halfling offered, and when Entreri took it, he handed him a second vial. "For the drow poison," he explained.

Entreri settled comfortably as the first potion filled him with warmth, and he tipped a nod to Regis before quaffing the second. "Off," he said to Drizzt, "with all speed." And he started away once more.

Drizzt looked all around. He didn't want to leave his friends in this dangerous place, not for a moment, but he knew that Entreri was right, and that Amber and hopefully Dahlia needed him. He dropped Taulmaril and the enchanted quiver at Catti-brie's feet.

"You take it," she said, but Drizzt just shook his head and sprinted away, hustling to catch up to Entreri.

Regis moved around the Forge, inspecting the work areas and pocketing more than a few items in that magical pouch he carried.

Bruenor went to the mithral door, nodding. He knew what lay behind it. It would not open, however, and he could find no handle to try to pull it in. He put his shoulder against it and pushed, but he might as well have been pushing against the mountain itself.

Drizzt and Entreri, too, had gone to that door first, then had rushed off to the far end of the room, angling down the corridor where some of the drow had run off.

Wulfgar, much-improved by Catti-brie's healing, sat up against the wall, resting easily and with Aegis-fang close at hand. If the drow came in, he would stand against them. Beside him, Afafrenfere lay on his back, working his arms up into the air in small circles, and his hands working in circles of their own, fingers lifting and closing as he tried to reawaken muscles that had been dormant for days. His voice was still thin as he explained the monk technique of feigning death to Wulfgar and Catti-brie.

Wulfgar listened intently, and with an amused expression, for the warrior barbarian hadn't even learned the art of retreat, let alone faking his death to fool enemies!

And Catti-brie did not listen at all, hardly aware of her surroundings.

For in her head, the woman heard a call, quiet but insistent, a plea, and one from some being beyond her, some great creature, perhaps divine . . . though its mental intrusion seemed too foreign to be that of Mielikki's song.

She didn't understand. She unwittingly clenched her hand.

The woman leaned against the wall. Wulfgar's laughter interrupted her thoughts and she turned to regard him, then followed his gaze and Afafrenfere's to the Great Forge centering the room, and to Regis, who was trying to drag an enormous warhammer, a weapon made for a giant king, it seemed—and indeed it had been crafted for just that reason—from the work table.

"What're ye about, Rumblebelly?" Bruenor called from across the way.

Regis lifted up his small belt pouch, which seemed barely large enough to contain his hand up to his wrist. With a wry grin, Regis slipped the bag over the end of the weapon's long handle, and smiling all the wider, the mischievous halfling continued sliding the pouch up, the shaft disappearing within, seeming as if the magic was somehow devouring it.

"And how're ye to get the hammer's head over that little bag, magical or not?" Bruenor asked, for indeed, it didn't seem possible.

"Well, come help me, then," Regis argued back, and realizing his error, he began extracting the handle from the pouch.

Bruenor gave a great "harrumph" and stood with his hands on his hips, but Wulfgar pulled himself up and started over.

Catti-brie started to call out to him, to jokingly warn him not to let the light-fingered halfling near Aegis-fang, but she was interrupted before she ever begin by an insistent telepathic call, a plea to her, she felt, but in some language she could not decipher.

She glanced at the mithral door just down the way and crunched up her face curiously, seeing that liquid was spilling out around it, steaming and bubbling.

"Water?" she whispered, and realized that the door had opened a crack. She gathered up the bow and quiver, slinging both over her shoulder and moved to the door. She easily pulled it wide, revealing a low corridor beyond. She lifted her hand, the light from the spell she had placed upon her ring stealing the darkness before her and revealing to her a series of puddles along the floor, fast evaporating, billowing steam, though the woman, protected from fire as she was, couldn't feel the heat.

"Girl?" she heard Bruenor call out as she entered the tunnel.

"Girl!" he yelled more frantically, but his voice was cut short as the heavy metal door swung closed behind her. Catti-brie went to it and pushed, but it would not budge. Strangely, she was not afraid, and the voice in her head beckoned her along. She made her way down the tunnel, pausing at one puddle where a broken pile of fast-cooling black rock lay. She found more of it along the path, like volcanic spit in a river bed, but she could make no sense of it.

She exited the tunnel into the steamy chamber, coming out right beside a pony-sized green spider that seemed to twitch at the sight of her. Catti-brie fell back and turned into a defensive crouch, her hand reflexively going to her bow. She shook her head and did not proceed, though, thinking that its movement must be a trick of her eye in the swirling steam of this place, for it seemed just a statue.

A beautiful jade statue, shining green against her light spell, and so intricate in detail as to appear lifelike. Still, when it didn't move, Catti-brie couldn't focus on it. The room around it seemed full of surprises, and oddly mixed shapes and items. To her right, beyond and above the spider, loomed tapestries of impossibly thick hanging webbing that shimmered and seemed alive in the pressing waves of steam.

Roving her eye out to the left and across the floor, Catti-brie noted an altar, black and shot with veins of red, as if carrying blood throughout the solid stone. Just past it loomed the ledge and a large pile of broken lava rock, steaming feverishly. Just past it lay the pit, with water raining down from above and steam billowing up from below, and Catti-brie felt herself drawn to the lip, to gaze in.

She saw the swirling cyclone of living water, and saw the fiery eye far below—and knew that fiery eye to be the source of the whispers in her head.

She closed her eyes tight and concentrated, trying to hear the call, and saw in her mind's eye this very room, and her focus moved down along the ledge, to a bridge, an anteroom, a lever . . .

Catti-brie opened her eyes, shaking her head for she could make no sense of this.

She heard the call of the fiery primordial again, and saw again the small room under an archway, with a lever.

The fiery beast wanted her to go to it, to pull it. She could feel its plea, its heavy heart, like a panther trapped in a small cage, or an eagle with its wings tied.

She started along the ledge, past the altar, and through the swirling fog, she saw a bridge crossing the chasm. Then she was upon it, halfway and more. And she saw a surge of water within the small room, rising up like a wave, and rushing out suddenly at her, a great breaker rolling over itself, barreling toward her to throw her from her precarious perch.

Catti-brie turned away and cast a spell, just in time to magically jump back the way she had come. The water crashed against her, hastening her journey, sending her into a flight that nearly flung her into the webbing as the water broke all around her.

Broke but did not dissipate. It flew together past her and rose up like some thick bear, watery arms outstretched and ready to batter her.

Catti-brie felt its animosity, saw its rage, and as it rolled in at her, she lifted her hands, thumbs touching, and burst a fan of flames into it. That minor spell hardly slowed the great water elemental, of course, but in its hiss and the resulting gout of steam, Catti-brie managed a retreat. She ran to the altar and skidded around it, using it as a shield so that if the elemental tried to break upon her and wash her away, the altar stone would serve as a small seawall and breakwater.

Her mind raced. She pulled Taulmaril from her shoulder, but shook her head and dropped it to the floor immediately, realizing that using lightning energy against a water elemental might not be a good idea.

Indeed, the only clear notion that cut through the jumble of her thoughts was the need for the opposing element, the need for fire.

And so she began spellcasting and the elemental charged, and she threw a fireball at her own feet as it swept upon her. Clenching her fist with her protective ring, she rushed away through the blinding flames, water battering her and crashing into her, and throwing her to the floor back near where she had entered the room. Instinctively she started for the tunnel, but scolded herself for her foolishness before she had taken her second step, for surely the malleable water elemental could rush along that narrow passage and even drown her against the door at the far end.

The elemental rose up around the altar, but not quite as huge, it seemed. The fireball had stolen some of its watery composition, turning part of the being to harmless drifting steam.

Catti-brie was already deep into her next spellcasting as the primal watery monster stalked in, rolling toward her like a giant ocean swell. Fires burned around her hands, sparkling and sizzling, and she punched them out, but not at the water elemental.

Instead she threw her last fiery spell, another wall of fire, running it the length of the ledge, splitting the bare area of the chamber in half and with the hot side of the wall burning back toward her and toward the door and the wall and the webbing.

When the water elemental didn't come through, Catti-brie leaped through her fire wall and taunted it.

How she could feel its seething hatred, as if she were a creature of the opposing plane of existence, as if she were a fire elemental instead of a flesh-and-bones human.

Despite her towering wall of burning fire, the watery beast threw itself at her, roaring like a wave, breaking like the ocean surf.

She jumped back through the wall of fire, into the inferno, and the elemental, so full of irrational hatred, followed. The water break swept her from her feet, but did not wash her aside, and she scrambled along, just inside the fire wall, and the elemental pursued. The water rushed in around her, roiling and boiling and bubbling, those bubbles popping and spraying the woman. But she did not feel the heat of the boiling water, as she did not feel the flames.

Steam mixed with rolling, angry fires, and she stumbled on, and when she felt no water around her any longer, she turned aside and dived back through the wall, into the clear and just past the altar stone.

And there back the other way stood the water elemental, much smaller now, but no less angry.

Catti-brie taunted it and held her ground, and again it charged, rolling in with the anger of a hurricane-driven tide determined to smash a wharf to kindling.

At the last moment, Catti-brie dived back through the wall, and more blue mist came from her sleeves, though it could not be seen in the swirl of fire. This spell was divine in source, calling to the stone beneath her hand, and she melded in with it, sinking her arm into it just as the water elemental fell over her.

She could feel the anger in the sloshing waves. The beast roared in her ears, hating her, needing to destroy her. It tried to pull her back to the cool side of the wall, but the woman held her ground, her arm literally rooted to the stone floor.

The elemental could not pull her free, could not take her away, and so it fell over her completely, holding its form around her, drowning her where she kneeled!

She could not draw breath. She swatted with her free hand, but the water would not wipe aside, would not leave its press on her nose and mouth.

She could not breathe, could not cast a spell. She felt as if a mountain giant was pressing a wet pillow over her face, and so she thrashed but she could not budge the giant.

Desperation drove her on—she felt as if her lungs would explode.

And then she was moving at least, back and forth in her jerking action, for now the mountain giant seemed more like an ogre.

Her enemy had diminished.

Catti-brie calmed immediately with that realization, conserved what little breath she had remaining. Darkness rose up around her, at the edges of her vision, as if the floor itself was swallowing her.

With that troubling thought, the woman reflexively retracted her enchanted arm, breaking her meld, and now the water elemental could pull her from the flames that bit at it and bubbled it to harmless gas.

But no, it could not, and the watery gag was gone, and even the steam diminished now.

Catti-brie rolled through her fire wall and lay on her back, gasping for breath. She feared that the elemental, too, had come through to the cool side, and would now fall over her once more, but no, it was not there.

It was gone, destroyed, melted to steam and flown away.

And the voice in her head returned, cheering, and she could understand it now and knew it to be the primordial.

It spoke in the tongue of the Plane of Fire, and Catti-brie understood that tongue, though she should not.

Images filled her mind—an explanation from the primordial? She imagined a humanoid that seemed made of magma leap from the pit and rumble down the tunnel. That magma elemental had opened the door, but the water elemental had pursued it, and had battered it to pieces back along the corridor and had broken it fully, over there, by the altar, where the steaming rubble remained.

The primordial had opened the door for her, to bring her in here, to pull the lever, to free it. She could feel its outrage, and when she looked around at the room, she understood that outrage to be wrought in violation. And not from the dwarves who had built this place, no, nor the wizards who had contained the volcano beneath the power of the water elementals. This outrage was new, an anger wrought in pride, an anger festering because the drow had dared turn this place into a chapel for the Demon Queen of Spiders.

Catti-brie pulled herself up from the floor, shaking her head, silently denying the primordial's pleas. How could this be? How could she understand the language of that otherworldly plane of existence?

Her gaze went to her magically brightened hand, to the ruby ring. She had thought it a simple ring of fire protection, a fairly common item, but no, she knew now. No, this ring's enchantment went far deeper, was far older, and many times more powerful, and it was a magic that had to be unlocked, for the wielder to prove herself worthy. And Catti-brie had done so by destroying an elemental from the opposing plane, an elemental of water.

Now with its magic fully engaged, this ring attuned Catti-brie to the Plane of Fire, and that magical connection deciphered the primordial's call.

And through this ring, she could call back to it.

Her fire wall came down then, the magic expired, but still some small flames burned, for they had caught the webbing, layer and layer stripped away as tiny flames sparked and climbed.

Movement turned her gaze to the right, to the jade spider, as it turned to her.

Movement to the left showed her a second spider, similarly turning to face her.

"They are mine," came a voice directly above and in front of her, and Catti-brie looked up to see a last layer of webbing burn aside to reveal a woman, an elf woman, hanging there, her arms outstretched. Her raven hair, shot with red streaks so similar to the altar stone, braided in a single line atop her head, and her face was marked with a multitude of blue dots. As she smiled and whispered the name of Catti-brie, those dots seemed to shift and join into an image.

A spider.

The newcomer drove her arms forward and the pole from which she was hanging broke in half over her back. She dropped to the floor to land gracefully, half the metal pole in each hand, and she snapped her wrists suddenly, violently, and each of those poles became two, joined by a length of cord, became a flail, and the woman put the weapon into a spin.

"Catti-brie," she said again, wickedly, and she laughed.

She turned her head left and right and called to the jade spiders.

"Come, my pets."

And they did.

And Catti-brie, her magic all but exhausted, stood with her back to the primordial pit.

347

CHAPTER 26

PROXY WAR

Drizzt and Entreri moved swiftly along the tunnel in short bursts, one darting to the next position at a bend or corner, then motioning the other to run past, to the next. They passed the back side of the lava-made tunnel to the primordial chamber, to find that it had been sealed by the drow, by a wall of iron with some new masonry work securing it. Drizzt paused there, staring at the new wall, thinking of this and the mithral door with its new adamantine jamb. The dark elves were protecting the primordial pit. They had taken this place as their home.

Drizzt knew this area of the complex fairly well, and he turned around to peer into the continuing tunnel on the other side of the corridor he and Entreri now traversed. He had battled a drow mage down there, along with the wizard's pet magma beast, which had carved these tunnels. From that mage, Drizzt had looted the ruby ring he had recently given to Catti-brie.

He waved Entreri past the opening of the lava tunnel, knowing it to be a dead end.

On they ran, leapfrogging past each other with practiced skill, and soon came to the entrance to a downward sloping tunnel, wide and smooth and recently worked, including grooves from, and for, the metal wheels of laden ore carts.

Down they ran for many strides, now side-by-side, for the tunnel was wide and straight with nowhere to hide. They came to a wide intersection, one passage forking left and down, the corridor continuing straight ahead, and a third passage breaking perpendicularly to the right. Unlike the other two, this third corridor was not descending.

Drizzt motioned for Entreri to hold this position, then started away to the right. The tunnel opened left and right into alcoves—mining stations, Drizzt realized, seeing the picks and shovels, and empty shackles staked to the stone.

"They've taken their prisoners with them," Entreri remarked, catching up to Drizzt in the culminating chamber of the wing, where three separate sets of shackles sat on the stone, mining tools beside them.

Drizzt led the way back, in full run, and turned down the main, central corridor and ran on for a long way. They found more side tunnels, more empty mining stations, and then a gruesome discovery: a pair of slain humans, very recently cut down where they worked.

"The drow have gone deeper," Entreri reasoned. "We'll find no living slaves."

Drizzt wanted to argue, but the reasoning was sound. They were far below the level of the Forge already, and the tunnel before them sloped more steeply and would soon open into the deeper Underdark.

"We have to return," Entreri said, or started to, but Drizzt held up his hand for silence.

Entreri looked at him curiously.

Drizzt moved over and put his ear against the stone wall, then pointed to that side. "The other passageway," he whispered.

As he neared the wall, Entreri, too, heard the rhythmic tapping of a pick against stone.

In their hasty retreat, the dark elves hadn't cleared all of their slaves, apparently.

The pair ran back up to the four-way intersection and broke to their right to the far fork. This one went on for some ways before they encountered any mining stations, but as they neared the initial one, they clearly heard the slave at work.

It was a woman, a human. She shrank back as they neared, covering defensively.

"From Port Llast," Entreri said, moving for the shackle and working fast to open the rudimentary lock. He looked at the woman. "We're here to free you," he said, and even as he finished, he pulled the shackle from her ankle. "Where is Dahlia?"

The woman wore a confused expression.

"The elf woman," Entreri explained, his voice growing more insistent, more frantic. "She carried a metal staff. She was with me in Port Llast. Where is Dahlia?"

"There are others," the woman answered and swallowed hard, clearly intimidated. She motioned down the tunnel.

"Wait here," Drizzt bade her, and he and Entreri rushed off. Within a few moments, a bedraggled man limped up to join the woman, then a third miner limped into the room.

Drizzt and Entreri found just a few alcoves in this area, and soon broke out into another wide, descending tunnel, and it seemed as if there were no more work stations to be found, for this place, much like the center tunnel, dived more steeply now.

Drizzt motioned for Entreri to turn back, but the assassin sprinted out ahead anyway, his eyes peering through the gloom. "Dahlia?" he called softly.

Drizzt moved up beside him and put a hand on his shoulder to steady him. "We have to go," he said. "We cannot pursue a drow army into the deeper Underdark."

Entreri looked at him, and for a moment Drizzt thought the man might simply lash out.

"We have wounded," Drizzt reminded.

Entreri's shoulders slumped and he gave a long and profound sigh, then turned back, but as he did, he caught some movement out of the corner of his eye.

There was, after all, one more slave down here. She wasn't working, though, when the pair came upon her, but sitting sullenly on a stone, facing the wall, head in her hands.

Entreri went for her shackle and just as she turned, Drizzt put a hand on her shoulder.

How the dwarf's eyes widened with surprise and joy! She grabbed at Drizzt as if to hug him, and blurted his name—or tried to, but found her mouth filled with that sickly green spew and wound up coughing and spitting the cursed mucus all over the floor.

"Are there any more slaves?" Drizzt asked, pointing farther along the descending corridor.

"Dahlia?" Entreri asked, an edge of desperation growing in his tone.

Amber gave an emphatic shake of her head and pointed to her work area, then down the hallway, and shook her head again.

So they rushed back, gathered up the three humans they had rescued, and headed back to rejoin their friends.

Artemis Entreri glanced back over his shoulder with almost every step.

Dahlia hesitated. Her twitch showed discomfort. Something was wrong, something out of proportion and beyond reality.

Catti-brie.

The name screamed in her thoughts repeatedly. This was the ghost who had haunted Drizzt's dreams. This was the woman who had ruined Dahlia's life with Drizzt, who had tainted Dahlia's love with Drizzt before it could even truly bloom. Were it not for her . . .

Dahlia found herself very near the altar stone then, facing the pit and Catti-brie, who stood across the block from her.

Dahlia moved to the right, Catti-brie similarly shifted sidelong to keep the stone between them.

"Dahlia?" the woman asked, and to hear this woman, Catti-brie, speaking her name stunned Dahlia as surely as a slap across the face.

"You are Dahlia, yes?" Catti-brie asked. "I have heard of you, from Drizzt."

The words hardly registered to the elf woman. All she heard was a grating sound, a screeching sound, an annoying cackle at the back of her mind.

The only word that came clear to her was, again, "Catti-brie."

Only when the woman reacted did Dahlia even realize that she had spoken the name aloud.

Dahlia's thoughts swirled back to the side of Kelvin's Cairn in faraway Icewind Dale, where Drizzt had spurned her, had betrayed her, had chosen this . . . this ghost above her. No strike had ever wounded Dahlia as profoundly as the one she had delivered upon Drizzt, and with the hope of killing him.

She had to kill him.

He was the source of all of her pain, of all of her misery. It was because of him that Dahlia had gone to Port Llast, had been captured by the drow, had been tortured . . .

She felt the tentacles of the awful illithid wriggling inside of her.

But wait, she thought, and she shook her head, for that mind flayer had told her the truth, at least. Where no one else ever had, the mind flayer had made so much clear to Dahlia.

"No, not Drizzt," she whispered, and Catti-brie wore a puzzled expression.

"From Drizzt," the woman reiterated, but Dahlia didn't hear.

"Because of you," Dahlia said pointedly. "Because of you, ghost!" She watched Catti-brie shaking her head, then bending low to retrieve her dropped bow.

The bow!

Oh, but Dahlia knew that bow! She thought of fighting beside Drizzt, of their brilliant teamwork when she intercepted his lightning arrows and re-directed the magical energy to more pointed ends.

She knew that bow, Drizzt's bow, and now this woman—this ghost held it, as if mocking her, as if mocking the love Dahlia had known with Drizzt.

A low and feral growl escaped her lips.

"Dahlia?" Catti-brie said, her voice calm and intentionally disarming. "Be at ease, Dahlia, I am not your enemy."

The altar thrummed to life before her, calling Dahlia to action, telling her to rise and vanquish this ghost, this woman who had caused her so much pain, this disciple of evil Mielikki.

Dahlia barely registered the stream of thoughts, but she surely understood the call and promise of the altar stone before her. She sent her flail into a spin, banging them together, building a charge, then pounded them repeatedly on the altar, and the throbbing black energy pulsed within and lent her weapon more magical power.

"Dahlia!" Catti-brie called to her, and Dahlia noted that the woman had backed from the altar, then had moved toward the tunnel to the Forge.

But she would not escape, Dahlia knew. Not from here.

"Destroy her!" Dahlia heard herself shout to the jade spider beside that tunnel, and surely the elf warrior would have been surprised had she stepped back from her rising emotions enough to decipher her own words, for how could she know the spider as an ally?

***

Wulfgar brought Aegis-fang up over his shoulder and swung it across with all his strength. With a resounding thud and a reverberation that ran back up the barbarian's arms, rippling his muscles under the tremendous vibrations, it struck the door dead center, right in the heart of the drider-like image of Lolth the drow craftsmen had constructed of black adamantine.

And bounced off, and neither the door nor the bas relief of Lolth showed as much as a scratch.

"Oh, me girl!" Bruenor yelled, pushing in past Wulfgar, who staggered aside under the weight of his own blow.

Regis, too, rushed for the door.

"Pick it, Rumblebelly!" Bruenor implored him.

Regis glanced all around the portal and the new archway, and ran his fingers over the smooth, cool metal. "Pick what?" he asked, completely at a loss and holding his hands out helplessly, for there was no sign of a lock or even a handle to be found.

"Bah!" Bruenor snorted and he hopped to the side and pulled Aegis-fang from Wulfgar, then leaped back for the door, Regis tumbling aside.

Bruenor noted the inscription on the warhammer's head, the symbols of his three gods overlaid, and from that reminder, he drew strength.

Great strength, the might of Clangeddin, and he slammed the warhammer into the door with tremendous power, rattling the stones of the Forge.

"Me girl!" he cried, and he hit the door again, as mighty a stroke as Wulfgar had delivered, at least.

"Me girl!"

He felt the power of Clangeddin coursing his veins, growing within him.

Tirelessly he pounded the portal.

But it showed not a scratch.

Catti-brie watched the woman slack-jawed, hardly believing the sudden rage that had come over Dahlia, who stood opposite the altar block, wildly banging her flail against the hard stone, her face a twisted mask of anger.

And Dahlia screamed to the spider, a pony-sized beast behind Catti-brie, and with another across the way, and, she then noticed, with thousands of fist-sized arachnids gathering on the wall of webbing.

Catti-brie turned fast, setting an arrow as she went. She called to the primordial, demanding help, as she drew back and let fly.

The lever! the ancient beast replied in her mind.

The spider shrieked horribly as the arrow blasted into it, throwing it back a skittering step.

"I cannot get to it! My way is blocked by enemies!" Catti-brie yelled in her thoughts and aloud, but in a language she could not consciously understand, a crackling, popping, sizzling series of sounds that made little sense to her human sensibilities—or to Dahlia's elven sensibilities as well, Catti-brie could see from looking at the woman, who paused in her drumming to stare incredulously.

A second arrow followed the first at the nearby jade spider, and a third and fourth went quickly after, and the spider shrieked and ran off down the tunnel.

Catti-brie pivoted, turning the bow upon Dahlia, who now stood on the altar, flail swinging easily.

"I don't want to kill you," she started to say, but the floor rumbled and rolled, a great roar from the primordial below, and Catti-brie was knocked to one knee as Dahlia leaped off the side of the altar, away from the pit.

Hissing and steam came from the pit and a burst of fiery magma leaped up over the ledge to crash down in a pile behind Dahlia and the altar, between the elf woman and the second of her spiders.

And not just normal, insentient lava rock—she heard its throaty grumble. She reached out to it through her ring, and it heard her call and rose up on two rocky legs. The jade spider nearby reared on its back legs and shrieked in angry protest and the magma elemental came on, unafraid.

"Brilliant," Dahlia congratulated, but seemed hardly concerned. Again she put her flail into a spin and now began advancing slowly on the woman with the bow.

"Drizzt is with me," Catti-brie said. "He is here, in Gauntlgrym—"

"Q'Xorlarrin," Dahlia corrected, and kept coming.

"You don't have to do this," Catti-brie pleaded with her. Looking past her, Catti-brie saw the jade spider go up into the air, its eight legs slapping and kicking at the elemental, mandibles biting in and breaking stone.

"Dahlia, I am not your enemy."

The elf woman laughed at her and continued her advance, now only a few short steps away. And from behind, Catti-brie heard the first spider's return along the small tunnel behind her to the right.

Dahlia charged and Catti-brie let fly, the arrow aimed for the woman's belly, center mass. Catti-brie winced, thinking she had surely slain this poor elf, yet the arrow did not strike home but simply disappeared.

And Dahlia's flail sparked with crawling, arcing sparks of energy all the more.

Catti-brie turned Taulmaril out defensively, like a staff, parrying the first strike. But Dahlia came in at her in a blur, spinning left and right, one flying weapon going out left, the other right. Desperately, Catti-brie worked her bow in a circle, creating a spinning wall to block, but it could not hold, and she was not surprised when a flail slipped through her defenses and smacked her painfully across the thigh, nearly laying her low.

And then she was surprised when Dahlia released the lightning energy collected by her weapon, the jarring bolt throwing Catti-brie back through the air, to crash in hard against the wall—and only the wall was holding her up.

Her mind spun as the elf stalked in for the kill. She tried to sort out her remaining spells, but they were few indeed, and none to lash out quickly or to properly defend.

"A ghost once more!" Dahlia cried triumphantly and rushed in, and Catti-brie dropped her bow and brought her hands up, at first defensively, but hardly thinking, she touched her thumbs together in a familiar pose and met the elf woman's charge with another fan of flame from burning hands.

Dahlia screamed and fell back, batting her arms at the biting fires, and Catti-brie looked at her hands, confused. She had no such spells remaining in her repertoire that day.

"The ring," she breathed, but before she could consider it, she saw movement from the side, from a charging, rearing spider, its mandibles dripping with deadly poison, and she fell to the floor desperately.

The rumbling belch of the primordial reverberated in the stone foundations of Gauntlgrym and into the Underdark tunnels below.

Drizzt, Entreri, Ambergris, and the three rescued humans felt it keenly, the tunnel around them growling with vibrations.

Drizzt and Entreri exchanged concerned looks, understanding the implications both for their companions back in the Forge and, for Entreri, the possibility that he would never get out of this dark place alive. They started ahead more swiftly, but Drizzt paused and turned to Ambergris.

"Turn left at the end of this passage and follow the right-hand wall of the next into the Forge," he instructed and the dwarf nodded.

And Drizzt and Entreri sprinted ahead, the assassin still laboring a bit on his wounded knee.

The companions in the Forge felt the growling, too, and knowing that Catti-brie had gone into that primordial chamber—and with Bruenor knowing exactly what was in that place—they pressed on furiously with their work on the door. Bruenor in particular threw himself against it, trying to wedge his fingers in between the door and the jamb that he might tug it open.

"Girl!" he cried. "Oh, me girl!" and he fought furiously with the metal portal. And he yelled for Clangeddin to give him strength, and sought the god in his thoughts and memories of the throne above.

"No, dwarf," came a call from the side, the weak voice of Afafrenfere. All the others turned to regard the monk, who was sitting up now, and even that with great effort, obviously.

"Not that god," Afafrenfere advised. "You'll not muscle the door."

"Eh?" a confused Bruenor asked.

"Three gods for the dwarves, yes?" the monk asked.

Bruenor started to argue, but stopped short and looked at Afafrenfere curiously, hands on his hips.

"Eh?" he asked again, but this time he was speaking more to himself than to the monk.

The snapping mandibles were barely a hand's breadth from her face when Catti-brie leveled Taulmaril and fired an arrow into the face of the jade monstrosity. The spider's shrill screech echoed off the walls of the chamber and it staggered back a shuffle of steps.

Catti-brie shot it again.

She turned to Dahlia and let fly another arrow, but low, to slam into the ground before the elf woman, the force and jolt sending Dahlia scrambling backward.

Catti-brie spun back on the spider and charged, drawing closer, and shot it again, and again. It tried to run away, but the woman pursued, pouring a line of lightning arrows into it, breaking it apart. One leg fell free, then a second and finally, with a great shriek, the spider rolled over and shuddered in its death throes.

And Catti-brie whirled back and shot the ground at Dahlia's feet as the stubborn woman came on. The elf warrior was holding a staff now, though, and not her flail, and she drove it down to the stone, and though she shuddered, it seemed to Catti-brie that her magical weapon had eaten the brunt of the blow. Indeed, it crackled once more with lightning energy, and Dahlia strained, it seemed, to hold on.

Catti-brie had no choice, and so she let fly another stream of lightning missiles, at the ground before the woman and at the woman, an explosive barrage that sent sparks flying wildly all around the center of the chamber. Catti-brie advanced, arrows flying, and Dahlia staggered under every blow, grunting and growling.

Sparks flew off and dived into the primordial pit. Sparks showered the webbing, burning into the flammable material and sending spiders scurrying all around.

Beyond Dahlia, through the crackling volley, Catti-brie noted the magma elemental standing tall, holding the thrashing jade spider up over its head as it stomped for the pit. She entertained the notion of bringing the elemental in against Dahlia, to catch her, perhaps, and hold her, for she did not want to kill this elf woman.

The elemental threw the spider into the pit and swung around to Catti-brie's call. It took a long stride at Dahlia, heading to Catti-brie's defense, but before it put its foot down to the stone, it hesitated weirdly, and seemed as if stuck in place, struggling mightily.

And Catti-brie understood and winced.

For in its dying fall, the jade spider had spat its webbing back at the elemental, the filaments grabbing hold well enough to tug it suddenly and violently.

The elemental pitched backward over the ledge, tumbling from sight and from the battle.

And Catti-brie shot Dahlia again, and the elf trembled violently as the energy of the staff crackled and jerked her around.

But Dahlia settled and screamed and charged, planting the pole and vaulting high just as Catti-brie shot the stone beneath her.

And Catti-brie also charged, fortunately so, for she slid down and crossed under the leaping Dahlia, and skidded up to her feet and ran off the other way, calling to the primordial, calling to her ring.

She leaped atop the altar and sprang away.

And felt very sickly immediately from simply contacting the foul stone.

She landed and she staggered, and she cried out against a demonic voice laughing in her mind.

She feared that Dahlia was coming in fast behind her, and with a staff bristling with mighty energy.

She knew she had to turn around and drive the woman back with more arrows, to overload the staff if that was possible, or at least to force it from Dahlia's grasp with the sheer strength of the teeming magical energy.

But she couldn't turn and she couldn't shoot, and it was all she could do to hold onto Taulmaril. Then she stumbled down to the floor.

And the demon in her thoughts, the Demon Queen of Spiders, laughed.

It was too much power—she should not have been able to hold it.

But she was, her hands tightly clenched on the staff, crackling lightning rolling up and down it, rolling up and down her, as well. The braid atop her head danced weirdly.

She watched Catti-brie's flight across the chamber, watched her stagger down to the floor, and Dahlia heard cheering in her thoughts even as her adversary heard the laughter of the Spider Queen.

Dahlia slowed, and winced. She thought of Drizzt, and not just that last encounter on the mountainside, but of their lovemaking, of their adventuring together, of their friendship.

She thought of Effron, and of how her companions—how her *friends*—had rescued her from him in the docked boat, and had then given her the time with him to heal their wounds.

And now he was dead, her boy, killed by drow . . .

But the memory shifted before she could complete the thought, before she could realize that the drow had done this terrible thing to her and to her son.

And instead, that line of thought swerved, leaping through connections that suddenly made perfect sense to the elf warrior.

Effron was dead because of Drizzt, because Drizzt had spurned her, and he had done so because of a ghost, because of this ghost, Catti-brie.

This disciple of foul Mielikki.

That last notion made little sense to Dahlia, who knew little of Mielikki and cared even less, but it didn't matter. For now it all made perfect sense.

Effron was dead because of Catti-brie; everything bad in Dahlia's life was because of Catti-brie.

And now she could find revenge. She charged. She planted her staff at the base of the altar stone and vaulted high into the air, screaming with unbridled glee and unbridled hatred.

Catti-brie came up to her feet and spun around to meet that flying charge, and Dahlia, landing right in front of her, could have ended the fight immediately, could have released all the power stored in Kozah's Needle in one mighty blast that would have melted the woman where she stood.

But no, that would be too easy, too mercifully quick.

Catti-brie deflected Dahlia's stabbing staff aside, then came up and across horizontally, bow held wide in both hands, to block a powerful downward chop.

The woman proved a decent fighter, parrying and angling her weapon appropriately to slide strikes harmlessly wide, but she was no match for Dahlia.

And Catti-brie knew it. Dahlia could see it on her face. She knew she was overmatched.

But she was not afraid.

For a moment, that puzzled Dahlia, but only for a moment. She understood that Catti-brie was buying time, and was she calling again to the primordial for help?

Dahlia drove on more ferociously, pounding her weapon heavily, driving Catti-brie back with each strike. And the woman was running out of room, closing in on the wall.

Dahlia increased her tempo, swatting and stabbing, rushing ahead and forcing her enemy ever backward, and when Catti-brie's back went against the wall, Dahlia swung mightily. Taulmaril came across to block, but as the weapons connected, Dahlia broke her staff in half, two equal lengths joined with a strong cord. The strike had been blocked above the halfway mark of the weapon, so that top half flew back over toward Dahlia as she drove the weapon down.

She was ready for that, however, and she caught it, and now stabbed freely beneath the blocking blow.

Catti-brie did well to drive her bow down to mitigate the attack, but as soon as Kozah's Needle touched her chest, Dahlia released a bit of its energy, enough to jolt the woman against the wall, her head cracking hard into the stone.

Dahlia retracted and dropped one of the two poles, then, confident that Catti-brie was too dazed to respond. She swung around in a full circuit, letting her weapon fly out to its full length and rejoining it into a single staff as she went. She came around with great speed and power and batted Taulmaril from Catti-brie's hands, launching it into the remaining webbing at the corner of the chamber, just to the side of the sealed tunnel meant for Matron Zeerith.

Hardly slowing, Dahlia slid one hand out wide and drove the staff sidelong before her, under the chin of slumping Catti-brie, lifting her up against the wall with Kozah's Needle tight against her throat.

Now it was personal, Dahlia thought, and she was pleased, and so was the voice in her head.

Now she could feel the woman's fear.

Now she could feel the woman's pain.

Now she could watch the light go out in Catti-brie's blue eyes.

"Now," Dahlia said, hardly aware of the words, "Mielikki will lose."

And Dahlia was happy.

***

Wulfgar pounded at the door while Regis crawled around the adamantine arch above it, looking for a lock or clasp or something that might spring whatever was holding it closed.

Bruenor, however, looked inside himself. He noted Afafrenfere, nodding his way in encouragement, then closed his eyes and sent his thoughts back to the Throne of the Dwarven Gods.

He heard the song of Moradin, the roar of Clangeddin, the whispers of Dumathoin.

He opened his eyes and moved for the door, nudging Wulfgar out of the way. He begged silence from Clangeddin, and begged for wisdom from Moradin.

Then he focused on the whispers, the secrets.

This was still Gauntlgrym, he was told, whatever the dark elves might be doing to deface the complex. This was still the realm of the dwarves, ever on and always before. The dressings on the door mattered not.

Not the black bas relief of foul Lolth nor the adamantine arch.

No, this was the same door, crafted of dwarf hands, set in stone by dwarf smiths, by Bruenor's ancestors.

He put his hand against the mithral.

He was friend here, royal of blood, noble of deed, he told the door, told the spiritual remnants the ancient dwarf craftsmen had imbued here with their love of their craft.

He was friend to Gauntlgrym, and this place remained Gauntlgrym.

The door itself seemed to breathe with life, the seal breaking as the portal swung outward.

And Bruenor charged in, Wulfgar and Regis close behind.

Catti-brie couldn't respond. She couldn't draw breath. The staff, crackling with power, crushed in against her windpipe. Her eyes bulged and she grabbed the staff in both hands, inside Dahlia's grasp, and tried to push back.

But Catti-brie was in an awkward position, her head bent slightly by a jag in the wall, and she hadn't the strength to push Dahlia away, nor the mobility to even twist her neck enough to get the press off of her windpipe.

And there was another power in the staff: a dark energy that she could feel as tangibly as the metal of Kozah's Needle. She thought of the altar, pulsing as if alive, and the feeling of weakness and sickness as she had stepped upon it flashed in her now-fleeting thoughts.

Now fleeting because she was falling away. The edges of her vision darkened.

She thought of Drizzt and wished she had said goodbye, but she was at peace because she knew that she had done Mielikki's bidding, that she and the Companions of the Hall had saved him.

In that notion, Lolth might win now, but Catti-brie had done as the goddess had bade . . .

A sharp recoil sounded in Catti-brie's mind, a shout of "No!" as profound as if she had screamed the word aloud.

This was not about Drizzt. Not now.

This was about Mielikki and Lolth.

This was about Catti-brie and Dahlia, proxies for the titanic struggle. Catti-brie could not be content with her efforts atop Kelvin's Cairn. Who would Drizzt be without her? How could he withstand a broken heart yet again?

Or Bruenor, her Da? Or Wulfgar or Regis?

She could not, must not, surrender until the end. She could not be satisfied with past victories when present battles raged.

She had but a fleeting moment of consciousness left, and in that instant, she recalled Dahlia's drop from the webbing, when the elf warrior had broken this strange staff in half across her shoulders.

Catti-brie's fingers played along the length of the metal pole; she sent the last vestiges of her conscious thoughts into that weapon to find its secrets.

Then she pushed out with every bit of strength she had left, a last, desperate gasp and grasp for life, and as she did, she tried to drive her head forward, meeting the press, and as she did, her fingers found the secret of Kozah's Needle and she released the staff into two parts.

The break of the weapon released her, so suddenly, and her head snapped forward, her forehead crashing against startled Dahlia's nose, slamming the woman backward in a stagger, and in that awkward shuffle, her staff, the focus of her balance, suddenly broken in two, Dahlia couldn't hold on.

Catti-brie, her teeth chattering from the sheer power contained within the weapon, yanked Kozah's Needle from Dahlia's grasp and drove the ends back together, trying to hold on to it.

She looked at Dahlia then, blood running down the elf's face from her shattered nose, and an expression on her face that Catti-brie couldn't begin to comprehend.

As soon as she had inadvertently let go of the weapon, a staff teeming with the imbued dark energies of the altar, Dahlia's connection to the darkness had diminished, just a bit, and beside those feelings of hatred for Catti-brie, of blame for the death of Effron, came the gentle images of Drizzt once more and the companions she had known, and the sea journey where Effron and she had found peace.

She thought of Drizzt and tried to reach for him more fully, but could not hold, his image fading from her to be replaced, to her surprise, by one she suddenly realized as more dear.

By the image of Artemis Entreri. She heard his words to her, of comfort in his own way, but of understanding.

And in them, the whisper of a better way and a better life, the distant whisper of hope itself.

And the turmoil of Dahlia, the great paradox of love and hate that had twined together throughout her life, that had carried her through murderous battles with her every lover, shocked her and infused doubt against the red wall of outrage.

She felt Alegni's violation once more, saw the murder of her mother, threw her infant baby from the cliff. Szass Tam leered at her, her dying lovers cried out for mercy she would not afford them.

The cackles of Lolth met the sobs of broken Dahlia.

She didn't know what to do, a voice screaming in her head to launch herself back at Catti-brie, a wound in her heart telling her to fall down and cry. She stumbled back from the wall and turned and had to get out of there, had to get away from this woman she faced, from the awful truth of herself and her miserable life.

She started to run for the far exit, the tunnel to the Forge, but in rushed the red-bearded dwarf, the huge barbarian, and the clever halfling—the other ghosts that haunted Drizzt Do'Urden, the other companions returned to life to stand with Drizzt against the dark lady.

Against Lolth.

Against wretched Dahlia.

Yes, wretched Dahlia, she knew, and she let out a cry, part anger, part remorse, part profound sadness, and she turned to her right, to the pit and thought to leap in and be done with the pain.

She took a running stride, but a sharp voice in her head denied her.

No! came the order she could not resist, the order from Lolth, the order relayed through Methil, hidden invisibly across the way, who spoke for Lolth.

Dahlia skidded to a stop and whirled around, then sprinted for the one remaining opening, the entrance to the sealed tunnel meant to serve as Matron Zeerith's chamber.

The remaining webs parted for her, and in her mind, she knew that the magical wall of iron would be dispelled, freeing her to the lower tunnels, saving her to fight and win another day.

Catti-brie watched the woman's run, and saw her companions entering the chamber, but only distantly did those images register. Her focus had to be the staff, Kozah's Needle, and the tremendous power contained within, curling tendrils of energy that battled her as surely as Dahlia had battled her. Her own lightning from Taulmaril arced and ran around the weapon, combining with the dark powers from the altar, and within those black energies lived a flicker of the Spider Queen, a conduit to the mind of the dark Demon Queen of Spiders.

In that staff, Catti-brie heard the thoughts of Dahlia, the telepathic exchange between the elf and the goddess. She felt the turmoil, the battle, light and dark, and she knew that Dahlia meant to end her struggle by leaping into the pit even before she saw Dahlia turn that way.

And Catti-brie, too, heard the denial, the darkness refuting Dahlia, the darkness dominating Dahlia, and as Dahlia spun around and rushed into the second tunnel, Catti-brie felt her hope for freedom that she could turn again upon Drizzt and his friends as an agent of Lolth.

Catti-brie could hardly hold the staff, and she, too, turned for the primordial pit, thinking to feed the god-like primordial beast this tainted weapon.

But mercy stopped her, mercy for Dahlia and her dismayed realization that Dahlia had lost and Dahlia *was* lost, and this realization turned her back fast the other way.

Kozah's Needle, teeming with power, flew spear-like into the tunnel behind the retreating Dahlia. It hit the wall just inside, and the resulting explosion shook the ground with the power of an earthquake, and as she tumbled down, Catti-brie feared that she had just broken the whole of the place, and perhaps had freed the primordial.

CHAPTER 27

NEVER FORGET

Drizzt and Entreri ran along the back corridor, passing the lava tube, an open tunnel to their left, a wall of iron blocking the passage to their right.

They paid it no heed, other than to use it as a guide-point in their rush to rejoin the others in the Forge.

But then they were flying, falling, tumbling, as a great retort rumbled all around them, dust and stones bursting out from their left, from around the magical wall of stone. Pelted and bounced around, the two crashed in across the way, Entreri several steps into the open lava tube.

"The beast," Drizzt breathed, picking himself up from the ground.

On he ran, Entreri, his limp noticeably more pronounced, struggling to keep up.

Entering the brightly lit Forge, Drizzt first noted Brother Afafrenfere leaning on the open mithral door on legs surely wobbly. He called out to the monk, who looked his way and pointed emphatically down the tunnel.

Drizzt never slowed, turning in fast, Entreri hustling close behind.

The two came into the primordial chamber, Drizzt leading and skidding to a stop as he took in the remarkable scene: the webbing, the dead green spider, the altar block, the pile of magma near the ledge, and the Companions of the Hall, standing together before a pile of collapsed rubble—right at the entrance to the lava tube, Drizzt knew.

Catti-brie leaned heavily on Bruenor, looking dazed and weak and covered with dust, and Drizzt ran to her with all speed.

"We found yer Dahlia," Bruenor said to him, nodding to the rubble.

Drizzt sucked in his breath. Entreri, who had heard, ran by him to the rubble pile and began hopping all around the broken stones and dust, shoving some aside.

"Dahlia!" he yelled and he threw a rock at the rubble and spun back on the others. "What did you do?"

Drizzt pulled Catti-brie closer, expecting Entreri to leap at her, but the woman straightened, stepped away from him, and lifted her chin resolutely. "She was not the elf you once knew," she said confidently. "She was possessed of a demon. She would hear no reason."

Entreri picked up another stone, swung around, and threw it with all his might into the pile. He sat down there, as if his legs had simply collapsed beneath him, staring at the stone.

"We should be leaving," Regis remarked. "Did you find the dwarf?"

Drizzt never stopped looking at Catti-brie or at the burn and bruise across her throat. "She is close behind, and with others we freed, as well," he answered. "And yes, it is time to go, and with all speed."

He took Catti-brie by the shoulders then, and pushed her past him to the waiting support of Wulfgar. He nodded to his friends, and they started back for the Forge.

"We have to go," Drizzt said to Entreri a few moments later, moving near to the man and bending low beside him.

"Then go," Entreri replied.

"There is nothing here for you."

Entreri looked up at him, and the assassin's crestfallen expression spoke to Drizzt before Entreri corrected the assertion with, "There is nothing for me."

"There is always something."

"Go, drow," Entreri said. "Your place is with your friends."

"You will find . . ." Drizzt started to say, but Entreri cut him short.

"Go," he said more firmly, and he turned back to the wall of broken stone.

Drizzt let his stare linger for a bit longer, but really had nothing more he could say. He rose, patting Entreri on the shoulder, and started away.

"I will never forget that you came for me, Drizzt Do'Urden," Entreri called after him, and for some reason he didn't quite yet understand, those words filled Drizzt's heart.

By the time he got back to the Forge, Drizzt found Ambergris and the three freed humans with the others. Catti-brie had no spells available to help the cursed dwarf, but Regis reached into his magical pouch and produced a potion he thought might be of use, and indeed, before the group of ten had even started off, Ambergris was already speaking once more, and nonstop as she recounted her adventures to any who would listen.

"Gutbuster," Regis whispered to Drizzt and Bruenor, nodding his chin at the recovering female dwarf. "I figured that it could cut through any sickly venom."

"Bwahaha," Bruenor laughed, and Drizzt was glad of his own smile. He was thinking of Dahlia, and with a heavy heart, and thinking of Entreri, with great sympathy.

Ambergris moved over to her dear friend Afafrenfere and placed her thick hand on his forehead as she began her chant, calling upon her god to infuse the battered man with healing warmth and strength.

Afafrenfere stood taller almost immediately and nodded his gratitude.

"I've some more magic prepared," the cleric offered.

"Use it upon yourself, then," said Regis, breaking away from Bruenor and Drizzt. "I'm not sure how long my potion will hold back the curse of the drow."

"Curse o' the damned drow," Bruenor muttered beside Drizzt, who nodded.

"Don't like seein' 'em here, elf," the dwarf went on. "Yerself excepted, o' course."

"Of course," Drizzt agreed with a grin.

Bruenor started to reply, but stopped short, and a curious expression crossed his face. He held up his hand to halt Drizzt's forthcoming question, and turned to the Great Forge.

"Bruenor?" Drizzt asked after a long while had passed, the dwarf just standing there, staring.

Without a word, Bruenor started across the room, for the forge. When he got there, he laid his axe, helm, and shield atop the metal tray leading to the closed oven doors. He looked around, ignoring the questions from Drizzt, and found a pole with a hooked tip and a pair of long tongs.

The others joined the pair then, Catti-brie and Wulfgar similarly asking what Bruenor might be up to, but still the dwarf ignored them all. He reached along the tray, between the blocking walls, with the hooked pole and used it to pull open the heavy oven door.

Inside, the primal fire burned angrily, and Bruenor nodded and smiled. Then he rushed around, collecting the tools he'd need.

"We haven't the time," Drizzt said to him when he figured it out.

"Hold the room," the dwarf answered, and distantly, his tone brooking no debate.

"Bruenor?"

"Just ye hold the room, elf!" the dwarf demanded. He looked past Drizzt to the others. "All o' ye!"

"We have injured," Catti-brie reminded him. "And innocents. Every moment we delay . . ."

The dwarf looked at her soberly.

"We have to g—" Catti-brie started to insist, but she stopped short and stared at the opened oven, and heard the call of the primordial. "The axe," she told the dwarf. "And the helm . . ."

Catti-brie looked to Bruenor, her expression suddenly one of excitement. To the horror of the others, she hopped up onto the tray and stepped between the guard walls, where it should have been too hot for any person to venture, and reached down to pick up the dwarf's implements.

"Girl!" Bruenor said with alarm.

Catti-brie glanced back with a wide smile, holding Bruenor's axe. She tossed it into the oven.

"Girl!" the dwarf cried and the others, too, gasped.

And in went the dwarf's shield, which was mostly made of wood, like the axe handle—and surely the primordial fires would eat it to nothingness.

Catti-brie held up the helm and inspected it. It was made of metal, one horn sticking out one side, set into a metal holding circlet, and the stub of a horn sticking out the other. Two rubies were set one above the other in the front, and Catti-brie focused on these, the others could tell, as she began to softly chant.

"Prepare yourself, and quickly," she told the dwarf. "Your hammer and mithral plating."

"Girl?"

"Listen to them," Catti-brie said to him. "To Dumathoin. He knows."

Bruenor closed his eyes and fell within himself, and pictured the throne, remembering the sensation, the sounds of the gods.

Like Catti-brie, he began to chant, but while hers was a mixture of songs, the melody of Mielikki and the foreign sounds of the Plane of Fire, his was the dwarven brogue, the song of workers and miners, an ancient song that had once echoed off these very halls, in ages lost to the world.

Catti-brie kissed the rubies on the helm and tossed it into the oven. She turned to Bruenor and motioned to the tongs, and the dwarf handed them to her. She turned and reached in, and dragged back the many-notched axe.

Its handle was smoking a bit, but seemed, amazingly, unharmed.

Catti-brie picked it up, examining the glowing metal head. She put it down before Bruenor, who began sprinkling it with silver flakes, then tap-tapped with a hammer, singing all the while.

Next came the shield, and the wood seemed a bit darker, but again unharmed, and the metal band around its edge glowed, and the relief of the foaming mug standard seemed to somehow have more depth to it. Catti-brie considered it for a moment, then laughed and cast an enchantment upon it as she put it beside Bruenor's work table.

Bruenor had just gotten to work on that shield, reinforcing the bands, when the woman pulled forth the glowing helm, and those rubies set in the front sparkled most of all, and indeed, small flames burned clearly within them. The horns seemed untouched, as did the leather inset of the item.

Catti-brie didn't put this down beside Bruenor's worktable. There was no need. She dipped it in the forge's water tray to cool it, hot steam shooting up with an angry hiss.

Then, as Bruenor continued his song and his work, the woman plopped the helm atop his head.

And Bruenor's face lit up with profound joy and he hoisted his axe.

And he sang, and tossed mithral flakes all around him.

The rubies glowed and Bruenor heard their call. He uttered a word that he did not understand, though Catti-brie surely did, and she nodded as the rubies flared with mounting inner fire.

The head of Bruenor's axe burst into flames.

Not flames to eat the weapon, though, but to enhance it, adding the enchantment of flametongue to an axe that had already known hundreds of battles.

Bruenor slid his shield over his other arm and extinguished the axe's fires with a thought.

"Now we can go, elf," he said, as if coming out of a trance. "Aye, now we can go."

Drizzt looked over to Ambergris, who was shaking her head in clear awe of the scene before her. He tapped her on the shoulder and pointed across the way, to the huge, broken drider and the weapon lying on the ground in front of it.

With a squeal, Amber Gristle O'Maul ran across to retrieve her beloved Skullcrusher, and when she returned, she looked to Bruenor and to the oven pleadingly.

"No, girl," the dwarf said. "Not now. I'm not for knowin' what just happened, but 'tweren't no simple bit o' smithin'."

"It was a gift," Catti-brie said. "To you. A gift of the dwarf gods, a gift from Gauntlgrym." She paused and matched intense stares with her dwarf father. "And it was a request."

Bruenor nodded. "Aye. A deal I'm glad to make."

"A request?" Regis and Wulfgar asked together.

"We've a long road," Bruenor replied, and started away. "And one that just got longer."

The others followed, Drizzt bringing up the rear of the line.

He looked back several times, toward the primordial chamber, thinking of Dahlia, thinking of Entreri. Truly the death of the elf woman stung him—more than he would have expected. Perhaps he had never really loved her—certainly not as he loved Catti-brie—but he had cared for her, and deeply.

She was at peace, he hoped. At long last, perhaps Dahlia had found peace.

And Entreri's last words to him rang in his head and in his heart. He wished that the man was leaving with them, out of this place and back to their own place.

But Drizzt took heart, confident in this one's skill and resourcefulness, certain that he would see Artemis Entreri again.

EPILOGUE

THE WONDROUS THINGS I HAVE WITNESSED, GROMPH BAENRE HEARD
in his mind, and the thought had been offered with excitement.
That alone alerted the archmage that something tremendous indeed
had occurred, for when had he ever known an illithid to show
excitement?

He felt a further communication, a request that he go to Methil with
all haste, and with the matron mother. Normally, the archmage would
have ignored such a request, but the excitement in Methil's thoughts had
surely intrigued him.

Within a short while, he and Quenthel joined the illithid in the anteroom of the primordial chamber.

"My elemental?" he asked at once, with surprise and alarm. "Where
is the guard?"

"Destroyed," Methil replied in his watery voice. The mind flayer's
tentacles waved toward the archway and the bridge beyond, motioning
them out.

The matron mother was no less alarmed, and surely more horrified,
when she crossed through the steam and mist to witness the defilement
of the chapel. One jade spider was missing, the other lying inverted and
quite destroyed back the other way, by the tunnel to the Forge. And most
of the webs were gone, the floor beneath the remaining strands littered
with the crispy bodies of scores of burned spiders.

"What is this sacrilege?" Matron Mother Quenthel demanded, and
Gromph looked to Methil for an explanation.

"The battle of gods," Gromph answered his sister a moment later, his voice full of incredulity. He lifted his gaze above the altar stone, to the missing centerpiece of this sacred chapel.

"The *darthiir* sacrifice," he mumbled.

Both he and Quenthel looked to the cave-in as Methil telepathically relayed the images of the last moments of the battle. The illithid started for the pile, the other two in tow. He held up one arm to Gromph, who joined hands with the creature.

Gromph nodded as Methil silently explained.

"What is it?" Matron Mother Quenthel demanded.

Gromph offered her his hand. "Come," he bade her.

Quenthel hesitated, looking at him and particularly at that strange mind flayer, suspiciously. When Gromph didn't retract his offered hand, though, she took it, and immediately she felt strange, lighter.

"Whatever you do, do not let go," Gromph solemnly warned as Methil led the way to the pile—and into it.

Quenthel did well not to cry out in revulsion and fear as her less than corporeal form slipped through the stones and dirt. Not between them, as a priestess or mage might do with some wraithform spell, but through them, as if her own corporality and that of the stones had somehow moved into different dimensions.

She could feel the stones slipping through her, and it was not a comfortable sensation.

When they came into an open area past the pile, the closed chamber was too dark even for drow lowlight vision. With a few words and a wave of his hand, Gromph created a muted red light. They were about halfway along the tunnel, the archmage estimated, glancing at his magically created metal wall a bit farther along.

"What is that?" he heard the matron mother say and he looked back, to see that Methil had collected something in their strange journey.

"The *darthiir*'s staff," Gromph said, taking Kozah's Needle, then handing it to his sister.

Methil pointed down at the rubble pile and waggled his tentacles, the emanating psionic magic pushing a few small stones aside to reveal a foot, delicate and light-skinned, the foot of a *darthiir* woman.

"She is dead, then," the matron mother stated flatly, for clearly Dahlia had been buried under tons of stone.

But a moment later, Gromph began to chuckle, and he and his sister watched as Methil became nearly translucent once more, then reached down and grabbed Dahlia's foot, sharing the psionic state with her.

Illithids were not physically strong creatures, but Dahlia slid easily out from under the pile. In that moment, she simply did not exist in the same dimension as the crushing stones.

Methil left her lying on the ground when he and Dahlia came back fully to their material state, and the *darthiir* did not stir in the least, and indeed, seemed quite dead.

But Methil knew better and he explained it to Gromph and to Quenthel.

"Strange are the powers of these creatures of the mind," Gromph remarked. "Often I am reminded to be glad that Matron Mother Yvonnel destroyed House Oblodra."

Quenthel could only shake her head and mutter, "Kinetic barrier?" without any understanding of the psionic dweomer at all.

"Come, and be quick!" Gromph said suddenly. He grabbed Dahlia's hand and held out his other one for Quenthel, who took it, then shuddered in revulsion as she grabbed hold of Methil's offered hand as well.

A few moments later, they stood by the altar, Dahlia lying atop it, the red veins in the stone seeming to pulse with life.

"Stay back," Gromph warned his sister. "When she awakens, she must release the held energy of the cave-in, residing now in Methil's offered psionic protection."

"Awakens?" the matron mother said, at a loss. "Release?"

Even as she spoke, Dahlia's eyes popped open and she jerked suddenly, her back arching so violently that she was lifted up into the air. As her physical form separated from the altar stone, they could see that she was still connected by a wall of black energy, pulsing with red lines of power, rushing into the stone. The primordial chamber shook once more, the altar taking in the force and seeming as if it grew stronger in doing so.

Dahlia fell back down, hard. She looked at them, but distantly, clearly dazed, and Methil fell over her, his tentacles wriggling up her nose and around her skull as he joined with her once more.

The illithid telepathically shared his understanding, and Dahlia's thoughts, with Gromph and Quenthel.

"Back to the anteroom," Matron Mother Quenthel instructed as she sorted it all out. "Let us await the arrival of Matron Zeerith."

And indeed, she was smiling as she made that proclamation, and Gromph could only shake his head at how this struggle of the goddesses continued to play out. When they got into the anteroom, Methil still connected to Dahlia, who walked zombie-like, her eyes empty, Gromph created an extra-dimensional mansion that the Baenre nobles and their blessed guest might relax in proper security and comfort to await the arrival of the Xorlarrins.

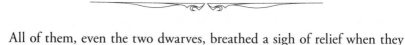

All of them, even the two dwarves, breathed a sigh of relief when they came out of the tunnels into the open air of the Crags.

"The road ain't far," Bruenor explained, pointing to the east. "She'll get us to Port Llast, and from there on to Longsaddle."

"For Pwent," Regis agreed, and the dwarf nodded.

The three humans they had rescued cheered at that thought, but Drizzt and Ambergris both turned to Brother Afafrenfere, for the monk had been hinting that he would not follow their road.

"Well, speak it clear, then," Ambergris bade him.

"It is time for me to go home,' Afafrenfere admitted. "To face my brethren in the hopes that they will forgive me."

"Was years ago when ye went with Parbid to the Shadowfell," Ambergris said. "Think they'll even remember ye?"

The monk smiled. "Not that long," he said, and Ambergris laughed.

And nodded as she looked at Drizzt. The drow knew her story, of how she had been sent to the Shadowfell as an agent of Citadel Adbar, as repentance for some . . . indiscretions. Knowing how Amber Gristle O'Maul had walked the gray areas of morality herself, Drizzt was not surprised when she reached up and patted her friend on the shoulder and declared, "I'm goin' with ye."

Brother Afafrenfere's face brightened immediately, but he shook his head and tried to insist that he could not ask that of her, that it was too far a journey, and through dangerous lands.

"Bah, but who's to speak for ye if not meself, who knows ye better than any?" the dwarf said.

Afafrenfere stared at her for a moment, then laughed in surrender. "I am not so sure that your presence will bolster my case," he said in a lighthearted tone. "But I welcome it!"

"The Monastery of the Yellow Rose?" Drizzt asked.

"Aye," said the monk. "In faraway Damara, in the Bloodstone Lands."

Regis's ears perked up. "Come with us to the road and turn south, then," he said to the monk. "Then turn south through Neverwinter and follow the Trade Way to the Boareskyr Bridge, and inquire of Doregardo and the Grinning Ponies all along your way. When you find them, tell them you are a friend of mine, of the halfling called Spider. They will see you to Suzail, where you can catch passage to Impiltur." The halfling nodded as he finished, his thoughts spinning back to the far banks of the great Sea of Fallen Stars, to Aglarond, to Donnola Topolino and a life he had known, and one whose echoes tapped profoundly at his heavy heart.

When they got to the main road and Afafrenfere and Ambergris turned to the south, it was all Regis could manage not to go with them.

He had a duty here, he reminded himself, repeatedly. To Pwent, trapped in Wulfgar's broken horn, and to Bruenor, determined to return to Mithral Hall.

But he would return to the city of Delthuntle and to his beloved Donnola, Regis silently vowed as he watched the monk and the dwarf walk away to the south, his other companions moving north for Port Llast, and with Longsaddle waiting beyond that.

***

They crept back into the complex they had declared as their home to witness the carnage and the defilement of their chapel. For Berellip Xorlarrin, the shock was complete. The webs had unfolded and the captive Dahlia was gone and the room prepared for her mother, Matron Zeerith, was buried now under tons of rock. She did not dare set the remaining goblin slaves to dig out that rubble for fear that it would lead to more instability.

The images in the Forge were no less troubling, beginning with, and centering around, the broken form of the great drider. The captive human was gone—even the dead monk had been removed. And those slaves they had not had the time to drag away had also been freed. The priestess cursed herself for not sending an assassin down into that remaining mining section, particularly when she remembered that a dwarf cleric had been among the few down there.

And the dead in the Forge, many, many dead, were all Xorlarrin allies, scores of goblins, a quartet of driders, and more than a dozen Xorlarrin drow.

With not a single enemy among them.

By all accounts, the invaders had gone and the apostate Do'Urden had gone, and the complex was back in Berellip's hands, but her mother would not be pleased.

According to Berellip's scouts, Matron Zeerith was only a day or two away, marching with the rest of the House and a sizable force from Menzoberranzan that would lead the way to Tsabrak's location in the east.

The only good news the priestess received came from the north, where Ravel, Saribel, and Tiago Baenre approached, so said her scouts. But even in this, there were whispers of trouble, rumors about many drow dead, many Xorlarrin dead, and even whispers that Weapons Master Jearth was not among the returning band.

It was all too much for Berellip and she went to her private chambers and tumbled down upon a pile of large pillows, seeking respite. She lay on her back, staring up at the webbing canopy of her bed, noting the designs in the intricate strands and letting them take her thoughts back to the chapel. What might she do to make the place more presentable to Matron Zeerith? To mitigate the rage she knew would be directed her way?

No, not her way, she decided, for she would blame Ravel for all of this. It would be a tricky proposition, she realized, for by doing so, she would also be implicating Tiago Baenre, and it was never a good thing to speak ill of a Baenre.

She would reveal Ravel's spying on Gromph—yes! This tragedy fell squarely on his shoulders. Ravel had found the apostate, so he had believed, and Ravel had taken the soldiers, leaving Q'Xorlarrin vulnerable, above Berellip's protests.

The priestess nodded as her plan unfolded in her thoughts. She would have to take care to absolve Tiago—if she did it correctly, she might even find Tiago on her side in this conflict, as he, too, tried to deflect blame onto others.

They would all try to deflect blame. That was the way of the drow, after all.

Berellip knew that she had to do so not only with her mother but with the archmage, surely. Gromph had taken a particular interest in this Dahlia creature, and now she was gone.

With that thought in mind, Berellip pictured the *darthiir* in the webbing, only in the strands of her own canopy. Perhaps she could find a replacement among the slaves they had brought back, she thought. Was Gromph done with Dahlia? Were they all? If so, another body up there might suffice, for how would they know the truth of the newer sacrifice?

The image above her became clearer, and nearer, and Berellip blinked as she realized that it was not an image in her mind's eye but an actual person up there. For a heartbeat, she thought of Dahlia and wondered if a handmaiden of Lolth had somehow saved the prisoner and hung her here for Berellip to find.

But it was not Dahlia, she realized as that form broke through the webbing and dropped upon her, as she recognized it as a man, and human, and one she knew.

Yes, Artemis Entreri made sure that Berellip saw his face and looked into his eyes as he deftly kicked aside her snake-headed scourge before she could awaken the serpents. And he made sure that those eyes were the last thing this witch ever saw before a fine drow sword cut her throat, ear-to-ear.

Entreri rolled off the pillows to his feet. "For Dahlia," he whispered.

He wiped the sword on the pillows and stripped the fine and valuable robes from the priestess, and was pleased to find that she wore a king's treasure worth of jewelry.

Now he could leave.

Tsabrak Xorlarrin at last came to the mouth of the deep cave and looked out from his mountain perch over the lands of the Silver Marches, over the kingdom of Many-Arrows. He squinted against the glare of the fiery ball in the sky, the infernal sun.

"Why would we deign to wage war in this wretched place?" Andzrel Baenre asked, moving up beside the Xorlarrin mage.

"Were it like this, I would agree," was all that Tsabrak would answer, and he chuckled knowingly.

"Set the guards," he instructed the Baenre weapons master. "Protect this place, protect me, at all cost!"

Andzrel narrowed his eyes, surprised that a mere Xorlarrin would speak to him in such a manner. For a moment, he harbored the notion of drawing his sword.

But then came a command from behind him, and in a voice he surely knew.

"Do," said Gromph, and Andzrel spun around to see the archmage, along with Tos'un Armgo and his half-*darthiir* daughter.

The weapons master bowed and rushed away.

"I thought you had vowed not to witness this," Tsabrak dared remark to Gromph.

The archmage shrugged as if it hardly mattered, and indeed, given the prize he and his sister had found and now kept in the extra-dimensional mansion in the anteroom of the primordial chamber of Q'Xorlarrin, it did not.

Gromph moved back into the shadows, taking the Armgo duo with him, and there they watched as Tsabrak began his long incantation. Heartbeats became an hour, hours became a day, and still he chanted.

But Tsabrak did not move, other than his mouth, standing perfectly still as if rooted to the stone beneath his feet, his arms uplifted and stretching forward, just under the lip of the cave's front roof, and up toward the sky.

The sun rose in the east, and still he chanted, and that infernal ball of discomfort had just reached its zenith when at last the call of Tsabrak was answered.

Black tendrils pulsed up out of the stone and into the Xorlarrin wizard's form, and ran up around and within him to his reaching fingers, then shot forth up into the sky.

And so it went, hour after hour, the daylight dimming with a roiling gray overcast, shrouding the western sun as it found the horizon.

Through the night, Tsabrak chanted, and the tendrils of the Underdark poured forth, and when the sun rose the next morning, it seemed a meager thing, and the land barely brightened, and those surface dwellers of the Silver Marches, orcs and elves, dwarves and humans alike, all battened their homes, expecting a terrific storm.

But no storm came, for these were not rain clouds, surely.

Through the day, Tsabrak chanted, and Gromph departed to a call from Methil that Matron Zeerith had arrived in Q'Xorlarrin.

The archmage had seen enough, after all, and indeed he was humbled by the power he had witnessed. Not the power of Tsabrak, he knew, for that one was merely a conduit, and indeed might not even survive this spellcasting. But the power of the Spider Queen as she reached into the realm of the Arcane, as she tried to claim supremacy.

As she stole the daylight of the region called the Silver Marches, preparing the battlefield for her drow minions.

The power of the Darkening, Gromph understood, and all the world would take note, and all the world would be afraid.

Matron Zeerith clearly was in a foul mood. Her weapons master was dead, slain in the cold north. Her eldest daughter, the First Priestess of her House, of her fledgling city, was dead, murdered in her own bed.

More than half the drider force she had sent here with her children had been slain, and nearly two-score of her House, including priestesses and wizards.

Oh, they had a sizable number of dwarf slaves in return, but that hardly mitigated the losses.

And the chapel!

Matron Zeerith had been told that it would be the shining jewel of her precious city, a place of solemn and god-like power that would serve her craftsmen well and please Lady Lolth.

She looked upon it now, webs hanging in tatters, rubble around the room and collapsed across the way, and with uninvited guests waiting for her.

The sight of Matron Mother Quenthel and Gromph standing beside the altar block did not improve Zeerith's mood. They were here to judge her, she figured, and to tell her how her children had failed the Spider Queen.

Likely, she thought, they were here to absorb Q'Xorlarrin into House Baenre's widening web.

A third figure was with them, a delicate woman standing atop the altar block in fabulous spidery robes. She had her back to Zeerith as the matron approached, her black hair bobbed around her shoulders—and shot with streaks of red, Matron Zeerith noted, much like the stone.

As Zeerith neared, the woman, the elf, turned around to look down at her from on high.

"Darthiir!" Matron Zeerith cried incredulously.

"Do you not recognize her, Matron Zeerith?" the matron mother asked. "You have heard the name of Dahlia many times, I expect."

"Upon the sacred altar stone, Matron Mother?" Zeerith asked. "Are we to sacrifice this wretched creature, then? Pray let me hold the blade!"

"Speak with respect to a fellow matron, Matron Zeerith Q'Xorlarrin," the matron mother advised, and as the words registered, a stupefied Zeerith stared at Quenthel.

Gromph began to laugh, and that only added to the tension and discord of confused Zeerith.

Matron Mother Quenthel turned to the archmage and bade him to explain, to introduce the elf woman standing atop the sacred stone.

Gromph stepped over and bowed respectfully to Matron Zeerith, then swept his arm back out to Dahlia. "Behold Matron Do'Urden," he explained, "of Daermon N'a'shezbaernon, the Eighth House of Menzoberranzan."

TELL THE WORLD
THIS BOOK WAS

Good	Bad	So-so